THE HIGH KINGDOM RETURNS

A FAT MAN'S HOLIDAY

KTK Press

Westlake Village, CA

The High Kingdom Returns:
A Fat Man's Holiday

by K.D. Fink

Published by
KTK Press
Westlake Village, CA
ISBN Print Edition: 978-0-9997171-2-7
ISBN E-Book (Kindle): 978-0-9997171-1-0

Design & Typography:
Proof Positive, Bloomsbury, NJ

DEDICATION

To my beautiful wife Joanne, who makes all things possible.

Let's stop for some KFC," said Theo, a dwarf who loved honey mustard on everything from steamed broccoli to extra crispy chicken strips at KFC.

"No time," said Dutch, a dyspeptic wizard who lived on Tums. "We've got to make up time from the Taco Bell run. The Demon Lord is hunting us now. Night is fast approaching and we've got to get under cover soon."

"Yeah, so?" I said. "Fuck the Demon Lord! There's always time for KFC chicken strips."

"Yeah, fuck the Demon Lord!" said Buck, the dwarf chief. "I love KFC coleslaw on top of my strips."

"Yeah, fuck the Demon Lord! And I love their 'masher taters' with extra gravy," said Burt, a blue-bearded dwarf who asked for a side of brown gravy whenever possible.

"Yeah, fuck the Demon Lord! I love their sweet butter corn on the cob — the way only KFC makes it," said Arnie, a corn freak, who probably crapped corn at every gas station pit stop.

"Yeah, fuck the Demon Lord! I'd love a couple of drumsticks to gnaw on the road," said Ornery, a dwarf very handy with an axe, but a real pain in the ass.

KFC! KFC! KFC! everyone chanted.

You don't begin a heroic quest on an empty stomach.

PROLOGUE

A full moon rose above Middlebrook University, whose bell tower chimed twelve times, reminding students that the library was closing. Students gathered their books and laptops and headed for the front entrance. On the fourth floor in the PR2800s Margie sat at her desk, making the final changes to her research paper.

"Is there *Justice in King Lear*? Hell No!" she said, unaware that anyone could hear her, as the fourth floor was usually empty at that hour.

Rufus Timmons looked up for a moment when he heard Margie, but he couldn't see her ensconced in her own corner of the library. So he returned to reliving, yet again, the coronation of King Fesbucket, in his worn copy of *The High Kingdom,* his favorite book in one hand and a McDonald's apple pie in the other. But then Rufus heard the voice again at a fevered pitch he couldn't ignore.

Margie sniffed the air. "SHIT! NOT Kung *Fu*! Not that camel piss you call cologne! I told you we're done, you bastard!" she said, expecting Chris, her ex, but not Ezekiel Watson, a mugger prowling the fourth floor for his next victim.

Margie lunged for her purse a nanosecond faster than Ezekiel. He pulled on the leather straps as hard as he could, but the purse wouldn't budge.

"Help!" she screamed, fighting like a wolf protecting her pups.

"Just gimme the fucking bag, bitch!" said Ezekiel, who smashed her in the head with his elbow. But Margie wouldn't let go. This was not going as planned.

"Bitch! You bit me!" he said.

Margie spat out a chunk of Ezekiel's arm on the linoleum floor, as if it were a tough piece of sirloin. Blood lust raged in her eyes.

"A classic has so many unexpected virtues, don't you think?" said a calm voice, seconds before a hardback copy of *The High Kingdom* slammed against Ezekiel's face, bringing him down hard, temporarily knocking him out.

"Thank God! Oh, Thank God. Bless you." She hugged the man, but couldn't quite get her arms around his waist. But she wouldn't let go.

"Rufus Timmons at your service, ma'am," he said, as Margie clung to him. "Listen to me. First, release me. Then go downstairs, and get the campus police, please."

Rufus sat on Ezekiel's chest, forcing the air out of his lungs and waking him at the same time.

"Hey fat-fuck, I can't breathe," said Ezekiel, as he regained consciousness. "You're crushing my chest!"

"Must be that second apple pie," said Rufus, patting Ezekiel's face. "You know, you get two for 99 cents at McDonald's."

CHAPTER 1

Yes, I'm Mr. Fat-fuck. I'm the guy who orders the whole, not the half rack of baby back ribs at Big Bob's BBQ Palace; the Triple-Triple not Double-Double burger at In-and-Out; the whole, not the half loaf of onion rings at the Burger Shack; the triple, not the double shot of El Patron in my margarita at Los Lobos. Life is short. The world has changed. I feel it in the smaller burgers at the Burger Shack; and I see it in the shitty little cappuccino cups they switched to at Rimi's French Bistro. Thought we wouldn't notice, the cheap bastards. Yeah, I'm the guy who enjoys a strip steak more than a strip show. Rufus Timmons, at your service.

I remember when you could stroll down to Jack-in-the-Box, bring home a couple of greasy tacos (also two for 99 cents), a Jumbo Jack and fries, cue up your favorite "adventure" tape, and settle back for a lovely evening of tacos, burgers, and "released tension."

I know that fat, ugly, socially awkward, but kind men have been releasing tension since the first cave man, Erg, jerked off to the big-breasted cave woman painted on the wall by his buddy Phil. Let's face it: ugly and socially inept men rarely get laid, and many refuse to pay for sex for reasons moral, medical, and monetary (not always in that order). But mostly moral: for who would add to the tragedy that is an escort's life?

How the world has changed. Imagine coming home to your man cave, as I did recently, only to find it robbed: your favorite "adventure" tapes gone, along with your HDTV and TV Guide. Too bad I wasn't there. I would have kicked the burglar's ass from here into next year. And the cops had more dangerous suspects to chase down: rapists, armed robbers, gang bangers. Reuniting one purloined HDTV with its owner wasn't at the top of their list.

Libraries, too, were once man caves, safe havens for scholars to think and dream, but that has also changed with the times. Library aficionados, even lowly Ph.D. candidates like myself, now pack a Taser with their thermos of black coffee as well as, in my case, a hardback copy of *The High Kingdom*, useful as both a reference and a weapon, a McDonald's Sausage McGriddle, delicious hot or cold (but order it with an extra sausage patty), a can or three of Pringles (love the BBQ and the Sour Cream and Onion), and a dozen High Five donuts, the best damn donuts in the cosmos. It's a sad, sad world when you can't enjoy, unmolested, a cinnamon crumb donut or a simple, yet marvelous, chocolate yellow cake donut without some scum-sucking dirt-bag invading your sanctuary. This is what our world has come to?

I was heading for the Middlebrook University library the next day, following the incident with Margie and Ezekiel. The library was this scholar's man cave, as well as a renowned center for F.S.S. Bartlett scholarship. That's right: the same F.S.S. Bartlett who wrote the wildly popular fantasy classic, *The High Kingdom*, the subject of my PhD dissertation. I longed for the library, its sacred confines, and my blessed books. I no longer spent my days dodging Improvised Explosive Devices (IEDs), and killing the monsters that planted them: Iraqi insurgents and Afghani Taliban.

I returned from those hellholes four years ago having earned my right to the quiet life of academia.

If only I could get those hellholes out of my dreams, I'd be in great shape. As Hamlet said, "I could be bounded in a nutshell, and count myself a prince of infinite space, were it not that I had bad dreams." Perhaps not a nutshell. But a cargo container should suffice.

Finally, I had the time to read fantasy and sci-fi novels at my leisure. Tucked inside my backpack was my laptop, a dozen High Five donuts, and my completed PhD dissertation. I also had an Anglo Saxon and Middle English dictionary, languages every Bartlett scholar was required to know. Terrance (Terry) Cornwall, a bibliographer in medieval studies, was helping me expand my vocabulary, and had been indispensable, in proofreading my dissertation's Middle English footnotes, for which I would be forever grateful. What's more, Terry had a Quaker's calm, quiet, reassuring faith in God. PhD candidates could be a neurotic tribe.

I had decided after reading my dissertation, "Bartlett's Disappearance on the Western Front and the Birth of *The High Kingdom*" for the hundredth time, that it was time to submit it to my doctoral advisor, Professor Thomas "Black Hole" Blakeslee. I dropped off one copy, now required, with the office secretary in the English department, and one with the Black Hole himself, a renowned Dickensian and legendary procrastinator. Students who had graduated years ago were just getting their final papers back. I knew it would be six months before Prof. Blakeslee could summon the courage to turn past the title page, and another semester after that to read the dedication. Which meant I had a year, possibly 18 months before he finished reading it and scheduled a dissertation defense committee to examine me on its merits. Assuming he didn't lose it, as had happened more than once: Hence, the department's office copy requirement. Ah, the perquisites of tenure. Practically speaking, I was free for the next 12 to 18 months.

Soon I would lose myself in one of the finest collections of science fiction and fantasy literature in the country. I'd reread the classics: *Stranger in a Strange Land, Foundation Trilogy, Dune, Childhood's End*, and many others. I'd read nonstop into the summer. Call it, "A Fat Man's Holiday." I earned it.

Later I would make a pilgrimage to Oxford University, where my literary hero F.S.S. Bartlett taught. It was an opportunity to examine Bartlett's letters at the Bodleian for clues to his disappearance on the Western Front in 1917. No fantasy novel was more realistically described than *The High Kingdom*. I wasn't foolish enough to say this to my colleagues in the English department, but I believe he journeyed to the High Kingdom.

In the meantime, I was on the other side of the campus, walking by the William Cooperman Hall where I heard tumultuous applause. Though the hall seated more than 2,000 people, I saw standing room only in the back. I felt compelled to join the throng, though I couldn't say why. I leaned against the back wall to see what the big deal was all about. A back wall is always a good place to observe events. Never get caught in the center of any room, unless you want to die. My daily experience in Iraq taught me that. Always scan your environment, no matter where you are. I took in the room and they were all kids, some faculty, but mostly college students happy to listen so long as the BBQ beef sliders, cherry slurpies, mini hot dogs (with mustard and ketchup), and finger sandwiches (rare roast beef, tuna fish, and some veggie concoction) didn't run out. However, I noticed a very small man, 5 feet 2 inches maybe, with a neat black beard standing next to an elderly, easily 70, beardless, man, a foot taller than his companion, who leaned on a strangely shaped cane with a handle like a Glock and tripod stabilizer at the bottom. Looked more like a weapon than a cane. They were also standing on my left, a hundred feet from me with their backs to the wall. They stood quite still, not speaking to each other, not moving, not even eating. Just waiting, I guess, for the show to begin. My military, my wartime survival habits relaxed for a few minutes. I felt safe in a room full of so many people and the BBQ sliders were beckoning me. Really tasty cherry slurpies, too. I grabbed a few sliders and a slurpie and returned to my position holding up the wall.

I wasn't planning on staying long. The week hadn't started out great and my books waited for me at the library, 50 novels in five stacks of 10, and time to forget all of the "stale and unprofitable uses of this world."

Tennessee's billionaire Senator Bobby Ross, the new Democratic nominee for vice president, was speaking. Ross had given a fat donation to Middlebrook University. Our school was awarding its lifetime achievement medal to a man who didn't look a day over 40. No doubt a plaque in the men's crapper commemorated this day. The broad smile of university president Gary Palazzo suggested, to me anyway, some serious cash had been deposited to Palazzo's private slush fund.

The buzz in the room was that Senator Ross also made obscene cash contributions to the POTUS fund for underprivileged students. That's right: POTUS, as in the President of the United States, Thomas McClintock, who was once a financially strapped student at Middlebrook.

Everyone who worked on his first presidential campaign loved "old man" McClintock as we called him. No president, since FDR, enjoyed the public's love like McClintock, who was credited with saving the U.S. economy from total collapse during the 2008 Wall Street toxic home mortgage debacle.

However, recently, the president hadn't been himself since his youngest son, George, a Navy SEAL, was killed last Christmas rescuing 250 British and American hostages from Indonesian pirates. No one expected McClintock to run for a second term. However, he confounded the experts when he announced he was running for re-election. Senator Ross of Tennessee reached out to President McClintock when his son died. The senator knew his own devastating personal loss when his wife and four children were killed in a plane crash on their way to a family ski vacation in Vale, Colorado. Tragedy forged a profound bond between the men.

When Vice President Fordham, 83, announced that he was retiring from politics, McClintock, 75, chose the young senator from Tennessee as his running mate. The press supported the choice and called Senator Ross the "Heir A-Parent," as Ross reminded McClintock of his lost son. It was the beginning of October, the undergrads had been back in school for a month now, but back in July at the Democratic Convention in Kansas City, Missouri McClintock and Ross were nominated. And the election was just around the corner.

"Ladies and gentlemen. Please welcome Senator Bobby Ross, the next Vice President of the United States of America!" boomed University President Palazzo, trying to sound like a big shot by predicting the outcome of an undecided election. Most of the students in the room, like me, didn't give a damn about politics and turned their attention to the free pastries, finger sandwiches, cherry slurpies, and BBQ beef sliders. Oh, and did I mention buckets of free Red Vines? And come on, really? The Veep has no job. He or she does squat unless the president dies.

I'm 6 feet 3 inches. Ross was at least 6ft 7 inches, with a body like an oak tree He took off the black suit jacket and threw it over his chair. Loosening his tie and rolling up his sleeves, he looked more relaxed than he probably felt. I grabbed another handful of Red Vines for the road, my third BBQ beef slider, and another cherry slurpie and propped up the back wall.

"Thank you, Mr. President, for your kind words," said Senator Ross, with a soft southern accent. "Like many of the students here, I remember a time when I didn't have two nickels to rub together. When I was a penniless scholarship student at the University of Tennessee. I caught a break when I landed a job washing dishes in the dining commons. I got free leftovers. Who could argue with that? Compared to the PBJ sandwiches, I ate like a king on turkey, mashed potatoes and gravy, collard greens, and cherry jello. I was in hog heaven, as we say down south, and I ate as much food as I ever dreamed of as a boy. My brother and I shared the same dreams, as well as the same bed until I went off to college. And I was happy knowing that I wouldn't end up in the coalmines like my daddy and his daddy. I wouldn't die, like them, from silicosis, Black Lung disease, God rest their souls.

"So you can imagine my satisfaction today in being able to share my modest success in life with hard working young men and women who remind me so much of myself. One of my greatest rewards in my life is knowing that I made a substantial investment in you all. Now I say investment and not handout because I expect R.O.I. — Return On Investment and that return, that profit is your future success and through you the success of our great country. So I'll be checking up on you, just to make sure you're all making progress toward your goals in life."

Senator Ross smiled widely and on one of the TV monitors setup throughout the auditorium, and I could see the edges of his teeth, which looked razor sharp. Must have been the light and nothing more.

I thought I'd despise this political hack, but I liked the man. He was modest and self-effacing. I didn't know any billionaires, personally. The billionaires I had read about or had seen on television were pricks or egomaniacs — or both. Everyone stood up to applaud Senator Ross.

I was in the back row, but still had a clear view of the stage, when he caught my eye. Why or how he zeroed in on my face in a crowd of more than 2,000 people, I'll never know. I looked at him; he looked at me and a voice, not my own, sounded in my head saying,

"I see you. Don't move. We must meet."

You'd think it would be no big deal to meet Senator Ross, but not with his fucking voice in my head. Very rude to seize my mind like that, in my opinion. My heart was pounding like a jackhammer and for those two or three seconds he was inside my head I felt as if he were two feet away. My feet were rooted to the ground like a tree and I couldn't move. *I couldn't move, dammit!* I was terrified — more frightened than at any time in my life, including my tours of duty in Iraq and Afghanistan. All I could think of was that I had to get out of that auditorium, or die, but I couldn't move my feet. I couldn't move my freakin' size 14 feet!

And then a different voice sounded in my head, **"Rufus, move your goddamn feet in 3...2....1...NOW!"**

At that moment the applause and an aide interrupted the senator who spoke to the aide, and for a moment the senator broke his powerful grip on my mind. That was all I needed.

Then his aide ran towards me, *fast*, at the same time taking my picture with his cell phone. I hate multitaskers. With a survivor's instinct, I dropped the slider, the slurpie, moved my right foot, then my left. I ducked down, left the room, and hightailed it back to the library where I hoped I'd be safe. You'd be surprised how fast a fat man can run when he's running for his life, as I was, or so I felt. I've always honored the scared shitless voice in my head that said, **"Run like the devil himself is chasing you. And don't run straight, you fool: zigzag!"** That voice got me through a war in Iraq and one in Afghanistan — in one piece — never running straight, but retreating, zigzagging, taking cover, finding refuge to fight another day.

So I made a mad dash zigzagging through bushes, inside buildings, across underground garages, all the way to the library, whose confines I knew better than my one bedroom apartment.

CHAPTER 2

I was right on time for my meeting with Terry who lived deep in the library's underground labyrinth. We were planning to evaluate recent acquisitions in English medieval literature. He saw the look of terror in my red face from the blood pumping there, about to explode through my forehead.

"Rufus, my friend," he said, "You look as if the devil himself is after you."

"I think he is," I said, "Or at least a close relative."

"Really? What happened?" I told him.

"I'm not even sure what it means, but I've never been so scared in my life."

"That's some admission coming from you of all people. Aren't you the guy who beat the enemy at his own game overseas?"

"I did, but I *knew* my enemy; could predict my enemy; could outthink my enemy and I always believed I had the Good Lord watching my back. This was different. This Senator Ross they were honoring over in Cooperman Hall took over my mind and body, in the most brutal display of mental and physical domination. I've never experienced anything like it. He literally paralyzed me in my tracks. I couldn't move! I couldn't get away!"

"But you *did*," Terry said.

"Only because another power in the room, also in my head, somehow helped me. I was a goner, Terry. I was one size fourteen shoe step away from death and maybe something worse though I can't say what exactly."

"But you're here now," Terry said. "Rufus, my dear friend, you've seen evil incarnate in the faces of the men you killed in battle. Human evil, powerful, full of controlled, and uncontrolled rage. I suggest this evil was not human. I don't what it was, but from what you describe this Senator Ross is not of this world. Maybe you shouldn't go home tonight. Stay with me and Mary tonight."

"I can't. I've got to prepare for 25 English 101 students in the morning. I'll be all right. This too will pass, God willing."

Terry put his arms on my shoulders and looked me in the eye. Then he turned around and searched through several drawers and removed two wooden crucifixes. He was a Quaker and though he didn't wear a crucifix, he knew its power in a crisis, real or imaginary. Thus one was always nearby. Terry had once used both crucifixes to subdue a gentleman who thought he was a vampire, who was threatening students. Turns out the vampire escaped from the local mental hospital and had found a home lurking in the library's Gothic literature section. Terry handed me a crucifix.

"Rufus, let's recite the Lord's Prayer," he said, and we did, as He did "deliver me from evil," blessed be His name, and his son Christ almighty.

I was glad I instinctively ran to Terry. He was strong in the faith and just the person to calm my nerves. I was also glad that most of the general public didn't know that the underground library existed, much less that it was eight stories beneath the main floor, built in the dot-com boom of the 1990s with a $300 million dollar gift from a Middlebrook alumnus who made billions off of some ingenious, short-lived software called Bamboozle, or some such name. Even the library's employees had a difficult time navigating its maze, which was lucky for me: for I'm certain the Senator's aide searched every floor and cubicle topside for me.

CHAPTER 3

I lost him, Senator," said his assistant Richard Leventine. "I'm sorry."

"Richard, this is the third time you've failed me, and I think the last," said Ross, who leaned against the door of the private suite provided by the university, blocking the man's exit. "That man's *death* is critically important to my success. You saw the gut on him. He should have been easy to outrun. He was about to give birth to *twins*. Now I'll have to employ additional resources to find him."

"You'd be surprised how fast a fat man can run when he's running for his life. Some big men are very light on their feet. Surely you're not worried about the prophecy, senator, *My Lord*," said Richard, who took a giant step backward, terrified.

"Don't *ever* contradict me," said Senator Ross. "As for a prophecy that some fool chosen by God will destroy me, don't be absurd. I've been eating such fools for millennia. Nevertheless, you lost him. Give me your camera. At least you took pictures of him."

His aide took another step backward, terrified. He knew what happened to those who failed this son-of-a-bitch.

"I'm sorry, Senator." Richard said, handing over his camera. "The man must be somewhere on campus. Please, give me another chance to find him."

"No, I so frightened him that he's in another state by now. No, this is for the best, Richard."

The senator took two steps forward and then he wasn't the senator. He looked like the senator and yet he wasn't. He was the same man and yet he wasn't: when his aide looked at his face it was the same face, but devoid of human expression.

The senator's arms were muscular but slender. He looked like a strong man, but not a powerful one, that is until the knotted sinews in his arms grew like an infection, as if something was crawling under his skin. He reached for his aide and without a word tore the man's arm off and ate it. Richard produced an anguished high-pitched scream that broke the water glasses on a nearby table, but only one scream before Senator Ross crushed his larynx. Ross then ate the other arm before ripping off his aide's head and devouring it, his jaw and razor sharp teeth now expanding like a snake's. A female aide from the university who must have heard Richard's scream entered the room unannounced, instantly lost her mind and ran around the perimeter of the room, like a cornered rat. The senator smiled in amusement as she ran around the room crying and shouting, "My baby, my baby!" The senator liked to play with his food until it bored him and the woman was boring him with her mindless gibberish.

"What fools these mortals be," He said, and snatched her when she came too close. He pulled her head off, first drinking the gushing blood from her neck.

"That was refreshing," he said after draining her body of most of its blood. He spread her legs and said, "Make a wish," before breaking them off her pelvis, as if he was breaking the wishbone off a Thanksgiving turkey. He threw her body parts in the heap with what was left of his aide, Richard. He opened Richard's phone and flipped through his photos until he found several good pictures of Rufus.

Another man walked into the room, dressed for a night at a Tiki bar: blue jeans, a yellow flowered Hawaiian shirt. Mike was one of Senator Ross' demon aides, only slightly more competent than the hapless Richard. He looked at the bloody mess as though nothing abnormal had happened.

"My Lord, I'll clean up here," said Mike, who got down on all fours and began cleaning up the scraps like a dog with a spilled bowl of beef stew: a hand here, a foot there, sucking the juices out of the carpet. He took out a bottle of Heinz pickle relish and another bottle of Gray Poupon's deli mustard and poured both on the remains before consuming them. The senator watched him with fascination and just for fun he kicked him hard in the ass.

"You missed a piece," said the senator, even though Mike was quite thorough.

"Did I, My Lord?" said Mike.

"Yes, you did. And when you're finished cleaning up, print this picture," the senator said and showed him the picture of a terrified Rufus on Richard's cell phone.

"I saw some dwarf scum in the back of the room," said the senator. "They, too, saw him run away. I sure he's the next 'Chosen One.' Take your crew and scour the campus for the fat man. Go to every department and see if anyone recognizes him."

"My Lord, what should I do when I find him?"

"Kill him of course, you moron, but bring me his head. It will make a nice appetizer with my Diet Coke."

CHAPTER 4

When I left the underground library it was almost midnight. I made my way home, still shaking from the experience with Senator Ross. Then I did what I always did when stressed: I had something to eat and took a Valium. I popped two English muffins in the toaster. Then I took out a frozen Stouffer's Lobster Newburg and put it in the microwave for five minutes. I sat down and waited at my small kitchen table where without warning I was back in Mosul, Iraq, with my unit. We were on one roof exchanging fire with insurgents on another roof down Saddam street, about 200 yards from our position. Although every other goddamn Iraqi street was named after that motherfucker. I waxed the sniper on the roof but not before the motherfucker put a bullet in Johnny Ayala's brain two feet to my left. I was covered in his brain matter. I can't begin to tell you in how many dreams I wiped brain matter from my face while offing that mother-fucking towel head. But even killing the sniper under fire wasn't half as frightening as having some *thing*, some creature, some shithead United States *Senator* seize my mind and fucking paralyze me. How the fuck was that even possible?

I was still trying to process what happened in that auditorium when I smelled the burning English muffins and quickly came out of my PTSD fugue-fun-fest. You never knew when PTSD would strike: a delightful waking nightmare. Thank God I wasn't on the freeway. I might have slammed into an SUV full of little girls on their way to a soccer game, like I did three years ago. Thank God, thank God, no one was hurt. I don't care how "well adjusted" you are or were, war follows you home. They never tell you that when you sign up. I pulled the muffins out and buttered each one; then I cut open the plastic pouch containing the Lobster Newburg and poured it on the muffins, by far the most delicious microwavable dinner with 50 grams of fat that I've ever eaten. I washed it down with a Corona and lime and finally started to relax. Nothing satisfied me like a delicious Stouffer's Lobster Newburg or mushu pork from Chen's take-out. It was just what the doctor ordered. Light years more effective than all the pills and shit they give you at the VA hospital.

After that I slunk off to bed and pulled my favorite Dodger Blue comforter up to my neck. I was still shaking and trying to process how that Senator Fucker seized my mind. Was that thing a man? I knew I was mentally tough from seeing some of my poor comrades break down under battle stress. I may have brought home my war demons, but I killed the enemy, defended my country, protected my buddies, and even defended civilians as best I could. With those thoughts I fell asleep, dead to the world and nearly woke up the same way.

I was in the middle of my oft recurring and delightful romantic-dinner-with-Halle-Berry dream. We were at Alfredo's Ristorante, a favorite of mine. I sat at the table, a half eaten slice of mushroom and pepperoni pizza in my left hand, gazing into her beautiful brown eyes when I was awakened by a scream and something hot on my face. I woke up wiping my cheek. I sat up in bed, frightened to find my face and chest covered in bright yellow goo.

"Get up now, laddie, if you want to live!" said a low voice, almost a growl.

"What the fuck?" I said, and saw a severed arm on my bed, between my legs, oozing fluorescent yellow goo all over my new Los Angeles Dodger's blue comforter, the one with Dodger caps and bats on it. Got it at Dodger stadium on Blanket Night when they played the Mets. It was so soft. Cost me fifty-five bucks. Worse than that: I didn't get to finish my pepperoni pizza with Halle, which really sucked.

In fact, I thought I was still dreaming until I looked up and saw a black-bearded dwarf staring at me, leaning on an axe dripping with yellow goo. The dwarf smelled just like Old Norse pipe tobacco, F.S.S. Bartlett's favorite brand.

"You were there yesterday! With that old man!" I said.

"Yes I was. But like I said, laddie, time to go."

"Go where?"

"Follow me."

Behind him I saw the lifeless body of a...thing. A creature. I would have said it was a man, but it was shorter and had dark, filthy black skin, though tough to say in the dark, except for the glow-in-the-dark yellow fingernails. The mouth was open and clearly he needed dental work, what with his mossy green, and two-inch incisors. He wasn't much taller than the dwarf. I assumed he made the scream that woke me. Yellow blood still gushed from a five-inch wound in his chest.

I got dressed in record time. It's weird I know, but I couldn't stop thinking of my Dodger comforter covered in yellow blood. I really loved it. It was so soft. I must be fucking crazy. It was really, soft, though. I had some Perrier sparking water on my nightstand and poured it on my face. The fizziness of the carbonated water foamed up the yellow blood, which I wiped off with a clean section of my comforter — it was so soft. We raced down the hallway of my fifth story apartment, out the exit, down five flights of stairs, where three more decapitated creatures greeted us.

The dwarf, I assumed he was a dwarf, since he was short, carried an axe, had a thick black beard, and said, "laddie" with a Scotsman's burr: hell, if it looks, sounds, and quacks like a duck, it's a duck, right? Thus, the dwarf led me to the alley behind my building to a candy-apple red Harley-Davidson Fat Boy, lowered to accommodate his shorter height. He wiped the blood from his axe on the wet lawn next to his chopper and slipped it into a pink sling case embossed with the Nike logo, which looked as if he was carrying an over sized tennis racket. Who knew Nike made the perfect axe case? And in pink! I also noticed he was packing a Glock 17 9MM on his left hip. I'm guessing, but maybe axes were a family tradition and were quieter than a Glock, apart for the screams of the axed. I got on the back of his bike and we took off in the middle of the night. If it hadn't been 3AM the sight of us would have attracted a crowd or a cop since I was riding without a helmet — the least of my problems, right?

Every three or four blocks we doubled back one block to be certain no one was following us.

"My name is..."

"Rufus Timmons," he said shouting over the engine noise.

"And you are?" I said.

"Buck, son of Lord Wessex of the High Kingdom," he said.

"The what?!"

"The High Kingdom, laddie."

"What were those things?" I asked.

"Goblins from the..."

"High Kingdom?" I said. I started to shake uncontrollably. This had all the makings of a nasty, dangerous, and most annoying adventure. It had to be a joke. Maybe my prankster pal Freddy the Finger staged this. He once sent me a notice for jury duty in flawless Elvish.

For my part, Iraq had been all the adventure anyone would ever need. I can't begin to tell you how many meals, *how many mushroom and pepperoni pizzas* I missed in Iraq!

"These goblins are from bad neighborhoods in the High King-dom," Buck said.

"Are you implying there are goblins from good neighborhoods in the High Kingdom?"

"No, you're inferring that. Don't be a fool, Mr. Timmons. What I'm saying is that you're damn lucky the Demon Lord thought three or four goblin soldiers could carry out the hit."

"Hit? Demon Lord?"

"Yes, the 'hit,'" he said. "You know...As in to kill you. We'd have been in deep shit if he'd sent along a demon with them."

"What Demon Lord?" I said.

"Senator Bobby Ross — *the* Demon Lord." Buck said.

"Oh," I said. "You mean that motherfucker at the university?"

"Yeah, that motherfucker at the university," said Buck.

"Oh shit," was all I could say. "He's a bad man."

"Bad doesn't begin to describe him."

We stopped at Jack-in-the-Box, always a good omen in my world. There was a ramp leading underneath the restaurant, where trucks could drop off supplies. We drove down the ramp and stopped by the loading dock and the concrete wall behind it. Buck took a remote control from the inside pocket of his black windbreaker and pointed it at the wall which slowly opened.

"Hey, Buck," I said, "I don't suppose we could stop for a couple of tacos first." He ignored me and we drove down a second underground ramp for at least ten minutes, until I was so nauseous I was about to hurl my Stouffer's Lobster Newburg. Finally we stopped. I've heard of underground refrigeration, but there was more than refrigeration down here. Lined up against one wall was a row of eleven Harley-Davidson Fat Boys side by side, as well as two Harley trikes with atypically wide tires and large trunks. Beautiful Harley hogs, every last one. There was a helmet on each hog. Each helmet had a small antenna fin on the top, so the riders could talk to each other on the road. Obviously, this was a safe house, but safe from what?

Something more: while each bike and trike was lowered, the engines were raised high and protected by three inches of steel plate. This little feature made the bikes adept on or off the road

— improvements very sweet and very expensive. I wondered what other upgrades they'd made.

"Follow me," Buck said.

"My ass is killing me. A wider seat might have save my left testicle," I said as I slung my left leg off the bike. He grunted twice and I wondered if that was dwarf laughter.

CHAPTER 5

On the left side of the Harleys was a red door with a glass porthole for a window. A light was on inside. Buck opened the door and entered and I followed behind. Inside, were eleven dwarves and an old man sitting around a twenty-foot oak table, with a gigantic Lazy Susan in the middle, laden with every imaginable fast food: fast food heaven or hell, depending on your point of view. There were tacos, burritos, two-foot long churros, double-double burgers from In-and-Out, roast beef sandwiches from Arby's, Kentucky fried chicken (KFC), chicken strips, cole-slaw and mashed potatoes and extra gravy (because sometimes the bastards don't give you enough and many people love extra gravy with their meal). There were even little packets of ketchup, honey mustard, and BBQ sauce next to the food. I love honey mustard. Oh, and they had my favorite potato cakes from Arby's and five of KFC's delicious carrot cakes. The food was hot and the combined smell of everything was driving me nuts. I hoped the introductions would be brief or even better over food. The aroma of all this great heart-stopping food compensated some for my Halle Berry romantic-dinner-dream-interruptus. I was still thinking of that mushroom and pepperoni pizza we never finished.

If I could honorably avoid it, my great hope was never to be a dead hero on the battlefield, but rather, just a regular guy dead from a massive cardiac infarction from Macho Man's breakfast burrito, with its bacon, egg, hash browns, melted cheese, green chiles, and salsa hanging from my mouth — wearing my favorite "Do Not Resuscitate!" T-shirt — just to dissuade any pain-in-the-ass do-gooder from helping out. That's a good death, a good life.

The dwarves all looked hungry — I assumed they were dwarves, though not everyone had a beard. I would wait for them to tell me first. I've read dwarves could be touchy that way. Each one was neatly dressed like Buck and about his height; each one had the same oversized Nike tennis racket case draped over the back of his chair. Most of them had short beards, neatly trimmed. No one had a beard long enough to tuck into his belt like the dwarves in *The High Kingdom*. But there were red beards, brown beards, blond beards, blue beards, black beards, even a green beard. Everyone stood up, including an old man in his seventies dressed in black Nike sweat pants, red tennis shoes, a powder blue, button down Oxford shirt underneath a black Members Only jacket, which made me smile. My dad loved his green Members Only jacket, always imagining how cool he looked. I never had the heart to tell him he was as dated as the transistor radio he took to every Dodger baseball game. He wore the damn jacket even after he walked past twenty of them displayed in the window of a Goodwill Thrift store. He didn't give a damn and wore it, along with his bell-bottomed jeans, from the 1980s into the new millennium. Like the old man, Dad didn't give up the things he liked, fashionable or not.

"Welcome Rufus Timmons, I'm Dutch," said the old man.

"It was you! You were the other voice in my head! I'm in your debt." I said.

"Yes, I told you when to move, but you had the strength to do it!" Dutch said.

"Don't worry about the debt you owe," said Buck, "We've got a job for you."

"Ok, I think. How'd you know they'd come after me? You said those creatures were associated with Senator Ross?" I said.

"Quite right, Rufus," said Theo, taking the last bite of an Arby's roast beef sandwich. "Goblins are in his employment."

"But why were you there to begin with?" I said.

"I had a dream you might be there," said Dutch.

"A dream?" I said.

"You aren't the only one with bad dreams," said Dutch, laughing. "We were in the audience when we saw him zero in on you. We knew then that you were the one he's been looking for. You showed real mental toughness in breaking the vise he had on your mind. Believe me, others have failed. That was the first test and you passed, barely."

"Barely is right. It was terrifying. What is he really?" I asked. "I mean besides the Senator of Tennessee and maybe the next Vice President?"

"He's a demon lord from the High Kingdom, masquerading as a human being," said Dutch. "He took over the Senator Ross' body and murdered his family, and over time most of the Senator's closest friends. And if he becomes Vice President, he will become President and he *will* destroy your world and mine and populate what's left with fell creatures."

"*Fell creatures*," I said. "Now there's term I never expected to hear outside of a fantasy novel."

"And as you saw tonight, he's brought other fell creatures with him. Hi, I'm Arnie," said red bearded dwarf who shook my hand.

"Yeah, what sort of 'fell creatures?'" I said.

"Aw, you know," said Arnie, "the usual assortment: trolls, demons, goblins, maybe even a dragon or two.

"This is terrible, but what's it got to do with me?" I asked.

"You've been chosen to destroy the "good senator." Buck said. "He knew, somehow, that you were on this side and he came to Middlebrook because he sensed you were in this part of the country. And he got lucky when you strolled into the auditorium by chance, if chance it was. Lucky for you we found you at the same time."

"You're kiddin' me, right?" I said.

"I wish we were, laddie," said Buck, "because you don't exactly inspire a whole lot of confidence in the courage department."

"Well, fuck you very much," I said, and the room went silent.

"That's the thanks I get for saving your sorry ass?" Buck said.

"You call me a coward before everyone assembled? What do you expect?" I said. "Need I remind you I was a warrior in my world? I served my country honorably in Iraq and Afghanistan."

"*I* know you did, but *I* still expect, I *demand* that we behave like brothers," said Dutch. "We *are* brothers and if we don't respect each other; if we don't display a common decency to each other, this quest is doomed from the start."

"If I am the person you say I am, which I seriously doubt, then I deserve at least a *chance* to prove myself and I apologize to everyone: for my words were said in anger. I'm truly sorry, Lord Wessex." I said, and stuck my hand out to shake Buck's hand, having, consciously, used the formal diction of the High Kingdom for emphasis, which was kind of corny and funny at the same time. Now this was really like living inside my favorite fantasy novel, my all time favorite book. And I wasn't sure I liked it one bit.

"I, too, was out of line," said Buck, Lord Wessex of the High Kingdom. "Truly, I do not know that I could have broken the grip he had on your mind. But I pledge my service and the service of my family to help you fulfill your, *our* quest," said Buck who stuck out his hand and clasped mine. The dwarves at the table nodded their approval. Was everything happening predestined, or had I eaten too many Hi-Five glazed jelly donuts while reading too many fantasy novels? It felt as if Buck and I were re-enacting some High Kingdom-like oath, which made me nervous, fearing that I wouldn't be able to back out of this thing whatever it was. Guess I'm trying to say that I preferred my adventures then and now between the pages of a book.

"Sit down Rufus, my brother, and have something to eat," said Buck.

Finally, we were going to eat.

These were my peeps, alright. In front of every dwarf were at least three cans of Pringles. I ate up to 10 cans a week. Nearly every flavor was represented: Cheddar Cheese, French Onion Dip, Cheddar and Sour Cream, Sour Cream and Onion, Honey Mustard, Jalapeño, Loaded Baked Potato, Memphis BBQ, Ranch, Pizza (a personal fav), Salt and Vinegar, Fiery Sweet BBQ, and Original. There were also limited edition Pringles such as Chile Con Queso, Chicken Taco, and Cheese Burger Pringles. However, in my experience you couldn't always find these special editions.

"Thank you, Buck, Lord Wessex of the High Kingdom," I said. "It will be my greatest pleasure to join you and my new comrades. And would you please roll me a can of Sour Cream and Onion Pringles."

"My pleasure!" said Buck, Lord Wessex. "Try the Chile Con Queso, too. They're a limited edition."

"Why don't we go around the table and introduce ourselves," said Dutch. "But before we do and before we eat, let's give thanks. 'To The One and his Son who provide this bounty and who selected each of us for this quest, we give thanks.' Let's eat."

I was closest to the Lazy Susan, and the dwarves had short arms, unable to reach all the food piled sky high. So I filled most of the orders. It was a good way to meet everyone. How people order food at a restaurant tells you a lot about them.

"Hi, Rufus, I'm Guido, could you toss me a Burrito Supreme? Oh, and some mild hot sauce, too? Thanks a bunch."

"Do you see a taco with 'Kev' written on it? It's mine: it got lettuce and cheese only on it. Send down some of that Scorcher hot sauce for me, if you please. I'm Kevin, but call me Kev, or Kevin, or the Kevster."

"Got it, Kevin." I said.

"Oh *Chosen One*, toss me wing and a breast, extra crispy from the KFC box, with two packets of honey mustard sauce. I'm Ornery. Oh, and some coleslaw, too, and a couple of potato wedges. On a plate." Not so much as a please or a thank you. I could see that Ornery with his sarcastic, *"Oh, Chosen One"* was going to be a major pain in the ass.

"Same for me, please, except, don't get grossed out, but I'd like ketchup with my KFC. I'm Chad."

"I like ketchup with chicken and potato wedges, too," I said, trying to make a little conversation between orders.

"But do you like ketchup on top of your coleslaw?" said Chad.

"Point taken," I said. "You've just grossed me out, Chad. Good job." Chad laughed as coleslaw juice and ketchup ran down the side of his mouth. In fact, he laughed so hard he spit up a piece of chicken on Ornery's potato wedges. Couldn't happen to a nicer dwarf.

"Be so kind and slide over a Big Mac. I'm Petey," said Petey, "And would you cut me a piece of that KFC carrot cake."

"Me, too," said Theo. "And throw a churro on top. There's a good man."

"Harold here. A Bonus Jack for me, and a churro, too, thank you very much. Pleased to meet you, Rufus."

And so it went. I took bites out of a Spicy Chicken Footlong from Subway while meeting, greeting, and serving. There was enough food for an army, all of it from local fast food restaurants — and all of it as auspicious a beginning for a heroic quest, even a fucked-up one as this one looked to be. And as if to prove the point, we passed around the largest bottle of Tums I'd ever seen, everything needed for a royal case of fast-food heartburn. Who wants to begin a quest with heartburn, right? Still, if they were as handy with an axe as they were with a Footlong from Subway, I was in good hands.

We shared our food stories, as we passed food back and forth around a table some 20 feet long and five feet wide. There was Larry, Guido, Kevin, Jake, Chad, Burt, Sam, Harold, Ornery, Arnie, Petey, and Buck. Larry loved hot sauce on everything. Guido preferred Kentucky Fried, but liked burritos, too; he wasn't a big burgers and fries fan. Kevin like tacos with just lettuce and cheese, but he also liked Bonus Jacks, though only when smothered in secret sauce. Of course, "secret sauce" is typically just some version of Thousand Island dressing, which is fine by me. I happen to love Thousand Island dressing. Jake missed his wife's home cooking and couldn't wait to get back to her in the small village of Feldman, a mile or two outside the capital city of Fesbucket in the High Kingdom. Chad was a collector and later showed me his rare collection of McDonald's Apple Pie holders going back more than 50 years. Sam would eat anything. Harold and Ornery favored BBQ, especially Big Bob's BBQ Palace. Arnie, Sylvester, and Buck weren't picky eaters as long as they got seconds. I sensed that each one of these fellows would have my back. I couldn't say how I knew this so early on. Every dwarf spoke with his mouth full of food, my kind of guys, and Buck had to translate Arnie's unintelligible rhapsody on fried onion strings. Of course, Arnie was preaching to the choir: I happen to worship fried onion strings, especially the onion strings at Big Bob's BBQ Palace. Ah, man, onion strings dipped in Heinz ketchup — delicious, man.

CHAPTER 6

I can't believe I've been chosen to take part in a real quest?" I said, after everyone had eaten.

"Quest schmest," said Arnie. "I think I can speak for my comrades in saying that mother fucker, the Demon Lord, Senator Ross, or whatever you want to call him — that prick stole our money and we mean to get it back for ourselves and the community of dwarves back home who were ripped off."

"What money?" I said, suddenly more interested *and* more motivated. Hey, I'm human right? Plus I got goddamn student loans to pay off. Graduate school ain't cheap, brothers and sisters.

"Right on, Arnie. You tell him. We're going to kill that miserable piece of dragon shit," Ornery said.

"What money? How did he steal all of your money?" I asked, wondering just how much it was and whether I stood to get a piece of the action.

"Classic ponzi scheme," said Buck.

"Why in the world would you invest your money with the Demon Lord?"

"We didn't realize he was a Demon Lord. He had the power to assume a pleasing shape and he tricked us."

"How so? And how much?"

"He represented himself as Charles Westinghouse," Ornery said. "A registered agent of Charles Schwab selling United States government debentures, T-Bills with a 10 year compounded interest coupon rate of 13%. Backed by the full faith of the federal government."

"I guess you didn't do your due diligence on this character," I said. "Besides, come on, doesn't 13% return on your money seem too good to be true in this, or any economy for that matter."

"Yeah," said Theo, "We were blinded by greed. Getting 13% ROI when the rest of the High Kingdom, even the elves, was earning 2%, 3% tops blinded us. Just too tempting."

"I *said* it was too good to be true," said Chad, a bald dwarf with a close-cropped blue beard. "But no one listened to me."

"In the sixth year," said Buck, "Charles Westinghouse disappeared and showed up here as billionaire Senator Bobby Ross and we're here to kill the son-of-a-bitch and get our money back for ourselves and our dwarf investors. Of course each of us get an additional finders fee of 1%. *And* we get to fulfill the quest at the same time."

"May I be so bold, again, as to ask how much money the dwarves lost?" I said.

"Three billion dollars," said Dutch.

"More really, as we reinvested the 13% return with that scum sucking demon, leaving us with bupkis," said Arnie, who seemed to have the numbers readily available. Although bupkis, nada, zilch, zero, squat, zippity-do-dah is never hard to calculate.

"I don't suppose if I help you kill this guy, that I might get a tiny piece of the action? I'd gladly settle for ½ of 1% of 3 billion," I said, laughing at the same time and figuring that even ½ of 1% of three billion dollars was exactly — a whole lot. Pay off my student loans, with more than a little left over for a lifetime supply of Pringles and Lobster Newburg. Let me tell you: Lobster Newburg on a Sour Cream and Onion Pringle is delicious.

"First things first," said Arnie. "First you have to prove yourself."

"Of course," I said. "I don't expect something for nothing and if this Demon Lord is as bad I think, the money, whatever the amount, is just a side issue."

"Good answer!" said Dutch. "And OF COURSE, WE HAVE TO PREVENT THE DEMON LORD FROM BECOMING VICE PRESIDENT BECAUSE HE WILL EAT THE PRESIDENT AND LAUNCH WORLD WAR 3 AND DESTROY BOTH OF OUR WORLDS...right fellas?"

"Absolutely, right, Dutch," said Buck. "However, I speak for everyone when I say: Dutch, isn't it time, already? He's got to be tested."

"Tested? What test?" I asked.

"Ornery, will you get it? The case is next to my bag," said Dutch, who had stuffed the last four inches of his churro in his mouth and was attempting to speak and chew at the same time. Took me years to master both those functions at once. Dutch was having a hard time of it.

"We might as well make sure before we waste his time and ours," Chad offered.

"Remember how the sword scarred the last applicant for life? Way cool," said Ornery, with an evil smile. "Of course that was before a troll ate him."

"Applicant? Scarred for life? Trolls? Who said I was applying for anything? If this is some kind fitness test, I can you tell right now I've been a little out of shape for a couple of years," I said.

"A couple? It would take more than a 'couple of years' to produce that gut," said Ornery, making a fist. "I bet if I punched you, my hand would disappear in that mass of pointless protoplasm."

"I wouldn't try it," I said. "I'd *toss* you across the room before you knew what hit you."

"A *dwarf tosser*," said Ornery, "I knew I didn't like this guy. Give me that sword. I'll run him through with it myself." He grabbed at a case that was at Dutch's feet, but Buck held him back.

"Settle down, Ornery," said Buck. "You know he deserves a fair chance to prove he's the one."

"The 'One?' One what? What one?" I said, feeling more panicky with every passing nanosecond.

"The prophecy's 'One,'" said Theo. "The Chosen One we've talking about all this time, Rufus. Couldn't we wait a few weeks? See how he does on the road? I like this guy."

"Didn't work last time. Fat boy here deserves to know now, and so do we," said Ornery. "The last two didn't pass and it would have saved us a lot in funeral expenses, if we'd known up front. Let's just get it over with."

"That's right, we had to stop the bloody quest when the last ones died before being tested first. Dutch, you said the sword arrived by mail just for this purpose. We need to test him now," said Petey, who took out his Glock 17 at least five times since I arrived, cleaning it and putting it back together, which was annoying. Great, an obsessive compulsive dwarf. What heroic quest is complete without one?

This Ornery fellow, and maybe Petey, too, was going to be a major pain in the ass, I said again to myself.

"Petey and Ornery are right. There's no time for a road test," said Dutch. "We've got to move our collective asses across the country. We've got maybe a week on the road before the Dark Lord pinpoints our location and destroys us. So let's do this now."

"Give me the goddamn test, already!" I said, exhausted and wanting a decent night's sleep. Shit. What a day! I realized then and not for the last time that real life fantasy adventures suck big time. But of course I already knew this tragic fact of life from my adventures in Iraq and Afghanistan.

Dutch brought out a case and opened it. The sword inside was less than three feet long. This little thing was the sword of a, or rather "The Prophecy?"

"Kind-a tiny for a magic sword, isn't it?" I said. "You could maybe kill a rat with it. And why do I need a sword? Wouldn't a Glock or an M-16 be more effective? I'll have to get close and spank the Demon Lord to death with this two foot rat-fucker of a sword."

"Rufus, you have much humor," said Dutch. "Now shut-the-fuck-up and take the sword in your right hand."

"A two foot sword. Dandy," I said. By now the dwarves were gathered around me in a circle. They were mostly finished with dinner, except for the fattest dwarf, Larry, who was on his fourth Burrito Supreme. They were now smoking cigars, pipes, and I even saw a few with doobies hanging from their lips and the sharp smell of marijuana filling the room. This was great theatre for them. I didn't give them any reason to think my results would be different than the last candidate who was scarred for life and then I suppose sent on his merry way. Weren't heroic quests to be a little more precise, a little more definitive, just plain more "together" than this. Maybe between the pages of a book they are. Real life is messy, isn't it?

The sword was made of a weird translucent material that shimmered and looked like see-through steel. For a magic and legendary sword, and here I was assuming it was magical and legendary; it was also quite nondescript. There were no jewels on the hilt; no heroic runes on the blade, no obvious ancient prophesy inscribed on a sword I swear looked transparent.

"*Take* the sword, Rufus Timmons," said Dutch who bowed as he presented the open case to me. Too weird, too much ritual. He clearly did not want to touch the freakin' thing. But then why should he if it burned and scarred the last poor schmuck.

I grabbed the hilt and held the sword aloft. My hand must have activated something because red and blue and gold gems stared out brightly from somewhere deep inside the hilt. Golden hues also glinted from inside the blade. The sword felt like it was an extension of my arm and that if I let it go it would stay in my hand. Then the craziest thing happened. The sword had an erection. It was no longer a two-foot long blade. It grew and was closer to five feet long. I stood up and slashed the air a few times and felt ready for anything. I almost cut off the Ornery's head as I swung it around the room. He ducked just in time. Lucky bastard. The sword filled me with joy, an inexplicable feeling of being God's agent for good. Funny, but the sword felt no heavier at five feet than at two.

"I name you, 'Le vendal ley de Rufus.'" I said in Elvish.

"The 'Tool of Rufus?' Hard to beat that for originality; doesn't sound so bad in Elvish," said Buck, who laughed with the rest of the dwarves. Even Dutch couldn't suppress a smile.

"I give you Rufus' Tool!" said Ornery.

"Rufus' Tool! Long may it wave!" shouted the dwarves, who laughed even louder, some of them rolling on the floor.

"What a relief," I said, waving the sword around. "So it's a good size sword when you need it to be. Still, won't the Demon Lord shoot me with a Glock or M-16 instead of stabbing me with *his* freaking sword?"

"The Sword seems to like Rufus," Buck said, marveling how it went from two feet to five feet in no time at all.

"So far so good," said Dutch, clearly pleased. "Evil's weakness is in its own vanity, Rufus. I know this Demon Lord. He'll want to prove he's the better swordsman, and defeat you and the One who sent you."

"Why don't you fight him?" I said. "Or Buck or Ornery or any one of the dwarves here, all of whom are better with an axe than I am with a sword, even a magical one."

"I would, we would if we could, but we haven't been chosen," Dutch said. "Heaven has other plans, Rufus my good man. Anyway that's my belief. And that sword will burn every one of us. But not you. Think about that."

"Could schmould, Chosen, schmosen," I said. "I think you've got the wrong guy. You're telling me there was no one more qualified than big, fat me?"

"You're it buddy," said Buck. "You've been chosen, though only God knows why. Hell, if you think you know better, you can always just walk out that door."

"Satan thought he knew better than God," said Dutch. "Thought he was smarter than God and so defied him and look what happened to him. Just as the Demon Lord thinks he is one step ahead of everyone else, and that we're all fools."

"Especially you," said Buck, putting a friendly hand on my shoulder. "Kindness and decency are not a part of his calculus. The so-called little things. That's how you'll defeat him."

"Buck may be right," said Theo. "But kindness also has a knack for getting other people killed. And you're obviously a nice man, a good man, Rufus. But are those heroic qualities? Don't know. No one does. There are lots of dead nice guys out there. Wish I could be more reassuring. Why you? Beats me."

"Beats the hell out of me, too" said Ornery, never one to miss an opportunity to insult me.

"He doesn't yet know that you possess a legendary sword, crafted in Heaven by the angels themselves," said Dutch, ignoring Ornery, "but he's a brilliant psychopath and believes he's invincible — that he has a sword more powerful than yours. And you can bet your ass he'll want to test his sword against yours. And he's had thousands of years of practice where you've had none."

"Oh, that's encouraging. But you're right," I said. "A swordsman without experience is like a Glock without bullets. Though there's more to fighting than just a sword — or a gun."

"Very true, fighting man," said Buck.

"The angels, huh? What's so special about my tool? I mean this sword?" I said.

Though I don't know about your *tool*," said Dutch unable to suppress his laughter with the dwarves. "As for the sword, I told you — it's from Heaven."

"Via the post office?" I said. "Come on, man. A magic sword delivered by mail just in time for a heroic quest? Do you still have the box, I'd like to see the stamps and return address."

"I promise you Rufus, if we all live long enough on this quest, my friend Lord Reggie will fill you in on the details," Dutch said. "USPS delivered the sword. I got it from Lord Reggie not two hours ago."

"I don't believe it. Not the same Lord Regginald the Magnificent, Elf Lord from the High Kingdom?" I said.

"The very same," said Buck.

"I know *none* of this is reassuring," said Dutch. "But we just saved your life, right? Right?! So have faith."

"I do have faith and 'the assurance of things hoped for, the conviction of things not seen.'" I said, holding Rufus' Tool in the air.

"And I'm in your debt for saving my life. And in an act of faith, I'm giving my sword a better name; No longer shall thee be known as Rufus' Tool. I name thee *Demon Slayer*, and may it do the job for which it was designed."

"All hail Demon Slayer!" said the dwarves and Dutch collectively.

"Should you begin to doubt, brother Rufus, remember," said Buck, "you can walk out at any time and we won't stop you. You can refuse the call. Free Will, Rufus: it's a bitch. But don't count on us to be there when you really wake up dead. With the Senator's resources, you can bet your ass or your head or both that he *will* find you *again* and he *will* eat you — count on it: next time he'll be there himself to make sure there aren't any fuck-ups. And he likes to eat his enemies and friends alive, with a Diet Coke, if the rumors are true."

"With a Diet Coke. How do you like that? Sounds tasty. Yeah, free will is a bitch, man," I said, finally realizing they were my only hope of survival. "Why is it guns will kill goblins from the High Kingdom, but not the Demon Lord?"

"The Dark Lord isn't from the High Kingdom," said Dutch.

"He's a demon of the High Kingdom, but he was a dark angel originally," said Buck.

"What the fuck is a 'dark angel'?" I said. "A euphemism for *one* evil prick?"

"Yeah, and a whole lot more," said Buck, sitting down with at least five pounds of fast food in his gut. He lowered himself gingerly on a burgundy velour E-Z-Boy armchair.

"He's a demon from the High Kingdom, thrown out of heaven with his master before time began." said Dutch somewhat matter-of-factly, "Listen up! Everyone give me your credit cards — and your cell phones. We're going off the grid. I brought cash for whatever we need on the road. We've got five, maybe six days before the senator pinpoints our location. If we don't reach our safe house in D.C. by then, we're all pretty much dead, anyway."

"Why D.C.?" I asked.

"Because now that he's the vice-presidential nominee, he's spending his time promoting the democratic ticket on the road and campaigning with President McClintock in the nation's capital. Still a hardworking senator in Washington makes for great media coverage. We believe you'll get your best chance to kill him in D.C. Make sense? Plus it's easier to plan our attack from our safe house in D.C."

"I guess that makes as much sense as any of this crazy shit makes sense," I said, still in shock and disbelief at this shit storm that had hit me. Man, did I feel fucked-up bad. At least I got one good meal out of it.

It was all just great, super freakin' great: I was at the top of the hit list of a demon lord from hell who was thousands of years old and had more sword fighting experience than a hundred Jedi masters. I could look forward to at least six days of practice, maybe less depending on traffic, with a sometimes short, sometimes long sword, reputedly from Heaven, that I *had* to use to kill the Demon Lord. Yeah, it could happen. Yeah, and I could grow wings and fly to heaven and meet up with Jesus Christ himself to talk about old times and about the man with a plan. In that moment I really wanted an "adventure" tape and a Stouffer's Lobster Newburg on a toasted English muffin, though, I just then realized *I* was the one on the English muffin.

CHAPTER 7

D warves, maybe six, killed our hitters, My Lord," said a goblin supervisor, who handed Senator Ross photos from the scene at Rufus' apartment. "Not to worry, my lord, we burned all the bodies."

"The other side has him." Senator Ross said, who examined the photographs. "What do I have to pay to find competent help? No, this is the work of just one dwarf, but quite handy with an axe. Come closer. I want you to see this for yourself."

Ross tore off his head.

CHAPTER 8

Mother always said, "There are two types of motorcycle riders: Those who have gone down and those who are going down."

Although I doubt it was from personal experience. I couldn't help but reflect on her wisdom as I traveled behind my posse, cruising east on Interstate 40, on my metallic, purple-flecked, three wheeled 1200cc Harley Davidson trike. Dutch also rode a trike, which I assumed from its large trunk stored essential camping gear. I had opened my trike's trunk and found it empty except for the more than thirty bottles of Extra-strength Tums, and two Glock 17 9mm handguns. There were also fourteen miner's headlamps, which made this claustrophobic academic exceedingly nervous. I was sometimes afraid of the dark, though embarrassed to admit it and "howlingly" phobic about being anywhere underground. I entered Taliban tunnels against every survival instinct known to man and I threw more grenades down those tunnels than I care to remember. Clearly Dutch, or someone had a plan unknown to me. I studied the gear and the 30 bottles of Tums and knew that indigestion would be the least of my problems.

For the other dwarves, they rode lowered choppers, like Buck's, declaring to the world that they were man enough, dwarf enough for a Harley Fat Boy, the perfect bikers' ride.

So here I was: an unheroic chump shanghaied onto a heroic quest: Me, Rufus Timmons, who did everything possible to avoid danger, even as a soldier. Falstaff, that lovable coward, was right you know, "discretion is the better part of valor." Surviving war means learning to play dead, retreat, regroup, and rethink an attack on an enemy's position. Retreating to fight another day was no dishonor. "Searching for the bubble's reputation even in the canon's mouth" did not compute in this soldier's software download. A heroic quest meant shit if it cost you your life, unless of course you saved your comrades' life or the life of an innocent civilian. Then it meant at most an honorable death, and at the very least it meant an honorable death. Fuck it. Any way you looked at it you were still dead, right?

Interstate 40 stretches from Barstow, California through the Arizona desert, the red mountains of New Mexico, the desolate plains of the Texas Panhandle, and the red clay prairies of Oklahoma. It runs through Arkansas and winds its way the length of Tennessee, up along pencil-thin roads through the deep forests of the Great Smoky Mountains, down through North Carolina and ultimately to the Atlantic Ocean. To make this trek on a Harley was for me a dream come true. Well, almost a dream come true: the one thing missing was the most obvious. A groovy, awesome looking biker chick on the back my bike clutching my fat gut in love with Rufus Timmons, AKA, the reluctant "Chosen One."

The truth is that only an idiot wears a short sleeve shirt on a motorcycle. On the first day of our quest, and thereafter, we wore faded Levis, JC Penney's flannel shirts for cold mornings and light long-sleeve white Penney's V-neck Ts in the afternoon, underneath black leather jackets with black Revzilla motorcycle boots. The dwarves had me outfitted from day one. The dwarves' bikes had saddlebags that contained not only traveling burritos, but also two Glock 9mm semi-automatic pistols. I stored my Glocks in the trunk on my Harley trike, but my sword's short length and intelligently designed sheath allowed me to wear it down the middle of my back. Dutch's Harley trike stored the world's smallest solar powered microwave, from Sunsizzle Inc. for popcorn and frozen pastry mini-breaks along I40.

Dutch said that our mission to destroy the Demon Lord was one of stealth, but tell me: what could be less "stealthy" than twelve dwarves riding choppers east on I40. You see it everyday, right? I guess hiding in plain sight had its advocates.

We'd been riding for more than four hours and my ass was killing me. My mom used to say, "Rufus, you have schpilkeez." Old world saying for having ants in my pants. I never couldn't sit still for long: Any family car trip more than an hour had me fantasizing about opening the car door and jumping into traffic to a speedy and certain death. It was nothing less than miraculous that I could still long enough to focus on a doctorate, much less finish my dissertation. I looked around, but no one else seemed bothered by riding for hours, which made me wonder where the dwarves got their riding experience, much less their bottom power. Were there Harley Davidsons in the High Kingdom? Gas Stations? Burger joints? Dairy Queens?

It was the middle of the fall season and, thankfully, it was overcast and cool while we rode. We stopped at the big yellow sign with the red heart in the middle, letting us know we had arrived at a Love's Travel Stop and Country Store, an all-in-one destination where you could buy gas or candy, take a shower, get a haircut, or chow down on a bucket of delicious Clucker's Fried Chicken with their famous apricot dippin' sauce. Love's Travel shops were all along I40. We got off our bikes, a blessing for my fat ass. I was walking to the store with our merry troupe when Ornery purposely tripped me and sent me flying head first into a man-size puddle of mud.

I knew many of the dwarves didn't respect me, questioned my fitness, my commitment, and my authenticity. I was relieved that no one laughed except Ornery, whose laughter stuck in his throat as I lifted him by his beard and slammed him against an ancient oak tree. I hated fighting and it always happened when my opponent underestimated me. You'd be surprised how fast a fat man can move when he's pissed. I looked again at the dwarves and I saw approval on every face.

However, if you're forced to do violence, few things gave me greater pleasure than to pound some sense into a bully. Not that you could pound sense into a bully. She's usually too stupid. That was a joke. *He's* usually too stupid. One had to be content with just kicking the shit out of him. In the army, especially if you were a nice, easygoing man, you meet your fair share of bullies, and by the time I'd dispatched a dozen, I'd become a competent fighter, sometimes dirty as dictated by the rules of survival, but always committed. I lost a few fights but I always did significant damage. Also, it was important for everyone to know I wasn't a pushover. I hit him hard just hard enough to break his nose, which was gushing blood down his beard. Ornery was no pushover. He came back and kicked me in the gut and I doubled over, and projectile vomited my breakfast burrito on Theo's boots. Ornery pulled a hidden knife from his boot. Lucky for me Buck threw his own knife and knocked it out of Ornery's hand.

"Let's keep it clean and friendly," said Buck, who laughed at my *unclean,* barf and mud-soaked body.

"I'm so blessed to have you as a companion, Ornery," I said, wiping my mouth as I swung my elbow into his temple and he went face down, unconscious in a puddle of greasy water. I looked to the dwarves to make sure they were ok with my actions.

"Don't worry about Ornery," said Buck, "We've all had to kick his ass from time to time."

"Yes, go ahead" said Theo, "but be his friend after you kick his ass. If you do so, he'll always have your back in a fight."

"You're sure?" I said, as I took some rope, tied one end to my Harley, the other around Ornery's feet. "I don't want to hurt him. I just going to drag some sense into him or he won't respect me in the morning." They nodded their approval. There was a very muddy field behind the men's room and a pail of soapy water. I poured the water on Ornery. I wanted him awake when

I dragged his sorry ass through the mud, but just once. You know, many people pay good money for a mud bath.

"Hey Rufus, what the fuck are you doing?" Ornery said, when he woke up hogtied.

"Time for your bath, Ornery," I said, "Hey Dutch, would you nuke one of those green Chile, bean and egg burritos for me, and grab me some Little Debbie chocolate cupcakes, if they have them, a family size bag of Lay's BBQ chips, and some Casablanca Pork Rinds? Oh, and a couple of cans of cold Diet Coke would be great. Thank you very much."

"Sure thing, Rufus," said Dutch. "You got to eat healthy if you're going to keep up your strength."

"What the fuck?" said Ornery, "A mud bath? You bastard!"

"Amen," I said. "Buckle up. It's going to be a bumpy ride."

CHAPTER 9

We were parked on the side of the road and surrounded by a host of fast food restaurants. It was five hours since I had kicked Ornery's ass. We stopped for gas and everyone was hungry, again! And a hungry dwarf, I discovered, is a surly dwarf. I made sure I gave Ornery my package of my Little Debbie chocolate cupcakes. His nose was broken and bandaged, but he smiled and took the cupcakes. We just got into New Mexico, with at least a day of riding before we even reached Amarillo, Texas. I was eating potato chips from a backpack. Ornery, I guess was still pissed off despite the cupcakes, and hurting from his chapped ass from the long ride. He saw me secretly eating chips while everyone was hungry.

"Hey, what are you eating?" he said.

"Just some chips," I said.

"What kinda chips?" Ornery said.

"Just some Lay's KC Masterpiece BBQ chips," I said.

"You know the rule: share and share alike," he said. "And I'm starving."

"Will you shake on it?" I said, as I tossed him my practically full family size bag of chips, as yet another peace offering.

We shook hands and both knew that giving up a family size bag of Lay's BBQ chips was a significant, even a profound gesture of goodwill, especially among foodies. Especially, on a quest of uncertain duration and outcome, when death could be around the corner or worse — the next Love's Travel Center might be 200 miles away. For now, though, we were safe. We were in the midst of fast food heaven.

"Where do you want to eat?" said Dutch, shouting above the traffic that whizzed by on the freeway.

South of I40 was McDonald's, Burger King, Taco Bell, the Waffle House, Carl's Jr., and Kentucky Fried Chicken; on the north was Clucker's Fried Chicken, Sonic Burger, and Denny's. You can imagine the argument that ensued with twelve dwarves, one wizard, and an overweight scholar, trying to agree on where to eat. Finally, Dutch stuck his cane into the air and shot a projectile high into the sky. We all looked to the heavens as it exploded in a burst of red, blue, and yellow stars that settled on one fast food restaurant: Pepe's Mexican Fusion restaurant. Ok, something new.

For better or for worse, we marched single file into Pepe's for dinner. When we walked out the dwarves and Dutch were all stuffed with buffalo burritos, escargot tacos, chicken and armadillo quesadillas, and queso cheese and Sweetbread nachos. I didn't eat much. Just wasn't that hungry.

Before we got to our Harley's I made a quick stop in a 7-Eleven next door to Pepe's for road grub: a mustard, ketchup, onion, and pickle relish chili dog, plus a can of Sour Cream & Onion Pringles, and a family size bag of M&M Peanuts. In the window of a car in front of me I saw the reflection of Buck coming at me from behind — with his axe drawn! Fuck...my only option was to turn around and throw my dog, my Pringles and my M&Ms at him and draw my sword, Demon Slayer.

"Defend yourself!" said Buck, who cleaved the Pringles can in two and slashed my bag of M&Ms. All those beautiful Sour Cream & Onion Pringles and M&M Peanuts scattered on the street. I never did find the dog. At least I covered Buck's shirt in pickle relish, mustard, and chili.

"What dah fuck!" I said and pulled Demon Slayer out from its sheath on my back. Buck swung his axe again. I blocked his first blow, and his second, but not before he got in a swift kick to my balls. I doubled over and he was on top of me in a heartbeat with his axe to my throat. That black bearded little fuck was on me like flies on shit, like white on rice. Who knew he could move that fast on such short legs? Ornery wasn't half as fast. His axe was a nanometer from my throat still. He kept it there.

"That was a decent parry to my axe, laddie," he said. "But never underestimate a kick to the balls. You can count on dirty tactics from the enemy. Permit me to show you some alternative moves."

Of course I knew this. I'd kicked more than one enemy in the balls in Iraq when the opportunity presented itself. A fight is a fight is a fight. It always gets dirty. Buck then insisted on showing me several parrying moves to counter both sword and axe while the dwarves and Dutch watched. Fortunately, it was at night and the dwarves blocked the view of any pain in the ass gawkers.

Then we left. As I rode, I couldn't help thinking of my lost chili dog, Pringles, and M&Ms. God, I loved fast food. But I wasn't a complete fool. I knew that our fast food nation couldn't survive forever. Health care costs were unsustainable. Epidemic levels of arteriosclerosis, diabetes, obesity, hypertension, cancer — all with direct links to half pound burgers with cheese and secret sauce, deep fried tacos, fried chicken with honey mustard sauce, chimichangas, pork sliders, filet mignon, rib-eye steaks, T-bone steaks, steak burritos, steak salads (yuck, a salad, really?), pancakes and sausage, pancakes and bacon, banana pancakes, strawberry pancakes, lobster and drawn butter, French fries, pepperoni pizzas, candy of every stripe, ice cream, chocolate sundaes.

And don't underestimate the lack of exercise in the general population. Need I say more? Maybe a little more: add to the above soda drinks with astronomical levels of sugar — a huge factor in creating diabetics. Ever notice most fast food joints have unlimited soda for their patrons? Why are the soda dispensers NOT behind the counter, but out in the open where you can refill, at no charge to you, a 64-ounce Coke, or Dr. Pepper, Hi-C Lemonade, or Orange Crush, or Sprite, or Root Beer or "sweetened" iced tea? Drink up America and overwhelm your pancreas. Drink up America and cover it with an extra dose of insulin. We've got your back, guaranteed!!

Throughout this great country, the home of the brave, the land of E Pluribus Unum, the place of 2 apple pies for 99 cents, fast food companies are slowly, but inexorably destroying the health of Americans. Can they have it both ways? Can they wean me or Americans off the destructive, but damn tasty menu to a healthier menu of salads, grilled fish, and tofu "meat products?" Fat chance. Free Will baby, it's a bitch. I wasn't having any part of it. And probably wouldn't unless my future wife, if there was to be a future Mrs. Timmons, laid down the law, a harsh unforgiving law like, "Pancakes or sex, Rufus? Pancakes or sex? You decide." Or in the absence of a loving and sexy wife, perhaps diabetes, or a stroke, or a myocardial infarction might change my ways. Or not.

Cokes, pancakes, and burgers were too damn tasty. Extra Thousand Island, if you please. I know gluttony is one of the Seven Deadly Sins, but it wasn't the worst sin and I knew I'd be ok, for my Lord, my God, my Savior, my Christ said, "I know you're weak, and yet you have kept my word, and have not denied my name." Come what may, I'd be fine, I hoped.

CHAPTER 10

We had taken an obscure exit off I40 just outside Albuquerque maybe 200 miles west of Santa Rosa, New Mexico. We threw down our sleeping bags and called it a day and fell asleep to the high pitched, cackling whine of desert coyotes.

"You sure it's safe to ride behind twelve dwarves after what they ate last night?" I said to Dutch, as we packed our bags the next morning for the next leg.

"I had terrible gas from that fusion-Mex all night," said Dutch. "Thank God we brought the Tums."

"You and me both," I said. "That's why I asked."

Speaking for myself, riding behind twelve dwarves seemed pure foolishness. No sooner had the thought occurred than a thunderclap of the foulest anal generated gas blew by us. It nearly knocked Dutch and me off our trikes.

"I see your point." Dutch said. "Let's lead this pack as we were meant to." We both rode to the front and stayed there. The dwarves were laughing behind us.

"Whatever you do, don't smoke," I said, "or this quest will go down in flames before it's begun. Hey, can I ask you a question?"

"Shoot," said Dutch. There was little traffic on I40 and we cruised well below the 75 miles per hour speed limit.

"I didn't want to put you on the spot back at the safe house, Dutch, but what do I get out of this crazy adventure? I mean, I believe in duty and honor and served in Operation Iraqi Freedom without reservation, but also without significant remuneration, unless you count a lifetime supply of bad dreams."

"Isn't saving two worlds more important than any 'significant remuneration?'" said Dutch.

"Of course it is," I said. "But you heard what they said at dinner the other night. That's a crap load of dwarf gold the Demon Lord stole from them. It's true?"

"Yes," said Dutch.

"Dwarves never do anything for altruistic reasons, if you believe what you read."

"Do you believe everything you read, Rufus?'"

"Of course not."

"There are exceptions," said Dutch. "Are dwarves greedy? Yes. Are they generous? Yes, and I know any of these dwarves will die for me and for you. It's true of man, too. Men murder, rape, and steal. But Men are also kind, generous, and heroic. What's your point?"

"How much money are we really talking about?" I asked, ignoring the truth about my species.

"I thought we discussed this: approximately 2 to 3 billion dollars, give or take a few hundred million," said Dutch, with a shrug and a laugh. "Dwarves are kinda funny: they want their money back — whether there's a world to spend it in or *not!*"

"Not an insignificant amount. Think I'll be included?"

"If you make it through this quest alive, if any of us do, then I think you'll see some money. The dwarves," said Dutch, "mainly Buck, felt you needed more 'seasoning' before they officially cut you in for any recovered treasure. They also wanted to be sure you weren't in this *just* for the money."

"I see. Well, I'm not in it just for the gold," I said. "I'm in it to stay alive! I know I won't last two seconds without you guys,

Ornery included. And honestly, I'd like to help. I don't like this likable Senator Ross. He scares the crap out of me. However, I wouldn't say no to a little dwarf gold; rich or poor it's nice to have money."

"Indeed. I know you're not in just for the money, Rufus," Dutch said. "I knew it the moment I met you. Besides, anyone who devotes his years to write a doctoral dissertation on Frank Bartlett's *The High Kingdom* doesn't do anything for money alone."

"Thanks, Dutch. I'll wait," I said, "for generous hearts to prevail. Just as soon as I'm deemed properly 'seasoned.'"

CHAPTER 11

One dwarf with food poisoning is manageable. Six dwarves with food poisoning is *unimaginable*. Twelve dwarves with food poisoning is an Extinction Level Event. Perhaps the armadillo tacos with chunky escargot sauce from Pepe's Mexican-French fusion cuisine was not the best choice. Mexican-French fusion cuisine: Now there's an oxymoron. However, poisoning usually strikes 2 to 4 hours after a meal. So maybe it wasn't Pepe's. Could have been everything else we'd eaten *including* Pepe's. Thank God I didn't eat there, but my brothers of the Harley Davidson thought the armadillo tacos with escargot sauce quite tasty, albeit a little chewy.

We were around thirty miles outside of Albuquerque when disaster struck. Arnie pulled to the side of the road. Then Theo, Burt, Ornery, Larry, and Buck. I had a pretty good idea what was happening. I stopped, opened the trunk on my trike, and tossed each dwarf a roll of Charmin and a bottle of Tums. They ran like jackrabbits into the middle of the Chihuahuan desert where a series of anal explosions rocked the peaceful silence of the desert. Never even try to predict how fast fast food can affect 12 dwarves, and one lactose intolerant wizard. Dutch followed soon after. Then I heard the pathetic sound of creatures whimpering at the desert sun. I couldn't tell if was a pack of sick coyotes or several howling, moaning, anally afflicted dwarves and a cranky wizard. I was spared as I only ate the plain guacamole dip and chips, which is why I still mourned the chili dog Buck knocked out of my hands during his training assault that night. But good news: everyone survived to eat another day.

CHAPTER 12

On I40 there are places that would never exist but for the small footprint by law enforcement. There was Blade Universe about 70 miles east of Needles, California. There you can buy switchblades, brass knuckles, and zip knives, where with the touch of a button the blade explodes from the knife at 100 miles per hour, as dangerous to its owner as to its victim. Imagine rubbing up against something and accidentally pressing the button. You'd slice off your cock before you were aware of it, nanoseconds before your scream and simultaneous heart attack. Knives at their best are dicey things, double-edged swords in reality. Hurts just to think about it. Christ said it, "He who lives by the sword, dies by the sword." Ain't it the truth. I just hoped it wasn't my truth, and that Demon Slayer had been delivered to save me, not destroy me.

Out on the long stretch of Interstate 40 you'll pass through rose-colored rock formations that look like dead relatives — together with prairie scrub, solitary pine trees, and cactus-filled deserts, all stretching beyond the horizon. Many small towns dot the landscape between Barstow and Amarillo, Texas.

In the tiny city of Santa Rosa, New Mexico, about 170 miles west of Amarillo, Texas, there is "Dave's Plumbing & Cleaning Supplies." Inside is a underground warehouse with a secret cache of weapons that could wipe out most of the state. It's located underneath an overpass on the I40, fifty feet from a lonely Pizza Hut.

Dave's Plumbing & Cleaning supplies has two levels: the first level discounts brooms, pipes, giant tubs of Lysol and Mr. Clean, plungers, plumbers' snakes, wrenches, and a variety of suction devices; the second level, one hundred feet underground is a warehouse the size of a football field, with every imaginable weapon of personal and mass destruction. We parked our bikes underground next to the loading dock and walked inside.

"Dave, my trusted friend, my brother," said Dutch, to the establishment's owner, "Time marches on, but your youthful face and good cheer lifts my spirit." Must be the standard bullshit greeting among arms merchants. This merchant of death, Dave, whose ancient visage resembled the sandblasted face of the Great Sphinx, hugged Dutch like a long lost brother.

"Right back at you, Dutch," said Dave. "Feels like centuries since I've seen you in these parts. You are thrice welcomed, my brother."

"Centuries?!" I gasped, forgetting that wizards and elves were immortal. Should I believe this? I found it hard, but they were from the High Kingdom. Far out, man. What a trip: a life of a 1000+ years. God spare me. Seventy, no more than eighty years will be a blessing and a relief, thank you very much.

"Centuries," said Dave who pulled the woolen cap off to reveal the slightly curved and sagging ears of a very, very old elf. He laughed and put his cap back on. It wasn't as though he really had to hide his ears; they weren't that different than my own. Elf ears were pointy like Mr. Spock's, but not as pointy. Also, that also didn't stop Dave from looking like an '80s punk rocker, in Ked's high tops sans laces, a faded black T, and 501 Levis with holes strategically sliced in each kneecap. He moved with the speed of a sloth. At any rate, he wasn't my image of a merchant of death and destruction. Still handsome is as handsome does, my mother used to say. Arms merchants were not high on her or the Buddha's list of noble professions. Although, I don't recall mom ever socializing with any arms merchants, despite the fact she was handy with a shotgun.

I looked around, marveling at the firepower in the middle of bumfuck nowhere, next to that lonely Pizza Hut, where I planned to have lunch and order a large pepperoni, mushroom, and pineapple pizza and some stuffed mushroom caps smothered in spaghetti sauce. But back to Dave's friendly Armageddon surplus store. We walked down one aisle adorned with flamethrowers, grenades, and spiked ninja assassin stars. Carefully, we placed two-dozen grenades in our shopping cart, and six handheld mortar pistols. We stopped at a wall with twenty chainsaws. Only the best of the best were represented.

"I like the STIHL 240 C-BE," said Dave, watching me lift and slash an imaginary enemy with two of the chain saws. "I modified it. It has half the factory weight with twice the power."

"Why, it's light as a feather," I said, marveling at its solid construction.

"Yeah, you can wield it in your left hand," said Dave, "and keep your Glock or sword in the right."

"We'll take 14," said Dutch. "Rufus, give Dave your keys."

"I'll have my man load the trikes," said Dave.

I threw my keys at him for no reason that I knew. They hit his leg and dropped to the ground and he picked them up. Probably bruised him. There was something about *Dave*, the arms merchant elf, I didn't like. Something disingenuous that I couldn't put my finger on that bugged the shit out of me.

"The usual discount?" Dutch said, who looked at me askance.

"Always, my friend," Dave said.

"Let's eat before we hit the road," said Dutch, who handed his keys to Dave.

I finally understood the need for Harley trikes. At the last minute, Dutch grabbed two mini-flame throwers of a type I'd never seen before. They looked like a sawed-off shotgun with a slightly flared muzzle, like a blunderbuss. It held three shells containing condensed propane mixed with napalm. Each cartridge was good for 120-second bursts of flame-throwing inferno. Not as hot as dragon fire, according to Dutch, but hot enough to incinerate 20 or 30 goblins on your ass, according to Buck.

"Sometimes you fight fire with fire," said Dutch with a shrug.

"I'm starving," I said. "Can we eat at the Pizza Hut?" All of the dwarves agreed.

"We need to use your practice room, Dave," said Dutch.

"We moved it recently to make more room for supplies," said Dave. "Follow me. When you said you were coming, I thought you might need it, so it's ready for you."

To practice what? I had no idea what they were talking about but we all followed them out of the main warehouse. We entered an adjoining building and down a long corridor where we entered a room without any furniture, only a soft padded floor and padded walls. Two guys who looked like thugs were sitting on chairs across the room. Each one had a chain and four-foot long pipe, looking at me with disdain, which isn't very nice, now is it? I looked at Dutch, but he and Dave had already left the room. The dwarves too were long gone. Shit, I thought. Another damn test. I didn't bother with the door. I knew it was locked behind me. Besides, I needed to focus on the threat 20 feet away. They'd be on me before I could turn the knob. Some fucking training program: let's allow two goons to beat the shit out of our sweet, our kind Rufus and see if he survives, which should quickly tell us if he's got skills — if he's got game.

Both the men wore black leather jackets. There was Mr. Red woolen cap and Mr. Green woolen cap; both caps covered their heads and ears. They had tough guy black half-leather gloves where the fingers are exposed to better rip out your enemy's eyeballs, and Red Wing work boots that could crush your shin or kneecap with little effort. The crazy thing was that they had beautiful faces that glowed and belied the fact that I knew they were there to kick my ass.

Like I said, this was to be a simple beat-down and they had chains and each carried a 4 foot lead pipe. They carried short swords sheathed behind their backs and had a Glock 9mm holstered at their sides. They obviously didn't want to kill me or they would have shot me as soon as I entered. No, they were just happy as clams to put some hurt and humiliation on me. I looked up and there was an atrium. There was dark Plexiglas around it so I couldn't see inside, but I was certain Dutch, Dave, and the dwarves were watching with eager anticipation. Especially Ornery. Another fucking test. I guess they thought these two biker punks could do the job.

"So what are you waiting for?" I said, and they got up. Neither one said a word during the fight. I considered just shooting them. But I knew that was outside the rules here, so I just pulled out my sword, the Demon Slayer, the "Tool of Rufus." And waited. They were no dummies. They circled me and I did my best impression of a slow, out of shape fat guy, panting heavily with each step I took — it was a good one, and not hard to fake. But, again, you'd be surprised how nimble a fat guy can be when threatened. Demon Slayer immediately perceived the threat and grew from two feet to five feet in a heartbeat, so fast it surprised my attackers. They were smart and came at me together. I backed away as one swung his chain at my head and the other his pipe. I cut the chain in two and it went flying, but the pipe grazed my shoulder before I could cut it in two. One of the flying chain pieces Demon Slayer somehow redirected at the head of Mr. Red, and knocked him out. I know I didn't have the skills to redirect the chain. Credit where credit is due. His cap flew off revealing elf ears. Mr. Green cap drew a short sword that also grew three feet in an instant. Guess, my sword wasn't the only magic sword in town. Anyway, I cut his sword in two and held him at bay with my sword about three inches inside his stomach. He pulled his cap off and he, too, was an elf. What a beautiful smile he had and a gold aura. He dropped his sword, backed away from the sword sticking three inches inside his gut, and bowed.

"Giles, son of Oregano, at your service," he said. "Thank you for not killing me. If it pleaseth you, may I attend to my wound?"

"It pleaseth me greatly, Giles, son of Oregano," I said. "Tend to thy wound." I don't know if he really talked liked that or whether he thought he might gain a little sympathy with his archaic bullshit High Kingdom speak. I guess it worked. I let him go. His companion was still asleep with a concussion. Elves or no elves, God only knows what they would have done to me if I'd been at their mercy.

The door swung open and Dutch and company came in and congratulated me.

"Is this what I can expect?" I said.

"What do you mean?" said Dutch.

"Is this your training program, you bastards?" I said. "To ambush me when I least expect it and see if I survive?"

"Well, not all the time," said Buck red faced and ashamed at the betrayal.

"Just some of the time," said Ornery, laughing.

"I'm sorry, Rufus," said Dutch. "We're on the road now and I felt we needed a quick assessment of your skill level. There are fell creatures on the road and we will depend on you as much as you on us."

"Congratulations, Rufus," said Buck. "Those were two tough Elvish hombres you took down. I'll feel a lot more comfortable with you by my side. I guess your military training wasn't total bullshit."

"No, it wasn't total bullshit," I said 'hangry,' hungry and angry at their brutal skills assessment. "Don't unexpectedly attack me again. I expect better from my comrades, my so called Brothers-In-Arms." Ornery laughed again, that miserable shit.

"There are flaws in your sword play," said Arnie. "The sword is not a bayonet, which is how you used it in the military, and partly in this fight."

"Exactly right, Arnie," said Buck. "How about this: your comrades will test you, but only to improve your skills, without 'great bodily harm' to your person. Fair?"

"Define 'great bodily harm,' " I said having little faith in their good intentions.

"We promise not to maim you, remove a bodily part, or kill you," said Buck.

"Agreed," I said, as if I had a choice. "Nor will I maim or kill any of you."

Everyone smiled at the victory of reason.

"Dave, join us for lunch?" Dutch said.

"I'd love to," said Dave, "but Italian food gives me gas."

"That never stopped us," Theo said.

"We've got smokers down here," said Dave. "I rip one at the wrong time in the break area and half the state of New Mexico goes up in a mushroom cloud."

"Hey, Dave, you prick, tell your Elf thugs no hard feelings. But the next time I'll kill them and you," I said, pissed at his role in the ambush. My black and blue shoulder throbbed with pain.

Dave gave me a withering 1,500-year-old stare. I gave it right back at him, a younger version. Fuck him. So except for Dave, a dealer in death and destruction, all of us loaded up on pizza, spaghetti, garlic bread, Caesar salad and, in my case, a liter of Diet Coke — and some Bengay for my shoulder. Dutch and I decided to trail our posse, with Buck riding point for the next leg of our journey.

CHAPTER 13

Some thirty minutes passed before yet another anal thunderclap disturbed my rolling meditation on the I40. This time seven or eight of the dwarves quietly maneuvered their Harleys in front of mine and ripped a collective fart right in my face. A cloud of methane ass gas enveloped me and as I choked on the fumes, those little fuckers were laughing their asses off. Those Dwarf-fucks did it again! And I fell for it, along with Dutch. We should have known better.

Even the bandanna that covered my nose and mouth was no protection. The shit powered Italian-food fumes were so toxic that they penetrated my badass bandanna as if it were made of gauze. But Dutch and I had our revenge. We knew the leader of the pack, Buck, had planned the attack. We sensed someone behind us and saw two New Mexico State Troopers on their BMW motorcycles. They followed a hundred feet behind us, and they must have gotten a snootful of the dwarves' anal blast because they looked none to pleased about it. I don't think there was anything in the penal code about farting in a cop's face, although I'm sure they were thinking about it as they continued to follow us.

Twenty minutes after the first assault Buck was giving hand cues to the dwarves for another attack. Dutch pulled out his collapsible wizard's cane ever so slightly out of his saddlebag, even as Buck and his conspirators drifted together. When they lifted their collective asses, Dutch shouted, "Gluteus blistex!" sending a bolt of blue fire from his tripod on his cane directly at the source, igniting the dwarves methane ass gas into roaring flames. The backs of the dwarves clothing ignited, burning right through their jeans, searing their hairy dwarf asses and testicles. The collective screams could be heard back in the High Kingdom. Buck screamed the loudest and almost lost control of his bike. Dutch and I almost fell off our trikes from laughter. Two state troopers pulled to the side of the road and fell off their bikes from hysterical laughter. They gave Dutch and me the thumbs up and then gave themselves up to laughter. Dutch walked over to them.

"Duermo felicitus, sweet dreams," said Dutch, waving his staff over them, and the troopers fell asleep. "They'll have a nice nap and remember nothing."

The dwarves pulled over to the side of the road and applied ice packs and Neosporin to their blistered butts.

"Lipsus demetris alloeis neosporis!" Dutch said, and a golden stream of light flowed from his cane, that encircled the dwarves, went between and through each dwarf, healing each one of his blisters and pain, restoring everyone to complete health. The enveloping aura from the golden light rained down the scent of pure jasmine, invigorating us all.

"Thanks, Dutch, lesson learned," said Buck. All of the dwarves grunted their thanks, still a little pissed off, not very thankful but very much relieved.

"Let's show each other respect and love," said Dutch, "and not fart in each other's faces from now on."

"That was awesome," I said. "Man, you're really a wizard."

"It's what I do," said Dutch.

The dwarves got out spare clothes from their saddlebags and dressed. Later we decided, after riding hours through the desert between New Mexico and Texas to take a collective piss. Dutch held up his fuck-you finger, signaling a restroom break.

We exited off Dead Sucka Gulch. We rolled up to the edge of what I assumed was Dead Sucka Gulch where there was a two hundred foot drop off the ledge and a variety of "dead sucka" animal bones at the bottom. We had drunk gallons of Diet Coke, as the dwarves and I were concerned with keeping their our slim figures, though mine kept expanding; we stood at the edge of the ledge taking a rhino piss into the gulch. If you've ever seen a rhinoceros piss at the zoo, you know what I mean. You're watching, looking at your watch and wondering whether the rhino will finish the same day. Our collective piss was taking some time, so I turned to Dutch.

"I want to marry an Elvish woman," I said.

"Your timing is impeccable," said Dutch.

"I've thought about it a long time, ever since I read about Princess Etherial and Prince Valspur. Maybe with my share of the dwarf gold, I could have *pied-à-terre* in the High Kingdom, you know, a little piece of the High Kingdom to call my own."

"I know what a *pied-à-terre* means, Rufus."

"For my Elf bride."

"First you should know," said Dutch, "that Elvish *princesses* live in palaces, not some *pied-à-terre* gingerbread cottage bullshit in the country. Moreover, Rufus, This isn't the best time to discuss your request, because for one: it's a pretty tall order; and two: you haven't done shit to distinguish yourself; and three: I've just finished micturating and I would like to put my dick back into my pants without discussing eligible Elven royalty."

"You don't believe in me, Dutch?" I said.

"I didn't say that. I believe in the prophecies; I believe in you, Rufus. But you're getting ahead of yourself. First: Let's kill the Demon Lord. When the time is right, if you're still interested, and still alive, I'll make the appropriate inquiries. But you better have some cash on hand. Elf Lords expect the groom to pony up, to show some serious cash on deposit to keep their daughters in the Elvish style to which they've become accustomed."

"You're right, Dutch," I said. "Bad timing. Hopefully, by then I'll have plenty of cash on hand."

"Yes," said Dutch, who put his dick back into his pants. "But like I said: you get through this adventure with all of your body parts, save both of our worlds, and I may be able to sell that to Elvish royalty, a minor house most likely. But no guarantee."

"Understood. Thanks for the vote of confidence. So other candidates have tried to kill this guy, this Demon Lord, and failed?" I said.

"No, others have tried and were eaten." Dutch said. "Very messy."

"Well, shit. Didn't they possess a magic sword like Demon Slayer? And didn't you and the dwarves back them?" I asked.

"Of course we backed them," said Dutch. "*We chose them.*"

"You chose them," I said.

"That's what I said," Dutch said. "But they didn't have your sword."

"No magic sword?" I said. "What the fuck. Why not?"

"It burned the shit out of their hands," Dutch said. "You're the only candidate who was wasn't scarred by 'Rufus' Tool.' The ones before you who *died* carried traditional weapons. Your sword couldn't or wouldn't help them."

"Fabulous, there was more than one?" I said. "Did you choose me?" I said.

"No. We were led to you. Go figure, but Ornery of all the dwarves had a dream about the university and when we checked the university's website, we discovered two things: Senator Ross, AKA the Demon Lord, was speaking and the cafeteria had a special on their famous BBQ French dip sandwich. So that's how we found you, but more importantly, the sword appears to like you."

"How? Why? None of this makes sense," I said.

"There's a lot in this world that doesn't make sense, my friend."

"Well, I want more answers," I said.

"Join the club. This is a holy quest, an unpredictable adventure Rufus; and dear fellow, you're not the only one on it!"

CHAPTER 14

I try not take things for granted. I'm in the habit of thanking God daily for hot showers, clean tap water, and flushing toilets. If not miracles, then commonplace stuff, marvelous, magical inventions from minds greater than my own. I marvel at the magical TV remote control, a wondrous device that enables me to spread out on my couch with a family size bag of Tostitos Cups, a party size bag of Lay's BBQ potato chips, 24 Grand Casa mini tacos, fresh guacamole, a margarita, and yet still wield total control over my Samsung 55 inch HDTV from the couch or anywhere in the room — all without moving an inch. Did I mention you could also add the crapper to my short list of miraculous creations? Think about it: only 200 years ago you'd leave the house to go crap in an outhouse, or in the woods, and risk wiping your ass with poison oak, or worse, taking an arrow in the back from some dumb-fuck who disapproved of Manifest Destiny and white folks stealing their land. Go figure. Today you can sit down on the crapper, release and flush, and your "waste products" are sucked into some pipe that ends up only God knows where, probably destroying the tuna population off the coastal shelf. But now I know the world *is* magical. Wizards, dwarves, goblins from the

High Kingdom appear in my own backyard. Dutch cast a spell that heals the scorched bums of twelve dwarves instantaneously! I possess a magic sword that chops up other swords like "butta." A demon lord seizes my psyche on my way to the library. Elvish arms merchants operate with impunity in the middle of the New Mexico desert. What more proof do you need?

On a less magical note, you never get used to the stench left in the bathroom after twelve dwarves make their "fast-food deposits." Bartlett excluded this information in *The High Kingdom*. I suppose it could put off a certain class of readers, readers with class I'm guessing.

CHAPTER 15

Even now few things in life were better than riding my Harley with my dwarf posse, through the golden sunsets of New Mexico and ponder why I was "chosen."

Maybe the Apostle Paul summed it up best. "God chose the foolish of the world to shame the wise and the weak of the world to shame the strong. For the foolishness of God is wiser than men; and the weakness of God is stronger than men." If true, God made the perfect choice.

While we're on the subject of the miraculous and magical, I looked up from my Harley trike at the night sky in the middle of the desert and couldn't help marveling at the vastness of the known universe. There are 300 billion stars in the Milky Way galaxy and more than a 100 billion galaxies, many so distant that it would take millions of years traveling at the speed of light to reach them. A human lifetime is but a belch on the lips of God, a hiccup in the cosmic throat of time. If 100 billion galaxies is not a miracle, I'd like to know what is. What idiot could look at what little we know about mathematics, or the laws of chemistry, and physics, and engineering, and think there is no God, no intelligent design and designer, and that it's all here by chance?

Which makes me wonder why would some higher power choose a porno jerkoff like me to realize his designs when there are thousands of morally superior men and women, far more talented, and with far better habits and life skills? Ah, what the hell, even Little Dojo in *The High Kingdom* wasn't the heroic type and look how much good Little Dojo accomplished before the dragon, Shraggle clawed him into thin little Philly Steak slivers, to feed to his baby dragonlings.

CHAPTER 16

H ey, I don't know about me, but you're all starting to smell a little ripe," I said after we stopped for a pee on the side of the highway, out of sight from the traffic.

"Yeah, Rufus, you don't exactly smell like a bed of roses," Arnie said with half a churro hanging from his lips like a really big doobie.

"Look who's talking, churro breath, but yeah, that's what I thought," I said. "I mean, aren't you supposed to occasionally wash your clothes on a quest? Didn't they wash their shitty undies by the river *Goldstein* in *The High Kingdom*? I think we're long overdue."

"Rufus is right," said Dutch. "Everyone stinks. I'll MapQuest the nearest Laundromat."

Five miles down the I40 was Wang's Laundromat & Public Showers, a half a mile south of exit 69, but right next door to a Tasty Freeze (TF), which from my experience made a mighty fine chilidog smothered in spicy mustard, relish, and diced onions. Plus they featured a $4.99 special where you could get two chilidogs, fries, and ice slush — any flavor, too! Multiply that by two: four chilidogs, two fries, and two ices for less than ten bucks. I'd call that the deal of a lifetime. Plus TF's ices were legendary: Screw the Diet Coke. I always pulled my hair out deciding if I should order a lime, grape, root beer, cola, raspberry, or a cherry ice. But now I had two choices! Cherry was my fav so I would order that *and* a lime ice slush. So while half of us washed our clothes and showered, the other half ate at Tasty Freeze. I love heroic quests, man.

Buck and the first half of the dwarves all came back eating donuts. Donuts, those bastards!

"Hey, Rufus, three doors down from Tasty Freeze there's a High Five donuts. Ever heard of it? Man they make a great crumb donut. Can't wait to sink my teeth into this here coconut cream donut with a raspberry-ice topping!" said Buck, as if to taunt me.

"High Five donuts?!" I said. "You gotta be kiddin' me. They're the best damn donuts in the universe. Aw, man. Maybe this quest *is* blest, after all."

"You screamed 'High Five donos!' once when you were sleeping, Rufus," said Theo. "Right before you screamed at your dead buddy, Jim, for stepping on an IED in Kabul."

"I talk in my sleep?"

"It's ok, buddy," said Arnie. "We've got your back."

You gotta to wonder: are heroes such damaged goods? I knew I was. Now, so did the dwarves.

Of course after eating all those dogs and donuts it was time for another collective bathroom break. I spent half the time on this adventure waiting for twelve dwarves to crap. All I can say is that dwarves have a very fast metabolism. Buck emerged from the men's room with a big smile on his face.

"I just left Arizona in Amarillo," he said. "I like your world. I was running out of holes in the High Kingdom where forests fill up fast."

"I guess so, what with a few million dwarves running around and crapping everywhere," I said. "I guess you walk in the forest at your peril."

"Oh, yes," said Buck. "We have a saying: the dwarf shit you don't see is the most dangerous shit of all! And if you smell something shitty, check your shoes."

"I'll remember that should I ever stroll though the woods in the High Kingdom."

"It's very difficult now to find a forest to crap in," said Buck. "Almost all the pines cones are gone, too."

"Pine cones?"

"You gotta wipe your ass with something," said Buck. "Pine needles are too messy and sharp and sting. So now there's a shortage of pinecones in the High Kingdom. Gas station bathrooms are miraculous. The toilet paper feels like silk compared to a pine cone."

"Pine cones? Sounds scratchy," I said, thankful once more for the simple blessings all around us.

"You bet your ass it is," said Buck; "I've had to forage hours just to find the right size. However, in the High Kingdom, pinecones prevent ass rash."

"Doesn't the pine sap cause your ass cheeks to stick together?" I said.

"Yeah, so, you pull your butt cheeks apart. Is that so hard?"

"I hope not," I said.

"Much, *much* harder starting a quest with ass rash," said Buck, a man with first hand experience.

"Indeed," I said, sympathetically scratching my ass. "It's uncivilized: like starting a quest without TP. Just plain wrong."

CHAPTER 17

There are monotonous days during every road trip that offer little in the way of inspiring landscape or even buildings of architectural interest, unless you include the new neoclassical colonnade at the Amarillo Sonic Burger. Oh there were hale times of grab ass and soap hockey escapades in the showers at the Love's and Pilot Super Stations, and those were fun until some dwarf hid the soap in a place unmentionable, in violation of time honored rules. Of course, no one would touch the soap after that and game soon ended in curses and the occasional fistfight. But a Tom's BBQ Pork Skins peace offering usually healed most altercations. The days went by like this as we traveled across the flat stretches of desert and prairie crossing New Mexico, Texas, and Oklahoma. The days were getting cold and the nights colder. We generally fueled up at a Love's or Pilot Super Station, where besides soap hockey, we could buy gas, grab a Subway sandwich, or a couple of buckets of Clucker's fried chicken tenders, smothered in their honey mustard, ranch, BBQ, or apricot dippin' sauces.

We passed through the Oklahoma flatlands, discovered its marvelous homestyle BBQ restaurants like Polly and Paul

Jackson's, "Hog Heaven BBQ" in Oklahoma City. We rolled in just before the lunch hour. We ordered a table full of beef and pork hot links, BBQ beef and pork ribs (with their famous sweet and spicy rub), BBQ chicken, garlic rolls and corn bread, BBQ beans, coleslaw, and ten pitchers of their fresh squeezed lemonade. For dessert we got two of their famous cheesecakes and fourteen of their fresh, individual piping hot-from-the-oven blackberry cobblers, with vanilla bean ice cream. It was hog heaven, all right. They'd seen a lot of bikers roll through, so twelve short people with beards riding Harley Davidson Fat Boys was nothing new to them. Hell.

We quickly passed through the flat, red prairies of Oklahoma, which changes into a lush green landscape with forested trees on either side of I40 as you travel east within 200 miles of Fort Smith, on the border between Oklahoma and Arkansas. Suddenly, you can't even see into the trees they are so thick, especially as you approach Lake Efaula, Oklahoma's largest lake, with its beautiful beaches, sheer cliffs, dense woods, wildlife, and more than 600 miles of shoreline. I camped there once with my dad. Though I never saw much of it on our quest. But now the fog was rolling in. It was getting dark and we were all tired.

We generally made camp off the side of the road, careful to stay out of hotels and motels that insisted on a credit card to register for the night, even if you want to pay with cash. Traveling with twelve dwarves didn't make it any easier. Dutch was determined to stay off the grid and we were all convinced the Dark Lord would find us quickly if we paid by VISA or Mastercard. These were my thoughts while as we rode.

"Stay alert! And stay on this road." Dutch said as he rode next to me. "The fog is getting thicker. Look for the *Rest Easy* motel. There's a sign you can see right off the highway. I'm sleeping in a bed tonight, even if I have to bribe the hotel manager with enough cash to retire on. This area is tricky, so, *again*, stay alert! It's easy to get lost. I'll hang back in the rear and guard our collective asses."

"Ok! No worries," I said knowing he was about to take one of his half awake, half asleep wizard naps. I would have never believed it possible if I hadn't seen him do it.

"Just to hear you say 'no worries,' worries me," said Dutch. "Signal me in an hour and we'll switch."

I had been leading my posse on autopilot, dreaming of elf maidens when I came out of my reverie and couldn't remember where we were or how long we'd been riding. I looked at my GPS compass and its LED display was moving all over the map. One moment it had us in Tennessee; the next in Oklahoma. There was condensation and moisture on the display. Everything was wet: my face, my leathers, my helmet, my eyebrows, eyelashes — *everything*, including the GPS. If there had been a *Rest Easy* motel, just up ahead, like Dutch said, we passed it long ago.

"Code five," I said through my helmet microphone, which meant "trouble," and everyone pulled to side of the road. "Does anyone know where we are? I think I may have veered off the 40 to another highway."

"Dammit, Rufus," said an angry Dutch. "Didn't I tell you to stay alert? This isn't a pleasure trip. We're moving targets and the Dark Lord has his sights on us; he's looking everywhere for us, but primarily for you, Rufus. I'm seconds away from calling him and telling him where he can pick you up, and take my chances with the next so called 'Chosen One.'"

"I'm sorry," I said, feeling like an ass. "I must have been daydreaming and taken a wrong turn in the dark. It's a nice looking forest — even if it's as dense as my Aunt Bertha's pound cake."

"You're as dense as your Aunt Bertha's pound cake," muttered Buck.

"Did someone say, 'Pound Cake?'" said Chad. "I'd love a piece about now, with an espresso."

Dutch was rubbing his eyes and looking at an impenetrable forest on both sides of the highway.

"Where in name of God are we?" said Dutch.

"Sorry," I said, again, "Maybe we'll know better in the morning."

Everyone was exhausted. My lower back and my ass were killing me, even with the plastic donut hole I'd sat on for the last 10 hours. I remember watching, with envy, riders on their choppers from the comfort of my dad's old '86 Chevy Impala. My Harley Trike's seats were comfy but still miles away, anally speaking, from the cushy seats in the family Chevy. In truth, I had the distinct feeling my hemorrhoids might burst and bleed out on I40. Dutch led us off an unmarked exit a mile up the road and rode up a short path into the woods, not too far into the forest, but far enough from the freeway to avoid any visitors.

CHAPTER 18

It was pitch black except for our fire. We got out our sleeping bags and half of the dwarves were soon asleep, too tired, if you can believe it, even for dinner. Six of us were cooking Bush's BBQ Baked Beans with Extra Bacon and a package of Walmart's Spicy Louisiana dogs when we heard the rumbling of at least three Harleys. The sound of the engines was unmistakable, as two blue and two red Harley Fat Boys rode into our camp. Fat Boys also described the riders, who looked as if they didn't miss many meals.

One rider, with brown teeth in the fire's light, wearing a filthy blue bandanna said, "Greetings, my brothers! My name is Phil and these are my brothers, Raymond, Farnsworth, and Lionel. Guess we're not the first in the Brotherhood of the Harley David-son to camp in this comfy little spot."

"Guess not. What do you want?" said Buck, none too friendly despite the unwritten code of the "Brotherhood of Bikers," especially among Harley riders.

"We come here now and then," Phil said. "Our camp is a 200 hundred yards west of here. Just hoping to share some of your hospitality."

"Why don't you park your bikes in your camp," growled Dutch, dead tired like the rest of us and anxious to get some sleep. "Come back and join us for dinner. We've only got dogs and beans, but you're welcome."

"Be right back! Thanks!" said Phil, who seemed to be the spokesman, while the others were silent on the subject.

The four bikers set up their own camp and came back in a hurry for some free grub. Good thing half the dwarves were asleep because these bikers were big fuckers and hungry. They cleaned us out of any hot dogs and baked beans that might have fed our sleeping comrades in the morning. After thirty minutes of silent eating the four bikers belched simultaneously waking up half of the sleeping dwarves.

"You're lucky we ran into you," said Phil. "There are strange things going on in these here mountains."

"Like what," I said.

"Like wolves for instance," Phil said. "I'd sleep with one eye open, if'n I was you."

"Thanks for the advice," said Dutch. "We'll say goodnight now."

Twenty minutes later they finally left. Ornery, half asleep, took the first watch. One by one we fell asleep. I'm a light sleeper, and was never a fan of the Great Outdoors. For me, roughing meant taking the elevator to the casino level at Caesar's Palace. Roughing it meant ordering room service at 3AM. Roughing it meant ordering smoothies and a Pu pu platter poolside. Camping was uncivilized, for nature freaks and mosquito lovers; I was proud to call myself neither. I also had a tendency to dream just this side of wakefulness. Which was lucky for us because I thought I heard muffled screams and woke up suddenly. Everyone looked accounted for, but then I heard the unmistakable scream from the biker's camp. I woke Buck and Dutch and pointed out the biker's huge campfire.

"I heard someone scream over there," I said. "Maybe it was just a bad dream. Ornery is supposed to be on guard duty. He must have fallen asleep."

"Go check it out, anyway, *Oh Chosen One,*" said Dutch, exhausted and still mad at me for getting lost. "Take a cell phone with you."

"Yeah, text us if there's a problem," said Buck. I headed for the biker's camp while Buck and Dutch went back to sleep. I started to shake uncontrollably. Do heroes shake uncontrollably?

So what if I didn't look, feel, or act like a hero. Mark Twain said a hero was anyone who could control his fear and act. I grabbed my sword, my Glock 9MM, and headed for their camp, despite my loose bowels. Before I took ten steps, I stepped in dwarf shit, probably Ornery's, who was on watch or supposed to be. Most auspicious.

I tried not to make any noise as I approached. I tippy-toed in near silence. Frightened fat men are the finest tippy-toe-ers in the world. As I approached I saw their campfire at least twenty feet across, not exactly the fire one cooks weenies or marshmallows over. Hunched over it were the bikers.

Only they weren't bikers, but trolls! Biker Trolls! Phil was now at least fifteen feet tall. He was roasting a long piece of meat over the fire. The meat had a pants leg around it, which Phil had scrunched up so he could hold it over the fire without being burned. The flames flared as fat and blood from the leg meat dripped into the fire. Cold sweat trickled down my spine. I crawled between the trees for a better look. The pants belonged to a park ranger, easily deduced from the ranger's hat sitting next to the fire. It looked like a pork loin except for the foot roasting over the fire.

"Toasty Ranger toes, my fav!" said Phil. "Lionel, toss me the KC Masterpiece." Lionel threw him the BBQ sauce, which Phil poured liberally over all five toes. He bit off a middle toe.

"Deeelicious, crunchy and munchy," he said. "Have a toe, Lionel, but save the big toe for me." Lionel bit off three toes, including the biggest toe and chewed them.

"Chewy, crunchy and munchy," said Lionel.

"I said *a* toe, not all three, and NOT the big toe, you inconsiderate pig," Phil said and clobbered Lionel in the face with a branch.

Phil grabbed the leg from Lionel, and poured more KC BBQ sauce on the toeless foot before devouring the entire foot, and half the leg in one bite. He chewed with his mouth open. Terrible manners.

On the other side of the blaze, Farnsworth was cooking a head with a beard attached to it. Oh fuck, a dwarf beard no less, crisping and turning to ash as the skull expanded and contracted from the intense heat: But whose head? Farnsworth popped the head in his mouth and bit into it as if it were a roasting chestnut.

"Ow! I burned my mouf!" he said, tears rolling down his face.

"How many time have I told you Farnsworth? Dwarf heads have to cool off before you eat them, yah dumb bunny," said Lionel. "Serves you right."

I texted Dutch just two words, BIKER TROLLS! Before I was lifted into the air.

"Look who stopped by for a late night snack," Phil said. "Hello Rufus."

"BIKER TROLLS!" I screamed before I pumped six shots from my Glock into Phil's head. His body just absorbed them. Phil didn't even flinch. What was up with that?!

Despite my terror, I flashed back on my Uncle Huston's love of pig's feet. He always kept a jar of them on his Lazy Susan. Whenever we visited Unc, my dad cooked burgers on half of Unc's old wagon-wheel grill, while Unc tended to his pig's feet on other. We'd chow down on the burgers and try not to watch Uncle Houston crunching and munching and sucking the marrow out of the two or three pig's feet he'd squeeze inside a hamburger bun. Fair to say we didn't visit Uncle Huston very often. Let me tell you, ranger toes looked every bit as unappetizing as pig's feet.

"Hey Phil, any ranger toes left?" said Raymond, "Nothin' like BBQ ranger toes."

"All gone." Phil said, "But we do have four dwarf toes left, and some man toes just around the corner, right Rufus?"

"May I be so bold as to suggest that ranger toes are too crunchy," Farnsworth said. "But they ain't too bad with BBQ sauce or honey mustard."

"Everything tastes better with BBQ or honey mustard sauce on it," I said to my amazement, well aware that I was about to become the next entrée.

"Of course, Rufus is right. And Rufus has ten toes left!" said Lionel. "It's a partay, a toe-fest!" My cell phone rang. I opened it. But I was upside down and it fell out of my hand to the ground.

"BIKER TROLLS!" I screamed, though I couldn't be sure anyone heard me. Reception was lousy in the mountains.

At the same time I dropped my phone on the ground, I grabbed my Glock 9MM and blasted Phil again, again in the forehead, which should have blown a hole through it the size of a ranger's foot. But the bullets were absorbed into his body like putty. Guess I couldn't believe the result the first time I blasted him.

Phil scratched his head as if a bug had bit him. His pal Farnsworth came to get a better look at my face and poked me in the stomach. It will always be a mystery to me why no one saw fit to mention — over breakfast, lunch, and dinner — that biker trolls were fucking bullet proof! It seemed like relevant information for almost any heroic quest. F.S.S. Bartlett never mentioned in his novel. But he could be forgiven, I guess, because they fought with swords in the *The High Kingdom*, not Glocks.

"Hi Phil. How's it going, my biker brother," I said, appealing to our shared membership in the Fraternal Order of the Harley Davidson. Safe to say, it wasn't working.

"Hey Rufus," he said with a wide grin of his brown teeth, still with bits of Ranger toes stuck between them. "I bet you're delicious broiled with a light Grey Poupon dressing. Lionel, be a sport and please pass me the Grey Poupon."

Unknown to me and contrary to popular belief, trolls are not made from stone, rather a rubbery substance that absorbed any blow to their body. You could open their gut with a sword and it would seal up again in minutes. Troll blood was a gooey mess: a yellow and green pus that smelled like puke. When I pumped a few 9MM slugs into Lionel's head, a gallon of troll pus flew into the fire, causing the fire to jump another twenty feet in the air. Troll pus contained a natural accelerant.

"Rufus has lots of man flesh on dem bones," said Farnsworth, pinching my right leg. "How should we cook him? Should we fry him in tempura batter and then slice him thin like sushi? I haven't enjoyed any man-sushi in quite some time, not since Officer Bob."

"That's brilliant, Farnsworth," said Phil. "That's using your ol' thinking cap. Now where did I put my sushi knife? I know it's around here somewhere. Farnsworth, check my saddlebags. Come to think of it, with what's left of the ranger, and if Raymond will boil some rice, I'll also fix us up some delicious spicy man-roll, with the tempura man sashimi."

"Is there enough of Rufus for tempura sashimi AND spicy man roll?" asked Farnsworth.

"Sure. There's plenty of Rufus to go around," said Phil, poking me in the gut. "I'll add avocado, Ahi Tuna, and bean sprouts and a touch of eel sauce. Scrumdidililicious!"

"We'll call it Spicy Rufus Roll in his honor!" said Raymond.

"That's so thoughtful of you, Raymond," said Phil.

And to think: not long ago I was sitting peacefully in the library, finishing my doctoral dissertation on F.S.S. Bartlett, with a thermos of espresso and a High Five Donuts variety pack. I had never heard of the Demon Lord or biker trolls, or Spicy Rufus Roll. What I wouldn't give to be back in my peaceful world with a cinnamon crumb donut.

Then I heard the most beautiful music I will ever hear: the thunderous sound of Harley Davidsons coming up fast and furious. The dwarves rode their bikes in and around and between the trolls. Phil was confused and couldn't decide whom to attack first. He dropped me to the ground and pulled off the large chain holding up his blue jeans. It was no ordinary chain. Between each chain link was a steel ball with razor sharp spikes, to break bones and sever flesh. I ran toward the trees to get out of the way and to figure out a way to help.

The dwarves surrounded the campsite. Each one held a revved-up STIHL 240 C-BE chainsaw.

The trolls were swinging heavy chains at the dwarves, but as everyone, except for me, knows, biker trolls don't move or think fast, except for Phil who was intelligent enough. For a biker troll, Phil was a genius. I shot Phil in the leg, hoping to slow him down.

"Bullets won't hurt it!" Dutch shouted.

"Now you tell me?!" I said.

"You gotta cut off his head to kill it," said Dutch.

"And how do I get to the head of a 15 foot troll?"

"Carefully," said Dutch. "Cut off his legs at the knee, and work your way up."

"Oh, sure. Why didn't I think of that? A piece of cake," I said.

"I'm down!" said Guido, who was knocked to the ground by Phil's chain. "I think my arm is broken or really bruised! I'm going to try and make it to the trees!"

When Phil dropped me, I scrambled for the safety of the dense forest. Guido made it to the trees with me, which is where he found me in a semi-catatonic PTSD fugue imagining I was back in Iraq.

"One down, three to go!" Theo said, as he sawed off Raymond's head. Green pus gushed forth like a geyser.

"Rufus! Snap out of it!" said Guido who shook me like a large buttered popcorn until I came back.

"Thanks, I needed that," I said, and looked around at the battle's progress.

All of the trolls had lost their legs, except for Phil, who was fighting furiously. Phil had taken down Buck, right off his Harley, with his chain, and was slashing wildly at Buck with a four-foot, razor sharp sushi knife. Buck barely escaped being decapitated.

Dutch jumped off his Harley, which continued into the trees where it stopped.

"Come on, you fucking midget," Phil said, as he circled Buck. Buck dodged the sushi knife, as he kept trying to rev up his chain saw, which wouldn't start. Phil kicked dirt in Buck's eyes and blinded him. Phil raised his knife for the kill, but howled and fell to his knees when his knife arm fell to the ground. Dutch had shot it off from twenty feet with his Uzi.

"Now Buck! Finish him off!" said Dutch. But Buck still couldn't see so I jumped out from my hiding place, pulling out Demon

Slayer. In an instant it grew from two to five feet in length and I cut off Phil's head.

"Well met, indeed!" said Dutch, who had his arm around Chad, who had cut off Lionel and Farnsworth's head, with assistance from Guido and Theo. Dutch and the others ran over to us and embraced me. Buck was still rubbing his eyes.

"I am in your debt," said Buck, who looked into my face with a new respect and shouted for all to hear. "Behold, The Chosen One! Let there be no doubt!"

"To be your comrade in arms means everything to me: there is no higher honor," I said and we embraced. Dutch looked at me just like my dad did when I was twelve. I had lost a close fight with my best friend Mark, a tougher kid who lived down the street. We gave each other black eyes and even though I conceded defeat, I still knocked out his front tooth. But he broke my wrist and pulled out a good chunk of my hair. I wore my Dodgers cap for months to hide the bald spots. The next day I invited Mark to the house and we both cried. I embraced him as still my best friend. He signed the cast on my broken wrist and I grilled hamburgers for us in my kitchen. You can fight the good fight and still lose. This time the good guys won.

CHAPTER 19

I felt conflicted killing Phil. I was covered in his green blood, slime, and pus. It was my first troll kill, but was Phil such a bad apple? True he and his companions roasted one of my dwarf posse on the campfire, and he had a sick proclivity for murdering, dismembering forest rangers and eating their toes with KC Masterpiece BBQ sauce. And had he almost filleted me for spicy man-roll. But for a 15-foot remorseless man-eating psychopath, he had a quirky sense of humor I appreciated. Yes, he did deserved to die, but I felt guilty that it should feel this good cutting off his head. He was a living creature. I guess taking any life sucks. Ah, but what the fuck, I'd get over it. Phil was just a charming psycho-path and I'd met a few in my life who deserved the same fate, including that prick Senator Ross, the Demon Lord.

Thank God the trolls were dead and we were alive. We quickly determined it had been Ornery's head roasting over the troll's fire. Ornery might have been a prick, but he was our prick, our companion. The memorial service for Ornery was brief but we honored him: everyone agreed Ornery was a piece of shit and that his family wouldn't miss him, and neither would I. That said, some of the dwarves said they would miss him. He was a dwarf warrior, loyal, who never shied away from a fight or from defending his companions.

Fortunately, there was a stream near the troll's camp and we washed most of the slime and pus off our faces. Though a hot shower is what I longed for.

"Great job, fellas. I never thought the cavalry would arrive in time," I said, when it was all over.

"Why didn't you warn us?" said Buck.

"What are you talking about," I said. "I texted you *and* answered your call on my phone. I screamed, 'BIKER TROLLS!' I can't believe you didn't hear me. Check your messages."

"I guess it doesn't matter now." Buck said.

"It does matter," I said, determined to prove I did the right thing.

"Relax Rufus. I got Rufus' text, Buck, and heard his screams. However, we have more important things to do," said Dutch. "Trolls travel with their wealth on their backs. Check every square inch of the choppers. Keep an eye out for secret compartments. Be quick about it."

Burt, a sturdy dwarf with a blue beard, walked over to one of the motorcycles.

"These are nice bikes, except the seats smell like troll shit," he said. "Haven't these monsters ever heard of a shower? Should we keep the bikes? Maybe sell them?"

"Keep them? Are you crazy? I can smell the bikes from thirty feet," I said. "They probably have tracking devices, too. Burt, we haven't got time to sell them. We've barely got time to burn them and get the fuck outta here," Troll shit makes just about any shit smell like roses. Besides, everyone agreed: very bad karma to ride a biker troll's Harley. We would burn the trolls and the bikes, including Ornery's Harley.

"I wonder where they got the bikes?" said Buck.

"Their vics most likely," said Dutch, as he wiped troll slime off his boots after kicking a tire. "Let's look one last time. The trolls have hidden their wealth. I'm sure we're just not seeing it."

I held my nose in the first go around and found dried body parts in Phil's saddlebags: hands, feet (some with painted toes!), arms, and several bottles of Heinz Ketchup, Grey Poupon, and hot sauce packets from Taco Bell. Gee, what could be better than cruising on the open road, and nibbling on a painted toe dipped in Grey Poupon or hot sauce? Does life get any better?

On the next inspection I noticed a blue thread dangling from the bottom of the engine plate that held the engine in place and protected it from road debris. The thread clearly originated from inside the bike. Perhaps the thread was inside a secret compartment. I thrust my pocketknife underneath the thread and a metal plate popped off. Inside was a blue leather pouch. I opened it and a mix of loose rubies, sapphires, and diamonds winked at me. The sun was coming up and I could see the stones were extraordinary even in the early light. They were more brilliant than anything I had ever seen. Not that I know squat about gems. For all I knew, the trolls could have picked them up at the 99-cent store. Their beauty stunned me. Should I just slip the pouch into my backpack? No one was watching. No big deal, right? Consider it partial payment for the Chosen One's work well done. Small compensation from those cheap bastards who excluded me from my fair share of recovered dwarf gold. Who would know?

I'm ashamed sometimes by my first reaction to things. I wanted to snatch and stash those stones and yet I felt a growing camaraderie with the dwarves and with Dutch, both of whom just saved my life! Some Chosen One, I thought. Still, I wasn't yet part of the contract between Dutch and the dwarves for even a measly ½ of 1% of any recovered dwarf gold. The jewels were all I had to show for my efforts. But fuck it and fuck them: I was better than that.

"Hey Dutch, we could all retire — even on 1/14th of the money from the sale of these jewels — if they're real." I said and poured diamonds, emeralds, rubies, and sapphires on a blanket the dwarves were resting on. They gasped. Even in the dim morning light the jewels blazed like stars dropped from the heavens.

"Retirement is overrated," said Dutch, who looked closely at the stones. "My oh my. I have never seen jewels of this quality before."

The rest of the company rushed over to look at the jewels and I could see the wheels turning in their brains, wondering what their cut might be. You see, there I go again imputing the worst motives to my comrades. No, dwarves *are* greedy bastards. But no worse than most humans and who the fuck cares, really? When your back is to the wall, you'll not find a better warrior and ally than a dwarf. If a dwarf has your back, it's your best chance to survive.

"Looks like you have a portion of that wedding dowry, Rufus," said Dutch. "All right, back off everyone: you'll all get your share of any loot. I'll hang on to the jewels for now. And Ornery's widow will get his share. Anyone else find anything of value?"

"Not me," said Buck. No one else answered.

"Right, that's what I thought," said Dutch. "If I find that anyone's holding back, I will be very disappointed." Two dwarves (no name calling here) each tossed Dutch a bag: one with gold bars and the other contained more gems.

"You *all* make me proud to be your companion on this holy quest," said Dutch. "Let's saddle up. We should have left already."

"Rufus, do me a favor and hang on to your gems," said Dutch, in a whisper no one could hear. "I'm watching our cash on hand and it's best if we have more than one person holding on to valuables we acquire along the way."

"Your trust inspires me," I said. The old man smiled.

I'm guessing dwarves haven't changed much since Bartlett described them in *The High Kingdom*. Dwarves were generous enough when it came to sharing anything dangerous, but if they happened upon a treasure first and no one was around, they wouldn't tell you about it. Dutch knew exactly what to say to them. Fortunately, dwarves also have a profound sense of honor and duty to comrades in arms, like the Marines in that sense: *semper fidelis* — "always faithful." Like the U.S. military, dwarves lived and died by that creed.

I thought about Dutch's comment about a dowry and the expectations of elf lords. Did he see something in the future he wasn't telling me? Dutch said if a mere mortal courted an Elvish maiden, he'd better have something to offer. Think about it: Elf Lord Wifflesmelf wasn't about to surrender his daughter's hand in marriage to anyone less than the ruler of the High Kingdom. In other words, no donut binging, beer swilling, fried chicken loving, taco devouring, and sex starved porno watching doctoral candidates need apply — *unless* you brought a small fortune with you. Perhaps Dutch was suggesting an elf maiden wasn't in my future. Or maybe I was just projecting me own fears and insecurities and they were legion.

As delightful as the jewels were, I discovered something disturbing among Phil's possessions: cell phones. I walked over to Dutch.

"Dutch, could you look at these," I said and showed him the cell phones. Dutch had been putting his chain saw in his trunk, where I saw all the cash I had a peek at when we first set out. Smart. Stay off the grid with cash, baby. Cash is king.

"Hurry up Rufus; let's get going; we've got to leave NOW! " said Dutch at first. "Oh, shit. Look everyone: Biker Trolls with fucking cell phones."

"Do you think Phil called anyone?" I said.

"More than likely,'" said Dutch. "Buck, check his most recent calls, quickly! We always assumed the enemy knew we were on the road — just not where. Now maybe they do." Dutch handed the phone to Buck who examined its calling history.

"Are we screwed?" said all the dwarves, ready for bad news.

"We dodged a bullet," said Buck, who was as handy with a cellphone as with an axe. "The most recent call, or text message on any of these phones was 48 hours ago."

"What about tweets?" I said.

"None," Buck said.

"Facebook postings?" said Dutch.

"Snapchats?" asked Theo.

"Nothing," said Buck.

"LinkedIn or Instagram?" I said.

"Nothin' ok?!" Buck said, his patience gone.

"With all of these social media outlets, Buck, we could get fucked every which way," said Arnie.

"I know, I know," said Buck, "But we're good to go fellas. Promise."

"Let's go," said Dutch. He threw the phones into the fire we'd started to burn the trolls and their bikes. The fire was raging and would attract someone's attention soon.

"Yeah, before those flames attract the Highway Pa*Troll*," I said and we all laughed.

CHAPTER 20

When we had ridden for an hour I rode up alongside Dutch and said, "I caught a peek at all that money in your trike when we first set out. Glad to see we still have a few bucks left. Where'd you get it all?"

"From your Uncle Reggie,"

"I don't have an Uncle Reggie," I said.

"Yes you do and you'll be meeting him soon. So get ready to be tested again. Uncle Reggie, Lord Regginald, likes to see things with his own eyes."

"Thanks for the warning this time," I said, "I can't wait to meet him. Hope he's everything Bartlett wrote about him. Sounds like a generous soul, at the very least. You know Dutch, we're down to thirteen."

"I know."

"It's not the luckiest number by anyone's measure," I said.

"You've made your point, Rufus."

"I'm just saying," I said.

"Anything?" said Senator Ross, who sat behind a black walnut desk in his senate chambers.

"No, my lord, nothing so far," said his demon servant, Mike. "But four of our biker trolls have gone missing in sector three."

"That's not far from here. Take the helicopter and see what you can find."

"Don't you think the Biker Trolls would have contacted us by now if they had run into the dwarves?" Demon Mike said.

"Not necessarily. Trolls think with their stomachs primarily," said Ross.

"And they love dwarf meat," said Demon Mike, "which I find tough and stringy. Gives me gas."

"Me, too. Take my new assistant, Jasper, with you. He's on my protection detail and former CIA. He'll know what to look for. And send in that new page. She's adorable."

"The police are looking into the disappearance of your last page, my lord," said Demon Mike.

"Give them our full cooperation. That will be all Mike. Oh, what's the new page's name?"

"Katie."

"Wonderful. Send in little Katie."

CHAPTER 21

We were racing through Arkansas as the sun came up. It's 280 miles from Arkansas to Tennessee on I40. But Tennessee is 455 miles long before you reach North Carolina. Tennessee is a bitch to cross. We knew the Demon Lord would soon locate the site of the troll fight and we prayed he wouldn't figure out we were there until we crossed Tennessee's long stretch of highway, and found cover under the forest canopy of the Smoky Mountains. It meant no stops other than bathroom breaks. Which was a bummer because Tennessee has the greatest BBQ shacks along I40. I practically cried every time we rode past a sign for Reggie's or Uncle Tommy's or Louisa's or Aunt Mabel's or Darlene's country BBQ pit.

By sunset I was riding with my posse deep in the Smoky Mountains. I was still occasionally shaking from last night's battle with the trolls, just as I did in Iraq whenever I shot some bastard. Destroying a life, even an evil one can damage you body and soul. Even the life of a biker troll, well, maybe not as much.

According to our justice system, a man's crimes are said to be mitigated by factors like child abuse. No one mentions or cares in the land of faerie that a goblin or a troll was evil because of a lousy childhood: both are considered evil incarnate. Since I now know they exist, I had to believe there were decent goblins and trolls who despised violence and hated their situation. I had to believe nothing was evil in its origin. Otherwise free will meant nothing. I also thought it prudent to keep such thoughts to myself.

This time Dutch was leading the pack, taking us along a secret path that only he knew. The dwarves looked like badass bikers with their beards and black leathers. I looked like a rotund academic who hadn't shaved in a week. Trolls aside, it was the most fun I'd ever had with my clothes on.

The night air was cold in October in the Smokies and we wore scarves around our neck and mouth. The cold increased with the altitude as we climbed. The leaves on the maples were showing their red and gold splendor. A month from now in November the different hues of red and gold would be gone, mostly. Regardless, the Smoky Mountains were beautiful all year long. Where were we going? I had traveled in this part of the country before and I thought I knew the area inside and out. I hiked through these valleys many times with my dad and my Rottweiler, Max. But I didn't recognize these mountains. It was getting dark, and I couldn't get a GPS fix on our location. I knew in my bones that these were the wrong stars for October. "Where the hell is the Great Square of Pegasus? And the Big Dipper!" I yelled into the speaker of my helmet. I heard laughter. "They should be plain as day in the night sky. We're lost!" I couldn't decide which was more frightening: biker trolls or missing stars.

"Relax Rufus," said Dutch through his helmet speaker. "We're not lost." We were now going downhill now on a road as skinny as a number 2 pencil. Buck almost drove his Harley off a narrow cliff, hidden beside the road in a misty cloud.

"Hey Dutch," I said again. "Where the hell is the Great Square of Pegasus? It's GONE! Where the hell are we?"

"You won't find these stars or mountains on any map," said Dutch. "These mountains hide from the moon and the sun, and are illuminated only by starlight when the earth faces The Halo Constellation. We're lucky our fight with the biker trolls left us enough time to be guided by The Halo stars."

I knew all the constellations from stargazing with my dad. *"The Halo Constellation?"* I said. "Never heard of it. There's *no* 'Halo Constellation.'"

"The Halo stars belong to the High Kingdom," said Buck.

"They've never appeared in your sky," said Dutch. "Until now."

"Why now?" I asked.

"To be honest, Rufus," said Dutch, "I'm not sure. With any luck the place we're heading may have some answers."

The stars cast an uncanny blue light on the road. The forest was so dense on either side of the road that you couldn't see more than a few inches into it. The starlight was bright and on a thick branch that grew across the road, five feet above us, behold, there was perched a large bird three feet tall, perhaps four with its pompadour. Its beak was gold, its body fluorescent yellow and red, its claws were emerald green, all topped off with a sky blue tuft of hair that stuck up from its head like a pompadour.

"Is that what I think it is?" I said. The mist was so thick the dwarves were weaving as we drove just fast enough to stay upright. So I got a good, long look at the magnificent bird.

"What?" said Dutch, focused on the thin road.

"Look up for God's sake! A Phoenix?" I said. "Looks just like its description in myth and legend — down to its emerald claws. Wish I had my iPhone: A Phoenix pic would be priceless."

"Your eyes do not deceive you, young man," said Dutch. "It is indeed a Phoenix and as good an omen as one could hope for given our current plight."

"But they're just a legend," I said. "Right, and biker trolls and goblins exist only in fantasy novels. What plight?"

"Legend or not, there are only five in the world. I've seen two Phoenixes in my lifetime, including this one. As for our plight, I'm certain the Demon Lord is doggin' us. I feel it. He's not far away."

"Oh, that plight," I said. "He won't find us on this road, will he?"

"No, indeed," said Dutch. "This road's enchanted, an enchanted blessing."

We descended slowly into the valley where it was impossible to see further than five feet. The roads were muddy and treacherous. It was slow going. To make matters worse, Dutch turned sharply to the right and then the left so many times that I wasn't sure if we were driving down or across the mountain.

I suddenly felt an inexplicable terror. Maybe it was from traveling so slowly on my Harley through the impenetrable mist — *that* and the blue light from the Halo constellation triggered a PTSD fugue: I was walking on patrol with my army buddies through the dense fog in the streets of Mosul unsure what was ahead or around the corner or on the ground or hiding on a roof. It was all real again. It was sheer dumb luck not to step on booby-trapped explosive device and dumb luck not to get picked off by some son-of-a-bitch sniper hiding in the mist and fog and killing us one at a time like that poor bastard Corporal Gillis who without warning dropped to the ground with an round to the head from a insurgent's Russian made SVD sniper's rifle. A second earlier he'd been muttering how happy he was to have finally heard from his girlfriend in Oklahoma City and then he was dead. Out of fucking nowhere. We had to scramble and drag his body inside an abandoned bakery. The person I really wanted to kill was our fucking Commanding Officer who sent us out in the fog. A dumbass CO will get you killed every time. That's what the fog leading down into a strange valley with stranger stars above had triggered.

Then I felt something hit me in the face. It was a bag of M&M chocolate covered peanuts. I remember saying something about fucking Mosul and Corporal Gillis through my helmet speaker.

"Rufus, eat the peanuts NOW!" said Buck. "You're hallucinating about the war. You're with your comrades who've got your back. Snap out of it!" And I did.

"Thanks, Buck. The M&Ms are just the thing." Buck knew what happened in war. Better still, he was becoming my friend. Plus chocolate and peanuts helps in most situations.

After hours of abrupt turns we emerged below the cloud cover only to see a sign for a Holiday Inn that was five miles away. However, the sign read, "Holiday Inn — Closed for Repairs." How strange is that? In the middle of freaking nowhere there was a Holiday Inn. Impossible. Of course it must be closed. Who could find it unless he was lost and stumbled onto it? For the next five miles I played this endless tape in my mind: "What the fudge? A Holiday Inn? No way." But 45 minutes later, there it was. Its electric sign flickered on and off, mostly off. The inn was dark, dilapidated and deserted from the outside.

The hotel's entrance was boarded-up, its bright yellow paint peeling and covered with green moss. As we approached the entrance, an old concrete circular driveway, the building disappeared! Was it magic? An illusion? A hologram? In its place stood a chateau, like that crazy Castle Lichtenstein in Germany. It possessed four turrets to guard it from surprise attack and like the Castle Lichtenstein, its tallest spire pierced the clouds.

We rode up and looked around and saw that the circular entrance was wide enough for all of our Harleys to sit side by side; and where we saw stained and chipped white concrete bricks there was now a pristine black onyx and gold tiled driveway with a ruby red brick fountain in the middle with its own self sustaining golden waterfall. That's where we stopped, all of us astonished, hoping this *wasn't* an illusion. Finally, a place to rest.

"Pray that it's real, everyone," said Buck, who smiled wide-eyed at the glorious castle.

"I hope they have decent room service. I'd love a grilled ham and cheese on sourdough with a chocolate shake," I said.

"All I want is a firm mattress and a hot shower," said Buck.

"Me too!" said the rest of the dwarves in unison.

"And maybe a Philly Cheesesteak with extra grilled onions," said Theo, who ordered one whenever he found it on a menu.

"I'd like an uninterrupted night's sleep," said Dutch. "And maybe some Mary Jane for my bong."

"Seriously? I said.

"It's relaxing and now legal in much of the country. Why not?"

"Ok, just saying."

"You want to see my medical marijuana card?"

"It's ok, Dutch, really," I said. "I think we all need to relax. It's been a stressful time. I was just saying."

"So just stop saying, *'just saying,'* ok?" said Dutch. "It's damn annoying."

"Ok, Ok, I was just, just, just damn glad we made it down that mountain in one piece."

"Good, now shut the fuck up and be 'glad'," Dutch said.

"Oh, go fuck yourself," I said under my breath. I guess even wizards need some down time. Damn testy, some of them.

CHAPTER 22

We sat on our Harleys in the circular driveway at the chateau's entrance, We looked up in awe at tallest spire which disappeared in the clouds when two young men came out to greet us. Both of the men, no older than 25, had some kind of bright rose and brighter gold "glow-thang" going on, respectively. The young man emanating a glittering gold aura was so beautiful to look at that his radiant smile made me happy, no small achievement. Elves can do that to you. Even the dour dwarves were delighted in his presence.

"Dutch!" he said, and bear hugged the old wizard, as surprised to see us as we were of him. "It's been too long since you graced us with your presence. What brings you to this side of the divide?"

"Everyone," said Dutch, "this is James, the son of our host *Lord* Reggie, master of this establishment."

I guess that explained the gold glow-thang. You'd expect no less from the son of the legendary Lord Regginald from the High Kingdom, right?

"James, we need to consult you father on a matter of some urgency. Is he home?" said Dutch.

"He's off hunting goblins with my brothers."

"Goblins in the Smoky Mountains, too?" Dutch said, looking even more anxious than when we found the trolls' cell phones. "Trolls and goblins multiplying in the United States of America? What's next? Dragons?"

"Did you say trolls, Dutch?" said James.

"I did, indeed. Biker trolls," Dutch said. "We just killed four of them off I40."

"I'd like to be present at that discussion," said James. "He'll be home soon and you can discuss this troubling news. I know he's spoken your name regarding the goblins and other issues of mutual concern. I'm forgetting my manners. Welcome to all. Please, everyone, come inside. You must be tired. We'll attend to your motorcycles and luggage."

"Are you sure?" I said. "We're covered in troll slime. At least we should leave our boots outside."

"Nonsense, Rufus," said James, who laughed. "Despite the troll slime, you're our honored guests. I won't hear of it. Dear friends, enter."

How did he know my name, I wondered. He spoke it as if we had been buddies these many years.

As we walked into the chateau I realized the dilapidated Holiday Inn sign was indeed a hologram meant to disguise the true nature of this structure, not that anyone was likely to accidentally stumble upon the place, unless they were looking for it and had the Halo Constellation to guide them. Because we weren't in Tennessee anymore, now were we? I wasn't sure. We certainly weren't under Tennessee stars. I walked into the chateau/hotel hoping to find a front desk, a room, a hot shower, a few restaurants, maybe even a Chinese noodle shop. You know, maybe something like the Venetian in Vegas. Oh, and by the way no one's troll slimed boots left so much as a mark on the gorgeous white carpeting in the lobby. But what we found instead was extraordinary. We entered a large room with four or five elf maidens in the background playing harps and music so beautiful that it gave me goose bumps. No hotel "muzak" track ever sounded, or looked so lovely. At several tables Elves, men and women, were playing what looked to be Texas Hold'em. I think a tournament was in progress as none of the players seemed to notice that 11 filthy dwarves, one smelly man, and a disheveled (and surly) wizard had entered their domain. I knew televised poker tournaments, as well as Internet gambling sites were very popular. Though I never expected to see elves succumb to a national obsession.

The game looked tempting. I wouldn't mind taking a little bit of their elf gold. Sure hadn't seen any damn dwarf gold on this quest. Then I realized it would be a big, very big mistake to sit down at poker game with elves. Reggie's son, James knew my name instantly. Imagine if he could just as easily read my mind, my poker face, or my poker hand?! I'd go bust in no time. Speaking of bust, every elf maiden I'd seen so far had a huge bust. Lucky elf dudes, right? Right then the four large busted elf maidens left their harps to attend to us. Without a word they split our entourage into four groups and led us to our rooms. The maiden responsible for our little group of Burt, Petey, Buck, and me, took us into one room.

"This is your room, Rufus," she said, with a voice like an angel, or what I thought an angel would sound like. "Each of your rooms is the same so I'll demonstrate all the features in this room."

"What's your name?" I said, thinking she would make a more than acceptable elf bride. With her golden hair cascading down her back, her skin a golden brown, and eyes the color of violets, to say nothing of her ample bosom (minimum 38DD). She was heavenly HOT.

"My name is Chantil Gemstone, *Mrs.* Chantil Gemstone," she emphasized, as if in response to my unspoken thoughts of romance and lust.

"Gemstone is right on the money," I said. Damn. Rufus, you old horn dog, I thought. Chantil must be a mind reader and one hell of a poker player. She's read your hand like a pro. What was my

Tell? My tongue hanging out, the heavy breathing, the drooling, or was it my laser-like focus on her big breasts? Fold your hand, buddy.

"Here is your telephone. You have only to pick it up and request something to eat or to drink. Our kitchens can prepare any food you desire. Grilled ham and cheese on sourdough with a chocolate milkshake, right Rufus?" said Mrs. Gemstone into the phone. She was a mind reader, oops.

Sure enough, we turned around and there was a grilled ham and cheese and a chocolate shake on a small table by the door. Man, I've heard of fast food, but then there's elvish fast. Woooo, baby!! Instantaneous room service was far beyond my expectations. This had to be heaven.

"That's too good to be true," I said.

"Nevertheless, it is true, Rufus Timmons, Oh, Chosen One," Mrs. Gemstone said, with impeccable manners and angelic voice.

"Please, just Rufus," I said.

"By my Grandmother Furkin's beard, seeing is disbelieving," said Buck.

I made sure I was the first to take a bite out of the grilled ham and cheese. I took a huge bite, almost half the sandwich, plus a gigantic swig of the shake.

"Best damn ham and cheese I've ever tasted," I said. "Have a bite, everyone."

"We would if you left any, you pig," said Buck, who devoured the other half.

"What about us?" said Burt, as Buck finished off the milkshake, too. "I'm ordering some mint chip ice cream as soon as I get to my room."

"Sorry, fellas, Buck make sandwich go all gone. Order your own," he said with his mouth stuffed with the remaining ham and cheese, which caused Mrs. Gemstone to laugh mightily for a good minute.

"Also, I must caution you about the showers," said Mrs. Gemstone sitting on the bed, laughing at Buck's grunts of happiness with his grilled ham and cheese. "They use the enchanted waters from the lake below. To bathe in such water is a heady experience for most mortals. Often it is the most pleasurable experience you have ever had in life. It is akin to being baptized in holy waters from the dawn of creation. Be careful not to spend too much time under the shower or in the bath." Geez, I thought, speaking of "heady" experiences, it sounded like the perfect place to jerk off, and it had been ages since I had any relief, much less the most pleasurable experience since the dawn of creation! Count me in. Everyone left PDQ. I guess I wasn't the only "creationist" in the room.

CHAPTER 23

When the others left, I lunged for the shower to test the waters, so to speak — and Mrs. Gemstone was right! Wow! Truly, the best experience I've ever had without a woman. Later, during the afterglow, wearing a green silk bathrobe, I sat on my bed dining on Lobster Newburg on a toasted English muffin (buttered), drinking a margarita, and looked down from my luxurious suite to the lake below. It felt as if the castle floated in the air, and I marveled at the lake some 500 feet below the chateau, on no map I'd ever seen, where sailboats, with red and blue and gold sails were docked at a white pier. But where did the lake come from? We saw no evidence of any lake as we descended into the valley, but the mist probably hid it. How was it possible to disguise, to hide the existence of a lake, much less a mountain range or the Halo Constellation? It defied the laws of nature. This Lord Reggie must be one powerful elf-dude.

The water of the lake reminded me of the brief time I spent in Maui with supply Sergeant Maureen Monroe. We had shore leave and we both stood at the window of our hotel room, holding hands, naked, and silenced by the surreal beauty of the white sandy shore and emerald green water that by the gradation of a few hundred yards became a deep cobalt blue. Of course, I couldn't take my eyes of the very real beauty of Sergeant Monroe's curvaceous figure, which also silenced me as we made love. One of the briefest, but happiest times in my life, until it ended, when I was miserable and heartbroken.

Again, I had that hovering feeling, as if I was floating on clouds, high above the lake. It was making me dizzy, and I was already a little drunk.

Thus far Lord Reggie's world felt like the happiest place on earth; and if there is one thing I distrust, it's happiness. The space was brighter, cleaner than the world I was from. I was in a world before mankind soiled it, or so it seemed to me. Was this a *real* slice of heaven? Every time I'd visited Disneyland, the other happiest fucking place on earth, I always felt like killing myself. But in the happiest possible way: like taking a header off the Matterhorn and, God willing, landing on Snow White, with my face buried in her 38 Double-D snow white breasts. At least I would die with a smile on my face. I can't speak for Snow White, however. I often imagined dying and going to a heaven which turned out to be just like an enormous Disneyland, only to discover by degrees that I had actually been sent to Hell! But Reggie's wonderful establishment, notwithstanding, made me long all the more for a loving woman to share it with.

Dutch told me that Reggie's place was one of the most secure locations in the country. Yet there were no guards anywhere, no security presence. Evil could obviously enter the valley or Lord Reggie would not have been on a goblin hunt when we arrived, correct? I wondered how close could the bad guys get to this chateau built like a fortress and surrounded by magic.

I wondered if Elves looked and lived like this in the High Kingdom. Was everyone tall and beautiful? All the women were at least six feet, and the size of their breasts gave me heart palpitations. Sorry if I sound like a pig. I'm not. I'm a gentleman, a gentle soul. Can I help it if I love big kahunas, lovely tatas, or ginormous bazooms? Please don't misunderstand me: lovely small-breasted, large booty women have their charms, too. In fact, all women have their charms. Without women men would have committed suicide long ago. Without women what would be the point of living? Adam who went into exile with Eve knew this. Maybe God said to Adam, "She's sinned. She's flawed. Leave her. I'll get you another one. A better edition." But Adam said, "Not a chance. Either kill me or send me away with her." How about that? Adam chose Eve over God, over paradise. Was it a test? If *I'd* been God, I would not have been too displeased. Perhaps while he was still sinless Adam should have chosen God over Eve to better plead her case for forgiveness. Then again, maybe Adam wasn't taking any chances that God would say no and made his choice accordingly. Ah, what do I know?

In all of our time here, brief as it was, I never saw one unattractive face, excluding my own, and, of course, those squat, hairy dwarves. Elvish men and women stepped out from the pages of *GQ* and *Vogue*. These elves, looked even better than those described in F.S.S. Bartlett's, *The High Kingdom* or in the countless fantasy novels and short stories I've read about elves. Where were their pointy ears like Mr. Spock? They curved upward slightly, but it wasn't that noticeable unless you looked closely. I had never seen or imagined seeing any man or woman as beautiful, much less emanating a visible aura. Except for Halle Berry, and my dad, who by halftime had a golden aura after the tenth Budweiser, who when he wasn't glowing, was in the bathroom pissing his brains out and missing half the game. Some of the elves glowed blue. Others glowed with a gold or silver aura surrounding their person. I think it was an individual elf thing. Every elf had his or her own special glow-thang. Even those elvish thugs whose asses I kicked glowed.

"What's up with all the hot women, and the auras surrounding everyone?" I said to Dutch. We were having a beer in the lobby watching the Texas Hold'em players.

"The elves here don't match your world's stereotypes, do they?" said Dutch.

"No," I said. "What happened to their pointy ears? Mr. Spock would be so disappointed."

"Here's the deal," said Dutch. "Maybe you should sit down because you won't believe me. They are the *same* as humans — only they were never thrown out of the Garden, like Adam and Eve. The ELVES *never* disobeyed God. They are without original sin."

"Holy shit. You're kiddin' me, right?" I said.

"Never been more serious," Dutch said smiling at my look of disbelief. "You don't believe me."

"So they never died, were never sent back to the dust they came from," I said.

"Right," said Dutch. "Until they choose to die and go to wherever God leads them, and I emphasize, 'where God leads them.' As opposed to man who thinks he can lead God, that God should follow him. Pride and arrogance. Elves always, always follow God. Get it? Got it? Good!"

"I don't know, man. I'm confused. I don't know what to believe," I said. "I've always questioned whether there was a real, historical Garden of Eden, much less a parallel Eden in the High Kingdom. I need time to wrap my brain around that one. I mean most of the Bible stories had witnesses to record it, who wrote it all down. Scribes some would say. Witnesses saw Moses part the Red Sea. Witnesses saw David slay Goliath. Even Jesus had the apostles to record the events — three of them anyway — who recounted much the same story. But who was the witness to the events in the Garden? Did God write it down? Did Adam recount the events orally to his heirs? Seth? But I agree, men are arrogant bastards, many of them, especially those with power."

"Yeah, Adam recorded it — through Seth and Seth through his children. Good guess. But take as much time as you need," said Dutch. "I'm tired and I'm going up to my room and sleep in peace for the first time on this nutty quest. I miss my wife, Giselle, who waits for me back in the High Kingdom."

I followed him upstairs for a nap of my own. Cool. Dutch was married. Was she an elf? A wizard? Maybe there *was* hope for me, too.

I must have fallen asleep a long time and only awoke to my phone ringing. It was Dutch.

"Reggie's back." He said. "We're meeting in thirty. Hurry up."

I looked at the clock and I realized I had been snoozing for three hours. I felt completely rested. I ordered Lobster Newburg again over a toasted and buttered English muffin and then got dressed. It took me five minutes to get dressed and the Lobster Newburg was waiting for me on a little dining table with a can of Diet Coke. I hadn't ordered a Diet Coke — and yet there it sat next to a tall ice-filled glass. What a great little meal before a powwow. I took an extra minute or two to stuff some of the complimentary shower soaps in my backpack. The soap was strangely invigorating and smelled of lilacs, gardenias, and jasmine all rolled into one bar. On the skin the soap felt soothing, like a baptism and a blessing — a soap-like epiphany. Now here's the crazy thing: the more soaps I packed, the more soaps that reappeared on my bathroom sink. Talk about accommodation! I headed downstairs, happy for no damn reason.

When I saw Reggie, Lord Reggie, I would have taken an oath on the Bible that I had known him my entire life. He had such a knowing, relaxed, and generous attitude towards everyone. I never would have guessed that the leader of the elves lived outside the High Kingdom and was working to defeat the Demon Lord, Senator Ross. He didn't look a day over forty, despite the fact that he was, according to Dutch, more than 1,700 years old.

We were talking about our encounter with the biker trolls when he said, "Rufus, could I examine the jewels you found?"

"Sure," I said, and poured the jewels from my backpack on the table.

"These gems," said Reggie, "are from the High Kingdom, from the mines of Thorzak, King of the Grey Dwarves. I saw these jewels grace his crown and the crown of his queen. How they ended up in a troll's hoard is a mystery. They are priceless, and they would make a fine dowry." Why was he looking so knowingly at me? Had Dutch betrayed my confidence? No way.

"In *The High Kingdom*, The Kingdom of Thorzak was destroyed more than two thousand years ago," I said. "You don't look a day over 40."

"We age very slowly and try to shield ourselves from the evil in both of our worlds," said Reggie.

"Wizards and Elves age slowly," Dutch said. "You should know this, Rufus. It's all in the Frank Bartlett's appendix."

"Cut me some slack," I said, "it's been a rough week."

"Dutch said you saw the evil one at Middlebrook University," said Reggie. "That he spotted you in a crowd of several thousand students?"

"The most frightening two minutes in my life. And I'm not so easily frightened. And I couldn't tell you how I knew that my very life was on the sword's edge."

"Good instincts. Indeed, it was, Rufus," said Reggie, "If he had captured you, he would have eaten you on the spot, no questions asked. It's a safe bet that he ate the aide who failed to catch you."

"Why does this sick bastard like to eat people?" I asked.

"They taste good to him," Lord Reggie said. "Like your Lobster Newburg."

"People sushi. I don't get it." I said.

"People sashimi. He eats them raw and whole. No rice required," said Reggie with no attempt at humor. He was deadly serious.

"Thanks for the specifics. I'll be sure to keep my distance when I finally meet up with the bastard," I said.

"That's the problem: you've got to get up close and personal to kill him."

"Yeah, that is a problem, isn't it?"

Just then a young woman came and sat down next to Reggie. She looked at me and smiled.

"Allow me to introduce my daughter, Katherine," said Reggie.

"Katherine," I said, "It is indeed a pleasure to meet you." I must have sounded like a phony bastard. I let out one of my habitual deep sighs and my belly jiggled. She had a massive pair of... a remarkable, nay, a majestic bosom.

"Please, just Kate," she said.

"Frank Bartlett left quite a mystery, bless his soul," Reggie said. "He wasn't much younger than you, Rufus, when I met him in Dreideldom. Bartlett's history of the High Kingdom was well received in this country as I recall."

"Yes," I said, "but as a work of fantasy fiction not history."

"Quite fortunate for us," said Reggie. "The last thing we wanted was a legion of fans finding their way to the High Kingdom and running amok in our peaceful countryside."

"Trolls? Goblins? Peaceful countryside? Really? Not from what I've seen so far. But why go to the High Kingdom," I said, "when the High Kingdom will come to you? You can be eaten by trolls right in your own backyard."

"An excellent observation, Rufus," said Reggie, who laughed. "And a fair shot across my bow. But we're here temporarily, until you, Rufus, fulfill your quest."

I looked at Reggie doubtfully, and at Dutch and the dwarves, as if they were alien invaders to my world, which is exactly what they were. Katherine immediately read my state of mind and said, "Father and welcomed guests, would you mind if I borrowed Rufus for a few hours to show him the beauties of the valley?"

"Of course you may, Kate," said Reggie, "but Rufus, may I borrow your sword for a few hours?"

I was loath to give it up, and not sure why or what to say. The sword felt like it was a part of me now. Besides it would burn Reggie if he tried to touch it. Dutch read my mind.

"Just put the sword on the table, Rufus," said Dutch. "It'll be fine."

"Sure, no problem," I said, and unbuckled my sheath, placing Demon Slayer, Rufus' Tool on the table.

"Katherine, be sure and show Rufus the Fountains of Gerald and Laura Joy," said Reggie.

No one voiced any objections and indeed the dwarves looked quite envious as Katherine placed her hand in mine and led me away.

CHAPTER 24

We walked and talked amid the singing waterfalls, chattering brooks everywhere whispering in sweet voices like the Siren's song saying, "Stay a while, friend. Don't rush, enjoy the beauty and the love — before you go forth to face the evil that you are destined to face." I know that sounds pretentious. I also knew I couldn't stay long at Reggie's Shangri-La or I would never leave. Above me were cliffs covered with lush green clover, blue vines, and blossoming rainbow flowers, intoxicating plants I couldn't identify, most likely native to the High Kingdom. I knew the elves had brought the plants since they gave off a scent unknown to me, but one filled with hope and love. Rainbows shined through the cathedral of waterfalls above us.

In Reggie's home, there were no speeding cars intent on turning me into road-kill. There were no video arcades, smart phones, or people texting instead of talking. Compared to my own world's seductive but alienating charms, Kate's cheerful voice and ample bosom provided a healing respite. When a beautiful, voluptuous elf maiden takes your meaty paw in her hand and pretends to find you even mildly interesting, who could ask for more? I could. But I wasn't going to get any. Ok, I'm a pig. Can one help one's thoughts? You try it. Here's a little test, a quiz really: try not to think of a beautiful woman with huge hooters. What is she wearing: tight blue slacks around her 40-inch hips? And a V-neck pink cashmere sweater packing 42 DDs? And her hair: long, deep brown almost black, stopping at her heart shaped ass. And then consider her eyes: are they blue, so blue they embarrass the sky? Or are they such a deep chocolate brown, so rich that you bite your lip in disbelief? But don't think of it. Banish it from your mind! Or can you?

That was one of my beefs with F.S.S. Bartlett's *The High Kingdom*: Where were the women? Where was the sex? Where were all of those elf maidens with their golden auras and large breasts? Most of the poor dumb bastards reading the book were male, single, nerdy, romantic, horny souls who'd never seen, much less touched a naked breast or had a chance to read about them in erotic, but tasteful prose, like Bartlett's. That bastard Bartlett left out all the good stuff. Those were the guys standing in line by the thousands when the movie adaptation was released. I know. For apart from Sgt. Monroe, my first great love, I was one of them, at least in spirit.

In *The High Kingdom* you knew Lord Gerald and Lady Laura Joy had the hots for each other. They were destined to be king and queen. So where's the harm in advancing the honeymoon a few months before the official marriage for the sake of the readers? A harmless handjob before they married 'twas not an unreasonable heroic quest-request to me. Or was it too much to add a description of their love making before the big battle, just to give Gerald, the future King, some incentive to return to Laura, alive with all his body parts intact. Geez, Loueez, the heroines should get to have hot sex before the big battle, right? Are not the rules, the standards, the conceits of faerie, of High Fantasy and the heroic quest total bullshit?

Why isn't good old fashioned fornication or a blowjob part of the world of Faerie and the heroic quest? Quest schmest. In many ways the heroic quest is a very limited literary genre. Even the one I felt forced to take part in. I agree that depicting dwarf sex is just wrong. I don't know if I could even read about steamy dwarf sex, much less watch it at the movies. I'd give it a shot, though. Worse case scenario: you close your eyes and listen only to the protestations of love and the grunting. For that matter, you don't meet so much as one dwarf woman in any of the 2,000 pages of the The High Kingdom. Why? Are they that unattractive? Do they have beards or hairy breasts? No one knows. Hmm... hairy breasts...hairy 44 double Ds. I could stand to see that on the big screen.

Why couldn't it also be a bit more like *The Godfather*, where you could count on Sonny Corleone banging anything in a skirt? Why couldn't we have a least one character — an elf, a man, or even a dwarf who was like Sonny Corleone — who wanted to bang anything in a skirt? I said that twice now. Maybe Bartlett could have included even a threesome: a man, a dwarf maiden and willing elf maiden. I could stand to see that on the big screen. Nobility and chivalry and good taste (and a PG13 rating) required a damper on all such normal or fairly normal human activities and I could see all of those admirable qualities in Kate. Although something told me I was not destined to know Kate in the biblical sense, nor was it healthy for an overweight academician to entertain such delusions.

Such were the thoughts that flitted across my mind as we strolled through gardens with purple and red orchids, coal black grottos, and sweet jasmine.

"May I speak to you as a friend, Kate?" I said, as we walked under one of the many beautiful waterfalls.

"You honor me with your friendship, Rufus," she said.

"I'm pretty sure it's the other way around," I said.

"What's troubling you?" Kate asked.

"How am I going to defeat this monster that's just as happy to eat me as kill me?"

"Probably happier to eat you alive." Kate said. "Don't look so glum, Rufus. Why do you think Dutch brought you here? He's got to feed someone to the Demon Lord and he's known the dwarves longer than you." She laughed. I wasn't laughing. Was she right?

Was I canon fodder? A Demon Lord appetizer? Like cheese on a cracker? Lox on a bagel? Chopped liver on rye bread? Cheez Whiz on a Pringle? Or just Lobster Newburg on an English muffin?

"Relax Rufus, I'm joking, I'm joking!"

"Very funny," I said, less than reassured. "I still I think they chose the wrong guy."

"They didn't," said Kate. "Trust me. You're the real deal, Rufus. And I say this because you seem so wrong for the part that I have to think that God must have a marvelous sense of humor and a good reason for choosing you. And if he's chosen you, he will back you — somehow. He chose you to shame the wise and the strong. Rejoice! He chose you and no one else. Rejoice!"

"Rejoice at being God's fool?' I said. "I can do that. I've been doing so all my life."

At that moment an elf lord interrupted us.

"My lady, your father has called a council meeting in fifteen minutes," he said. "Your presence is requested."

I wasn't exactly rejoicing when we returned. Dutch and the dwarves were already seated around a red table made of a volcanic rock that seemed to rise from the foundations of the earth. Fifty people could have sat around that table, and there was not so much as one lazy Susan on the table, which depressed me a little bit. The Chosen One's gotta eat, correctamunde?

And I was getting hungry again. You'd think a master of hospitality like Lord Reggie would have five lazy Susans on the table all bulging with a few choice hors d'oeuvres, some delectable "appe-teasers," tidbits, such as crab stuffed mushrooms, a cheese assortment, sliced pepperoni, blinis and caviar, cracked crab and shrimp, oysters on the half shell, bacon, chocolate soufflés, ice cream, maybe some cheese and blueberry blintzes, OJ, champagne for mimosas, lobster, chocolate cake, sponge cake, sausage, eggs Benedict, hash browns, seafood burritos, egg salad, chopped liver, corned beef, latkes and applesauce, French fries, beef and pork sliders, sticky buns, butter croissants with honey — get the picture? But nope: nada, nothing, zilch. He's was an Elf Lord, for God's sake. Money was no object; so where was the grub? Good thing I ate my Lobster Newburg before. Plus there were also four or five men, a few more fucking glowing elves I hadn't seen before. They were built like NFL linebackers and each man shouldered an Uzi. Were they security? Then I saw it: the Navy Trident. This did not bode well.

"This can't be: You're Navy SEALs?!" I said.

"Captain Danny, at your service," said one of the men who bowed without giving me his last name or his Elvish house name, as was customary with SEALs. When you met one or several SEALs as I did it the army, they never ever gave up any personal information about themselves. Smart. Although Lord Reggie didn't mention his house's name either, but then again maybe lords don't have to. But Reggie's house seal looked to be an apple tree filigreed in gold, whose fruit was the ruby gems that hung like fruit from its branches. This tree was on every wall in the chateau.

"Your servant, Sergeant Rufus Timmons of the 2nd Battalion 7th Army War Dogs," I said respectfully.

"Your battalion did good work in Iraq and Afghanistan," Captain Danny said.

"Thank you," I said. "Many good men, my best friends died there, though it sounds like a cliché to say so."

"Even clichés begin with a truth," said Captain Danny, "Nevertheless the cliché is true and we're still losing good men in Afghanistan so little girls can go to school in safety and become women who can realize their God-given potential."

"It all comes down to that, doesn't it?" I said. "Stopping motherfuckers from throwing acid in their sweet, innocent faces. Saving the sheep from the wolves."

"Yes it does, sir," he said, saluting me, a lower ranking officer. Why? I returned his salute. All this saluting and bowing to the "Chosen One" was making me uncomfortable.

"I was just telling everyone before you arrived that we're leaving in the morning," said Dutch.

"No way." I said. "I thought we were going to spend a week or two making plans for the next leg of our *fabulous* adventure."

"Sorry about that lover boy," said Dutch, "but the enemy is moving fast. It's already mid-October."

"What's the rush?' I said. "The Election is three weeks away."

"Doesn't matter," said Dutch, "Three weeks will slip by in a wink. We're leaving in the morning and heading for our safe house in Washington, D.C. From there we'll be better positioned to strike at *Vice President* Ross, the Demon Lord, after the President's reelection."

"Yeah, McClintock's reelection is a sure thing. The polls have him ahead by 15%. But geez, we just got here." I said, sighing loudly again.

"Quit your damn sighing," said Buck. "I'm getting sick of it. I never met such a chronic sigher."

"Shut the fuck up, Buck," I said. "I'll sigh whenever the fuck I feel like it. You fart more than I sigh."

"Please excuse their crudeness, Lady Katherine." Dutch said. "Buck and Rufus are loyal comrades and sometimes good friends."

"The fuck we are," Buck said.

"The fuck we are," I said.

"You see my lady, pals through and through," said Theo. "Maybe we'll be welcome here on the way back."

"Not a chance in hell," said Lady Katherine, smiling. "Seriously, you are all welcome here anytime."

"Ah, shit," I said. Turning to face Katherine, I added, "Please forgive my uncouth language: Shit is merely common American vernacular for, 'Tis a pity we must leave so soon.'"

"Yes," she said, "I get that a lot from Americans. Shit, that is." She smiled and now glowed a bright blue. It was gold before. Shifting auras. Groovy. At least her breasts were the same size. She exchanged a look with Captain Danny and I suddenly I understood. I'm not blind, you know. They were in love and I wouldn't be returning. That was ok. It was clear I wasn't meant to and they should only be happy. Lucky guy.

Everyone stood up when Lord Reggie came into the room, followed by an elf lady dressed in a purple leather pants suit. She was holding a large matching purple pillow. Could it be my sword, Rufus' Tool, Demon Slayer, as it was small, little more than two feet long.

"What's up?" I said to Dutch who stood next to me. Dutch was silent.

"Thank you for loaning me your sword, Rufus," Reggie said. It was my sword on a purple pillow, like royalty, as if before me it had belonged to kings. Why was it wrapped in brown butcher's paper? I didn't get it. If it was regal enough to be delivered on a purple pillow, why the butcher's paper? Wasn't that like wrapping a king's crown in toilet paper? Reggie unwrapped the butcher's paper and sure enough there was my tool, my Demon Slayer. It was the same sword, a very simple sword: no jewels glittered from inside the hilt, except when I held it, and no runes of any kind on the blade that I had ever seen. Thankfully, Reggie and his boys didn't mess with the sword and it was returned to me just as I left it. Or was it?

Reggie bowed as he presented the sword to me without touching it. When I looked at it closely, it *was* different, translucent, the blade, that is. For the first time it shimmered and sparkled as if it were alive. What's more, there were symbols floating around inside the sword, but they were so faint I hadn't a clue what they were. When I held Demon Slayer it quickly grew to about five feet, but I couldn't tell where the blade ended exactly. The blade was different somehow. Something changed. What did the elves do to it? What did Reggie do to it?

"Rufus," said Reggie, "Dutch may have told you that Demon Slayer is from beyond my world and yours. It is made from holy steel, forged by the angels themselves."

"It will always be just good ol' Rufus' Tool to me," I said. "No kidding? Holy steel. Groovy. I've heard of holy water, but holy steel? Made by the angels. Pity they didn't send an angel to wield it. Would've simplified my life considerably. Too bad they didn't send a holy Glock or a blessed Uzi."

"You're out of line, Rufus," Dutch said.

"Maybe. But who uses swords these days?" I said. "Oops, did I just 'unceremoniously' burst a sacred ritual transfer from Lord Reggie to moi? Damn."

Dutch stepped on my foot; Kate was not pleased, in fact she looked a little pissed at my lack of etiquette. Hey, just being honest. Funny, that a pissed elf princess, is not a pretty elf princess, despite her gigantic breasts. Really nice breasts. Ok, amazing breasts. Maybe the nicest pair of 44-double-Ds I'd ever seen. And believe me when I say I've gawked at my fair pair, I mean share. Reggie was unfazed. I guess in his 1,700 years of life he had encountered more than one reluctant hero, as well as some awesome breasts. He even managed a smile.

"Rufus," Reggie said, "focus your attention on me and not on my daughter's bosom, will you please?"

"What? Bosoms? What bosoms? Huh? Who, Me? Yah gotta admit they're pretty damn impressive — of course NO disrespect meant." I said, embarrassed.

Elf Princess Katherine tried her best to look nonplussed, but her pressed lips and narrowed eyes belied her equanimity. She folded her arms on top of her huge hooters, said nothing, and simply stared into Captain Danny's eyes. Larry and Burt, standing behind me were laughing their asses off. Most disrespectful, I thought.

"Focus? I'll try, though I make no promises. What's that inside the blade?" I said. "I thought I saw something. But it was so faint, I wasn't sure."

"Those are sacred runes," Reggie said, pointing to symbols literally floating in the sword.

"They weren't there when Dutch gave me the sword." I said, losing my focus *again* when the elf broad in the purple leather pantsuit dropped the purple pillow and I caught sight of what must have been her 38 DDD bosom, breasts, machanga, hooters, hangers, which themselves had a purple aura. Imagine doing the motorboat with those glowing "auraing" purple breasts on your face. That's what I was thinking. Why did all of these elf babes wear low cut blouses. Didn't seem to bother the elf dudes any. Didn't the elf dudes have lustful, sinful thoughts at all about the big breasted elf babes? Oh wait, they were without sin, so, I'm guessing even their lustful thoughts were not sinful thoughts, by definition. I shoulda been a theologician. At any rate, I'd already forgotten Katherine. She was clearly spoken for by Captain Danny. But the elf princess with the purple pillow... she was looking my way. I think she dug me: Ah, Rufus, you ol' horndog, you. But would there be time — that enemy of every heroic quest.

"That's because this sword has been hidden for 2,000 years," said Reggie, "and went dormant after so long. The icons appeared now because you woke it up when you first touched it and it recognized you as chosen, and its current owner. And this ground, this chamber is on holy ground, so sword became more alive, fully awakened."

Reggie sighed almost as deeply as I. Although, it would be one of the saddest days of my life when I left Reggie's Pleasure Palace, I could tell from his exasperated expression it would be one of his happiest.

"Rufus! Over here! May I have your attention, please!" said Lord Reggie, who raised his voice as loud as any elf lord with superior class and restraint might. "I'm going to activate Demon Slayer's final powers NOW."

"'Final Powers?' What the fuck? So what was I using: a beta version?" I said, in mock outrage, and at the same time doing by best to make eye contact with the purple elf princess with the glowing purple breasts. "Great. That's just great. Did you hear that Dutch? You gave me the 'trial version.'"

"In a manner of speaking, I'm afraid so," said Reggie who touched the sword's icons in some secret sequence that lasted about 30 seconds. "I've got to do this quickly to avoid being badly burned."

"Thanks, Dutch," I said, "You gave me the Beta version of Demon Slayer?"

"Sorry, Big Man, who knew?" Dutch said.

"Even the Beta version is very powerful," said Reggie. "But without pressing the runes in their proper sequence you would never be able to unlock Demon Slayer's full strength. I'm the only one from the High Kingdom who remembers this sword. Rufus you may take Demon Slayer." Reggie lifted the butcher paper and handed me the sword without touching it again. Yet his fingers were burned from touching the icons on the sword even briefly.

"It feels like my old friend, Rufus' *Tool*, ha ha!" I said. "Does it come with a set of instructions? A user's guide perhaps, a help menu, FAQs?"

"Demon Slayer will teach you and *now* has the power to heal you, as well. It is the only weapon that will destroy the demon known to your world as Senator Bobby Ross. Bullets, rockets, even a cruise missile will bounce off him like a rubber ball. Demon Slayer will cut off his head and remove a great evil from both of our worlds. And he fears who might wield it against him."

"Not me he doesn't," I said, "Remember? I met the guy; and holy sword or no holy sword, Demon Lord Bobby Ross fears nothing about me. However, he sure scared the shit out of me. Lord Reggie, I've been trying to tell everyone that maybe they've got the wrong man for the job. And at least half of the dwarves agree with me. I think you should fight him or it."

"That's bullshit," said Buck. "You're the man, the Chosen One, the Troll Slayer. I have 1000% confidence in you, Big Man. If you can't kill the bastard, no one can."

"I don't decide who is the Chosen One, and neither do the dwarves," said Reggie. "Demon Slayer decided, and the powers that made it. That alone should comfort you."

"I'm ain't comforted," I said. "I'm telling you there are better candidates out there."

"Undoubtedly," said Reggie. "There is a simple test."

"Oh, fuck me, not another test, for God's sake! Ok, I believe you! I believe you! Shit. Too late."

Captain Danny and his three colleagues drew their swords and came at me. They circled me. But I was distracted by what I was feeling with the sword in my hand. Demon Slayer felt like it was knitting, fusing itself with the sinews in my arm and hand, and with my mind. The first blow came from an elf with shoulders like a NFL tackle. It was automatic: my sword arm parried his blow and cut his sword off at the hilt. Demon Slayer did the same thing with the other four elves that attacked me. I wasn't aware I was even moving that quickly. I could see the dwarves were astonished. However, Captain Danny's blade scratched me a good one across my upper right arm. It bled profusely for about ten seconds than stopped. The gash had been healed.

"That's right," said Reggie, "your sword has healing powers, but try not to put it to the test."

"As in 'do not put the Lord your God to the test.'" I said. "I get it."

"By the Blessed Virgin," said Theo, "you *are* the Chosen one."

"It's the sword, not me, Theo," I said.

"It's not just the sword, Rufus," said Reggie. It's the sword *and* **you**. Did you feel it becoming a part of your body and mind?"

"Exactly. How did you know?" I asked.

"It happened to me, too. I was ten years younger than you when I received the holy Blue Glacier," said Reggie who pulled a short sword from his side. The sword grew to six feet in length and true to its name it was ice blue and looked ice-cold to the touch. "But even my blade is no match for yours, my son."

"I am thrice honored to be called your son. It is more than any Timmons deserves, Lord Reggie. Sorry I'm such a smart-ass, perhaps dumb-ass is more fitting."

"I believe in you, Rufus," said Lord Reggie. "You have much humor and innate kindness and I believe Demon Slayer recognizes both. Remember, Demon Slayer does not do the fighting. Rather it brings out the best fighter in Rufus Timmons: The Chosen One. However, you cannot be complacent. You must still train and you've got to fight Ross with all of your heart and mind, to be worthy of '*Rufus' Tool.*'"

"I know, I know, but I just can help thinking, that sword play is a little dated."

"Vanity," said Lord Reggie. "Don't underestimate the power of pride to delude oneself, especially in a demon. Ross is a psychopath and a megalomaniac and he will want to defeat you — man-to-man, sword-to-sword. And then eat you."

"What if he gets impatient and realizes his sword isn't working. Won't he just shoot me with his Uzi."

"Dutch, will you do the honors," Reggie said.

"Ah, fuck, not again," I sighed mightily.

Dutch pulled out his Glock 17 and fired four shots in rapid succession. Demon Slayer parried all four shots, destroying the bullets.

"Ok, asked and answered," I said. "But dammit Dutch, warn me next time , will you?"

"Besides," said Kate, "the Demon Lord *wants* to *eat* you. There's a lot of meat on your bones, ha! ha! And I doubt he wants to bite into 9MM slugs."

"I just hate bullets in my meat, don't you?" I said. "I guess I'd better not lose this sword. I'll be sleeping with it under my pillow."

"Don't get corn-holed without it," laughed Theo.

"Corn-holed?" I said, but no one answered. Strange.

CHAPTER 25

The next morning was as foggy as the day we arrived. Our Harleys had been gassed and washed by our hosts. I was going to miss Kate's gigantic hooters almost as much as ordering room service. Delicious BBQ spareribs, French Fries, and coleslaw arrived as a midnight snack, almost as soon as I hung up the phone. For breakfast I had one last Lobster Newburg with scrambled eggs on an English muffin, and a large orange juice.

"Be careful where you camp," Reggie warned. "You may want to risk a hotel, if only for one night. We have reliable evidence of goblins in the Smoky Mountains."

"First trolls, now goblins," said Dutch, still weary from our fight with the biker trolls.

"Do the best you can do and hope," Reggie said, who lifted his arms in a parting benediction. "May the Lord give you peace and joy at your journey's end."

"And may the God of the dwarves and of all creation guide you on the path of the righteous," Buck said, who knew the correct response.

"Amen," said all.

We rode for hours. The fog made it slow going. Although, it was easier going down the mountain and we could ride a little faster. We didn't see the phoenix with its ruby claws and purple head feathers, but I saw a blue unicorn peek out at us from the dark forest on the left side of the narrow highway. I know I saw it, but the dwarves and Dutch gave me grief and said I had drunk too much elf wine at Lord Reggie's pool bar, despite the fact that they knew I was strictly a Diet Coke man. But later Arnie confirmed my sighting. I *did* see a blue unicorn. Can you believe it? Thank God, and thank God that after three hours on the road, I saw the familiar stars from the Pisces constellation. The Halo constellation was gone. I was back in my own world. A good thing, indeed.

I knew we had left the enchanted land when at last I saw the neon sign for Colonel Sander's Kentucky Fried Chicken, which was located inside a Love's Travel Center. In this part of the country you either saw a KFC or a Clucker's Fried Chicken. I preferred the Colonel, as I really loved their original recipe and the Colonel's coleslaw, finely shredded and sweet. I also thought the Colonel made the best honey mustard dippin' sauce. Though some of the dwarves were disappointed when it wasn't Clucker's. As we sat down to enjoy our food, Theo felt compelled to give us his depressing goblin assessment, giving me indigestion before our meal.

"You know, of course, where there are goblins there are also flesh eating lupines," said Theo, who always sat on his Muslim prayer rug before offering grace to the blessed Virgin and before every meal. Go figure.

"For God's Holy sake, do we have to talk about this before we eat?" said an irritated Dutch. "Theo, please, shut-the-fuck-up."

Dutch was unintentionally funny, though no one laughed, because for all that's holy, every morning, come rain or shine, Theo would lay down a red and yellow Muslim prayer mat, pointed in the direction of Jerusalem, and repeat the Lord's prayer and a "Hail Mary." Besides being a devout Catholic, who constantly prayed to the Blessed Virgin, Theo was also a fierce warrior who would gladly lay down his life for his friends. But Dutch was tired. How old, how ancient was he? I didn't know. One thousand years old, 2,000? You could see the weariness in his face from the beating his body took from riding his Harley across the country. Believe me, you needed strength in your arms and serious stomach muscles to ride all day. Add sleeping in the woods to the equation, and even an immortal wizard would be exhausted. Dutch needed a dwarf to help him out of his sleeping bag most mornings and onto his feet. A few days like that and I, too, would be a cranky old bastard. When I looked into his eyes, I realized he didn't exactly volunteer for this quest. I heard rumors among the elves that Lord Reggie yanked him out of retirement. I loved the old wizard. I'd do anything for him.

There was silence as everyone ate. Lupines, I knew from *The High Kingdom* were wolves the size of grizzly bears. Out of respect for Dutch, the silence lasted five minutes, but you couldn't shut up dwarves for long. Not when they're eating Colonel's Sanders fried chicken, Original Recipe. Soon they had their happy faces on and were humming strange deep melodies as they ate, no doubt old dwarf battle songs.

Every dwarf I've ever met loves fast food and my comrades told me there was no fast food in the High Kingdom. Imagine a world without KFC or McDonald's or Taco Bell or In-N-Out hamburgers or High Five Donuts. It's too horrible to contemplate. We were eating Kentucky Fried chicken, happy just dippin' and dabbin' the Colonel's Original Recipe in honey mustard, barbecue sauce, and ranch dressing. So happy were we that everyone broke into a chorus, laughing and singing, "Ninety-nine Goblin Skins on the Wall." It was politically incorrect for our world, but it went like this:

99 goblin skins on the wall: 99 goblin skins
Take one goblin skin off the wall: 98 goblin skins on the wall

99 lupine skins on the wall: 99 lupine skins
Take one lupine skin off the wall: 98 lupine skins on the wall
99 demon heads on the wall: 99 demon heads
Take one demon's head off the wall: 98 demon heads on the wall

Many of the patrons joined in though they looked confused with "Lupine skins." You couldn't expect anyone to know about lupines without reading *The High Kingdom*. Even Dutch eventually joined in when the count reached ten goblin skins on the wall. After the singing, after everyone was finished eating, a concerned expression returned to Dutch's wrinkled face.

"Are you surprised that there may be lupines and goblins here?" I whispered to Dutch.

"Yes." he said.

"I'm not," I said.

"Explain," he said.

"The scientific term for this phenomena," I said, "is 'Invasive Species.' It occurs when some asshole's imported an illegal animal as a pet into the U.S. such as a boa constrictor from the Amazon jungle. When the stupid fuck gets bored with his pet, he'll try to sell it; but he's unable to sell his Amazon boa constrictor because it's illegal to own one in the first place. So the motherfucker releases the boa constrictor into the wild where it multiplies. In Florida some shit-head released a pair of Brazilian Green Iguanas, a lizard the length of a teenager. If the Demon Lord brought goblins with him and has allowed them to run amok, then you could be looking a serious infestation."

"Brazil?" said Buck.

"Yeah, a country in South America, about 8,000 miles south of Florida."

"A five and a half foot lizard? You're joking, right big man?" said Buck, who had listened in on our conversation. He had taken to sometimes calling me the "Big Man," instead of Chosen One.

"No joke," I said. "Some of them are more than six feet long. They sit so high in the trees that animal control can't reach them and the iguanas have a nasty habit of shitting on people below."

"I'd rather face an army of Green Brazilian Iguanas than a pack of lupines and armed goblins." said Dutch, who was dippin' his last chicken tender in ranch dressing. "I pray we brought enough fire power. Hell, if they're already in the Smokey Mountains, they've probably tunneled into every national park in the country. So, if you're right Rufus, this country could have a major infestation that would take years to clean up."

Before we left I pulled Dutch aside and said. "So what's this great plan you and Reggie have concocted? Will I be able to get close enough to kill Senator Ross? Does the plan stand a rat's ass chance of success?"

"Yes," said Dutch, "It has exactly a rat's ass chance of success, *if* we have the element of surprise."

"Who'd ever suspect that we were up to something, right? I said. "Just eleven dwarves, a wizard, and one scholar traveling across the country on a pack of noisy Harleys. Plenty of surprise there. Why it happens everyday."

Dutch blew a series of marijuana smoke rings and sent them hovering above my head. And then he couldn't stop laughing. Laughing in the face of small chances and long odds. I can respect that.

CHAPTER 26

We left KFC and were filling our bikes with gas at Love's when I noticed a smallish teenage girl with her thumb out, hitchhiking by the side of the road. She had beautiful, more red than brown, auburn hair cut short, a pageboy cut like Halle Berry. From the back she looked fourteen. Her face told a different story: a life of pain. She reminded me of a kind, sweet, abused girl, Courtney Bevelson, a student I helped in the English composition class I occasionally taught for new students at Middlebrook University. This petite redhead stood on the corner, hitchhiking in worn Red Wing work boots, faded Levis, and a black leather jacket. She was cute as a pixie, with freckles on her face and an upturned button of a nose. Her auburn hair was bewitching, and flashed red in the dusk of the setting sun.

We passed her and Dutch said, "What do you think, Rufus?"

"I think we should pick her up before someone takes advantage of her."

"My very thought," Dutch said.

I swung my bike around and drove up beside her.

"Where are you headed?" I asked.

"Washington, D.C." she said.

I looked at Dutch who smiled and said, "We're headed for East of Eden."

"Thrown out of paradise were you?" she said. "Fine by me. Paradise is for fools."

"A cynic," I said

"A realist," she said.

I made room and she hopped on the back of my bike.

"Cluckersfriendoelvosh?" said Dutch who rode up beside me and gave her hard look before asking her the question.

"Hey, same to you, buddy," she said. "Is he some kind of foreigner?"

"No," I said. "He just wants to know if you're Elvish or speak it. "Cluckersfriendoelvosh means, 'Clucker's chicken is always shared with friends.' It also means that you're good luck, 'little chicky baby.'"

"Elf! Hey, I ain't no *elf.* I know I'm small for my age, but you ain't got no cause insulting me. 'Little chicky baby, my ass!' Cluck off, buddy!" She said to Dutch.

"No insult was intended, young lady," said Dutch, "but aren't you a little young to be hitchhiking."

Aren't you a little old to be riding a Harley?"

"Touché! The name is Dutch and you are?"

"Beca. I'm 23 and a damn good judge of character, old man."

"Short for Rebecca?" I said.

"Wow, nothing gets by you, genius. Yeah, it's Rebecca. What else you wanna know."

"That's enough for now," said Dutch. "Rufus, focus on the road."

Beca put on her headphones and we got the message. I turned to Dutch with a puzzled expression.

"Clearly not from the High Kingdom," I said.

"She has an air of mystery," Dutch said through the speaker in his helmet. "I'll give her that; and don't you like a good mystery? Maybe she is simply an enchanting young lady without any magic."

"You mean less than enchanting," I said. Beca was rocking and grooving to the music, shaking her head back and forth. "I only hope she doesn't morph into some throat slashing she-demon while I'm sleeping."

"Rest easy," Dutch said. "I've had a fair amount of experience unmasking evil creatures and she's not one. Willful to be sure, but not evil."

"Just hearing you say 'rest easy' makes me uneasy," I said. "I can live with willful, but tell me master unmasker, how'd those biker-trolls fool you?"

"I'm not infallible, asshole," said Dutch, "but there *is* something here I don't understand. Be on your guard."

"Oh, that's comforting. Maybe I should sleep with one eye open."

"You should always sleep with one eye open," said Dutch. "That's the first rule for any quest. Forget that and you're as good as dead."

"Yeah, right," I said to the soundest sleeper on the planet. I loved the old wizard's pithy sayings, especially this one. I thought it best not to remind him that he was sleeping contentedly while biker-fuck Lionel and his troll posse were roasting Ornery's head over a raging campfire that should have singed his wizardly eyebrows even 200 yards out.

After riding two hours we stopped at a 7-Eleven for some snacks. The dwarves took the opportunity to foul the bathrooms after eating too much KFC. They were surprised and delighted to have a cute girl in their midst. Beca got off my trike to stretch when Buck walked up to her.

"And what brings a young lady to be in our company?" asked Buck.

"You'll need more than a friendly dwarf demeanor, rare as it is, to fool these eyes, grandfather. My business is my own concern," said Beca, removing her ear-buds, and sounding far more educated than she had with Dutch and me.

"Maybe I should wash out your insolent mouth with soap, you little imp." Buck said.

"I'd like to see you try," she said.

"You should have left her by the road," said Buck, as he passed by me and Dutch into the 7-Eleven.

"No, you made the right decision," she said, and patted me on the back before she put on her headphones. Her hand felt very warm, and while I was beginning to hope she'd never take her headphones off, I was thrilled beyond the power of words to describe how it felt to have her warm body pressed against mine.

CHAPTER 27

We'd been riding for about 30 minutes when Buck lifted his middle finger. One finger whether the fuck-you finger or another signaled a code one, so we pulled over to the side of the freeway. The traffic noise was making it increasingly difficult to hear each other through our helmet speakers. Buck counted Harleys.

"Burt's missing," said Buck.

"What do you mean, Burt's missing? Damn it!" said Dutch.

"Count the bikes if you don't believe me," said Buck. Sure enough one of bikes was missing. One of the little guys was gone!

"It's Burt, damn it," said Dutch. "Let's just leave the little fuck. He's been a royal pain in the ass anyway; nothing but, 'Where's the mint chip ice cream? They're out of mint chip ice cream? 7-Eleven's can't they run out of mint chip?' Good riddance I say."

"You know we can't leave a comrade-in-arms," I said.

"Comrade *in arms*, you say?" said Dutch, waving his. "The only thing in his arms is mint chip ice cream, mint chip cookies, mint chip Oreos — I've had it with his mint chip bullshit. He's putting us all at risk."

"I'll go back for him," I said. "And for the record, Dutch, mint chip Oreos *are* cookies."

"Oh, sweet Jesus, save us," said Dutch, "another moron."

"You can't go back, Rufus. Could be a trap," said Buck. "We all go back."

We found Burt stuck in the freezer case at the 7-Eleven. He was still hopelessly reaching for the last carton of mint chip ice cream in the freezer.

"Hey fellas," Burt said, "I knew you'd come back for me! Rufus, be a good man: reach in with your longer arms and snag the last carton of mint chip." We dislodged Burt and with my longer arms I got his ice cream.

Unfortunately, a lot of employees and customers were laughing and snapping selfies with Burt stuck in the freezer. Dutch took his cane, aimed his tripod tip, and vaporized every cell phone with blue lightning. Then he waved his cane around the room and a stream of gold stars filled the air.

"Dormitus felicitus!" said Dutch, and everyone in the store slumped to the ground asleep.

"Oh, that won't draw attention," Beca said, laughing and also monitoring the people outside the store.

"They won't remember anything," said Dutch.

"I just pray no one posted any selfies or uploaded any of this on YouTube, which would pin point our exact location," Theo said.

"Pray now and pray hard, Theo," said Dutch.

"Let's rock, you clowns!" said Beca, still laughing at Burt who had freezer frost and mint chip ice cream on his beard.

We jumped on our hogs and through my helmet speaker I heard Theo begin thus: "Dear Lord, forgive Burt's stupid obsession with mint chip ice cream and protect us on this holy quest to destroy evil. We ask this in your son's name, Jesus Christ. Amen and thank you." Theo had the best manners in the group. He always said thank you.

CHAPTER 28

We lost some time rescuing Burt. So we had to ride for another five hours. My ass was killing me when we passed a road sign for Clucker's Fried Chicken three miles away at a Love's Travel Center. Five or six of the dwarves shouted, pleaded in unison through their helmet's speaker, "Please, please, can we stop at Clucker's?!" I knew the drill: they wanted to eat, but also to buy a bunch of chicken strips to stuff in their saddlebags for the road. Even through my helmet's internal speakers I could barely hear them over the Harleys and the traffic. It was, however, easy to hear their cries of joy when Dutch sighed, "Oh fuck it," into his helmet, meaning he would stop. Beca also tapped me on the shoulder with a thumbs-up.

I'll say this for our fast-food nation: travel any interstate highway and you'll never starve. In fact, I don't think interstate trucking would be as efficient without all the food outlets, as well as the Love's Travel Center with its showers, grocery stores, Subway, Clucker's Chicken, Taco Bell, KFC, McDonald's, and Carl's Jr. You could find anything at a Love's: shirts, sweaters, pork rinds, booze, GPS systems, lottery tickets, and more.

We pulled into the Love's and everyone went inside. It was the dinner hour. The sun had set. It was dark and the line at Clucker's was long and made longer by eleven dwarves. The restaurant was filling up fast. I took a pen and paper and walked the line taking the dwarves' dinner orders.

"Hey fellas," Dutch said, "why don't you grab some tables after Rufus takes your order."

I was making my way down the line when three men got in line behind us. They were biker dudes and wore leather jackets with, "Satan's 'Angles' Las Vegas" embroidered in purple and gold. I didn't have the heart to tell the morons that Angels was misspelled. The jackets must have cost a bundle. Considering we were in Tennessee, they were far from home. Their hobnail work boots made a painful racket on the floor when they walked into the restaurant. They wore thug-like black gloves cut off at the knuckles. One of these mutts fixed his laser-like gaze on Beca. Beca dropped her wallet, picked it up, revealing the wings of an eagle tattooed just above her ass that some might consider suggestive. I almost had a heart attack when I first saw it. She's that sexy. One of the biker-fucks pulled out a $100 bill.

"Hey sweet cheeks," he said, "The Benjamin is yours if you drop your wallet again."

"What's your name?" said Beca.

"Charlie," said the biker. "What's yours?"

"Well Charlie, I'll forgive your rudeness because I'm certain your IQ is smaller than the 'Benjamin' in your greasy hands."

"Really now?" said Charlie. "Can you repair a carburetor on a '65 Harley Flathead?"

"In my sleep," Beca said.

"I think you're prejudiced against honest labor?" Charlie said.

"I'm not prejudiced against honest labor. I'm just appalled by bad manners," said Beca.

"Appalled and probably outraged, too," said Charlie who with his posse laughed. They glared at her. She left and sat with the dwarves. The biker-fucks glared at us and had a stupid confab, no doubt, discussing their next move. I'm sure fighting dwarves was not in their plans. Hungry, angry dwarves are like frenzied sharks feeding on a wounded fish. Fish all gone. Bikers all gone.

We walked past the bikers as we left. When Beca walked past their table, they got up and surrounded her. Charlie waved the Benjamin Franklin in her face.

"Come on, let's have a peek at that tat," he said. "We'll pay for the show. It'll be fun."

Before I could pound the guy, Beca grabbed the hand of the biker-fuck, Charlie, and broke it at the wrist. Then she applied two precise groin kicks to the other two. She seemed to grow during the fight. The bikers collapsed to the ground, their hands cupped around their testicles. Charlie clutched his broken wrist in agony.

She pulled Charlie's filthy hair, put her thumb in his left eye, looked into his face and said, "Having fun now?"

We were flabbergasted by her Kung-Fu, Chung-king, Kung-Pao, or whatever style of martial arts she practiced. And then I thought: had I behaved any better than Charlie & Company in the presence of the elf ladies at Lord Reggie's? Openly lustful, openly rude, I was lucky Captain Danny didn't deck me for how I looked at his beloved fiancé, Lady Katherine; or Lord Reggie for how I gazed at his daughter. Or Mrs. Gemstone: she should have given me a fat lip, but instead served me the best darn ham and cheese sandwich I've ever eaten. Or the elf babe in the purple pants suit, with her huge glowing purple hooters, who delivered the much improved Demon Slayer to me. She should have clobbered me, too. I was ashamed of myself. Was the Chosen One a royal jackass? A unforgivable pig? I think so. I owed them all an apology. I just hoped they would forgive a fool in over his head on an impossible quest to save the world.

I was also glad that the biker-fucks didn't morph into fifteen foot trolls at the restaurant. We all clapped and patted Beca on the back, including me. Some of the customers stood up and applauded. For my sake, I was relieved that our earlier confrontation hadn't escalated beyond words. She was tougher than she pretended to be. I've never been in a fight with a girl: to lose a fight to a girl would be humiliating. Not that I didn't meet some tough ladies in the army. Personally, though, when I think about it: I'd rather have my ass kicked by a woman than to kick her ass. That's a beating I could always accept. To raise my hand against any woman is unthinkable. Well, that's not entirely true. I once killed a female insurgent in Baghdad. She was pointing an RPG at my buddies. Pulled the weapon right out from under her skirt. Though when we examined her we discovered she wasn't a woman but a man. That's war for you.

I was impressed, attracted, and a little bit afraid of Beca. I'll admit it — she made me a little nervous because of her dangerous and unpredictable skill set. Who or what was she?

Dutch and I stood apart and talked quietly.

"Was I hallucinating or did she grow half a foot while she was fighting?" I asked.

"Then we were both hallucinating," said Dutch. "I don't trust her."

"I still like her. Should we get her own Harley?" I said.

"I don't want my own Harley," Beca said before Dutch could answer. "I like riding shotgun with Rufus, thank you very much. Let's roll, Big Man."

"You have your answer," said Dutch, laughing nervously. "Just don't piss her off or talk behind her back!"

CHAPTER 29

I had my answer and it was enough to set my heart pounding like a jackhammer, as we rode together on I40. Like I said: I felt her pain. There was trauma in her past. I marveled at her toughness. She had transcended her painful past whatever it was. And that was easy to fall for.

I couldn't get her out of my mind as we rode together. I was in trouble. Beca had *it*: a cute girlish quality to her, but something more. She could be 70 and she'd still have it. I couldn't forget seeing her on the side of the road with her thumb out, hitching for a ride. Forget all the kick ass ninja shit. There was no denying *it*: this petite young woman with an auburn pageboy, white tank-top, firm but well concealed breasts, and a booty big enough to accentuate her small waist was the *it* girl. A curvaceous rear on a short girl with a slender waist *is* God's gift to man. Add her sass to her curvaceous ass and I was on the brink of annihilation. Tell me I'm wrong. Dutch saw the adoration (ok, and lust) on my face, but said nothing. Well, when I feel it, when I lose it, I'm in trouble.

Falling in love is perilous. Do you know what I mean? The kind of love that convinces you that's why you were created. You wake up in the morning drenched body and soul in a spiritual, sexual, and emotional high that nothing on earth compares to: not a million bucks, not full tenure at Harvard, not the power to heal the sick or raise the dead. I mean nothing compares to this kind of love; it's the greatest feeling in the history of creation. You could be unemployed, penniless, living on the street, wondering where your next meal is coming from. You could have been beaten, thrown into a concentration camp, tortured by the enemy. But if you have that kind of love for someone and she has it for you, then you are — you are the happiest man on earth and wouldn't trade places with anyone. Could this meeting with her, so random, so accidental be an intentional part of this fucked-up quest? Was this part of His plan, God's plan for me to meet Beca, to heal my miserable heart, just like in Bartlett's *The High Kingdom* between Lord Gerald and Lady Laura? Probably not. Could it be that all of the fantasy novels I've read had softened my brain?

Of course, love's opposite: to so love someone and not to have it returned is like a death, a living death, a pain so intense that it needs no description. Because if you've experienced it you understand; I had not forgotten what it felt like; I had wanted to forget what it felt like because the last time I had a hard time getting up again; A broken arm will heal itself in three or four months; a broken heart will heal itself, but it takes longer and it leaves a scar. If left untreated it will suck the joy out of everything that follows. But love is stronger, and as my buddy Ben Jonson once wrote:

"...*Except Love's fire the virtue have,*
To fright the frost out of the grave."

As I drove, Beca would rub up against me occasionally and I could feel the heat of her body against mine. I felt my face flushed with excitement. I looked in my rear view mirror and she looked back at me, smiling innocently. She knew the effect she was having on me and she was enjoying my torment. So was I. After her smack down of the bikers, every dwarf wanted a chance to ride with her and to get to know her better. Even Buck came round.

"Young Lady, unless I may call you Beca," said Buck, "I would take back my unkind words at our first meeting, if you'll forgive me and ride with me."

Beca was an emotional young woman despite her bluster and tough talk. She grabbed Buck and pulled him close enough and kissed his bearded face. I thought Buck was going to cry (He did shed some tears, but said road dirt got in his eye. Right.) So for days I didn't see much of her, except when we stopped for dinner.

The next day Dutch and I sat in a corner booth at the Taco Bell eating our breakfast burritos. I sat silently, while he finished the last bite of his burrito drowned in hot sauce. Outside the dwarves surrounded Beca, each one trying to impress her with war stories of killing dragons and dragon gold; and the best ways to eviscerate a goblin, or skin a lupine.

"Are you thinking what I'm thinking?" I said.

"I'm a wizard, not a mind reader," he said.

"I'm thinking we know nothing about this girl, this kick-ass, teenage kung-fu master. I think she is hiding something from us," I said.

"Yah think?" he said as if I'd just told him the earth was round. "Yes, she is hiding something from us and it disturbs me that I have no idea what it is. I hate the fact that she's able to hide from me. She wants to ride with us. So let's see what happens."

"Right," I said, in complete agreement. "We'll ride with her — it's the only way to find out." I wouldn't dare tell him how I really felt about her.

"Right," said Dutch, "Let's lock her in the stall of the ladies' room next time we stop for gas."

"Very funny. And you said you weren't a mind reader. She can't hide forever. We'll learn soon enough," I said, not really giving a damn what we found out. I knew enough.

The dwarves were grumbling. Again, they needed a bathroom break. If I had eaten as many Clucker's chicken strips and Burrito Supremes as they had, I'd be on the goddamn toilet 24/7.

We pulled into the next Love's Travel Center and parked the bikes. It would take some time for eleven dwarves to crap. After I finished the call of nature, I walked over the beef stick section to check out the different varieties of beef jerky they carried. Most beef jerk and spicy beef sticks are processed in airtight, vacuumed sealed packages and they tasted like prepackaged, prefabricated pseudo-jerky. I was looking for the old fashioned beef jerky, the real thing like Trapper Jack's, that comes in unpackaged, individually sliced sheets. The FDA or some unit of the food police forgot to ban it and some gas stations still carried it in plastic tubs that you could reach inside of and grab ten or twelve pieces with your hands. That's where you find the best jerky. After perusing the many brands of beef jerky I moved on to the aisle for beef sticks, Slim Jims and the like, a viable dissertation topic if ever there was one: *How the West Won: Beef Jerky, and Its Derivatives*. Dutch gave me the eye and the finger that it was time.

We stood just outside the store counting dwarves as they left the Love's Super Store. You'd be surprised how easy it was to lose one of the little guys.

Burt was finishing up a carton of mint chip ice cream and Theo said a prayer to the Blessed Virgin before eating a Hostess Pink Sno Ball, with one still stuck to the greasy package.

"Hey, Theo," I said. "Pink Sno Balls, cool. You know the rule."

"But this is my last one and what about Burt."

"Burt's mint chip is already gone. So do the right thing, Theo." Buck said.

Theo knew the rule only too well. Everyone knew the rule. Only yesterday a fight broke out between Arnie and Chad over a disputed Strawberry Pop Tart. strawberry jam and dwarf beards flew everywhere. Not pretty. Arnie and Chad were still not speaking to each other. A Pink Sno Ball split between them in the spirit of reconciliation would go a long way to heal recent wounds.

"You know what to do," I said. "I was going to eat my Oreos tonight, but I'll add them to the Sno Ball and you can take all the credit for restoring Arnie and Chad's friendship. You know the routine. You know they will do anything for a Pink Sno Ball *and* Oreos. 'Blessed are the peacemakers:'"

"For they shall be called the children of God," Theo said. "Oh, all right."

I knew Theo had *at least* five more Pink Sno Balls in his backpack, and who knows how many packages of Twinkies and Zingers, which I had a sudden craving for.

Dwarves are the chipmunks of the High Kingdom: they have cheeks capable of holding a 7-Eleven. When Beca arrived she saw us standing there, blocking the path to our bikes, She was one of the sharpest crayolas in the box so Dutch could hardly finish saying, "Hey, Beca, you're an amazing person..." Dutch began. "But..."

"That's precisely why you guys need me on your quest," she interrupted.

"We think it would be better for everyone if you were on your own now," Dutch said.

"Wait a sec, Dutch," I said, "No one agreed to that."

"Relax," she said. "Trust me: If I wanted to kill every last one of you lovable goons, I would have done so by now."

"Oh, that's reassuring," I said, less sure of my support, but still madly in love.

"I'd never have shared fried chicken with you, Dutchy," she said, "or *three pounds* of spicy BBQ chicken wings with the 'Chosen One.' I have principles, too. In fact, I won't share Clucker's chicken with anyone I plan to kill. There are rules, lines you don't cross. Besides, you need a better plan."

"What makes you an expert?" I said.

"I know that eleven dwarves, one retired conjurer, yeh, Reggie told me he forced you out of retirement, and an extra chunky academic can't possibly have a good plan, At least not a plan that will get Rufus close enough to kill good ol' boy Senator Ross, once we locate his digs."

"I didn't say a word to her, Dutch. Swear to God," I said, placing my hand over my heart.

"You both talk in your sleep," said Beca. "Regardless of what you think, *candidate* Vice President Ross is now twice as hard to kill with Secret Service protection. After President McClintock is reelected you can multiply that by a factor of 100. Not that he needs a government security detail with his demon bodyguards surrounding him 24/7? He'll probably eat his secret service team one by one. So, yeh, I think you need me."

Even Dutch was stunned that she knew our plans, and her incisive analysis of our plan's weakness. How the fuck were we going to get close enough to that bastard. Dutch never really offered a solution for that.

Dutch pointed his staff at Beca and said, "Omini patri velociraptor! Reveal yourself!"

"Relax Dutchy-boy," Beca said who took three invisible steps to kiss the old man's cheek.

"Who and what are you?" insisted Dutch.

"You grew by several inches as you fought those biker-fucks," I said. "Dutch and I both saw it. Didn't we Dutch?"

"That was just a little adrenaline pump," Beca said. "I'm an independent contractor, under no enchantment, except my own. Ask Lord Reggie, if you doubt me."

"I think she's very enchanting," said Buck, chiming in.

"And so do I," said Theo.

"Me, too," said Arnie, and so it went down to the last dwarf.

"And while we're on the subject of killing the Demon Lord," Beca said, "Rufus needs more swordplay, more practice, more people to ambush him when he's not expecting it."

"We'll be happy to accommodate him," said Buck, who with six of the dwarves wrestled me to the ground to prove the point. I think I peed my pants from laughing.

"Nonsense," said Dutch. "Rufus' Tool, his Demon Slayer will shield him."

"Review your words, oh, mighty wizard," said Beca. "I don't care who made that sword. Even it if was God himself, a sword needs a swordsman; and the Demon Lord will cut you down without more practice. How long do think *that monster's* been practicing?"

"She's right, Dutch. I can't rely on my sword alone to defeat Senator Ross. Wouldn't be fair to the sword. Don't put too much pressure on Rufus' Tool. The last thing it needs is a case of 'projectile dysfunction.'" I said, and kissed the flat of the blade. How I found myself defending this impudent girl I will never know. Well, I was in love; that's how I know. My mother would say she had spunk.

"Text Reggie," Beca said, "He'll vouch for me."

"Alright, ride with Rufus, for now," said Dutch looking weary as he leaned on his cane. "You've made your point."

We weren't so bad off: we had eleven dwarves, a wizard, an overweight Operation Iraqi Freedom vet, and a cute little red headed ninja assassin with us on our journey into the unknown. Finally, fourteen comrades. Lucky fourteen. Just saying.

CHAPTER 30

We rode all night and the following day. We traveled along the edge of the Great Smoky Mountains. According to Reggie's source, deep in the mountains Senator Ross had a coal mining plant that satellite infrared analysis showed was honeycombed with endless tunnels — tunnels that were not there two years ago. We hoped Senator Ross might be there. So we stopped in Gatlinburg, Tennessee, a popular Smoky Mountain tourist resort, and registered at the famous Four Seasons hotel.

Our plan was to ride our Harleys into the mountains, hoping to surprise Senator Ross at his coal plant, and kill him if possible or at least gather some useful intelligence. We planned to ride our hogs a small distance into the mountains, but hike most of the way on foot. Little choice, really. If we rode our bikes to the mining plant itself the bastard would hear us a miles and kill us all.

"We're right next to the Demon Lord's power base; so it's safer to stay in a hotel than to camp: the Four Seasons should suffice." Dutch said. "We've earned it, but we must really stick together. No one wanders off for ice cream, chicken wings, beef jerky, pork rinds, Ho Hos, burritos, tacos, Red Vines, tobacco, Sweet Tarts, Abazabas, Doritos — understand?"

"Not even a Big Mac?" said Burt.

"Especially *not* a Big Mac," said Dutch. "The Senator's campaign posters are everywhere in town and so are his agents. Dwarves attract attention. We stay put."

"I hope you're not suggesting we stay in one room?" I said.

"That's exactly what I'm suggesting," said Dutch. "We order room service and hunker down."

"I was kind of hoping you weren't going to cheap out at the last minute, Dutch." I said. "Fourteen in one room?"

"We must be prepared for the unexpected. We're on a bloody heroic quest, not a holiday. And heroic quests have contingencies and unexpected fuck-ups," said Dutch trying to justify cheaping out, as we approached the front desk of a hotel known the world over for safety, luxury, and class.

"Even at the Four Seasons?" said Buck "It's the best hotel in the world."

"I don't care if it's the best hotel in the galaxy." I said. "Who in his right mind wants to share one bathroom with eleven dwarves? For God's sake, Dutch, I've been doing just that the length and breadth of this entire fucked-up quest. I want my own freakin' room or I'll take my chances out in the wild with the Demon Lord. Besides, we have a young lady with us now. Let's do right by her, I say. The Chosen One has spoken."

"Alright, alright!" said Dutch. "We'll get adjoining suites with two bathrooms!" said Dutch. "Beca can have her own bed."

"Vast improvement," I said, with as much sarcasm as I could summon. "Sharing a bathroom with six dwarves is like sleeping with six instead of eleven Water Buffaloes. It'll do, I guess. At least Beca will have some privacy."

In the end we stayed in the one very large, three-bedroom penthouse suite with three bathrooms. That I could live with. Dutch grumbled at the surcharge for a party of fourteen, but I laughed. I couldn't believe the Four Seasons would permit six much less eleven dwarves, a old man, an unchaperoned girl, and a portly scholar in single suite, even one with three large bedrooms. We didn't need extra beds, just blankets; dwarves sleep quite comfortably on the floor. By unanimous agreement, Beca got the king size bed in the master bedroom to herself. All the more impressive was an 80-inch Samsung High Definition TV. But why the suite was on the first floor puzzled me. Weren't penthouse suites usually on the top floor?

Room service was a not new concept for the dwarves: we ordered hot fudge sundaes, chocolate croissants, burgers, quesadillas, spicy chicken wings, shrimp platters, pitchers of beer, an unending stream of coffee, lattes, cappuccinos, and diet cokes because Diet Cokes are sugar-free and good for your figure. Then we kicked back, turned on the 80-inch Samsung, a penthouse perk, and watched *Jeopardy!*, *Wheel of Fortune*, and a marathon of *Law & Order: Criminal Intent*. You could be on a different planet, circling a distant star, and still find a *Law & Order* in your star zone.

For *Jeopardy!* we divided into two teams: one with Buck and seven dwarves and our team with three dwarves, Dutch, Beca, and me. We murdered Buck's team in the categories political families, and potpourri. But they ran the category, "Beer and Skittles," as one might expect, and "Fantastical monsters." The *Law & Order: Criminal Intent* episode featured a serial axe-killer that caused the dwarves no end of laughter. They all agreed that no serial axe-killer worth his axe would wield an axe the way the TV killer did. "TV," they snorted contemptuously, "always gets it wrong." Then Theo demonstrated the proper way to decapitate, eviscerate, and obliterate an adversary or regular citizen with an axe. Most instructive, although I think he was just trying to impress Beca with his acrobatic and formidable axe skills.

It was 1AM before everyone decided to go to bed. But even with three bathrooms, nonstop flushing continued until about 2AM when everyone fell asleep, except for me. Lately, I couldn't fall asleep without my sword, Demon Slayer, in my arms. The sword had become a part of my soul. So I recited my traditional bedtime prayers: "Testicles, spectacles, wallet, watch, and Demon Slayer." Beca had heard me recite this litany each night since she joined our merry group and laughed herself to sleep in the other room. Anything I could do to bring a smile to her sweet face was fine by me and I fell asleep. And don't know why I stuffed the pouch of troll jewels into my underwear, but I did.

I was in the middle of a dream, sitting on the shore of Emerald Lake below Reggie's chateau, holding hands with Beca. We had just emerged from the lake in our bathing suits: Beca emerged from the water sans the top of her bathing suit, only beads of water clinging to her tan breasts. I turned to her and tried to focus on her beautiful grey eyes, but my eyes and my fingers strayed and I reached for a handful of her 42 Double-Ds when my dream took a more sinister turn. I dreamed a large crack in the wall was opening up and I then screamed. Suddenly it was more than a dream as at least two powerful creatures popped a foul smelling hood over my head and zip ties secured my arms behind my back; I could only hope I woke my friends in time.

I didn't know who or what had captured me, but faster than you could say, "Twinkies" I was seized, bound, lifted to my feet, and dragged through the crack in the wall that snapped shut like the jaws of death.

CHAPTER 31

The bag on my head smelled as if some poor creature died inside and was left to rot, or like a fine Stilton. I was marched, pushed, and prodded with some kind of sharp object. My poor ass felt like a pin cushion and I could feel the warm flow of my blood from both cheeks running down each leg. Something or someone grabbed the hilt of my sword, but screamed in pain and dropped it like a hot potato. I heard Demon Slayer clang as it fell to the ground. I pretended to fall and searched blindly for my sword but couldn't find it in the few seconds I had before being yanked to my feet. I despaired of ever seeing it again.

It sounds crazy, but without Rufus' Tool, without *my* sword, I had no interest in living. Without my Demon Slayer I had lost everything that meant anything to me, far more than any amount of dwarf gold. I can't explain the awful despair I felt. How could a sword affect me so? But it did and I couldn't, I wouldn't be without it.

At least I hadn't crapped in my pants from fear, though I had every reason to. I thanked my stars I was spared that indignity. I thought to myself that this couldn't be happening: we had been in a ground level suite of the *Four Seasons* for God's sake! Abductions don't happened at the Four Seasons. Certainly not without a complimentary buffet to follow. Now we were moving down a steep grade, down into the bowels of the earth. To where I could not say. Google Maps was not going to help me here. At least I knew, I prayed, I was still in, or under Tennessee, in the Great Smoky Mountains.

It was a good thing I'd eaten those hot fudge sundaes and chicken wings and the tempura shrimp platter because we marched for hours, and if it turned out to be my last meal, I could die with that. When we finally stopped they sat us down with our hoods on so that we couldn't see them or each other. I think we were left alone in the room, a large stinking room with dimly lit torches that burned some sulfurous chemical. I couldn't see my friends but I could sense movement in the room. Fortunately, they hadn't taped my mouth so I decided to risk it.

"Dutch are you here?" I said.

"I'm here Rufus," he said, right next to me. "The goblins must have left or they'd have clobbered you by now. Quickly, everyone count off so we know who's missing."

Beca was missing.

The goblins came back. They took off our hoods and were busy examining the items they took from us, including 14 chain saws, which meant they had our Harley's too, and Dutch's cash. Man, were we screwed. Then they searched us individually, but they missed my family jewels, ha! ha!

Geez Loueeez, they had the worst breath and horrendous teeth: yellow, green, brown, black, all in various stages of decay. Sad to say there was no dental plan in the Demon Lord's employment package. I could smell the pipe tobacco on Dutch who was next to me.

"Dutch," I whispered, "What the fuck is going on?"

"Goblins," he said.

"No shit, Sherlock," I said. "What are you going to do about it?"

"My God they stink," said Dutch, still in shock. "I will have to investigate how they traveled to this world."

"Now is not the time, I think," I said. "What the fuck, you never told me they are fluorescent yellow and glow in the dark."

"You never asked." Dutch said. "They're naturally filthy creatures and black is just the accumulated grime from not bathing over the years, plus makes it easier for them travel at night."

"Are you sure?" I said, "Goblins were described as 'black as night,' not *yellow* in The High Kingdom."

"Have you forgotten your High Kingdom Lore?"

"What lore?"

Dutch started to chant,

"Sin free, eldest of all, the elf children
Dwarf the hoarder, never lends money;
Man the mortal, master of take-out;
Black hearted Goblins, nasty corn-holers."

"Right. I don't see the relevance, to be honest," I said. "High Kingdom lore. How could I forget? But could you run that corn-holing thing by me again?"

"No joke, Rufus, Goblins are notorious corn-holers, butt fuckers, fudge packers, sodomists — rapists." Dutch said, laughing for no apparent reason. He was still in shock, I think.

"Do you see me laughing, ol' wizard of wizards?" I said, scared shitless.

"They'll rape your mother, your cat, your dog, your goldfish — anything with a hole in it," he said. "Yellow or black, these goblins will strip us of all our possessions, and then they will corn-hole us unmercifully, until we will wish for, beg for death."

"Kinda gives 'Chosen One' a whole new meaning, doesn't it? Just my luck to be corn-holed in the Smoky Mountains," I said, beginning to think this crazy quest had a logic of its own, not to mention a twisted sense of humor to do this awful thing to the Chosen One. Chosen for what? Corn-holing? Priceless.

"Yep, let the good times roll," said Burt, who heard us a few dwarves away.

"Strange that the good Professor Bartlett never mentioned this little known, but relevant fact from *The High Kingdom*." I said. "Not exactly something you'd expect in the Land of Faerie."

"Oh, Bartlett wanted to!" said Dutch. "'Be my guest, Frank, and watch sales of *The High Kingdom* plummet,' I said to him. Some things are better left unsaid. In the end he took my advice and sales of the trilogy continued unabated. But where is Beca?"

Everyone had counted off except for Beca. Where was Beca? Did she escape? Was she in the bathroom when we were kidnapped? Beca strongly supported Dutch's suggestion that we stay together in one room.

"Did she betray us?" Buck said, which is what everyone was thinking.

"Never," I said.

I sat there stinking from the bag that had been on my head when I remembered a conversation I had with the dwarves while we chowed down at *Endless Chili Dog Night* at Der Weiner Schnitzel. I asked dwarves and goblins hated each other.

"Why do dwarves and goblins hate each other?" said Buck. "Well, it was back in the dreaded goblin wars, that goblins first made it their practice to rape dwarves and their wives in the High Kingdom. To punish the goblins, dwarves habitually disemboweled goblin warriors, and fed them to the crows. But we never hurt the goblin women and children. We would not lose our souls by killing innocent goblin females and children. But goblins use their females and young as shields in battle. So, sometimes it was unavoidable."

As I looked around the cavern I saw piles of clothing all around us: blue jeans, shirts, blouses, tennis shoes, backpacks, belts, canteens, all of it new stuff, most likely from the hikers and campers caught unaware while sleeping peacefully under the beautiful stars of the Great Smoky Mountains. Did any of these souls survive? I saw no evidence of it. "Payback's a bitch," said Buck, surveying our present circumstances. "Pucker up, brothers."

I felt my own anus pucker up, cramping shut with a snap. I was glad that goblins were fluorescent yellow, not black. You could avoid the negative and prejudiced images and stereotypes in our culture associated with being black. In my world some of the most talented and beautiful men and women were black, yellow, and brown.

"I'll never believe Beca betrayed us," I said.

"Thank God she escaped," said Dutch, thinking his best for her, as he was very fond of her, as we all were. She loved us and we all felt it. "I would hate to think of what the goblins would do to her."

"Me, too," said Buck.

"Me, three," said Burt.

"Me, four," said Theo, as so it went down to the last dwarf.

I was happy, too, that she escaped and wouldn't consider the possibility she hadn't. Though I'd be happy if the sun was shining on my face, and happier still if my head and shoulders didn't smell like Stilton cheese.

CHAPTER 32

The goblins had searched us and stripped us of all of our possessions: our money, credit cards, even my Automobile Club of America card. I would have given half of my illusory dwarf gold to see an Automobile Club tow truck plowing through these goblin soldiers.

I was still bereft at losing Demon Slayer. What could I do except hope it showed up, which seemed doubtful — the one thing in this world that could kill the Demon Lord, now gathering dirt in the goblins' tunnels. I was surprised that Losing Demon Slayer filled me with such a profound grief. I felt an emotional loss as keen as losing one of my buddies in battle. But why? Get a grip, I told myself: it's just a sword made by the angels in heaven, but Beca was gone. How could I continue with the quest without her? A kingdom for Beca and my sword!

Goblins left and returned hours later and dragged us to our feet. They marched us out to a courtyard where a throne stood on a five-foot high dais. The courtyard was large, at least five hundred feet in diameter. Our hands were tied in front with chains. I felt as if I had a hand squeezing my balls, which were turning blue for lack of circulation. All caused by the freaking jewel pouch. Then I realized the irony: what good were the world's jewels if it cost you your *own* "jewels?" No one seemed to notice me, or my blue balls. By my count 115 soldiers and an equal number of goblin females and their imps lounged around waiting for the show to begin. We were all waiting for something to happen.

One nutty thing about the goblins: they all wore surfer clothes. Cypher Kelly Nomad shorts in Yellow Peel and Solar yellow; Gunsmoke shirts in green and black. Goblins were decked out in JC Penny's sleeveless T-shirts. They all had at least one piece tucked into their shorts: a Glock 9MM, a Smith & Wesson .45 semiautomatic, or a funky looking Walther MPK submachine gun.

The goblin then did something incredibly stupid: they piled high all of our weapons at the foot of the King's throne: our Glocks, Uzis, chainsaws, headlamps, flamethrowers, even Dutch's cash. I think they wanted to impress their King, when he showed up, with all the booty they had seized. Very impressive and no more than six feet from where we stood chained. Several goblin imps by my guess no older than ten or eleven were on the King's dais messing around with our weapons until their mothers screamed at them and they huddled with their moms to await their king's arrival. It was a big crowd waiting for the big show.

Then the Goblin king emerged from the shadows, walked up the short staircase to the dais, kicked a few goblin imps in the ass who were too close to his throne, before he sat down. He surveyed his dominion, looked up and down the courtyard, and assessed the situation.

"Why are these bitches and their miserable imps here?" the king said. "This is not a *public* execution. They have no business here. Get them out of here." said the Goblin King who smiled at the assembled dwarves. Three of his personal bodyguards escorted the females and their children off the square, presumably to their living quarters somewhere in the tunnels.

The king was a snappy dresser: black Quicksilver shorts, a yellow-flowered Hawaiian shirt, yellow Maui Jim sunglasses, and some groovy looking red Nike high-tops. Not a bad looking fellow if you could look past the unbathed yellow skin, facial skin tumors, brown teeth, and fingernails black with grime. He wore a crown; only it was one of those little princess crowns, with fake jewels, that you see little girls don at Halloween. I'm not kidding. I would have laughed my ass off if my balls weren't killing me. The crown was made of cheesy plastic and at least six sizes too small for his massive, wart-studded noggin. How do you tell a goblin king he looks like an idiot? You don't, unless you want to die a most painful death. Isn't that the problem with being king, or president, or chief? No one tells you the truth, especially if you rule through fear.

The second thing he did when he sat down was to pick his nose. He tried to cover the fact with some deft fingering from the left hand covering his right index finger, but he was working it, digging deep into his nostril. In fact, most of the goblin guards were emulating their king, picking the two flat holes in their faces that passed for noses, or scratching their own and sometimes their buddy's ass. I adjusted my "jewels," *again*, which provided some relief, wondering what the goblins' next move would be. I didn't have long to wait.

The king must have been near-sighted because he bent over to look at us and came much too close to eleven lethal, battle-tested dwarves than I ever would in his position. But kings in their arrogance are often blind to their own mortality. The Goblin King laughed merrily when he saw our fearful faces, especially when he recognized Dutch. Dutch saw it too and sighed.

"How in the world did *you* get here, Gorporlin?" said an angry Dutch, who didn't give a rat's ass about being polite when we were all dead anyway. "I see you haven't missed many meals." Evidently, this was how you addressed the Goblin king, if you didn't want to look weak.

"Nice to see you, too, Dutch," said the King. "I see you have the usual dwarf-scum tagging along. Who's the fat boy? Oh! He must be 'The Chosen One.' The Demon Lord can't stop talking about him."

"Fuck the Demon Lord. You haven't answered my question." Dutch said.

"We tunneled, of course, to this truly hospitable country," said the king. "In a land where no one believes in goblins, we have prospered."

"You're right, if you call eating rats and cats prospering. But don't lie to me, Gorporlin. You couldn't tunnel beyond the barrier without powerful magic," said Dutch.

"Well perhaps our good host Senator Ross gave us a few pointers," King Gorporlin said, as those in the King's Royal Guard stood by and picked their noses, farted, and scratched their testicles.

"That's what I thought," Dutch said. "You don't have the brains."

"The Senator will be very unhappy he wasn't here to greet you. He's looking forward to meeting all of you, especially the Chosen One over there," Gorporlin said, pointing to me. "The Senator returns soon from fundraising, and he's promised us extra dwarf gold for your capture. Maybe even enough to buy a McDonald's franchise."

"Try the twenty piece Chicken McNuggets for just $4.99," I said, not knowing why. "Get the meal deal, with fries and a large coke for a buck more. Better value, and downloading the McDonald's app to your smart phone will save you and your minions even more. But good luck, your Royal Anus, getting your hands on any dwarf gold: I haven't seen so much as a goddamn farthing."

"Thank you, I'll remember that, Oh Chosen One," said King Gorporlin. "In the meantime, Dutch, I've been looking forward to killing you for years, in the traditional style, of course."

"Of course, I'd expect no less, you rotting sack of feces," said Dutch, defiant to his last breath.

Gorporlin swept his sword from its scabbard. His guards dragged Dutch before the king. As the king raised his sword to decapitate Dutch, one of his guards was faster, and cut off the king's head.

The shock of it froze every goblin in the courtyard. The king's head rolled like a bowling ball, off the dais stopping in front of Dutch's feet.

CHAPTER 33

The goblin assassin jumped off the dais and morphed into Beca. Beca was a shape shifter! Though there wasn't time to discuss the fact. After dispatching a few goblin guards, she cut off Dutch's chains with Demon Slayer, which went through his chains like butter. Beca tossed the hilt of Demon Slayer to me. I grabbed it with my right hand feeling joy pulse through my veins. Demon Slayer attached itself to my sinews: Demon Slayer and I cut off the rest of the dwarves' chains; then we grabbed our weapons, cash, and then the slaughter began in earnest.

Dutch, Buck, Beca, and I killed more than thirty goblin soldiers before they fled. We killed even more on our way out of the tunnels. Their screams were terrible as we blew off, sawed off, and cut off goblin arms, shoulders, heads and pumped goblin bodies full of 9MM parabellum slugs from the Glocks and Uzis. But not the women and children. Thank God they had retreated to their living quarters and were not in the tunnels.

Nevertheless, it's never like the fucking classic Hollywood war movies where the good guys are all smiles as their guts spill out on the floor. Killing in Bartlett's, *The High Kingdom* was sanitized. Our killing was up close and personal, and bloody as hell with what felt like endless screaming from the goblins we killed.

I never felt such terrible guilt in my life. Still a large contingent of goblins escaped and retreated up various tunnels. They had clearly trained for a disastrous retreat, even as it unfolded. It was Iraq all over again and I looked forward to a new batch of waking nightmares in the future.

I can't help thinking we must have killed women and children in the firefight, although I didn't see any. This is what still drives me crazy. This drove our boys crazy when they came back from Iraq and Afghanistan. Yeah, they killed the bad guys; it's the murder of innocent women, boys, and girls, caught in the cross-fire that drove them mad. Even if it was murder in self defense, such as killing a woman about to throw a grenade at your buddies. It can still drive you mad. It wasn't like killing the trolls, who were eating Ornery and absorbing bullets like they were mosquito bites. The goblins looked like human beings, if uglier. They were built like us: had arms and legs like us. They talked and felt like us; their bones shattered and sprayed blood like ours; and they screamed like us. Dutch saw the horror on my face, said nothing, except exhorting us to advance. We kept running and running and running.

Thanks to Beca's impeccable sense of direction, we escaped the goblin tunnels. We knew the goblins had marched us a long time, but we were pleasantly surprised to find that we were only a couple of miles away from Gatlinburg. Have you ever noticed that when you are going somewhere for the first time it seems to take forever to get there, but the return trip home seems almost miraculously short? Why is that? We felt as if the goblins had marched us a hundred miles, but it wasn't so.

That's how it was going down the mountain to Gatlinburg. We hustled our collective asses down the mountain in no time. The dwarves ran with a chainsaw in one hand and an ax in the other. I had Demon Slayer and an Uzi. Our guns were loaded, our swords were drawn, and our chainsaws on idle — prepared for anything we might meet as we raced down the mountain.

We surprised five large goblin soldiers on patrol, hoping to capture and enslave the unwary camper. Buck cut off the heads of two, Beca eviscerated the third, and Dutch shot the last two. We also ran over a couple of campers sleeping in their tents. We couldn't tell them there were goblins; so we told them there were three murderers, escapees from the local prison still at large on the mountain. They made it down the hill faster than we did.

Further down the mountain we looked behind and fifteen goblins were on our tail, a minute or two up the trail from us. During our escape, I had grabbed one of our flamethrowers and waited for the goblins to get within a hundred feet but I couldn't blast them. I just couldn't do it. Beca grabbed the flamethrower out of my hands and blasted them, incinerating every last one.

We reached the Four Seasons in the dark knowing that our Harleys were gone. They weren't at the hotel and so the fucking goblins had our bikes, too. Still, we were free.

CHAPTER 34

What now?" I said to Dutch. "Will the goblins will attack us here?"

"Not during the day. They won't risk the locals discovering their existence, or that they live only a few miles away." Dutch said. "But we've got to get as far away from Gatlinburg as we can before nightfall. They'll come for us tonight, regardless. We killed their King. There *will* be payback. Even though they have no leader, a goblin commander will step up and lead them."

"That'll be tough without our Harleys," said Arnie, who had a nasty wound on his forehead, bandaged with part of his shirt. He ducked just in time to avoid decapitation.

"No shit," said Theo.

A shot rang out and hit the light above us where we stood in the hotel's driveway.

"Did I mention they have they have snipers in those trees?" said Dutch, pointing to the forest high above us. "Let's get inside and decide on alternate transportation." It was still two hours before sunrise; we entered the Four Seasons with alacrity.

"You can bet your ass they'll track us using the mountains for cover, probably riding our own Harleys," Buck said, fingering the edge of his ax. He nodded approvingly at the yellow blood on the blade. "Still good as new."

"We don't have time to buy new bikes," said Beca. "We were damn lucky to get most of our weapons back."

"Buck's right, of course. They'll track with our own bikes. I think we should buy a large mini-van, a bus if we can find one, with four wheel drive, just in case we need to go off road with it." I said.

"Hey, that's what I was thinking!" said Beca, surprised that we might share an intelligent thought.

"But how are we going to pay for it?" I said. "My Mastercard limit is not high enough. And I doubt anyone will take the troll jewels without verifying that they're real and we haven't the time for that nonsense."

"I grabbed most of my cash in the tunnels. I hid part of it in our room here. Together, it should be enough to buy a used bus," Dutch said.

"Before we do anything, I want to ask the assistant hotel manager about the property we left in the room," Buck said.

"Right. Did he do anything with our clothing? Did *he* take any cash?" said Dutch.

"Speak of the devil: here he comes now," I said.

"Welcome back my friends!" said Geoffrey, the assistant manager, suddenly pale from the loss of blood in his surprised face. "I was worried something terrible had happened to you. Have you had breakfast yet?"

"No, we haven't," said Dutch, looking at him with a gimlet eye.

"Well, then please allow me to treat everyone to the breakfast buffet," he said. "Follow me. You're going to love all the wonderful choices: omelets, bacon, fresh squeezed orange juice, caviar, champagne, your hearts' desire."

Free food was like manna from heaven for any dwarf and some of the dwarves forgot their suspicion of this man, but not all of us. Arnie walked across the lobby at that moment.

"All of our clothes and belongings are gone!" he said.

"Not at all," said Geoffrey. "I put them in storage when I didn't see you today. No worries. Go and eat and I'll retrieve everything you left in the room." With that he left us standing in the buffet line.

"Dutch, please: allow me to apply a woman's touch. Permit me to have a little chat with him," Beca said, fingering the edge of her knife.

"Wonderful idea my dear Beca," said Buck, who was now her biggest fan.

"Could he be in league with the goblins?" I asked while I heaped bacon and sausage on my first plate of food.

"I noticed he was wearing a solid gold watch. A Rolex Presidential, if you can believe it," said Theo who loved his old stainless steel Rolex Submariner, a gift from his father, a cutlery salesman in the High Kingdom.

"Can't buy that kind of bling on an *assistant* manager's salary — at the Four Seasons or any hotel," said Buck.

"Damn right. I'll have a nice chat with him," said Beca, who speared bacon and sausage, a couple of maple waffles, and some fresh fruit with her knife.

"If he is league with goblins," said Dutch, "he deserves the same fate. Our sweet Beca is just the person to discuss the matter. Needs a woman's touch. Now, let's eat."

"Here's the rest of your cash, Dutch," said Beca, two hours later. "Count it. See how much is there. *Geoffrey* said he wanted to make amends."

"What'd he say, exactly?" said Arnie, his mouth full of eggs and sausage smothered in hollandaise. The buffet was great.

"Should I cut his throat?" said Theo.

"Hey, there's $150,000 here," said Dutch. "That's three times what we had left."

"I took what I found in his safe. Had to slice up his hand a bit to get him to open it," said Beca. "He said the money's all ours after 'our terrible ordeal.' I just assume I'm getting 1/14th of any money recovered on this quest, right?"

That got everyone's attention. The silence was deafening. The dwarves looked at the ground sheepishly. Even Buck was at a loss for words. Dutch broke the silence.

"Safe to say we're not Geoffrey's first victims and you're damn right, young lady: you get 1/14th of all the money recovered now and in the future of this quest. And bless you, again, for saving all of our lives," said Dutch, loudly, like an incantation, if only to remind the dwarves how close to death they had been. Dwarves have an uncanny ability to forget such things when money's involved.

"I knew you'd do right by me," said Beca, looking up to Dutch who stood a foot taller.

"Come here, please," said Dutch. Beca stood in front of the old wizard. He embraced her, held her, and kissed her several times on the top of her head the way a father might kiss his daughter. Beca looked up at Dutch, as if his fatherly embrace was payment in full. "You're family now, dear Beca."

"Amen!" I said in unison with every dwarf.

"God's blessing on you, Beca. And take as much of this cash as you like," said Dutch who handed her the entire amount.

"It really belongs to everyone and I don't need any right now," Beca said. "Would you hold it for us, Dutch?"

CHAPTER 35

It was already past 11AM and we had yet to visit auto dealerships, which were just opening. The Four Seasons assistant manager approached us in the lobby, directing his comments to Dutch.

"We feel terrible about the bikes being stolen," Geoffrey said, using the Royal We to try to avoid personal responsibility. His hand was bandaged and blood seeped out and stained his French shirt cuff and the carpet in the lobby. Beca had done quite a number on his fingers. "But we have insurance for occasions like this one. If you will fill out this form." He tried to hand Dutch a paper with a shaking hand.

"We haven't got time to file a claim, *sir*." Dutch said. "You can do it for us. Right now we need to find transportation for fourteen."

"Allow us to make a call," Geoffrey said. We have an associate in town who sells vans and buses. And please consider your breakfast on the house."

"You do that, Geoffrey and get back to us, quick!" said Beca, as he gave Beca a terrified look and hurried back to his office. "He's so dirty. He said he only took our cash and three of our bikes, but that the goblins took the rest. Said goblins threatened to kill him if he didn't supply the occasional guest for their pleasure."

"So, he's a murderer," said Dutch.

The assistant hotel manager at the Four Seasons had a friend, Chuck, a used car salesman, whose lot had a 1995 yellow and red tricked-out school bus with 4-wheel drive, and 450,000 miles. The negotiation began when the salesman, Chuck, said, "Why 450,000 miles is nothing on a school bus. I have seen school buses rack up more than a million miles. She'll be the best $20,000 you ever spent."

The negotiation ended when Beca said, "We'll give you $7,500 for the Piece of Shit bus and you have my personal guarantee I'll run back and slit your throat if it breaks down." Many of the dwarves pissed their pants they laughed so hard. Chuck agreed to the deal and despite the danger we faced down the road, we all knew it was a good ride.

A school bus was a great choice because it not only had room underneath the seats for our backpacks and handguns, but someone had also removed the last four rows of seats in the back, which created space for our precious chainsaws, Uzis, Kalashnikovs, and flamethrowers. We also had an XM25 Grenade launcher, and an extra flamethrower we took from the goblins' hoard. The bus had black gangsta rims, shades on all the windows, so you could blackout the interior if you wanted to sleep during the day. It was a sweet ride.

Everyone boarded the bus, fastened their seatbelts, and chatted amiably. Dutch volunteered to take the first shift as driver. I stood, held my arms up for silence and the dwarves looked up to me, as if they were school children waiting for instructions from their teacher. There was a strong breeze blowing throughout the bus. I can't begin to describe the wondrous feeling I had looking out over a sea of bearded faces, buckled in their seats like little kids. Dutch drove down Main Street and we all saw something attached to the side of the Four Seasons. Stapled to the side of the hotel, courtesy of Beca, was assistant manager, Geoffrey, who was screaming and slowly dying. I will never forget the victims' piled clothing and backpacks that filled our room in the goblin tunnels and thought only the Good Lord knew how many innocent, unsuspecting tourists were worked to death and raped in the goblin tunnels thanks to that Judas, Geoffrey.

CHAPTER 36

Let's begin this leg of our journey together by singing the Happy Bus Song," I said, while Dutch drove and smoked his pipe. "I'll sing the first verses to you and you can pick it up from there."

The wheels on the bus go round and round,
round and round, round and round,
The wheels on the bus go round and round —
Early in the morning — EVERYBODY!

The birds in the air go chirp, chirp, chirp,
Chirp, chirp, chirp.
The birds in the air go chirp, chirp, chirp —
Early in the morning.

The dwarves in the bus say, we're so cool, we're so cool.
The dwarves in the bus say, we're so cool —
We escaped the goblins this morning!!

The wheels on the bus go round and round, round and round.
The wheels on the bus go round and round —
On such a lovely morning!

After a couple of hours, I took over for Dutch, who sat next to me, watching the road and blowing blue, red, gold, yellow, and yellow smoke rings — all the colors of the rainbow. The smoke rings traveled throughout the bus, hovering over the dwarves heads like halos until, Burt, the last of nine angelic dwarves fell asleep. Only Theo and Buck were still awake in the back. Buck came forward and took over driving. I sat next to Beca who used my stomach as a pillow while she slept. Buck threw me another pillow and I gently placed it under her back for support. We had all been praising Beca for her courage. I looked at Buck and he looked at me. I considered pinching Beca to be sure she was asleep before I said anything.

"I think I'm in love with her," I said to Buck.

"I think we're all in love with her, Rufus Timmons," said Buck. "No dwarf has ever witnessed such bravery or battle skills in a woman before and most dwarf women defend themselves well in battle."

"No, you don't understand. I think I am truly in love with her, not just as a warrior, but also as a woman. What should I do?"

"Be patient, Rufus. You're the Chosen One and there is no question about that. You're a brave man, too, my friend. But she's a shape-shifter and no one here has experience with that. And she's got a temper; so she is wonderful and very dangerous at the same time — more dangerous than any of us know. So, if you want my advice, I would say let her come to you on her own terms."

"Sage advice, Buck son of Lord Wessex. You're a true friend. She loves you, too. She would die for you, too."

"Thank the Lord of Creation," said Buck holding up his left hand, which had a thick gold wedding ring, "Or I'd be as heart-sick as you."

"What's your wife's name?" I asked.

"Deborah, and this quest has taken me away from her far too long. I want to go home, yesterday," he said.

"Why don't we ever hear of dwarf wives? I said. "I've never heard you or any of our comrades mention whether they are married."

"They are our best kept secret," Buck said. "If we let them... no that's wrong... dwarf women are powerful... we don't control them... they do what they want, but they love their husbands so profoundly that for our sake they are rarely seen in public. If they were, their beauty would break too many hearts. So they live and work behind the scenes and raise confident, powerful children and are their husbands' chief blessing in life. I would be worthless on this quest but for my Deborah's strength. She's my height with long black hair like the blackest coal; radiant eyes like the stars; and a bosom that would give most men a heart attack. Please, you must kill this Demon Lord soon so I can get back to my Deborah."

"I feel ashamed for all the cracks I've made over the years about dwarf women," I said.

"Don't be," said Buck.

"But they were made out of complete ignorance," I said. "Maybe I'm wrong, but I don't remember Bartlett ever writing a single word about them in *The High Kingdom*, though that's a pretty lame excuse."

"Rufus, we've heard all the jokes and they mean nothing to us. Dwarves are fierce warriors, as you know, so when a laddie is born into a dwarf family or clan, it a cause of great rejoicing. But when a dwarf lassie is gifted to us, and it's rare for reasons unknown, you can multiply that rejoicing by a factor of 1,000,000, which is still too small a number. For God is more deeply embedded in the heart of every dwarf girl. The love a dwarf wife gives her husband is his chief reason for living. It's certainly mine. Everything else: money, power, victory in battle means little by comparison. Ask any dwarf warrior. He'll tell you the same."

"I believe every word," I said. "I promise to do my part to get you and all of our comrades home as soon as I can." Never before had I considered the depth of passion and love that Buck had for his wife. I felt honored by his candor, realizing for the first time on this quest that all of my comrades had someone in the High Kingdom yearning for his return.

I took a short nap and had my first PTSD nightmare back in the goblin tunnels. Great, I thought, it's started. I woke up teary-eyed thinking back on what I had done in the tunnels. I was still troubled by the slaughter. Dutch blew on his pipe and gave me a sidewise glance. Buck was driving and focused on the road. Arnie and Theo were lookouts for any Harley's on the road, as well as lupine riding goblins off the road. Nothing so far.

"It's good you feel terrible for the killing done in the goblin tunnels," said Dutch, who sat beside me, puffing on his pipe, and reading my mind.

"A few of the goblin men were unarmed." I said.

"Collateral damage," said Dutch, "They simply couldn't get to their weapons in time and would have killed you if they had."

"So you're saying killing unarmed, defenseless goblins isn't murder, just collateral damage if their intent was to kill me?"

"You bet your ass. I'm saying you acted in self-defense in a war," said Dutch. "You did this, *we did this* to save our lives, *and you,* suffered another brutal psychological trauma, no different than the injuries you suffered in Iraq and Afghanistan."

"Why didn't King Gerald suffer from PTSD after he slaughtered lupines, goblins, trolls, even evil men in the battle for the High Kingdom? He felt no guilt at all. And yet soon I'll be forced to kill more goblins and damage my soul beyond recognition. It's so fucking depressing."

"You were born with different values than Gerald, in a different place and time. Listen to me, Rufus. You've broken God's most sacred law against taking life, any life. If you felt nothing, I'd be worried and I wouldn't trust you. Thank God you feel terrible. You're a moral man, a man I'm proud to serve with. Which brings me to Beca: I love her desperately, but when she kills there isn't a shred of regret in her. And that worries me." Fortunately, Beca was driving, with her headphones on, and singing during this conversation. I don't think she heard what Dutch said, which might have hurt her feelings.

"You may be right. She may have no regrets when she kills. But I know this," I said. "She loves us and will never betray us. We're her family. I feel it every time she rests her head on my fat gut, even if you can't. She possesses a savage love for every one of our comrades. She will die for us if she has to. You said it yourself, Dutch: she's family now. You saw her nearly break down when you hugged her and kissed her and made her our own."

"I pray to God you're right, Rufus," said Dutch. "Because I really do love her. I couldn't love a daughter more."

CHAPTER 37

Interstate 81 goes through mountainous terrain before it crosses from Tennessee into Virginia. We pushed our vehicle past the speed limit. Toward the late afternoon we found ourselves climbing in altitude on I81 with a dark forest looming on either side, and night closing in. One good omen was that we found of all things, a Clucker's Chicken House at a Pilot Travel Center. We stopped, gassed up, and got 10 buckets of breasts, wings, and thighs to go. We kept driving, planning to eat when we camped. But the smell of all that delicious food drove us nuts. We probably waited all of five minutes before a collective shout out of, "FUCK IT! LET'S EAT!" We attacked the fried chicken and what's fried chicken without Clucker's famous gravy, dippin' sauces, potato skins, and coleslaw, which we ate with gusto, kind of redundant when applied to dwarves. Even though it was messy and spilled on the floor, it was so good and filled us with energy for what was to come and for what might be our last meal.

"Pull off the Mountain View exit and let's drive into the forest," said Dutch.

"Why here?" I asked.

"Just a hunch," said Dutch. "I'm hoping there *is* a mountain view off this exit and that it *is* on high ground. We'll build a defensive perimeter there."

We drove maybe five miles on that road, steadily increasing in elevation, deep into the mountains. From there we got off the main road and climbed up the side of the mountain, until we came to, Mountain View, the highest point in that area. We could see everything for five miles in any direction. Of course, we wouldn't be able to see a damn thing when it was dark. Still, we had an advantage fighting from a position on high ground. We couldn't take a chance of having to fight out in the open near I81. We'd have been destroyed on the highway. And a good defense is often the best offense. Let them come to us. We'd be ready.

It was getting dark and we quickly chopped down trees and carried large stones, creating a good makeshift defensive perimeter around our camp. We sharpened branches, buttressed by large stones; we pointed the branches outward at a 45 degree angle, hoping to impale our enemy in the dark. According to the dwarves, goblin trackers were impossible to outwit. They *would* find us. Their sense of smell was as good as any bloodhound, maybe better; plus they had our Harley's to help them with our scent. The only question was how long before they found us and how much firepower would they bring?

We waited, and while we waited we took turns, two at a time, going into the woods for a colossal Clucker's crap, though most of us were constipated from anxiety.

At first we couldn't stop talking about what had happened in the goblin tunnels and couldn't stop praising Beca for delivering us from a certain death. I was the only one who wasn't saying much. I was behind a four-foot wall of trees and stones. I was actually wiping tears from my eyes. I was still disturbed by the slaughter in the tunnels and the slaughter to come, and my part in both.

Assuming we lived to see the morning, many of the dwarves wanted to find a mall and buy red Nike tennis shoes like the ones worn by the dead Goblin King. I can't speak for every part of a dwarf's anatomy, but they do have big feet. That's all they could talk about. It was all a bit exasperating. They had narrowly escaped a major corn-holing and torture fest at the hands of the goblins and 24 hours later they had to find the Goblin King's red Nike high tops. So they asked me to keep a lookout for a Sam's Shoe Outlet if we got out of this mess. They just crapped their brains out in the forest, but were still thinking of their next meal. While they readied and cleaned their guns, they wouldn't shut up about the hankering they had for the Original Six Dollar Burger at Carl's Jr. I liked mine with guacamole and a big onion ring on top with extra Thousand Island dressing. Man, I'd love a burger. It had been a while since we had a good burger and onion rings. It seemed inconceivable that I might never enjoy another Six Dollar Burger. I'll also admit the Goblin King's red high top Nikes were cool and that I wouldn't mind a pair myself. I liked his Maui Jim sunglasses, too.

"Hey, maybe they're not coming." I said.

"They're coming," said Dutch.

"What makes you so sure?" I asked. "They just took a hell of a beating."

"No matter. Buck, what would you do if the goblins killed the King of the Dwarves?" Dutch asked rhetorically.

"If you killed our king, we would find you and we would kill you. But first we'd hang you from a hook in your back which would give us enough fun time to play with your body parts; That's what the dwarves would do and I'm confident the goblins could think of something much more unpleasant."

"That sounds unpleasant enough for me. Life's a helluva thing to happen to someone." I said, out of the blue and for no damn reason other than as an existential musing that popped into my head, based solely on the shit I'd seen go down in two battle zones, and one just hours away.

"It certainly can be if you're called," said Dutch.

"Called?" I said.

"Called to lead an extraordinary life; called to do extraordinary things," said Dutch.

"Such as destroying demon lords and fabled monsters?"

"Yeah," said Dutch, "Those qualify."

"I wouldn't give an Elvish fart for another hotel," said Dutch to Buck loud enough for everyone to hear.

"Do elves really fart?" I said. "Because I don't see Katherine ripping a burner, cutting the cheese, or cranking a cheese ball back at the chateau. Do their farts smell bad?"

"Of course elves fart." Dutch said. "Even Princess Katherine. Elves are flesh and blood creatures. They eat, crap, make love — even fart on rare occasions. But no one's farts smell as bad as yours."

"Who is Princess Katherine?" said Beca.

"Just some awesome Elf Babe Princess we met at Lord Reggie's hidden chateau who Rufus had the hots for," said Arnie.

"No, I didn't," I said. "She gave me on a tour of the chateau's waterfalls. That was it. Nothing more. I was getting on Lord Reggie's nerves so she took me aside to give her dad some relief."

"You get on everyone's nerves," said Theo. "But we saw how you stared at her big breasts, her super-sized bazooms. Even Reggie called you on it. Don't deny it."

"Yeh, so? I said. "All the elf babes there has super-sized boobs. You had to be blind not to notice. I noticed you noticed, too, Theo. It was an 'Event Sociological.'"

"What the hell does that mean, 'an event sociological?'" said Buck. "Geez, what bullshit, Rufus. Just own up to it, Oh, Chosen One. You're a big breast maniac."

"Look, if you enter a room in our world you'll see women with large AND small breasts. When you entered a room at Lord Reggie's Elf chateau, ALL the women had large breasts, which is extraordinary OR an 'Event Sociological,'" I said.

"Nice try, Big Man," said Beca, who left to check our defensive perimeter.

"Thanks everyone," I sighed. "That was a big help. And elves may fart, but Buck's farts were conceived in Hell." I closed my eyes.

"Buck's farts are homicidal," said Theo. "Which is to say I want to kill him when he rips one."

"My farts smell like roses compared to your atrocities, Theo," Buck said.

"Remember that little boy who fainted at Clucker's when he walked through a cloud of Buck farts?" said Burt.

"How 'bout the time Ornery ignited his own fart while smoking?" said Arnie, "God rest his soul."

"You know, Dutch, I'm glad that elves fart on rare occasions," I said, opening my eyes. "Because once I..."

"Shut up Rufus, and everyone else, too!" said Dutch. "We have serious issues to decide. There's a large goblin infestation in this region, which means the goblins have tunnel access to most of the hotels in this region. Right now they are tracking online hotel registrations for parties with ten or more guests staying for the night. We have to tell Lord Reggie. They may be kidnapping innocent civilians, too."

"Dutch we're in the forest, not the Four Seasons," said Theo.

"Don't you get it?" Dutch said. "I just said that the hotels and motels aren't safe anywhere between here and Washington — even if we survive the night and we're get back on Interstate 81 north, we have nowhere to sleep except outside. By now Senator Ross knows the Goblin king is dead. He's sending reinforcements that may not make to tonight's fight, but they're on the way. We'll have to drive straight through Virginia to Interstate 66 east to D.C. without stopping, if we hope to reach our safe house alive. We're never staying in another hotel while our quest lasts."

"We can always sleep in the bus," said Larry, one of the worst farters among the dwarves.

"Everyone sleeping in the bus? You gotta be kidding," said Burt. "Eleven farting dwarves *and* Rufus? I'll take my chances with the goblins."

"How long will it take to reach the safe house, Dutch?" said Buck.

"We should reach D.C. by the late afternoon," said Dutch, "assuming we don't break down or get waylaid by the Demon Lord's agents. And once in D.C. at least two or three hours, maybe more, to locate the safe house."

"I think if we can stay on the side roads, avoid the Interstate as much as possible, and quickly pass through any mountains and forests unscathed, we may reach our destination." Beca added.

"I agree," said Dutch.

"Do you really think the goblins are coming for us this far north?" I said.

"How many times do I have to say it? We killed their king," said Buck. "They're *coming*."

CHAPTER 38

At dusk we built a small fire after building our defensive perimeter. The dwarves wanted s'mores, a big hit. Dutch melted his with blue fire from his cane, which was the craziest looking blowtorch I've ever seen. Everyone else held them on a stick over the campfire. A delicious last treat. Besides, fire didn't matter: goblin trackers would find us.

I was praying for just one uneventful night with all of these characters, but it wasn't meant to be. I suppose if you're traveling with eleven dwarves, a wizard, and a cute, possibly psychotic, yet irresistible shape-shifter, you'd be a moron not to know you're also a shit magnet. I was afraid.

Everyone looked as if they were sleeping peacefully, or so we hoped it appeared. In reality, we created bundles of leaves, branches that when covered by blankets looked as if we were asleep. Actually, the dwarves were sleeping and hiding in the tree branches above our campsite, armed with their chainsaws, Uzis, Kalashnikovs, and M-16s. Dwarves hate heights, which every goblin knows. I knew this too and suggested this ruse. My War Dog buds and I used this trick in Paroon, Nuristan, a forested section in Afghanistan. We hid in the trees and when the Taliban soldiers came through we killed them all, and none of my buddies was hurt. We hoped to get the drop on our enemy and wipe out the first wave of the goblins. It was agreed, with one dissenter, that I would sleep on the ground, among the fake dwarves and snore loudly, thus giving the ruse the appearance of reality: just me, my Glock, and Demon Slayer. I was not thrilled and worried my friends might shoot me if I failed to slip into the woods fast enough as goblins approached my snoring hulk. A raccoon came by and sniffed my body from stem to stern and left. Buck and Theo were on the outer perimeter and would signal when the enemy approached. Between the two of them, not a mouse could escape unnoticed, except, I suppose, if they were asleep on the job. But Beca wasn't snoring. She moved unseen around the camp signaling that we were surrounded. The motherfuckers who got the drop on us at the Four Seasons would have to do better this time.

Beca's signaled there were fifty goblins creeping silently toward us on huge wolves, lupines they were called them in the High Kingdom. As they approached, I slipped into the woods and circled behind them. Beca followed me. When the goblins were ten feet from our camp they blasted our counterfeit bodies with countless rounds from their sawed-off shotguns, Glocks, and Kalashnikovs. Billionaire Senator Ross armed his monster allies with decent weaponry. Then the lupines shredded what was left of our lifeless forms. They looked puzzled by the absence of blood.

Then we blasted them: the dwarves and Dutch above them and Beca and me behind them. The first wave was joined by more lupines and goblins, who shouted "Aieeeeeee!!!" shooting wildly in every direction and hitting nothin' but air. By the time the enemy realized dwarves were slaughtering them from the treetops, the dwarves changed tactics, dropped to the ground, moved soundlessly between the trees and high foliage killing the bewildered goblins at will. Beca and I and Buck flanked an enemy attacking them from every direction, trying not to hit our comrades in the process. Friendly fire can be a bitch, especially in the thick of it. BUT MAN... DID... WE... FUCK... THEM... UP!!

Though described in *The High Kingdom*, lupines were new to me. Giant wolves, easily three times the size of my beloved Irish wolfhound, Shamus. Truly, only seeing is believing. Strange that we didn't see any lupines in the goblin tunnels. Maybe the lupines protected the female goblins and their children. I took out Demon Slayer and my Uzi. Demon Slayer and I cut off the heads of three goblins while my Uzi blasted the heads off two lupines. However, one lupine got a partial 5-inch claw in my left shoulder and ripped me a good one. Fuck that hurt.

I caught my breath long enough to see how my friends were doing: they were holding their own. Dutch blasted several Lupines with his Kalashnikov, and blew apart goblins with bursts of blue fire from his cane. Of course, the dwarves were having a field day with their axes and lightweight chainsaws. Yellow goblin blood and red lupine blood drenched the trees and our campsite: we were soaked in it.

But they kept coming. My arms and legs were spent, but Demon Slayer healed the clawed hole in my left shoulder. When I felt that I couldn't lift Demon Slayer one more time, we heard the extremely loud and disturbingly close sound of UH-60, Black Hawk attack helicopters. Goblins with Black Hawks? No fuckin' way.

I had seen and heard Sikorsky UH-60 choppers, or Black Hawks in Iraq. I knew them well and their firepower frightened me even back then. Was the Demon Lord in possession of Black Hawks and finally joining the battle with his goblin servants? Was that possible? But then we heard the terrible screams of our enemy shot from above by a Saco 7.62 mm M60 general-purpose machine gun. The battle was ours.

Beca shape-shifted from human to goblin and back again, as she slipped in and out of the trees (and goblin ranks) killing the enemy, which was insanely dangerous for her with bullets flying everywhere.

Soldiers dropped from the Black Hawk, three or four soldiers at a time: in all, about twelve Navy SEALs, but they fought like a 100. They used our perimeter defense and fired on our enemy until fifty or more goblins and dozens of lupines were piled high. When another fifty had been killed the surviving goblin regiment fled.

Dutch, Buck, and Beca came out of the forest where they were "cleansing" the area of stray and injured goblin soldiers. Dutch was the only one not surprised by the SEAL team. "Holy Moly," I said. "How did you know we were here?"

The captain of the SEAL team removed his night vision goggles and helmet and I laughed. It was Captain Danny from Reggie's home in the clouds! I guess Captain Danny's golden aura followed him wherever he went. Like all the elves I met at Reggie's Shangri-La, Captain Danny projected a serenity that complemented the warriors' creed. It was still hard to believe there was a United States commissioned Elvish SEAL Team.

"I bring greetings from my father, Dutch," said Danny.

"How can I possibly express our gratitude, Lord Daniel?" said an exhausted and grateful wizard who bowed.

"How about, 'Thanks for saving our collective asses, Danny Boy.'" I said, surprised when he laughed and embraced me. The guy had a great sense of humor.

"High praise, indeed, oh, Chosen One, Sergeant Rufus Timmons of the 2nd Battalion 7th Army War Dogs," said the Elf Lord. "Dutch, we'll need help piling up the dead. We don't want the locals discovering they have a goblin and lupine infestation. We'll obviously need to burn everything, quickly."

I couldn't believe the calm of Captain Danny. It's always the gentle-men, the quiet soldiers who are the toughest. I have never met a rude Navy SEAL or a bullying Green Beret. Quiet, tough, good people.

"How did you know we'd be here?" I said, rotating my left shoulder that had healed but was stiff. Theo was limping from buckshot in his ass. The Navy SEALs would patch him up.

Fortunately, we'd set up a good defensive perimeter because besides Theo, no one was dead or seriously injured.

"Lord Reggie lost track of your GPS, Dutch," Captain Danny said, directing his comments to the wizard. "That's why I was dispatched as soon as it reappeared. We were surprised when our drone showed us pictures of goblins riding your Harleys. They led us right to you."

"Thank Lord Reggie for me Captain," said Dutch. "He must have lost track of us when we were in the goblin tunnels."

"Captain Danny, have you found more Goblin infestations around the country?" I said.

"You ask too many questions, Rufus," said Dutch. "Please, go help the others with the bodies."

"Any idea how many are here?" I asked, ignoring Dutch. I had a right to know. This was my country, not his.

"Too many," said Captain Danny, who avoided a specific answer to my question. "And they breed like rabbits. Dutch, you've enraged them by killing the king."

"Gorporlin's death was long overdue. I'd met him a few times in the High Kingdom, and barely escaped each time. But I didn't kill him," said Dutch. "The person with that honor is in the forest cleaning up. Her name is Beca and she rescued us in the goblin tunnels where we were captives."

"Lord Reggie said you might have a shape shifter contractor in your company," Danny said turning his attention to me.

"So she was telling the truth," I said. "Told you, Dutch. She knows Lord Reggie. Listen, Captain Danny, I want to apologize for my behavior at Chateau Reggie. You know, with the elf ladies."

"Yes, Elvish women can be overwhelmingly beautiful, especially for mortals. Don't give it another thought, Oh Chosen One," Captain Danny said who laughed as embraced me with powerful bear hug. "Lady Katherine sends her greetings."

"Really?" I said.

"No," he said and laughed and I laughed and we left it there.

I thought the SEALs were listening to me and Captain Danny, but they were focused on Beca who had just walked up behind us. She was dragging two dead goblins, one in each hand. Beca was in her pint sized, cute little red headed girl mode, which belied her strength, as she swung the goblins over her head and launched them to the top of the pile with their dead comrades. One of the SEALs stepped back, in awe at her effortless display of power.

"Hey, Chunk, why aren't you helping me with the cleanup, dude?" Beca said. "Plenty to go around."

"Who's Chunk?" said Dutch, with a half knowing, half laughing expression on his face.

"It's her new name for me," I said, a bit embarrassed, but loving the attention. She came right up to my face, though she was still more than a foot below my face.

"All I'm saying is that Chunk here could stand to lose a few and what better way than to haul some dead goblins a few hundred yards. Am I wrong?" she said, and stuck her hand under my shirt and rubbed my belly, most disrespectfully.

"That's enough of that young lady," I said, removing her hot hand from my stomach. "Show a little respect for your betters."

"My elders, perhaps, but not my betters, and a little respect *is* exactly what you've earned. Come on, oh Chosen One, let's go find some more bodies. We'll make it a 'togetherness day,'" she said and held my hand.

"Beca, my dear," said Dutch, "There's someone you should meet."

"Dutchy, *should* isn't in my vocabulary." she said.

"Captain Daniel, United States Navy, ma'am."

"A SEAL, if that Trident on your chest is for real," Beca said.

"It is ma'am," the Captain said.

"Boy, I'll say! You're the real deal, all right," Beca said looking admiringly at his Navy SEAL battle gear and powerful physique. "Hey, Chunk, I'm going to whip you into this kind of shape, if it kills you."

"Captain Danny's spoken for," I said, hoping she was pretending to be hot for Captain Danny, the way the dwarves said I was for Princess Katherine.

"I'm sure he *is*. He better be! A Navy SEAL Elf!? Danny, did you say? Who'd a thunk?" said Beca, moving even closer the Elf SEAL, and doing an excellent job at making me jealous.

"I send you Lord Regginald's, my father's greeting," Captain Danny said. "I was instructed by him to ask you a few questions should we meet and should you be willing to answer them."

"Oh, that's what this is about. If you don't get too goddamn personal, I guess it's ok," Beca said."

"Thank you. Do you remember where you were born?" he asked. "And when you discovered your powers?"

"Asked and answered. I told your dad I don't where the fuck I was born. No birth certificate to the best of my knowledge and if there is I haven't a clue where to find it. I discovered my powers when I was three or four. My foster father tried to put out his cigarette on my arm. The second it touched my skin I shape shifted into a wolf and ripped out his fucking throat. Then I dragged his worthless carcass into the nearby woods where my mother and I buried him. He's rotting in hell where he belongs. Pretty much smooth sailing after that."

I said nothing and it was the smartest thing I never did. I wanted to hold her in my arms and never let her go. She could morph into a wolf and rip *my* throat out for all I cared. She was still a major pain in the ass, like now calling me Chunk, a fat bastard in front of everyone. I was nuts about her; all the dwarves were nuts about her; I also knew her love would never be smooth sailing. She was damaged goods, one of the walking wounded. Hell, who wasn't?

"Have you met any others like yourself?" the Captain asked.

"I'm it, as far as I know," said Beca.

"When your quest is completed Lord Regginald would be honored to meet you," said the Captain. "Until such time, he also asked if you would accept a small gift for your service."

"Depends on the gift," Beca said.

Captain Danny removed a small wood box covered with gold filigree and powerful Elvish runes around Lord Reggie's family crest, an embedded silver filigreed apple tree adorned with red apples cut from the brightest rubies. Nice presentation box. The silver tree I recognized from seeing it everywhere in Chateau Reggie: embedded in the lobby walls, on the door posts, on the soaps and toiletries, every dish, and on every silver knife, fork, and spoon in the joint. Beca bowed as she accepted the box, which shocked the hell out of Dutch and me. We never knew she possessed any good manners. She opened the box and inside was a bracelet.

"Hooyah! It's the most beautiful bracelet I've ever seen! Is it bugged?" she said, and examined it closely from every angle. Satisfied it wasn't, she gave Captain Danny a huge hug, a little too huge for my liking.

"What is it? Let me see. Let me see!!" said Buck who couldn't see over me.

"It's a silver bracelet," I said, making room for him, "with the brightest rubies, sapphires, and emeralds you will see in your lifetime."

"But who would set such stones in silver?" Buck said, his eyes large with wonder.

"No one would. It's not silver," said the Captain, "and those are not rubies, sapphires, and emeralds. The bracelet is platinum, and the stones are known in the trade as, "fancy colored diamonds." They are red, green, and blue diamonds mined and cut by the finest dwarf craftsmen in the High Kingdom. The bracelet and setting were both created by my father's good friend, the late Harry Winston. And *no*, it is not bugged, but it has my father's blessing upon it which bestows power and grace, and means you *are* in his prayers."

Even I, The Chosen One, heard of the legendary Mr. Harry Winston. He was the jeweler to royalty and Hollywood's movie stars. He donated the Hope Diamond to the Smithsonian Institution. Ok, so The Chosen One likes to read the tabloids while waiting in line at Walmart. But what does Lord Reggie know about Beca that I don't?

"I'm honored. You know, I'm really a nice person," Beca said, looking at Captain Danny and the bracelet. "Sure I'm rough around the edges, but what can I say? I can't abide assholes. But I love these dwarves. They're a hoot and good people. I love Dutchy, and you, too Chunk, oh, Chosen One," A another nickname I hoped the dwarves wouldn't start using. Beca jumped up and kissed me on the cheek. She kissed me, not Captain Danny.

"I feel the same way about you, too, shorty." I said, blushing, and kicking the dirt a little. Then I walked away to think about what just happened. I walked back into the forest for one last reconnaissance.

"Lord Reggie thinks very highly of you, Beca. He can't thank you enough for keeping an eye on this motley crew," said Captain Danny.

About a hundred yards into the forest, I heard a whimper. I approached the sound warily, convinced it might be a trap. Better to be paranoid and alive than inquisitive and dead. The source of the whimpering seemed to be a large, dead lupine. It must have weighed 400 pounds. Unlike most heroes, I threw a couple of rocks at it, from a safe distance, just in case it was a trap. Who knows? The lupine could be thinking, "Maybe I can rip his throat out before I die." Or a goblin with the same thought and a remote control, at safe distance in the woods, who'd earlier taped a couple of sticks of dynamite to the dead creature. It happened all the fucking time in Iraq. Some decent soldier would go and see if he could help a woman face down in the street, thinking, hoping she was still alive. Just as soon as our guy gets close enough, some motherfucker hiding in a building 100 yards down the street presses his remote control and blows the dead woman and our comrade into a 1000 pieces. Just because you're paranoid doesn't mean they're not after you. I'm paranoid and for good reason, thank you very much Operation Iraqi fucking Freedom. Human beings would have vanished from the face of the earth but for our paranoia.

The dead lupine looked "really, most sincerely dead." It didn't move. I approached with Demon Slayer in hand. The whimper was coming from underneath the lupine. I dragged the body a few yards and, lo and behold, underneath was a baby lupine, burrowing into his mother's body, crying for its dead mother. I could tell by the umbilical cord that the mother had given birth before dying. The pup was chewing through a short five-inch thick pine tree branch as if it was a pacifier. If this was a lupine teething, I thought it best not take it away. Instead I took the little guy into my arms, branch, and all. He couldn't have been bigger than a raccoon, a really big raccoon. He had been burrowing into his mother's side trying to hide from me. But when I cradled him, he nestled in my arms.

I cooed, "Hello little guy. Hi baby boy." He stopped crying and buried his head into my armpit. I rocked him in my arms when accidentally I pushed up his right lip, revealing two-inch, razor-sharp incisors. Oh, shit, maybe this wasn't the brightest idea.

Beca, Dutch, and some of the dwarves had come looking for me. Beca saw the lupine in my arms and there was little pity in her expression.

"Put it down," said Beca, pulling out her Glock. "I'll kill it fast. It won't feel a thing."

"You're can't kill this innocent creature?" I said.

"Look what they become," she said, pointing her Glock at the dead mother. "They're monsters."

"Yeah, and look at human babies and what some of them become," I said. "Are you going to kill every baby because of a few monsters?"

"I never met a good lupine, have you?" she said.

"This is the first one I've met and I'm willing to give it half a chance. I'm not going to let you kill the little guy without a vote," I said. "Just remember, *everyone*, he's an innocent creature of God."

"God?!! Seriously?" said Beca, laughing. "You mean the Devil, don't you?"

"Rufus is right," Dutch said. "Nothing is born evil. Not a goblin, not the lupine, not even the Demon Lord, curse him: He, too, was given a choice. All is foreseen, but free will is given."

"Hold on there, Dutchy boy," said Beca. "Let me try and get my head around that last statement: God's sees all outcomes, but still hands out Free Will?"

"It's called a paradox, Beca," I said, "meaning..."

"I know what a paradox is college boy," she said. "I just don't buy it."

"God can do anything, even the logically inconsistent. When you've aged, when you're older you'll understand," I said, giving her some college boy shit.

"I've a hankering for ending your aging right here, right now," she said. "Right after I stop the aging of your lupine puppy."

"We could use a good watch dog." Buck said, getting back to our original subject.

"Dog? You mean a grizzly bear. A lupine separated my brother from his legs," said Larry, a lover of hot sauce on everything from chicken to apple pie. "They're evil creatures. We should destroy it at once."

"How could he be evil? Look at him," I said. "He's snoring in my arms. He's so sweet." Beca seized him from my hands, held him up. The the little guy starting crying.

"Hey genius, your *He* is a *She*!" Beca said, giving it right back to me. "Trust me, you never, *ever* want to meet an angry lupine bitch."

"She's a cutie patootie. Whoever wants to kill her speak now, or forever hold your Glock!" I said, rocking her in my arms. There was silence. Ok, there was some, ok, a lot of grumbling but nothing more.

"Alright, Mr. Softy, what do we call her?" Beca said, shaking her head in disbelief.

"You won't regret it. I'm calling her Wendy. She reminds me of Wendy Darling in *Peter Pan*," which was one of my favorite stories growing up. I always loved Wendy, and had many childhood dreams of flying with her to Never-Never Land. I also had some sexual dreams with Wendy Darling, but I think this is not the place to recount those. I rocked little Wendy darling in my arms, as she snored.

"I like that," said Buck. "Wendy Timmons, of the family Rufus. I think we should make Rufus her primary caregiver. What say ye?"

"Yea!" said everyone.

I gave the sleeping Wendy a kiss on her sweet little head.

CHAPTER 39

We thanked Captain Danny and his team of Navy SEALs. Their medics patched up our hurt. My shoulder was healed, but sore and stiff. The SEAL medic breathed easier when he verified the healed wound wasn't poisoned. Then he rubbed a little Ben Gay cream on my shoulder and its heat soothed my sore muscles. With the SEALs help, we burned the dead. We waved goodbye as they took off in their Black-Ops helicopters.

As I took the first shift driving on I81, I got to thinking and said, "What the fuck? Why isn't Captain Danny-boy flying all of us to D.C. on his war birds? Sure would save us a lot of time on a dangerous road."

"No pets allowed," said Beca, with reference to Wendy. "It's that mutt's fault."

"Funny," I said. "But Wendy's not a mutt. She's our pet, our mascot, our *family.*"

"Says who?" said Beca.

"Says the Chosen One. That's who," I said. "And we voted on it."

"Last time I checked, we only voted not to kill the lupine bitch," said Beca. "Mascot? Family?"

"You'll see. She's going to grow on you," I said.

"You got that right," said Beca. "In less than a week she'll be a 100 pounds — ten times her current weight. You'll see."

"Who said Captain Danny is going to D.C.?" said Dutch. "Besides, he couldn't get within 500 miles of the nation's capital in an unmarked Black Hawk. Even if you received permission to enter the air space, how would he explain our passengers: twelve *Elf* SEALs, eleven *dwarves*, and an *uberwolf* with no evolutionary antecedents? Immaterial, really: an unidentifiable Black Hawk would be shot down in South Carolina, long before ever reaching Washington D.C. And is it my imagination, or has that lupine bitch grown?"

"Understood, Dutch. Asked and answered," I said. "Yes, look at our little girl. Seems as if Clucker's chicken agrees with the little munchkin, doesn't it Wendy, my darling?" I cradled Wendy, rocked her in my arms, and scratched her head as I fed her another Clucker's chicky strip. She was getting good at taking food from my hand without taking the chicken *and* my fingers with her razor sharp teeth. Good thing I carried leather gloves in my backpack.

Our school bus had morphed into a party bus, with Beca, our official cheerleader conducting our dwarf choir, singing some of her favorite songs. Her personal fav (and one of mine) was, "Material Girl." Beca, one sexy dancer, had a beautiful voice; a mix between Janis Joplin and Karen Carpenter, a raunchy sweetness that gave me hope (and a hard-on) that she might shape-shift into a the real dancing Madonna, or Halle Berry, or Jennifer Lopez. Sadly, she never did shape-shift into Madonna; neither would she ever shape-shift in front of us, except in battle. The only sexy celebrity she became for us was Beca, a star of hope on our quest.

Anyway, the last thing Beca wanted to do was to excite eleven dwarves who all missed their wives. Could sink a heroic quest in no time. It got me thinking though: what's it like to be married to a shape-shifter who could become Madonna, Halle Berry, Beyoncé, or even Marilyn Monroe for you? Jackpot, baby! Truth be told, Beca was pretty damn cute herself — a jackpot herself. But I sometimes asked myself, was "Beca" really Beca?' God, I hoped so. What was her true shape? Was Beca a shape-shifted form, too? Whatever she was, I just hoped she didn't have a dick, right? That would be such a major depressing bummer. My army buddy, Jake, once told me he went to a massage parlor in San Diego for a massage with a "happy ending" and discovered that the masseuse not only had great looking breasts, but also a nine inch dick. Made Jake go limp PDQ. Nothing wrong with she-males, but hey, whatever happened to truth in advertising? Be just my luck if Beca had a dick. Wouldn't that be a pisser.

We drove on Interstate 81 for three hours when we saw a billboard for a Johnny Ray's New and Used Cars off the next exit.

"Take the next exit. Let's visit Johnny Ray and give him the 'business,'" said Dutch.

"What's up?" I said.

"We're getting rid of the bus." Dutch said.

"What's wrong with it? Everyone loves it."

"He thinks we're being tracked in it, Mr. College Graduate," Beca said, jabbing me in the ribs. She scratched Wendy's head and Wendy emitted something between and growl and a coo. She growled, though, only when Beca stopped scratching her head.

"She likes you," I said.

"As an appetizer maybe," said Beca. "I'd dump this high-tech bus in a heartbeat. Was anyone watching the bus during our little firefight? No. Let's get rid of it."

"Exactly right, Beca. Too easy for a goblin to have planted a tracking device during the battle." Dutch said

"You're telling us now?" I said.

"Exactly right. We don't have the time to tear this bus apart looking for it and thanks to our wonderful Beca we have the money to exchange it for something comparable." Dutch lit his pipe and blew furious smoke rings that settled above everyone's head like so many dunce caps. Then he gazed into the mountains as if he could see a swarm of goblins moving silently from tree to tree, getting closer and closer to us.

After that, it wasn't hard for me to imagine that the enemy was on the move again. And we knew Captain Danny's Elvish SEALs wouldn't be joining the fight.

Still I wondered: why the fuck didn't we just fly direct to Washington? Why the road trip? Or why when we were staying at Lord Reggie's chateau, Reggie didn't ask Captain Danny to drop us off just outside Washington, D.C., say somewhere in Maryland. Would that have been so difficult? It would have been the most direct route. We could be plotting right now in our little safe house, wherever that was, how best to kill the Demon Lord. Even if you only watched CNN, you would know that Senator Ross was in D.C. more often than not. We'd have more chances there than anywhere else. What the hell were we even doing in Tennessee?

Then it occurred to me that had we flown the entire distance, we'd never have met Beca or become aware of the goblin infestation in our national parks. I wouldn't have rescued little Wendy. I guess quests have their own logic and one just has to have faith in the power that put you on the freaking path to begin with. I had to arrive at Lord Reggie's before Demon Slayer's full powers could be revealed. The "Chosen One" wasn't the only one on a quest. So were the dwarves and Dutch, I had to assume. Would not life be diminished without the knowledge of Clucker's Chicken, a national treasure? Or the comradeship created by backtracking miles to unstick Burt from the ice-cream freezer. That stuff is priceless, like riding across the country on a Harley Davidson, with Beca behind me, fulfilling my boyhood dream of riding with my very own biker chick, whom I could even imagine loved me.

Besides, who knows, we could have been shot down in a plane. If the Demon Lord had agents searching the airport's database for parties of ten or more flying, he may have easily spotted twelve dwarves about to board a plane. In good conscience, we couldn't fly and put so many innocent passengers' lives at risk.

And what if this really is a full blown, divinely ordained quest, maybe it was the "Quest" itself or God himself who prevented us from boarding a jet or helicopter for the first or last leg of this crazy journey. Faith, man. Comes down to that sometimes.

CHAPTER 40

We stopped at Johnny Ray's New and Used cars, but there weren't any SUVs or trucks that could accommodate us. We drove through small Tennessee towns like Jearoldstown, Fall Branch, Locust Spring, over the mountains of Warriors Path State Park, through Blountville, and finally Fairview. Most of the small towns in northern Tennessee had at least one car lot, crappy used cars and some decent trucks, the solid Ford 150 the most common.

In Fairview, however, one used car lot featured a super-duper stretched out, tricked out black 2009 Cadillac Escalade Limo. It was as long as our school bus, if not as tall. It had seen its share of senior proms, decked-out as it was with stained red shag carpeting with cigarette burns throughout and numerous ashtrays. The ashtrays were clean, but the interior smelled like cigarette smoke thinly disguised by pine tree air freshener. When you have stupid prom kids smoking up a storm in a car, especially one with red-shag carpeting, it's impossible to remove the smell. But the dwarves smoked pipes, so it wasn't as big a deal to them as it was to me. Also we were pressed for time, so I couldn't sweat the small shit. The limo's jet black exterior made it all but invisible at night and it came with some groovy technology: a 40 inch HDTV, its own compact cell tower, bullet proof windows, and a three inch thick stainless steel sun roof.

"This little darling was confiscated from a Mexican drug lord by the feds," said the salesman, a Mr. Teddy Gunderson.

"A Mexican drug lord in Tennessee?" I said.

"Silvio Chavez. Loved the Grand Old Opry and Graceland," said Gunderson. "Used to visit them every week until he was arrested with 15 kilos of cocaine and 25 Uzis stashed in the secret compartments of this very limo. And notice the holes in the trunk. Lots of air in case you have a special someone you need to pack for a short trip, if you catch my drift. Even your big dog can sleep in there."

"So show us the secret compartments where weapons were stowed," I said, "There needs to be easy access from *inside* the limo."

"Oh, yes, everything's available from inside the limo," Teddy said.

"It better be. Or it's totally useless," said Beca, echoing my thoughts. "Rufus, by God, those are good questions," said Dutch. "Didn't know you knew so much about secret compartments."

"I don't," I said. "I've just seen a lot of lousy mobster movies, with too many plot holes."

"You're gonna love this," said Teddy who pressed a button underneath a Lazy Susan built into the middle of a thin seven foot long black onyx table.

A false bottom retracted electronically under the table and in the ceiling, revealing separate compartments for your weapons of choice. You could conceal a dozen chainsaws inside. If the police stopped us for any reason, the secret compartments in the table, ceiling, and trunk allowed us to hide all of our weapons.

"I'm impressed," said Beca whose mouth dropped in awe at the black stainless steel custom designed compartments, perfect to hide her pump action, model 870 Remington sawed-off shotgun, an American classic.

"Check this out and be astounded," said Teddy Gunderson, who kicked an ashtray-shaped device on the floor. Integrated side panels slid back under the seats to reveal more space for contraband. "At the time of his arrest Silvio had a body stored under a seat. The body was getting a little ripe from the summer heat, which tipped off the cops that something was most definitely rotten in Graceland, and I ain't talkin' 'bout Elvis."

"Looks like Silvio spared no expense," I said, and stuck my head just above the sunroof. "This is a great location for a sniper."

"I bought it at auction for a very reasonable price which I'd like to pass on to you folks today," said Teddy. "It's yours for $25,000 cash plus your bus; or I'll trade it for the bracelet you are wearing young lady." Leave it a used car salesman to instantly spot an original Harry Winston.

"I wouldn't trade this bracelet for all the limos in the world," said Beca.

"Your bracelet is without equal. Clearly, a Harry Winston one-of-a-kind creation. Just beautiful," said Teddy, "and so are you, if I may be so bold."

"But no bolder," said Buck who stepped between them and loosened the safety on his ax. Teddy got the message. I smiled at Dutch, who nodded approvingly at Buck.

"I meant no offense," Teddy said quickly, as he look at the deadly faces surrounding him. "And as a token of that, I will practically give you the limo for the paltry sum of $20,000 and your bus."

"No paperwork?" said Dutch.

"None," said Teddy, whose face was white with fear as he looked out at the deadly expressions staring at him that only a drug lord and used car salesman could appreciate.

"Then here is your cash," said Dutch, who took out $20,000 from his satchel and handed it to him, as well as the keys to the school bus.

"Perfect. And here are the keys to the limo," said Teddy, sweating on a cold October morning.

Perhaps there were heroic quests that had been launched from a stretch limo, but I couldn't name one. One of the coolest features were the bulletproof blacked-out window; you could see out, but no one could see in or shoot in. There were plugs for all of your electronic toys. Best of all, the previous owner left an unexpired handicapped sticker on the front and rear license plates, as well as a blue handicapped placard hanging from the rearview mirror. Parking this monster would have been a bitch, particularly in D.C., but the handicapped stickers meant we could park anywhere, anytime, for as long as we wanted — and that was pure gold.

However, the limo had too much flash and not nearly enough anonymity for Dutch. At least it was black, with black rims and bright red brake calipers. It was invisible at night. Maybe the stenciled orange flames on both sides, running down the entire length of the limo was a bit much. But I loved the red shag carpeting, the minibar, and the HDTV. I had already missed too many episodes of *Jeopardy!, Law and Order, Pawn Stars, Blue Bloods*, and *Charlie Rose*. The limo had also been updated with enough electrical outlets to simultaneously charge everyone's cell phone, which was of no use since Dutch collected them back at the beginning of our quest, believing the enemy had signal sniffers or satellites that could pinpoint our exact location. The Trolls' smartphones freaked him out and made him more paranoid, if that was possible, about electronic surveillance. I saw his point. Although, I secretly used a public telephone, just once, at a Lowe's Superstore to call the English Department to check the status of my dissertation. "Black Hole" Blakeslee signed for it, and had it in his possession, which was good enough for now.

A new set of wheels is always groovy, even without the new car smell. The dwarves put on their sunglasses. Buck started chanting, "Partee! Partay! Partee! Partay!!" until the limo was a rockin' and a groovin' to classic and modern tunes. Come on, who doesn't love Marvin Gaye and Tammi Terrell or Smokey Robinson?

Motown, baby, was where it's at. The Beatles and the 1960s and '70s music, man. Timeless.

The central controls for the stereo and air conditioning systems were right at the driver's fingertips, where Dutch was sitting. I was surprised to find that he had pretty good taste in music, especially dance music, and loved such classics as Donna Summer's, "Bad Girls." Beautiful Donna Summer: may she rest in peace.

The center of the limo had a taller ceiling to accommodate a sunroof; below the sunroof the floor was lowered a few feet, enough to allow six dwarves and one shape shifter to dance the Greek Kalamatiano, OPA!! And every dwarf wanted to dance with Beca. She could really shake that booty.

Those testosterone levels plummeted when Dutch turned on the big screen TV and the first image we saw was Senator Bobby Ross, the Demon Lord being interviewed on *Meet the Press*.

"Sit down everyone," said Dutch, "and take a good look at the enemy, the monster waiting for us in Washington. He's a formidable adversary."

Everyone sat down and watched the verbal battle between Senator Ross and the host of *Meet the Press*, Mitch Dunnelly.

"Senator Ross," said Dunnelly, "Experts inside the Beltway are saying that although you are one of the youngest vice-presidential nominees in history, you also have one of the thinnest résumés, and that you will ultimately prove a drag on the McClintock ticket."

"Well Mr. Dunnelly, I've been thoroughly vetted by the Democratic Party elders, by the FBI, the CIA, and President McClintock himself. Furthermore, I believe my résumé speaks for itself."

"Well, if by speaking for itself you mean your complete lack of foreign and domestic policy experience, then yes, it does," said Dunnelly. "If by speaking for itself you mean your zero sponsorship of any significant domestic legislation in the last six years, then indeed your résumé speaks volumes."

"I think you're being very unfair, Mr. Dunnelly," said Senator Ross." The fact of the matter is..."

"I know I'm always about to be lied to whenever a politician says, 'the fact of the matter is,'" Dunnelly said, "But please continue."

"All due respect, and I question how much respect is due, owing to your insulting tone, Mr. Dunnelly. However, the questions are fair ones. And I am proud to say I've contributed to dozens of top-secret foreign policy meetings at the White House and in Congress as a member of the Senate Foreign Relations committee. I've voted with both sides of the aisle to condemn Iranian aggression in the Gulf: I voted for the sanctions on Russian aggression in the Ukraine. I've spoken out against discrimination against women wherever it occurs in our country and abroad. True, I haven't traveled extensively outside the United States, but I have visited foreign leaders whenever they visit the capital and Great state of Tennessee. May I remind you Mr. Dunnelly that we live in the 21st century, the age of the Internet when international video conferencing is as easy as turning on your computer. So trust me and I hope the American people trust me when I say I am very much aware of what happens around the world and how best we as Americans should lead and respond to the great events of our time. And the same is true with respect to my contributions to our country's domestic agenda. Just ask the leader of our party, President McClintock."

"Geez, I like this guy," I said. "He's good. His southern accent is so soothing."

"Too soothing," said Dutch. "Dunnelly doesn't realize it, but he's about to become lunch."

"Yeah, lunch," said Buck. "The Demon Lord, the honorable senator from Tennessee is going to eat this insolent Dunnelly. You'll see a CNN report that Dunnelly's gone missing and his family too, if he has one."

"And sooner rather than later," Dutch said.

"In the belly of The Beast," said Theo.

"That's not how it works in a democracy, Dutch," I said.

"No, Rufus, that's how it works in the real world," said Beca backing up the old wizard.

We listened enthralled at the dangerous game Dunnelly played with no clue for how dangerous his guest was.

"Speaking of the President," said Dunnelly, "would you comment on the allegation that you bought the vice presidential slot with a $10 million contribution to President McClintock's fund for disadvantaged students at McClintock's alma mater, Middlebrook University? Some say that was a critical factor in the President's decision to put someone as young and inexperienced as you on the democratic ticket."

"Only a very cynical man would level such a mean spirited accusation." Ross said. "But as we say down south, 'That dog just won't hunt.' By the grace of God and hard work, I am a billionaire. Although once I was as poor as a church mouse, a scholarship student like many others. So I've spread my wealth whenever and wherever I thought it would do the most good. As the saying goes, money is like fertilizer: to do the most good you've got spread it on young, tender plants. I've made it a point to spread my money on young people at colleges and universities all over this great country. Ten million dollars is a fortune for most folks, but it is not a lot of money for me, especially when it results in the improved lives of wonderful young men and women who will all one day pay it forward by helping others, in turn, who are less fortunate. Isn't that America's greatness? That we reach out to all of our children and to people in need: college students, single mothers going back to school, older gentlemen and ladies retraining themselves for a high-tech world — and what is the result but a stronger, more talented, and more loving America. I'm proud of every dollar I've contributed and I plan to contribute much, much more. As you know, my own family died in a plane crash not very long ago. I have no immediate heirs really, other than the children of our great country, so help me God. Any other questions, Mr. Dunnelly?"

"I'm afraid our time has run out, Senator Ross," said Dunnelly. "Thank you, for joining us today. And join us next week when Senate Majority Leader, Henry Bushnell will join us. Thank you and have an All-American week!"

"Thank you, Mr. Dunnelly, it's been a privilege," the Demon Lord said, who got up and left with his entourage.

"Geez Louise, I'd vote for the guy," I said. "Damn compelling and fast on his feet in an interview."

"He better be. He's had a few thousand years to prepare," said Dutch.

"What were those things guarding the Senator?" said Buck. "By my grandfather's beard I could feel their evil from here."

"We all could," said Dutch. "They're demon shape shifters, demons incarnate — no offense Beca."

"None taken," said Beca smiling. "I'm no demon. I'm just a little red headed girl with a special gift. But I think that's what Lord Reggie was worried about when he sent Captain Danny to check me out."

"His demon bodyguards surround the Senator 24/7. They're his most loyal and his most dangerous servants," said Dutch. "Only Demon Slayer can kill one."

"Great, more pressure," I said. "Beca, I hope you know how rare and how precious you are — to all of us."

"Until you made me part of this family, I never would have believed it," she said. "I'd love to meet one of those demon-shape shifters. Show them how it's done."

"When he shook hands with Dunnelly, Ross looked as savage as a house troll bitch in battle," said Buck. "Dunnelly, that poor bastard, is a dead man walking."

"Count on it," said Dutch.

"House trolls?" I said.

CHAPTER 41

When Senator Ross stepped into his limousine his was fuming. He got the better of Mr. Dunnelly, he thought, but was angry at the man's insolence. It wouldn't do to eat a member of his staff. Something more was required.

"Mike," the senator said to his demon chauffeur, "Take me to Mr. Dunnelly's home address. When I'm president, I'm going to enjoy turning every one of these worthless human beings to ash when I start World War 3. Then I'll bring the rest of our family here. For now though, that SOB Dunnelly has stimulated my appetite. I'm hungry. I want a full course meal. I'll eat Dunnelly's family while he watches. And then him." Senator Ross opened the refrigerator in the limo and removed a bottle of Heinz 57, Heinz Ketchup, Gulden's Deli Mustard, KC Masterpiece BBQ Sauce, and a jar of Gray Poupon in anticipation of the night's festivities. Twenty minutes later his chauffeur parked the Lincoln Town Car across the street from Dunnelly's house.

"We're here, My Lord."

"Wonderful," said Senator Ross.

CHAPTER 42

In our high profile limo we did our best to stay invisible to the world, which was impossible, but we tried by keeping the blacked out windows rolled up and no dwarf drivers. So Dutch, Beca, and I did most of the driving. Most of the dwarves were content to stay in the back playing chess, or Texas Hold'em for a percentage of their heretofore contracted for, but unrealized, and some would say, nonexistent dwarf gold. Beca was driving.

"So, just how bad is this motherfucker?" said Beca.

"The Demon Lord? He's pretty bad," said Dutch. "Think of Senator Bobby Ross as a fallen angel. In the First Age of the High Kingdom a very powerful spirit convinced other lesser spirits to revolt against God. Here we'd call him Satan. In the High Kingdom he was called by the elvish term Swentavanaburq, which translates, loosely, to Shithead. Shithead settled in the High Kingdom and brought many of these spirits with him. Almost all of them were destroyed when God pursued and destroyed him and his kingdom. But a few of Shithead's demons hid themselves and slept for thousands of years. Senator Bobby Ross is the strongest of these spirits, Sons of Shithead you could call them. Ross and his demon buddies have the power to incarnate themselves into human forms, but this makes them vulnerable to a human death, although not by human weapons. Demon Slayer was designed by heaven's own sword makers to kill the human body as well as the demonic spirit of these fallen angels."

"How do we stop the Demon Lord from becoming Vice President?" said Beca.

"We can't," said Dutch. "Too many forces beyond our control."

"You're right," said Beca. "We can only deal with the aftermath."

"It's game over, when he's VP," said Buck, who was listening behind us. "And he will be elected. McClintock is ahead in the polls by 20 points."

"You say the Demon Lord is vain?" said Beca. "How vain?"

"No more than any other psychopathic demon leader." Dutch said. "He's full of himself, so over confident that it may be possible for Rufus to get close enough to wield Demon Slayer."

"Talks a good game, this reasonable, soft spoken southern senator," I said. "He's a smooooooooth operator."

"Behind closed doors, unmasked, he is a soulless, heartless cannibal," said Dutch.

"Rufus needs more practice with Demon Slayer," Beca said.

"Thanks for the vote of confidence, Oh Beca The Realist," I said, disappointed in her assessment. "Although I'm inclined to agree with you."

"From what you've said, Dutch, the Demon Lord has had thousands of years of practice with his sword, that is, when he wasn't sleeping in limbo." Beca said.

"You're not setting me up for failure, are yah Dutch?" I said.

"You have something the Demon Lord doesn't," said Buck, who had been noticeably quiet during this conversation.

"Tell me, oh Buck the Magnificent," I said.

"Me," said Beca. "And I'm tired. Would you drive now, Rufus?"

We decided the best time to make a pit stop was in middle of the night. No one mentions the pleasures of driving 60 hours with unwashed dwarves from *The High Kingdom*; We couldn't chance looking for a Love's Travel Center for a quick shower, much less a Clucker's chicken or a fast food joint on the main highway. The back roads would take longer to reach Washington; so we had to stop at whatever mom and pop restaurants we could find along the way.

We found no shower, but we did find great takeout at Delores and Dave's Diner, just across the street from an old moss covered Civil War cemetery: real homemade fried chicken, mashed potatoes with porcini mushrooms in a brown gravy. Oh, my was it delicious. Instead of mashed potatoes you could get sliced thin, garlic French fries with real chunks of fried garlic adhering to every fry. I ordered both: garlic mashed potatoes *and* garlic fries. Dipped in Heinz ketchup, the fries were nothing less than heaven on earth. Delores and Dave's diner would have put Clucker's out of business if they ever decide to franchise the joint. For dessert we ordered 14 individual pies for the road: apple, blackberry, peach, and banana cream.

You didn't have to travel too far off the beaten path of I40 or I81 to find the best homemade American cuisine. And by American I mean every type of ethnic delight: BBQ, Greek, Southern Fried Chicken, Mom & Pop Burgers, Italian, Chinese, Indian, and anything else you can imagine. I just wish we had more time to explore. Delores and Dave's was a real treat and the real deal.

Little Wendy seemed to double her weight overnight. She was the size of a large raccoon when she came into our lives. Lupines must grow rapidly as a survival mechanism in the High Kingdom. She didn't crap much, just kept putting on weight and muscles. The little darling was a scrappy 100 pounds, the size of a German shepherd, as Beca predicted. Had Beca been to the High Kingdom? How did she know? Sometimes I could swear Wendy was growing right before my eyes. She had an insatiable appetite that disposed of chicken bones, and any other leftovers, not that the dwarves believed in leftovers. She licked the pie tins and would have eaten the tins too if I didn't wrestle them away from her. God I loved that pup. She would chase her tail, which made me laugh. And if I said the C word (cookie) she would dance on her hind legs. Wendy looked at me with more love in her eyes than my own mother (who, BTW, loved me dearly).

Lately, Wendy preferred sleeping in the trunk, which could be popped from inside the limo. Our little girl functioned as an early warning system for us. She was our eyes, ears, and especially our nose for anything dangerous we weren't aware of when driving or parked.

At 2AM we saw a Walmart in the distance. It was well lit and crowded. So we decided to sleep there for the night. More than 75% of the 900+ Walmarts in the United States permit RVs to stay the night. There were at least 100 vehicles parked there: cars, SUVs, motorhomes, anything, and everything with two to four wheels. There were motorcyclists who pitched tents not quite big enough to cover the length of their sleeping bags and even a couple of lovebirds entwined in the back seat of their yellow convertible mustang, covered by a canopy of stars.

At 3AM a fleet of 20 bikers rolled in with some nasty looking biker chicks. They were welcome, too. All of the men and women had tattoos of skulls, eagles wings, and drug parapher-nalia up and down their arms and exposed backs. The biker ladies should have been a sign that they were half-way civilized, but it wasn't so; they were assholes, since only assholes would rev their engines loud enough to wake the dead in the middle of the night. lights turned on in the motorhomes. Old men and women turned out to see if we were under attack by aliens. It should have been no big deal. Even assholes were welcome to sleep at Walmart.

I long admired individual Walmarts that welcomed everyone to sleep in peace in their parking lot; it was a compassionate gift for all Americans on the road looking for work, for family, or for America. On our journey we met families sleeping in their cars, or in campers with no other legal place to park. Even many bikers preferred to throw down a sleeping bag at a Walmart than to sleep on the side of the road in a desolate area. I watched these bikers from the blacked-out, bulletproof windows of our limo and had an excellent view of this new adversary.

These bikers rolled in and saw our luxurious limo and assumed we were rich and an easy target. Their leader, a bald man with a tattooed leopard on his neck, made a sharp turn to circle our limo. His posse joined him, riding around the limo like so many Indians circling a covered wagon with defenseless settlers.

When they had finished their little show of intimidation they stopped and the leader got off his bike, patted his biker chick's ass for good luck, I assume, and approached our silent limo. The dwarves were asleep through most of this, which was a good thing because they would have killed them all in a few minutes. Beca and I wanted to jump out with our AK 47s and blast the bastards, but Dutch held us back. Wendy growled loud enough for us hear her warning.

"Let's see if Wendy is up to earning her keep," said Dutch.

"I hear her growling in the trunk," said Beca. "She's just a baby, still; I say we blast the fuckers."

"Wait, just a second. I think Wendy darling wants to help." I said, surprised, but pleased to hear Beca wanting protect my baby girl.

"On my signal," said Dutch, "pop the trunk and release the hound!"

The biker leader strolled over within fifteen feet of our limo and shouted,

"Come on out and nobody gets hurt," he said. "We just want your money, motherfuckers. We won't hurt you, much." When no one answered he took his gun and fired it at the front windshield. The bullets bounced off the bulletproof windshield.

Dutch signaled and I popped the trunk. Wendy had heard enough, and flew out of the trunk and lunged for the leader, who pissed in his Levi 501s. One hundred pounds of roaring lupine caught him by his left boot and bit off his leg at the kneecap, which she carried back to her place in the trunk. It would make a nice snack between now and breakfast. The biker, in shock, collapsed to the ground and was losing massive amounts of blood.

His biker bitch snatched him up and used the chain hanging from her belt to tie a tourniquet above his knee. She threw him over his Harley and raced off to the nearest hospital, to save his worthless life. The rest of the pack took off behind them. Some of the folks parked around us came out to thank us. I got out of the limo and checked to make sure Wendy was secure in the trunk.

"Where can I get a dog like that?" said one elderly man who with his wife stepped out of their RV. He and his wife were a both dressed Levi overalls, red denim shirts, and blue clogs.

"Well, you know," I said, "rescue dogs come in all shapes and sizes down at the animal shelter."

"Well your pup did quite a number on those criminals," he said. "I'm Bill and this is my wife Jane. Could we thank him, personally?"

"He's not a he. He's a she," I said. "Her name is Wendy."

"We've got some beef bones in our refrigerator," said his wife. "Do you think Wendy would like them?"

"I think she would love them," I said, as Jane went back in their RV, which had their road names painted on the side in fancy red italic script, *Mr. and Mrs. Sunshine*. Jane came out with two, foot-long beef bones, still bleeding on the white butcher paper she unwrapped.

"Could we meet your pup?" Bill said. "We love dogs."

"You bet," I said, as I popped the trunk. "Wendy darling, come on out and meet some friends."

The people were smart and courageous. They knew animals. When Wendy jumped out of the trunk, they stood still and let her approach them. Jane held out the beef bones on the butcher's paper and I walked with Wendy to the bones, to reassure her these were good folks. Bill and Jane shook a little when Wendy purred, but they stroked her massive skull as she sniffed the bones.

"Nice Wendy," they said. "We love you."

"It's ok, Wendy," I said, "You can take the bones. They're a gift from your friends Jane and Bill." She took both bones in her maw and carried them back to her trunk where she settled in for the rest of the night. By morning the beef bones and the biker's leg would be gone.

"Thank you," I said. "That was very kind of you. I know Wendy will enjoy them."

"Your dog is a hero," said Jane.

"We think so, too," I said. "Have a happy and healthy journey."

"God bless you and Wendy," they said and went back to their RV for the night.

We went to bed and woke up around 9:30AM when our hero Wendy howled to go out to pee. People must have been watching last night when Jane and Bill fed Wendy because outside our trunk waiting for Wendy were boxes of Milk Bones, more beef bones, BBQ chicken and burgers from the many portable grills folks carried in their vehicles for the journey.

Fortune also smiled on us when we discovered a Denny's right next to the Walmart. Hallelujah! And Demon Lord or no Demon Lord, not no how, not no way, not no one would force us to miss out on the Denny's Grand Slam Slugger breakfast: two fluffy buttermilk pancakes, two sausage links, two strips of bacon, two sunny side eggs, hash browns, orange juice, and endless coffee.

We all wanted to thank Walmart for allowing us to sleep in their parking lot. So Beca, Dutch, and I went into the store with our shopping lists. An hour later we emerged from Walmart with pork rinds, Lucky Charms, Trix, Tillamook beef jerky, KC Masterpiece BBQ potato chips, Ben & Jerry's Cherry Garcia, Häagen Dazs Mint Chocolate Chip ice cream (for Burt), a dozen or so Slim Jims, Sweet Tarts, and lemon drops. I love Sweet Tarts and lemon drops. Oh, and 20 boxes of Milkbones biscuits for Wendy who loved crunchy dog cookies. There was a sliding access door to the trunk from inside the limo and I just threw in a few boxes. She liked the cardboard box too, which was like a cracker for the little munchkin. Dutch handed me a bag.

"Rufus, would you please store these under your seat?" he said.

"What are they?" I said.

"Headlamps," said Dutch.

"Headlamps?" I said.

"Flashlights worn on your head, yah moron," said Beca.

"We'll need them later," said Dutch. "Don't worry about it."

"Just to hear you say, 'Don't worry about it,' worries me," I said.

CHAPTER 43

Our tricked-out stretch limo was drawing a lot of attention, which was another reason stay off the main drag. Add eleven dwarves and we were lucky no one could see inside. However, the dwarves had to get out of the limo, just to stretch their wee little dwarf legs and have a snack or they would go nuts from the confinement. Slim Jims only went so far. We couldn't keep them cooped up in the limo. I'd have gone nuts too, if I couldn't get out occasionally. You can find a McDonald's anywhere in the universe. I hear there's even one in Hell (the food is never cold). Can't imagine what the secret sauce is there. So it was no accident or surprise to run into one on the back roads of rural West Virginia. I couldn't wait to order a Deluxe Breakfast: Two hotcakes, hash browns, scrambled eggs, bacon, sausage, and an English muffin for $4.49!! Nowhere in America could you find such value.

No one there had ever seen a limousine like ours. A dozen or more people stepped out of the restaurant to see if celebrities had landed on their doorstep. The Demon Lord had many spies and it's hard to miss eleven dwarves lined up, all singing the McDonald's theme song,

"Na-na, na-na-na! I'm loving it!"
"Na-na, na-na-na !I'm loving it!"
"Na-na, na-na-na! I'm loving it!"

Of course if you gave them a 20 piece Chicken McNuggets, they'd wipe their collective asses with it — because, as everyone knows, chickens don't have nuggets. But hell, the McDonald's theme song worked well with whatever your favorite fast food was. While they were singing McDonald's theme song and eventually pissing off customers and employees, I thought I saw, from the corner of my eye, two very dark men slip out the back. Was that yellow peeping through a rip in one of the men's baggy Levi 501s? They were hiding something in their baggy jeans. Guns? It was wagging. A tail? No fuckin' way. Could they be goblin spies? Dutch turned to Buck and whispered something to him.

"Stop singing that asinine song!" Dutch said to the dwarves, up and down the line. "Dammit! you're attracting too much attention! Get your food and let's go. Everyone's in the limo in ten."

Ten minutes later we were all in the limo — well, all of us except Beca.

"Listen up, everyone. I think we've been made," said Dutch. "We are going to have to stop eating at any fast food outlets for the rest of our drive and possibly ditch the limo ASAP."

Beca stuck her head in the limo and said, "Maybe not. We need the limo — now more than ever."

Buck, Dutch, and I followed her into a small forest of trees above a hidden ravine behind the restaurant. The dwarves waited in the limo. Behind the trees at the bottom of the twenty-five foot ravine were two yellow bodies, covered in grime, goblins dressed like tourists.

"Those were the guys in McDonald's," I said. "But what's with the tails? Goblins don't have tails."

"These goblins were born here and not in the High Kingdom," said Dutch.

"Born here? Then they're American citizens!" I said.

"Very funny, Rufus. Actually, they dock their tails in the High Kingdom," said Buck who walked up from behind and looked down on their bodies. "Usually when they turn from a mere imp into an adult goblin, around thirteen years old."

"A twofer: Two for the price of one: a circumcision *and* Bar Mitzvah," I said. "Must be one hell of an infestation if he was born here. Those goblins look at least 25, not that I'm the best judge of a goblin's age."

"I'm afraid you may be right," said Dutch.

"Beca, how did you know?" I asked.

"Hoorah!" she said like a Marine grunt, "I shape-shifted into a goblin bitch in heat and waved my junk, and said, 'come and get it boys.' As they were taking out their little yellow dicks, I snapped their little yellow necks."

"Sweet Jesus," I said. "I'm glad you're on our side."

"I checked their phone histories. They made calls minutes before I ended their miserable lives. We've been outed," Beca said and waved the goblins' cell phones at Dutch and Buck before tossing the phones into the ravine.

"We should go on foot," Buck said. "It's mostly mountainous terrain now. It will be much harder to track us than on a back road highway. Dwarves can march for days without rest."

"But Rufus can't," said Beca. "Very bad idea."

"Slightly overweight Bartlett scholars don't, as a rule, hike," I said.

"Slightly?" Beca said, and couldn't stop laughing for the moment.

"Dwarves are safer in the mountains on foot. Ditch the limo. We should get going, now," said Buck.

"No!" Dutch said. "We're going to hightail it out of here in the limo and reach D.C. If we go on foot we're dead in 24 hours, even less. We've have proof Beca's right. It's a race now to survive and no more fast food before we reach our safe house. Beca's absolutely right: the limo is our only hope for survival."

"Geez," I thought. "This had been a cool adventure so far. We drove in our tricked-out limo, stopped for breakfast, lunch, and dinner, sang old dwarf battle songs, danced to Beca and disco, defeated the goblins, even partied with the elves in their magical, hidden kingdom. But now we had to fly like eagles through the West Virginia back roads to D.C. or die.

We'd been driving for almost three hours and everyone was glum. Every time we passed a fast food outlet at least one dwarf cried out, "Stop!"

"Farewell BK Whopper," said Chad, mournfully, as we blew by a Burger King. Beca put her arm around his shoulder to comfort him.

We were ready for anything — anything but a freak snowstorm in October. Or was it a freak storm? The presidential election was just days away, even as we closed in on the position of our safe house in the nation's capital.

One minute we were looking at a forest of green pines, sycamores, golden maples, and the next minute a heavy snow was falling. Before our eyes the road was covered in white and the branches of forest trees were laden with snow. And a shadow of fear showed on Dutch's face. It felt as if something was about to strike us from the void. Was the Demon Lord *that* powerful that he could change the weather at will? Did his power stretch that far that he could command a snow storm in late October?

"This is the work of the enemy. We've been found," said Dutch. "It's the snow. He's deliberately trying to slow us down."

"How the hell is that possible? It's the end of October. It doesn't snow in late October," I said. "Besides no one knows where we're driving. How could the Demon Lord hit us with a snowstorm from such a distance?"

"He knows it's his time," Dutch said. "He's on the verge of becoming the second most powerful man in the world and he can take a chance like this. The two goblins at McDonald's gave him our location."

There was a very loud howl from the trunk. Either Wendy wanted her dinner or something had frightened her — and nothing frightened her.

"Wendy is your answer. She's afraid. Those goblins got their message through," said Beca, waking up from her nap. You always think Beca's sleeping when she is listening to every word around her. Can she do both?

The snow was coming down so hard that we couldn't see through our windshield and we pulled to the side of the road.

"What's up?" Buck said.

"We have a stage one," said Dutch.

"What the fuck is a 'stage one?'" I said. "I wish someone would have given me a goddamn playbook at the beginning of this heroic quest. How am I supposed to know a stage one from a stage three? What's a goddamn 'stage one'?"

"The enemy is upon us," said Buck

"Oh, fuuuuuuuuuuuuuccccccccckkkkkk," I said.

"Yeah, it's an 'oh, fuuuuuuuuuuuuuccccccccckkkkkk moment," said Beca, who instinctively popped the trunk for Wendy who left the trunk and took up position underneath the limo.

"Everyone!" Buck shouted. "Position yourself for a Stage One!"

Every dwarf reached under his seat, cracked open a window and stuck the muzzle of an Uzi and pointed them at the forest on either side. We waited.

Burt cracked the sunroof and peaked outside.

"I'm worried about Wendy," I said. "Is she safe under the car?"

"Safer than we are inside it," Beca said.

"Dragons! There be dragons!!" Burt yelled he dropped to the floor moments before a deafening swoosh!!! Our sunroof was gone!

An evil fate: we were on an empty stretch of road on the forested side of Interstate 66, less than three hours from Washington. I looked up through the missing sunroof. In one fell swoop our limo had become a convertible. But the Chosen One was here this time. I said that to myself as I started to shake. Come on, really? Who wants to be a goddamn hero?

"Fuck the dragons,'" said Buck. "Let's kill them all."

"Dragons means demon riders," said Dutch. "How many?"

"Two," said Buck, "and closing fast."

"Could be worse. Could be four." Dutch said. "What shitty luck, and we're so close to D.C. Get out the machine gun. We'll give them a good fight."

No sooner were the words spoken than we heard another swoosh above the limo that sounded like a sonic boom. The dragon had ripped off the trunk. Theo shot wildly at it with the machine gun but the bullets bounced off the dragon's tough hide. Each dwarf grabbed a Glock, a chainsaw, and his axe.

Beca opened her door, stuck her head under the limo and whispered something in Wendy's ear. Wendy stepped out from underneath the limo, dropped down on her haunches so that Beca, with her M16s in hand, could roll onto Wendy's back. Then Wendy ran for cover into the forest.

"Beca!" I said. "What are you doing? Come back!"

"Love you!" she said and was gone.

"Forget about her. She can take care of herself," said Dutch. "Focus everyone. Dragons have scales top to bottom," he continued. "But they're sitting ducks between the scales, so leave the chainsaw, keep the axe. Take out anything you can shoot or throw with." A dwarf could split a watermelon with his axe from 150 feet and, given the opportunity, any of them could cleave a dragon between the eyes.

"Your weapons will not harm the demon riders." Dutch said. "Rufus must destroy the riders, or we're finished. Run for the trees!"

Great. No pressure. Luckily I stopped the car close to the trees, so it was more like a trot. We jumped out, dragged the machine gun with us, and took positions behind the limo and the trees. I couldn't see Beca anywhere.

One thing you should know: Dragons do not breathe fire, thank God. All that medieval fire breathing dragon horseshit was just that: horseshit from the Middle Ages and fantasy literature. Dragons haven't got one noble bone in their rancid bodies. They not heroic like the giant majestic hawks in *The High Kingdom*. They're scavengers, gigantic vultures, eaters of carrion — and goblin meat, when they can get it, or sometimes a bit of man flesh, if their demon masters are feeling generous.

It's also a documented fact that dragons are dirty fighters. By dirty I mean a dragon will first cover you in dragon piss or dragon shit, swoop down and disembowel you with its tail or claws while you're temporarily blinded. Even a pet dragon, raised from infancy with love, is unpredictable. Try to train it to catch your Frisbee and it will happily rip your arm off, just cuz. They are very smart, like a poodle, a very angry poodle. And poodles are damn smart.

The demon riders must have thought we were small pickings because only one demon rider attacked us. The demon riders wanted to torture us for a while, for sport while the other one watched, probably filming it for his master. Very sadistic, very voyeuristic, and very poor battle tactics, I would say. Shock and awe baby, that's how you win. Overwhelm the enemy with superior forces and superior numbers. If they had attacked simultaneously, two demons and two dragons at once, we'd have been in deep dragon shit, especially me. Maybe I could handle one demon rider, but two? No fucking way, man. But as has often been said, "Evil will, by evil — will be all fucked-up, man." Or something like that. Bottom line: we caught a break.

The two of them were high in the sky deciding who would make the first run. Then one took the plunge. The dragon's wingspan must have been a hundred feet. Quite majestic, really. The demon rider lay flat against its back. As the dragon plunged to within a hundred feet of us, the demon took his weapon, a long stick-like thing, fired it, and hit Theo with a burst of blue flame. The concussive force threw Theo against a tree so hard that we could all feel the impact. No one could have survived it. The demon trained his weapon on Buck and fired. He missed, but the blast radius knocked Buck to the ground. That was enough for the dragon to swoop in for the kill. Despite what Dutch told them, the other dwarves fired on the dragon from behind the limo, but the bullets bounced off the dragon's scaled hide, and were absorbed by the demon like putty. Buck was on his feet, running for his life as Dutch sent a blast of blue fire from his cane, but even that had no effect on the demon or the dragon.

From out of the trees sprang Wendy, my sweet, fearless, darling lupine. Beca had waited behind the trees with Wendy, but now they rode together. Beca aimed her M-16s at the dragon, which was gaining fast on Buck, about to drop its payload — 200 pounds of toxic dragon shit, certain death. Buck lunged for the trees as Beca fired a precision burst of thirty rounds from each weapon. Thirty rounds that squeezed between the scales covering the dragon's breastplate and into its heart. The dragon screamed before it plunged from the sky, crashing in the middle of the snow-covered road. Blood mixed with snow and created a red skid mark 200 feet long. But not before releasing its payload. The demon rider got off his dead dragon covered from head to toe in dragon shit. We all laughed as hard as we could without bursting an appendix. The demon rider was not amused. If we couldn't hurt a demon rider with bullets or missiles, at least we could humiliate it with laughter.

The rider approached my companions, casually, as if he had nothing to fear and all the time in the world to kill everyone. The demon was neither of this world nor of the High Kingdom; and he thought nothing in either world could harm him. He stopped long enough to seize Theo's body by the beard and dragged it with him.

I was expecting the demon to be eight feet tall with rows of razor sharp teeth. Instead the demon looked like an accountant or your next-door neighbor. He was average height. He wore blue Levi's Dockers, a blue and red-checkered short sleeve shirt, and black Reebok tennis shoes. True, the demon rider was covered in dragon shit, but he was so ordinary looking that he'd be eating your arm before you realized a demon was chowing down on you. Surprise!

I left my place in the trees, stopped in front of Wendy to pet her head. He was about a two hundred feet from Beca and Wendy.

Beca held her ground out of sheer stubbornness. Wendy roared a challenge that could be heard from the capitol steps.

I took up my position in front of Beca and Wendy and waited with an Uzi in my left hand and Demon Slayer in my right. I shot the demon with at least twenty rounds from my Uzi, if for nothing else than to verify its invincibility to human weapons, and to fool the demon into thinking that was the best I had. The bullets were just absorbed into his body. I stood in front of my girls, waiting.

"Stand behind me, Rufus. I can handle this guy." Beca said.

"I just blasted him for God's sake," I said, "There's only one weapon that's any good. Now move back, dammit, he's almost here." Beca stepped back a few feet. "Dammit Beca, move back! Give me room to maneuver."

"One thing, *oh Chosen One*," she said sarcastically, "His blade has poison on it. If he draws your blood, I've got to suck it out of you fast or you die."

"How do you know this stuff?" I said.

"You can smell him a mile away. And he's covered in dragon shit. You think his blade is sterilized? Think, Rufus, think!"

"Ok, so sometimes I lack common sense — an academician's prerogative. Now back up! I'll handle it!"

The demon rider stopped fifteen feet from me and I almost gagged: he stank like nothing you've ever smelled in our world. Dragon shit: a combination of rancid meat, vomit, human excrement, and death! He extended his jaw like a snake and bit off Theo's left arm, chewing and swallowing it in two large bites, slowly so we could see the blood and bones and watch in horror. He was enjoying himself. He smiled as he chewed and laughed when Theo's finger got caught between two teeth.

"Demon-dude, didn't your mother tell you to chew with your mouth closed?" I said. "And what's that smell, dude? Don't you bathe? That can't be *just* the dragon shit." The demon made no answer, but took his long staff, aimed it at me and fired. I brought up Demon Slayer to block the burst of blue fire and prayed. Demon Slayer recycled the energy back to the weapon and vaporized the Demon's staff. Pretty cool, right? Unfortunately, it didn't faze my enemy.

"Demon-fuck, is that the best you got?" I said with a laugh. I kept an eye on his buddy upstairs, high in the sky. I was surprised he wasn't helping out, what with a dead dragon and the fact that I just vaporized his buddy's weapon. I guess Demon-fucks don't back each other. Was there was no esprit de corps between demons? Sad isn't it? Yet another disadvantage. They didn't believe in teamwork or even in the brotherhood of Demon-fucks. Two against one: much greater chance of success. My dear friends, helpless though they were, nonetheless formed a half-moon behind me with their weapons poised to strike; though if I died, they would all die. We had our love and faith in each other and in the Son of the One who was always on our side, regardless of the outcome. The demon took another chunk out of Theo, and wiped his bloody mouth on his shirt.

"When I finish with my meal," the demon said, who munched on Theo's fingers, "I'm going to eat your girlfriend. Living meat is so much tastier. Her fear smells delicious. By the way, nice sword. Where'd you get it?"

"Walmart," I said, "$29.99. The sheath was an extra ten bucks." The demon laughed, but my friends were silent.

"Sounds like a good deal," said the demon.

"It will be when I cut off your head. Hey, man, can't you do anything about that smell?" The wind blew from behind him and I was close to hurling.

The demon ripped a thirty-second belch and vomited some of Theo's beard and blood on his Reeboks.

"Dwarves," he said, "they always give me indigestion."

"Didn't your mama teach you never to belch in public? You've got terrible table manners, oh demon-fucker. Do you mind if I call you demon-fucker? Since I don't know your name."

"I've had my fill of dwarf for today. I'll eat you now," said the demon as he withdrew a long black sword from an invisible scabbard. I pulled out my translucent Demon Slayer, all two and a half feet. Uh oh.

"Bad time for Projectile Dysfunction," I said, though not really worried. Just a little worried.

"Kinda short for a sword," said the Demon-fuck who laughed, a horrible gurgling sound in its throat. But then Demon Slayer had an erection and grew another four feet and the demon stopped laughing.

"Go for it, sucka." I said, and assumed a defensive posture, drilled into me by Buck the Indomitable. I faked being nervous by shaking, just to give this bastard a false sense of superiority.

He tried some fancy bullshit parrying move, but Beca and Buck had parried the crap out of me: Every day after breakfast, before lunch, after dinner, when I least expected they'd ambush me until I knew instinctively where the blow was coming from. Parrying was in my freakin' dreams. I parried the shit out of the demon, back and forth, forward, and backward, and it was fun in its way. Finally, though, in the process, I found my opening and cut off his sword arm. It's not about victory. It's about process, right? That sounds cool. But it's bullshit. It is about victory and enjoying the look of horror on the face of that overly confident demonic shithead.

"Oops, that must really hurt." I said, and saw the look of surprise on his inhuman face as he stared, dumbstruck, at his arm and his sword lying in a puddle of steaming, puke-stinking black blood.

I decided to be merciful and cut off his head quickly. He crumpled to the ground and his buddy three hundred feet above us bugged out.

"I'm so proud of you, Rufus," Beca was first to say, checking my chest for any wounds. Her warm hands felt great. "You're clean, yah big goon. You're lucky."

"Good work, Rufus, but this was a test," said Dutch, pointing a finger up to the demon rider hightailing it. "These guys are scouts. Congratulations, young man; you're on the grid. After killing one of his captains, the Demon Lord will know you wield a famous sword with training by dwarf masters-in-arms. I predict he'll be both furious that you escaped yet him again, pissed that you killed his demon dragon-rider, but *more* worried about the prophecy that God's fool is coming for him."

"God's fool? Beca said. "Boy, you can say that again."

"Hey, thanks a lot. I can call myself God's fool, but you sure as hell can't."

"I just call them like I see them," said Dutch who laughed long and hard.

"You can't hire a demon dragon-rider off of Craigslist, or Facebook," said Beca.

"Oh, a 'Chosen One." I said

"It won't be easy for the Demon Lord to replace that dragon rider," said Beca.

"Walmart, $29.95, my ass!" said Buck who gave me a bear hug. "Nice touch, Rufus. At least he doesn't know the name of the sword or its origin."

"Neither do I," I said. "All I know is that it's from Heaven, which is good enough for me. Bring it on, baby. I can't wait to meet Senator Bobby Ross, that SOB. Ok, not really. I hope I'm up to the final test. Let's get what's left of poor Theo and give him a proper burial."

"Are we just going to leave the demon's sword?" said Buck. "It could be useful when the next one shows up."

"Do not touch it! It's pure evil, Buck," said Dutch. "Made in hell for unspeakable crimes. It's bound-up with evil spells that would lead the Demon Lord right to us. And it has lots of germs. Bad idea all around."

Dutch held his cane out and shot a lightning bolt at the sword. It was undamaged. I chopped it into pieces with Demon-slayer, making it useless.

"Rest assured the surviving demon rider is talking right now to his Demon Lord," said Dutch. "He'll be back with reinforcements. I fear that if we don't reach Washington by nightfall, we never will."

"What about Theo?" I said.

"Buck would you gently place Theo in a body bag and place him on the dance floor in the limo. We'll bury him in D.C. with full rites and honors. *Stouffersalis frozenalis!!*" chanted Dutch softly, waving his staff over Theo's body parts, freezing them.

" 'Stouffersalis frozenalis'? Really, Dutch!?" I said.

"No disrespect," said Dutch. "Those are Theo's frozen body parts, not Theo. He died a hero's death trying to save our lives. 'Greater love hath no man.' We both know Theo is in heaven with his ancestors and with God. So relax."

"I accept that, but you're making me hungry, Dutch," I said, trying to lighten the mood a little bit.

"You were born hungry," he said and managed a smile.

Before we left, Buck got out the emergency gasoline can from a secret compartment and doused the demon and burned his body as best as earthly methods could. The dragon was a bigger problem. We attached six grenades to strategic areas of its body, took the remainder of the gasoline, and set the dragon on fire. A few seconds later there was a tremendous explosion.

"Good enough for government work," I said to Dutch as we drove away.

"Punch it. We haven't much time." Dutch said.

CHAPTER 44

od, please get us to our safe house, in one piece," I said to myself and to no one else. I had no idea where in Washington D.C. our safe house was located, but now I could understand the anxiety Abraham Lincoln, under death threats, might have felt sneaking into Washington like a thief in the night.

Lincoln was President-elect, but already there were people bent on assassinating him before he could reach D.C. and take the oath of office. At a train stop in Baltimore, before he enter the capital, the famous detective Alan Pinkerton who was in charge of Lincoln's protection detail, disguised him with a soft felt hat, not his traditional stovepipe; then Pinkerton instructed Lincoln to pretend to be hunchbacked to disguise his true height. Thus attired, Abe made it alive to D.C. ready to lead the nation.

We were driving east on Interstate 66, heading into the capital. From I66 we took the Curtis Memorial Parkway heading east, which leads to the Francis Scott Key Bridge. The bridge drops you three blocks east of Georgetown University. We stopped at the bridge, make a quick right turn, and drove a short distance along the Georgetown Waterfront to a small park called Sequoia. It was pitch back. The park was deserted. We buried Theo with his prayer mat and rosary and intoned prayers to the Mighty One who created the dwarf race, as well reciting Theo's daily prayer to Mary, the mother of Christ — he was with them both now. We sang heroic songs to prepare Theo's waiting ancestors, all of whom Buck seemed to know for the last ten generations. Who would greet him on the other side first: Mary, Christ, or his dwarf ancestors? You tell me. I say all three. We would send his share of the gold, of which, I might add, we had not a farthing, to his widow, as well as his share of the troll jewels — far my part, he could have my share. I already missed Theo. I loved him and would see him again when it was my time.

I wouldn't want you to think all I was interested was gold, but I sure felt it was a loss-leader item, like a brand new Corvette for five grand, a fiction made up to get you to the dealership, or in my case to get me to sign up. Ok, ok, it's true I was a dead man anyway if I'd refused and gone back to my apartment. The Demon Lord would have found me. I didn't have the cash or resources to stay off the grid. But I still felt duped, like an enlisted soldier in the army. "Oh, you want to fly helicopters? No problem. Just sign here and take this aptitude test," the recruiter says. Following boot camp you're told, "We regret to inform you that you have as much aptitude for flying as a hippo. Here's your M-16. There's the enemy. Go kill him or we'll court martial you." The army got real, real fast. The goblins, demons, trolls got real, real fast. The Demon Lord was real. The only thing unreal was that the task to destroy him was appointed to me. A big old softy who cries every Christmas at *It's a Wonderful Life*; who can't pass the animal shelter without crying knowing that they're putting down, no, call it was it is — murdering dogs and cats who no one will take home and love (mea culpa). Enough whining.

It was night and there was no sign of anything overhead. We weren't sure if the Demon Lord had battle troops in the city, but he certainly had spies. The sky was clear. Lucky for us, it looked like we had escaped his flying fortress, as we drove through the outlying parts of the city.

We continued our drive into the city and arrived at an underground parking garage, near the Quincy City Central Metro Station, underneath a high-end mall above with a Saks 5th Avenue, Bloomingdales, and a Barnes & Noble bookstore. I think we were directly below Bloomingdales. Our stretch limo had no sunroof or trunk, but it still had its handicap placard, and we parked it across two handicapped spaces, where we knew it would likely remain undisturbed, or towed, not that we gave a damn at this stage. I guess an underground parking lot was as good a place as any for a safe house.

"Hey, was that a Denny's just down the street?" I said.

"What Denny's? I didn't see a Denny's." said Burt.

"You're slipping, Burt," I said. "I'm sure it was a Denny's."

"It was a Denny's, Rufus," said Dutch. "But would you focus on something other than your stomach right now?"

"Don't ask the impossible, Dutch," said Buck. "I sure would love a Grand Slam Slugger about now."

"Show some leadership, Buck," said Dutch. "Don't get these dwarves worked up. This Quest is far from over and we're still vulnerable right here, right now."

"Is this the place, Dutch? Where are we in relation to the Lincoln Memorial? Are we within walking distance?" I said, like a dumb hick visiting Washington for the first time, which I was.

"No, we're not too far from the memorial, but too far to walk," said Dutch. "Hang in there, Big Man. I'll take you there myself when the time is right. We'll reach the safe house in a few hours. Keep moving, my friends." We all followed him single file, with Wendy bringing up the rear, protecting our collective asses.

"I'd still like to see the Lincoln Memorial one of these days." I said again, to everyone annoyance.

"You will, Rufus," said Beca. "Just not now. Right about now you should shut-the-fuck-up."

I laughed and almost fell down the dark staircase. I couldn't see my goddamn feet, even with the headlamp Dutch bought for each of us at Walmart. I was glad I didn't fully understand their purpose at the time. Dutch also lit the way with his cane. I finally understood the purpose of the fourteen miner's headlamps loaded in my Harley Trike at the beginning of our journey, which felt like a lifetime ago. The goblins must have inherited the headlamps with our stolen choppers. More important than the headlamps was the fact that I still had a stash of four Clucker's chicken strips left for our journey to the center of the earth.

CHAPTER 45

If I had known that our final destination, our safe house, was miles below the earth, I would have gone back to my apartment and taken my chances with the Demon Lord. Tunnels freak me out.

All of the plumbing and sewage pipes for the building followed us down into the bowels of the planet. I never knew a building to have such a wealth of pipes running in every direction, to infinity and beyond it seemed, far below the underground parking lot. It seemed odd, very odd indeed.

I do not say thousands of feet lightly. We walked for hours down endless staircases, through tunnels leading to more staircases and tunnels. What were the builders expecting: a thermonuclear attack?

"Hey, Dutch," I said. "I hope the way out is a lot shorter."

"It is, Rufus. Not to worry."

"Oh, fuck, not that, 'not to worry' bullshit again," I said, worrying all the more.

Finally, we stopped our descent, reaching the first of a series of tunnels in the black labyrinth that confronted us. I assume it was ground zero for the planners and builders, a place for some part of the population to retreat to during a nuclear attack on the United States. There could be no other explanation.

It's hard to get your sense of direction, of time, much less your equilibrium in the dark, even with the headlamps. The tunnels were round and man high, but there was no lighting above or below. At least the floor was smooth and easy to walk on. We followed the pipes in a westerly direction when we came to a dead end. Dutch cleaned just enough caked-on dirt, grease, and rat turds off the wall to reveal the outline of a door handle flush against the smooth wall. How do you open the mere outline of a door handle? Clearly, no one had been here in some time, or they wanted to make it appear that way.

Dutch tapped the wall three times with his staff, and muttered some words under his breath that no one could hear and the door handle slowly and silently pushed itself out from the wall. Dutch turned the handle, pulled the door open and we walked through, into another dark tunnel. Dutch closed the door behind. The door and its handle disappeared and the wall we had just passed through was blank. Was it magic or some DARPA or CIA technology unknown to the public? I assumed we were in manmade tunnels of vast proportions.

If I was feeling claustrophobic walking down the endless staircases, it became worse when Dutch locked the door behind us. It was clear and frightening that there was no way I could ever return the way we came. I just prayed I wouldn't let out a tunnel-collapsing howl, as I often did as a claustrophobic boy whenever I felt boxed in. Some goddamn things plague you for life. Maybe I forgot to mention this. I felt a howl rising to the surface. Beca saw my panic when Dutch shut the door leading back to the surface, back to life and she held my hand and wouldn't let go. She looked into my eyes and the howl slipped back into my subconscious. I looked into her eyes and saw only love and understanding.

"Be patient everyone. We're getting closer," Dutch said, but we were all exhausted and no longer even bothering to count the minutes or our steps.

"Don't worry, Rufus. We're not lost. Dutch will find his way in this darkness of hell faster than a Costco customer searching for free samples." said Arnie, who rarely, if ever spoke up unless to say, "Any more honey mustard?" Arnie was a foodie and a warrior and I loved him.

"That's damn fast," I said, knowing how quickly I myself could traverse Costco's aisles on the hunt for free sausages, mini burritos, green chile tamales, enchiladas, fried chicken patties on mini sesame seed buns, carnitas and salsa, chips and salsa, pita and salsa, orangeade, muffins, lox and cream cheese on a bagel chip, or any food product they were hawking that day. If you were fast and aggressive you'd hit enough free sample stands to make lunch out of it. Though Costco customers were tough and competitive, especially the retired old broads in their 60s and up. They'd push you aside, elbow you, step on your foot, especially if they were getting a free sample for a loved one: a doddering old husband, a grandson, or granddaughter, or simply trying their best to shove enough free food down their own gullet to call it lunch.

A tiny, wrinkled Mrs. Greenblatt, around 100, not five feet tall, elbowed me in the balls once to get to two lousy meatballs in a garlic cream sauce. Thank God I had already eaten fifteen of them. Tasty little meaty balls compensated for my big sore balls. It was worth it, though, especially if you topped it off later with a hot dog and a Diet Coke, or a Polish knockwurst and a Diet Coke for a $1.62! Where in American can you buy a Polish knock for a buck sixty-two — with a Diet Coke? Nowhere on this planet, man. Plus the condiments were free. You could practically ladle on the deli mustard, ketchup, diced raw onions, and pickle relish for no additional charge. God bless America, the home of the brave and the $1.62 Polish knock. Arnie interrupted my reverie:

"You can bet your last Clucker's chicky strip he's that fast," said Arnie, who saw I was in a panic.

"Thanks, Arnie. I feel better now," I said, wondering how he knew I had four strips left. "Hey, if I'm not hallucinating, isn't that a Kentucky Fried Chicken box?"

"See any honey mustard packets?" said Arnie.

"Where?!" said the dwarves collectively.

"You can see that from 100 feet in the dark?" Beca said, as we walked near the box. "Don't touch it. Could be booby-trapped, yah big booby."

"It's KFC. Of course I can see it. I'm wearing a damn headlamp," I said. "Do you really think someone would booby trapped a box of KFC *a billion feet underground* on the chance that a pack of starving dwarves and a fried chicken crazed Bartlett scholar would stroll by? You're right, ok? Suicide Fried Chicken bombers, SFCBs strike when you least expect it, at least according to the FBI. Yup, booby trapped KFC boxes explode all day long. I saw it everyday in Iraq. Why not here, a billion feet underground? The perfect location."

"You're damn right I'm right, smartass," said Beca. "The world *is* that fucked-up. Evil fucks plant bomb vests on children; they steal UN food shipments so that little boys and girls starve in Africa; they drop Sarin gas on kids in Syria. Is it such a stretch to imagine some fucker planting a bomb down here?"

"It's possible, IT'S POSSIBLE! You've convinced me. Just not probable," I said and grabbed the box anyway.

I opened the box, which was empty. No wing, no breast, no thigh, not so much as a lousy drumstick — or C-4. Just an empty, greasy box. We passed the box up and down the line so at least we could all sniff what we were missing. It was more masochistic than sadistic. Everyone took a hit, some more than once. A collective sigh went up through miles of solid rock.

"Yah big, dumb bunny," said Beca, who looked at the collective lot of us with disbelief. A dumb bunny. Maybe the nicest thing she's ever called me. I could live with being a dumb bunny.

"This can only mean either we're not alone or there's a KFC just around the corner," said Dutch, trying to be funny. No one laughed. I took out my four hidden Clucker's chicken strips wrapped in five napkins soaked in Clucker's fried chicken grease. I'd save those. I tore off a small piece of a chicken strip and distributed the strips down the line.

"Hey, everyone, did you hear that? There's a KFC not far from here," said Chad, who was, like moi, hungry all the time. "I think I can see it!"

"Me too," said Larry, still nibbling on the little pieces of chicken strips.

"You're hallucinating, yah morons. It was a joke. Snap out of it! Dutch was joking. There is no KFC, Cluckers, Burger King, or Taco Bell, except for five miles above us," Buck said. "So, suck it up, everyone!"

"Thanks for the chicky, Rufus! God bless you!" everyone intoned as they ate the strips.

The gastronomic meter of despair was in the red zone. Making matters worse was the fact that each of us was lugging a plastic bag from Walmart with all sorts of goodies in it, which we weren't allowed to touch. Dutch repeatedly threatened us if we ate anything. He told Burt he'd turn him into a rabbit if ate so much as a carrot from the bag of vegetables he carried. My bag contained Mrs. Bee's Brownie Bites and I dare not even contemplate what Dutch would do to me if I ate them. I mean no one can eat *just one* of Mrs. Bee's brownies. So in addition to all of our weapons we had to carry food. I felt as if I was on patrol in Mosul, and in a sense I was, except for the Walmart bag. I'm glad I shared my last chicken strips with my comrades. I think it took the edge off for everyone.

Again, the fact that we were miles below the earth caused me to panic again and again. Beca saw it and wrapped her arms around me, or as much of me as she could wrap around, and my labored breathing stopped, though my heart was beating wildly for freedom from this oppressive confinement and wildly for her.

We stayed on the path Dutch had chosen, despite the hundreds of side tunnels we passed. It felt like an entire day had passed before we came to another dead end. This time we faced a huge metal wall 100 feet long and 50 feet high. On the far left hand side of this expansive slab of metal was a small, humble, lonely little door no taller or wider than one of my dwarf companions. There was an intricate keyhole in the middle, staring at us from behind its cobwebs, as if it had been waiting patiently for its family to return.

Was there a way inside? Dutch took out a large intricate key from inside his Members Only jacket and inserted it into the keyhole and turned the key, but the door wouldn't open, no matter which direction he turned it.

"This has to be our final destination. There has to be a way inside," said Dutch, who was nose to nose with the door, singing softly through its keyhole in languages unspoken in a thousand years. He stepped back. Nothing. No change to the steel door.

"Oh, for God's sake, no one said anything about a magic door with a faulty keyhole," said Dutch, who banged on the door with his cane, angry at this impasse.

"What *did* they say?" I asked.

"Obviously, that there would be an accessible door with a working key." said Dutch who held up the key. "It shouldn't need a password, not even the several thousand in my vocabulary."

"Do something wizard-like. It's your job," said Kevin, sweetly, but beyond stupid, just asking for trouble. "It's your job" would get under anyone's skin, especially a testy wizard, already frustrated.

"Shut the fuck up, Kevin. *Dormiritas catatonis le Kevster!*" said Dutch and waved his cane at him. Kevin keeled over, out like a light.

"Was that necessary? Did you kill him?" I asked.

"Probably should have, but no. I just put the annoying little bastard to sleep. If I get this door to open you can drag his sorry ass inside."

"Come on, Dutch, don't be a prick," I said. "It was an innocent enough question; and one we're all thinking. Kevin's a good guy."

"You're right. I feel terrible. Not really. Sorry Kev," Dutch said, looking down on Kevin's catatonic body. "At any rate, I once knew every spell from the San Fernando Valley to the High Kingdom."

Dutch tried again: This time he took out a sheet of yellow legal paper and recited incantations, threats, legal pleadings in Greek, Latin, Pig Latin, Elvish, French, English, Spanish, Spanglish, Goth, Anglo-Saxon, Icelandic, German, and finally, even dolphin (weird high pitched shit): all to no avail. Finally, in despair he dropped to the floor after uttering my favorite incantation, "Please baby, please baby, please baby, please baby, OPEN!" All without success.

"I guess wizards are human after all," said Buck.

Dutch removed the key and I'm sad to report we then did violence to the door. We shot it through the keyhole with our Glocks. We blasted it with our Uzis and M16s. We fried it with our flamethrower. We stood back while Beca shot an RPG at it, and finally Dutch planted C4 plastic explosives to the door and detonated it. Everything failed and what's more unbelievable — the door was undamaged. Not a nick or a scratch. You had to admire the builder's powerful magic.

"Did I forget something?" Dutch muttered in despair. He sat down with us on the tunnel floor, cupped his chin in his hands and was silent.

"Ah, fuck it!" I said, expressing everyone's frustration, especially Dutch's.

Lo and behold, to everyone's astonishment, a flashing blue neon sign appeared on the gigantic wall, with a recorded voice that said, *"Ah, fuck it! Say the magic word and win $100."* And then the wall lit up like a Christmas tree with green and blue and red and yellow and orange flashing neon signs blinking on and off in every section of the wall:

"Welcome to the Hotel Armageddon!"
"The Only Good Commie is a Dead Commie."
"One Damn Nuke Can Spoil Your Whole Day, Girlfriend."
"Coke Is the One."
"No Exit"
"It's Dark Down Here"
"Who Turned Out the Lights?"

"Where's the Beef?"
"This is Your Brain on Nukes."
"Make Love AND War"
"Got NUKES?"
"What Happens in the Bunker, Stays in the Bunker."
"You Get More from a Kenmore"
"Rise and Shine — Ooops, Make that Rise and Glow!"
"Ford Tough!"
"Hope and (spare) Change!!"
"Stayin' Alive!"
"Keep the Faith"
"Go with the Flow"
"Go with the Glow!"
"Hell No, We Won't Go!"
"Give Peace a Chance"
"Extra Cheese, Pleeze"
"Watch the Fro, Daddy-O"
"Right On! Right On! Right On!!!"
"Fuck the Establishment, Man"
"Never Trust the Man, Dude"
"Make America Grape Again!"
"I'm fucked; you're fucked; we're all fucked! Hooray!! Fuck It!"
"Love is the Answer"

And then the signs stopped flashing and disappeared forever.

"Maybe you should try the key again, Dutch," I said. Dutch inserted the key and this time the door opened.

"Rufus," Dutch said, "you are indeed the Chosen One. 'Ah, fuck it!' My oh my! Of all the possible passwords. Those were groovier times."

"Funnier, too." I said.

"Lord Reggie said access might be difficult," Dutch said. "He wasn't joking."

"He knew about this place?" said Beca.

"He gave me directions, and the key!" Dutch said. "Reg said the 'pad' would be fully stocked, but who knew it would be such a bitch to get inside."

"Ah, fuck it" became an inside joke for the remainder of the quest, and beyond. And so we marched into our safe house, and what a wonderfully warm 1950s welcome it gave us. Whoever conceived and built this retreat from the world, had planned to spend a long time down here. It was as cozy as Mole's home in *The Wind in the Willows*, but in dire need of its own spring cleaning.

CHAPTER 46

I felt immediately at home, as if I had entered the quintessential bachelor's pad: the walls were covered in dark brown mahogany paneling and dust. The paneled ceiling was slightly arched, as if you were in a very large, very expansive ship's cabin. In the middle of the family room were fourteen velour La-Z-Boy recliners covered in dust facing an old 1950s RCA color TV with a 15-inch screen. I hoped it was a color TV, but at 15 inches, who cares? It looked like the set my grandparents bought in the mid 1950s. When my family visited we all pushed our chairs within a foot or two of the damn TV just to see the frickin' screen. Each La-Z-Boy had a flimsy tray parked next to it with enough room for a beer, a couple of hot dogs, peanuts, Raisinettes, and Red vines. I turned on the TV and the St. Louis Cardinals were playing the Los Angeles Dodgers, in glorious black and white. Awesome!

The kitchen had a cherry wood theme, but more impressive was the world's largest Sears Kenmore refrigerator/freezer, fully stocked. Someone had filled it and the cupboards with enough provisions to last us through World War 3. I was ready to abandon the quest altogether, and hang out until such time as the nuclear winter had passed.

"Who stocked the fridge?" I said. "Steaks, chicken, fish, condiments, even Mint Chip ice cream!"

"They didn't come in by the front door," said Dutch. It hadn't been touched in decades."

"The front door is a war door," said Buck.

"Did you say Mint Chip?" said Burt, sprinting to the Kenmore. "I just love heroic quests."

"A war door?" I said.

"Yeah, a war door," said Buck. "No more than one dwarf at a time can pass through the door. Impossible to storm this place, except maybe from the back or the side."

"Unless the enemy could breach that gigantic slab of metal next to the tiny door. Very clever design," I said.

"We build our dwarf cities, our strongholds the same way," said Burt who already had Mint-Chip ice-cream dripping down his beard.

"Yeah, and only the Chosen One could have guessed that password," said Beca. "Must be a rear entrance, through those blast doors."

There was a solitary door, next to the TV and family room, and behind it another door, both with electronic keypads. They were blast proof. Three long tunnels branched out after passing the second door: Fortunately, someone stuck a Post-it note with the combination for each door. Guess they figured if we gained access to the safe house, we were supposed to be there. But a Post-It note? Some security protocol, right? Go figure. The three tunnels merged at the second blast door. If you were coming out from your bedroom you had to lock the door behind you before opening the first door. The same protocol coming and going. And along each of the three tunnels there were bedrooms.

This was also the thinking after the 9/11 terrorist attacks, when the airlines installed two blast doors on every plane to safeguard access to the pilot's cockpit. But this joint was decked out in the 1950s. Someone had either updated this place or the concept had been thought through by some genius in the 1950s, before airplane hijackings became popular in the decades.

We didn't care much about secure doors or even rear entrances. We just wanted to sleep, for a month if possible.

"This place is amazing." I said, asleep on my feet. "We're only missing 'Goldilocks and the Three Cheerleaders.'" Beca didn't laugh and punched me on the arm.

"Ouch," I said, "What was that for?"

"Wake up, lover boy!" said Beca. It dawned on me that Beca *could* shape-shift into one of those hot cheerleaders every night. Fat chance, fat man.

"Hey everyone," I droned, "we're finally safe. Let's talk in a few weeks. Goodnight to all."

"And to all a good night," said Dutch.

"Stay awake, lover boy," Beca said, keeping me on my feet, "and I'll show you to your room." I followed half asleep, behind her cute, heart-shaped tush, to a bedroom where I fell into a queen bed big enough for two regular people or one single, solitary Chosen One.

The dwarves followed behind Dutch, each to his own bedroom, except for our darling Wendy, who slept in the family room in front of the first blast door. Good luck getting past a now 200 pound lupine bitch.

CHAPTER 47

I woke up to discover Beca asleep next to me. I put my clothes on hoping to finish dressing before she woke up. I was just getting into my pants.

"Hey sexy," she said, groggy from the long sleep. "What time is it?"

"Looks like 2:30 in the afternoon," I said, trying to see the clock from my position, jumping up and down with my back to her, hoping to get my pants and shirt on without giving her a full-on frontal view of my jiggling gut.

"Sorry if I startled you when you woke up," she said. "You try sleeping surrounded by ten snoring dwarves and a wizard who casts spells in his sleep. And *yes*, I can see your big gut. Don't worry about it. I'm going to help you work it off."

"What? How?" I said, my blood pressure rising, among other things.

"Don't worry about that now," she said, looking where she shouldn't. "Don't you smell that bacon? Those dwarves are eating *all* of it without us. You like bacon, right?"

"Do I ever! It's my second favorite thing in the world. If we don't get there soon, it will vanish," I said, the gastronomic urge taking precedence over other urges. "Smells like someone made pancakes, too. I'll see you in the kitchen."

"Wait for me," she said. "I dress fast." Beca jumped out of bed in her underwear and her bra. Oh, by the grace of God, she had a heavenly body: strong legs and arms and bust that was larger than I ever imagined, held in check by a tight-fitting sports bra. She had no shame about dressing in front of me. Maybe she just felt I was one of the guys, you know: her comrade-in-arms. That's how I treated women in combat roles in Iraq, with decency and fastidious respect.

"For God's sake, Rufus, put your tongue back in your mouth. Haven't you ever seen a woman before?" She laughed at my red-faced embarrassment.

"Never one as beautiful. At least not in some time," I said. She jumped into my arms, wrapped her legs around me. I caught her. Her face was inches from mine. She kissed me quickly on the lips. I kissed her back. She kissed me back hard. Only this time she was a comrade in my arms.

"Why would He make the 'Chosen One' such a lovable goof-ball?" she said, kissing my neck.

"Maybe, *He* chose a lovable fool: to show the wonders He could work with such inferior materials," I said.

"Now don't go all Biblical on me," she said. "Come on, Rufus. I'll bet I can eat more pancakes than you."

"There are many things you can do better than I, but that's not one of them."

We had all overslept. When we woke, the first thing we wanted was bacon, bacon, and more bacon. The refrigerator was filled with everything one dreams about after fasting for two days: orange juice, bacon, waffles, eggs, hollandaise sauce (store bought), pancakes, hash brown potatoes, fresh fruit, coffee, espresso, English muffins, blueberry jam, strawberry preserves, even cold fried chicken — from Clucker's no less. We joined Buck, Dutch, and the dwarves already around the table, with a lazy Susan that kept spinning like the earth around the sun, with hands darting in and out.

"Hey, what are those big tubes in my closet?" asked Petey.

"There are four in our closet. They look like pneumatic tubes," said Beca. "Ours look like escape pods."

"How many are there?" said Buck

"Thirty in all," said Dutch. "I counted them while you were asleep. Beca's right: they are escape pods. After breakfast I'll show everyone how they work, or how I think they work, just in case we need them."

"How can they be escape ponds? Is there an opening at the top of each tube?" I said. "Do you think each one travels miles through solid rock? Are you sure they're not for our dirty laundry?"

"For our sake, let's hope they're not for our laundry, but lead *safely* to the surface," said Buck.

"They're our last hope of survival should our bunker be compromised. I can't imagine what they cost to build," said Dutch.

"They're a huge part of all that government waste one hears about," said Beca. "A *huge* part."

"Guess if you're craving a Denny's Grand Slam Slugger, you could ride the tube to the street level. Gotta to be one hell-of-a ride." I said, thinking more about my stomach, than about Beca's insight — or the terrifying prospect of traveling through four miles of solid rock to reach the surface. Not sure a Grand Slam Slugger was worth the risk.

"What's our next move?" Buck said, addressing his comment to no one in particular, though we all waited for Dutch to answer.

"We need to explore our immediate surroundings." Dutch said. "No one knows the full extent of these tunnels; they were created during the Cold War when the United States government sought a network of safe houses beyond the reach of radiation from a hydrogen bomb, yet close enough to retreat to in the time it took an ICBM to reach Washington, about 30 minutes. I suspect there's a direct entrance to these tunnels from the White House. It makes sense."

"Are they more places down here like our groovy pad?" I asked.

"Maybe, but we have no way of knowing without leaving our 'groovy' pad," Dutch said. "Certainly there is an underground command center for the President of the United States. So everyone gather round."

Dutch walked over to a map of the underground tunnels covering the wall behind our La-Z-Boy recliners. He used a Bacsu steak knife as a pointing device. The map was yellow and gray with age, and showed tunnels going in every direction: north, south, east, and west — hundreds, maybe thousands of tunnels — far too many for our small group to survey if we had fifty lifetimes.

"These tunnels," he said, pointing to a group of tunnels on the map's south quadrant, "led us here; and here are the tunnels that branch off from them that we know nothing about. We don't have time to explore all of them, but we need to explore a few, if only to get a better sense if anyone or anything is nearby."

"I'd like to know who left the KFC box. Someone left that box, which could have been an IED!" I said, mocking Beca's warning at the time.

"Which you were stupid enough to pick up, despite my warning," said Beca.

"You're joking, right?" said Chad, who wore a Chicago Cubs hats covered with official state pins. "If you ask me, one person with a box of KFC isn't much of a threat. Speaking for myself, I've explored enough tunnels for a lifetime. Like Rufus, I'd rather take a pneumatic tube to the surface; that's where I'm going. I signed up for a White House tour tomorrow at 2:30. Besides, I want to make sure the tubes work."

"Hey Chad, great idea!" I said. "Let's go together. Been a long time since the tubes were tested, if they ever were."

"Don't be idiots." Dutch said. "The Demon Lord has agents everywhere in the capital looking for you. You killed one of his captains, Rufus, and they know what you look like. You can bet your ass the other demon high in the sky filmed everything for his Lord, who's focused on you and your famous sword. He doesn't know the origin of Demon Slayer but he's worried now that you and your sword could kill him."

"I'm betting he's obsessed with being the new Vice President, right Chad?" I said. "I'm betting he's got his subordinates working on getting rid of President McClintock and not on us at all. He can't be bothered with me right now. He's VPOTUS."

"Yeah, and we know Vice Presidents of the United States don't do shit," said Beca. "Trust me, he's got nothin' better to do than hunt you Oh, Chosen Knucklehead."

"Good one, Beca," said Buck. "Count on it. His agents will be looking for you to do something stupid. And sightseeing, behaving like a tourist is right up there."

The TV was on in the background. Suddenly the volume increased announcing a Special Report from CNN. It was Wolfy.

"Good morning, everyone. Wolf Blitzer here, reporting to you live at the scene of a horrific murder in our nation's capital. Police have discovered the grisly evidence of cannibalism and murder at the home of Mitch Dunnelly, the highly respected host of *Meet the Press*. While investigators are withholding details of the crime, our sources say there are no survivors. It's almost too shocking to believe what we've been told. However, according to our inside sources, Mitch Dunnelly and his entire family have been eaten alive. We have graphic pictures of the crime scene we will show you following this message from our sponsors. Please be advised these pictures are not suitable for children."

"Oh, but they're suitable for adults?" I said. "I'd love to see pictures of the cannibalized Dunnelly family."

"I told you he was a dead man," said Buck.

"Turn the TV off," said Dutch. "I don't want to hear anymore, but Rufus, that's what's waiting for you if you go to the Lincoln Memorial or the White House by yourself."

"Really?" I said. "I don't agree. He's already met me. I'm small potatoes. I'm not that important. No one's looking for me. He'll catch up to me later. Geez man, he's Vice President of the United States of America! He's just won the brass ring, the whole enchilada; the Super Lotto, man. He couldn't care less about me or any of us."

"Don't be a schmuck," said Beca. "He's concerned about both. I'm confident he's pretty good at multitasking."

"How can you be so sure he knows we're in D.C.?" I said.

"It's where *he* would go. The Demon Lord knows the direction we were heading and he knows we're not here as tourists, Rufus." Buck said. "He knows we're here to kill him and to recover our dwarf gold. This is our best chance to get our gold back. We're so close. Don't fucking blow it, Big Man."

"Of course they know we're here." Beca said, staying glued to the subject. "The Senator, the Demon Lord may be damned for eternity, and an insane cannibalistic monster, but he's been smart enough to fool a lot of very smart people. It's won't be easy to kill him, or get close to him, or to elude his minions much longer."

"Minions, schminions," I snorted. "Ok, have it your way. I'll stay put with you, buried beneath four miles of rock." I felt a claustrophobic, a buried-alive panic attack in my near future. I kept the feeling to myself. Seeing the Lincoln Memorial wasn't my only reason for wanting to escape this grave-like bunker, despite its well-stocked refrigerator.

"I want to meet the Demon Lord on our terms, not his," said Dutch, drawing my attention to the map and pointing to the tunnels. "Look Rufus, here's the White House and here are our tunnels. There must be tunnels near the White House, even though this map doesn't show them. There *has* to be underground access nearby. I have connections at the White House, Rufus, and we'll get you to the Lincoln Memorial. Just not now. So buckle up. We're leaving our cozy hideaway to get see what's beyond our cozy little safe house."

"Lead on. 'Hell is for heroes,'" I said quoting Steve McQueen, the essence of cool. He always got his man and his lady.

"Yeh, and you're the most unlikely, most reluctant hero I've ever met," said Buck.

"Let me tell you something, Buck-o: Every hero worth his or her testosterone or estrogen is a reluctant one, or should be," I said with a nod to Beca. "As far back as Prometheus: Do you think he brought fire to us because he wanted to? No, it was Mrs. Prometheus nagging him night after night: 'This house is freezing, Prometheus! Do something, Mr. Hero! Do something! I'm freezing my ass off, Prometheus. Prometheus!! Are you listening to me?'

"'Put on a damn sweater,' he told her, but do you think she listened? No, Mrs. Prometheus wanted indoor heating. She's the one who insisted on fire. Pissing off the gods was the last thing Prometheus wanted. But he couldn't take the nagging any longer. So Prometheus steals fire and pays for it."

"And you're telling me this why?" said Buck.

"I'm telling you this because being chained to a mountain by the gods and having an eagle rip out your liver every night, for eternity, is a goddamn pleasure compared to a nagging wife, or — a smart ass dwarf. And by the way, as for your lost dwarf gold, you can all shove it."

I knew Buck would get even with me during our next practice session with Demon Slayer. Demon Slayer or no, he was a formidable attacker and I expected to pay for my remarks in blood and bruises. That's life isn't it? Words have consequences. Still, it had to be said.

"Can you *fire* a 'Chosen One?'" said Buck.

"No!" said Dutch. "End of discussion. Now collect your weapons, grab some snacks, and practice a little civility. Would someone please wake up that mutt in the corner? It's time for him to earn his keep."

"He's a she, Dutch." I said.

"Whatever," said Dutch.

"Wendy, darling, wake up," I whispered in her ear, "we're going out for your constitutional." She stood up and stretched her hind legs like a cat, all 200 pounds of her. She yawned and the size of her five-inch incisors caused the dwarves to take a collective deep breath, relieved that she was on our side. The dwarves stroked Wendy's fur gently, as she moved around the room, marking each dwarf as family by rubbing her fur and her scent on them. She settled on my feet and look up at me with a love not even death could separate. Beca scratched her head. Her purring shook the cutlery on the kitchen wall.

"We'll retrace our steps," said Dutch, "from where the tunnel branches off north east. You remember: the tunnel with the empty KFC box."

"Hell, man," I said, "anything that smells like KFC must be worth risking our lives for."

We headed back the way we came, our noses sniffing for the scent of that chicken.

"There had to be dwarves involved in making these tunnels," Buck said, as we trudged up a familiar tunnel. "Only dwarves could produce such magnificent tunnels."

"No, not the dwarves, talented though they be: just the American taxpayer's dollar hard at work." Beca said. We all looked at her.

"Yah, think?" said Burt.

"What, I'm not allowed to read the papers or the GAO's annual report and wonder where the fuck all the big money's been siphoned off to?"

"GAO?" I said.

"The Government Accounting Office! I'm ashamed of you Rufus," she said, "You should know that acronym."

"Guilty as charged. You analyzed the GAO annual report for hidden spending?! Beca, you never cease to amaze me. "

"Thank you," she said. "I'm glad you noticed. I'm not just a pretty face, you know."

"No, of course not," I said. "You're so much more. Right fellas?"

"Hear, hear!" said every dwarf.

"Right on," said Dutch.

CHAPTER 48

The vastness of the tunnels never ceased to amaze me. Time-and-again we came out of a tunnel into a plaza capable of holding thousands of people. The planners had to have imagined a population of millions of people living here in post-Armageddon America. Who among the planners of our underground labyrinth decorated and stockpiled our magnificent safe house? That and KFC is what you think about when your belly's full. I was walking with Wendy and petting her when I smelled something very *un*-Original-Recipe-like.

"What's that God-awful smell? Sho' don't smell like the Colonel's Original Recipe. See it, about 25 yards ahead?" I said. "What are those fluorescent yellow piles on the floor?"

"Goblin shit." Buck said.

"Thank God I saw it before I stepped in it. The shit you don't see is the most dangerous shit of all.'"

"Amen, brother," said Beca, laughing her ass off.

"Sage words, *Oh, Chosen one*," said Buck, also laughing.

"But why is it fluorescent yellow?" I asked.

"The obvious answer is the most likely," said Chad, who had slain hundreds of goblins in battle. "So they don't step on it in the dark. Goblins are yellow and goblin tunnels are usually pitch black, except for the light you bring."

"Why didn't I see any in the goblin tunnels?" I said.

"Again, the obvious answer is the most likely,," said Chad. "They clean up after themselves."

"Amen, brother," I said, and Beca laughed some more.

Yellow crap must be an evolutionary trait, I thought. Yes, a favorable survival mutation for those who had the yellow crap gene. Favorable in that those with the gene were less likely to step in goblin shit than their brown shitting brethren. Not only would the goblins who crapped brown be more likely to step in it, but brown crapping goblins were more likely to be killed off by rest of the tribe who got just plain sick and tired of stepping in their brethren's brown shit. A surly goblin is a killer, as everyone knows. Needless to say, goblins who *also* stepped more frequently in their own brown shit were less attractive as mates and so failed to pass on the brown crap gene. Thus those with yellow crap gene mated more often and more successfully. Hence yellow goblin shit that glows. Of course, it was just a theory, but I might write a monograph on this phenomenon when I returned to my studies.

"Makes sense." I said. "I guess we must leap over it as goblins do: one small leap for man, on giant leap...ah shit." Before I knew it, my leap was one pile short and I had fluorescent, yellow goblin crap on my Nikes, all inside the little grooves on the bottom of my left shoe.

"Dwarf experts agree that the different shades and brightness of scat can reveal the goblin's age and sex, plus or minus a year or two." Petey said.

"That's a little more than I care to know about goblin shit." I said, despite my previous disquisition.

"Petey knows more about goblin shit than any dwarf alive," said Buck, pointing to a huge load inches away from his right foot.

"A rare gift," said Beca.

"Thank you, Buck and Beca," Petey said. "Yes, my Uncle Milty was captured and eaten by goblins. They left Uncle Milty, or to be more precise, Uncle Milty scat on my aunt's doormat." Petey paused and examined the yellow loads like an entomologist examining a new and rare dung beetle.

"By the size and color of these various loads," said Petey, "I can say with confidence that the larger loads belong to an adult male approximately 40 years old, with a slight limp; these smaller loads belong to a slightly younger female, and the color and shade on your shoe, Rufus, points to a young goblin around fifteen."

"Thank you, Petey," said Dutch. "Delighted to hear that daddy goblin is a family man — pity about his slight limp."

"Probably a family," said Arnie, "just passing through. But where to is the question."

"Looks like they were in a hurry," Beca said.

"How so?" said Dutch.

"Look fifteen feet ahead and to the right," said Beca. "It's a half eaten Big Mac."

"Oh My God!! Did you say a Big Mac? Who in his right mind would leave a Big Mac *half eaten*?! That's madness! I'd give all of my nonexistent dwarf gold right here, right now for a Big Mac, or a double-cheeseburger." I said.

Then the dwarves started cursing, too, because they couldn't leap successfully across the scat on their short legs.

"Ah, shit," said Buck.

"Goblin scat." I said.

"Goblin shit," said Beca, who with Wendy and Dutch were the only members of our party who managed to avoid stepping in it.

"Smells fresh everyone," said Dutch, pulling out his Glock. "Lock and load!"

We walked for hours, but never ran into any goblins. Maybe they had a hideaway down here, too. At least we scraped off most of the goblin shit by the time we got home and entered through our secret back door.

We left our shoes on the mat outside the back door and entered.

Who knew what the Demon Lord knew about our operations. So like smart soldiers we never entered our safe house from the same tunnel, especially since there was more than one entrance.

As we opened the first blast door, on our way to the kitchen, there were sounds coming from the family room.

"Who left the TV on?" said Dutch, irritated.

"I hear a familiar voice," Beca said. "A female voice."

"It's Vanna!" I said.

CHAPTER 49

We entered the second set of blast doors to the family room with our weapons drawn. However, the unmistakable fragrance of freshly baked cinnamon buns shattered my focus.

Sure enough, it was Vanna, alright, from *Wheel of Fortune*, but the voice that solved the puzzle belonged to a female goblin sitting on *my* recliner. There was also a male goblin sitting next to her in Buck's favorite purple recliner and Buck was none too pleased about it. A goblin teenager stretched out on the floor in front of them. Oh, and the boy had a lupine pup lying across his lap. More importantly, next to the TV, against the wall, rested an M16, an AK47, and a old rifle with a barrel three inches in diameter, which I didn't recognize, but looked like a grenade launcher, a precursor maybe to the modern Russian RPG. The goblins didn't bother to reach for their weapons: we had them surrounded, our weapons aimed, ready to blast them. Even a growling Wendy signaled her readiness.

They were eating cold Clucker's chicken from our refrigerator, itself a death sentence, and watching *Wheel of Fortune* on our tiny TV. Petey and Buck cocked their Glocks and almost killed them on the spot for hijacking their Clucker's chicken strips. We had our weapons cocked when the female goblin said, "Rock-and-roll your baked brie," which, of course, was the answer to the puzzle, which I might add she accomplished on very few clues.

Dutch motioned everyone to stand down. Then he started to laugh, quietly at first, then very loud, and we had to wait some time before he stopped.

⊹═══ ═══⊹

"I'm Gormog," the goblin said, "and this is my wife, Farsog, and my First Born, Sam. Chicken anyone?"

"Shush, Muppin!" Farsog said to the howling, frightened lupine pup. "He's really very sweet, once he gets to know you. He lost his mother recently. Sam, Muppin wants you to hold him." Wendy looked at the pup and wailed: two motherless lupines meant to be together.

"We were going to leave right after *Jeopardy!*" said Gormog, "but it's so nice here and *Wheel* really sucks you in. We're very sorry."

They were defenseless and I wanted to hear more of their story. Before we blasted them. And by the lowered weapons of the dwarves, I think they felt the same way, despite our missing chicken.

"I know how it looks," said Farsog.

"Really?" Beca said, "Tell us: how does it look?"

"It looks like we're goblin hitters, who got sloppy," said Gormog, "that's how it *looks*."

"That's right," said Buck. "I say we take them out to the tunnel and waste them, right now."

"Let's not be too hasty." I said. "We know how it looks; let's find out how it *is*. Look at the mistake we almost made with Wendy. And look what a great and loyal watch lupine she's become."

"Yeah, a watch lupine who is eating us out of house and home." Kevin said.

"She's saved your ass more than once, Kevin." Beca said.

"Why, she'd give her life for any one of you." I said. "I say we let them speak their piece — before we waste them."

"Yeah, ok, speak your piece and then we'll blow you to fucking pieces," Kevin said.

"A quick question," I said. "I'm guessing dad's packing the AK47; mom's sporting the smaller M16, but what's junior got leaning against the wall?"

"Oh, that's an M79 grenade launcher. A little old school, but effective." Gormog said. "Sam, lift your shirt."

"Really, Dad?" he said.

"Really, Son." Sam pulled up his oversized LeBron jersey. Underneath was a belt with at least seven M79 grenades attached to it.

"Thank you, Sam," a nervous Dutch said. "You can drop your shirt now."

"They're all duds. Not a single live grenade. See for your self," said Gormog. Burt pulled three grenades off Sam's belt.

"The grenades are light as a feather, completely inert," Burt said.

"You think I'm going to let my little boy carry live grenades?" said Gormog.

"Ok, everyone," I said. "Let's hear them out."

"We didn't come here to make trouble for anyone." Gormog said. "We'd like to defect and help the Chosen One."

"So many dwarves in the High Kingdom have been raped, even my grandmother, by goblin soldiers in the High Kingdom," Burt said, unconvinced. "How do I know you're not a rapist, too?"

"How dare you accuse my husband of that terrible crime!" said Farsog, angry and in tears. "Our weapons are empty. My husband is a gourmet cook. He had never hurt anyone in his life and the only female he has ever touched is ME!"

"It's ok, Farsog, it's ok," Gormog said and put his arms around his wife. "I know the reputation of our soldiers in the High Kingdom and it is shameful. Our parents were enslaved by the Demon Lord and were brought here against their will from the High Kingdom. But we were born in Tennessee, under the Great Smoky Mountains. Everyone is a soldier in a goblin community, but not everyone fights. I carry an empty gun and to be honest, I've never even fired it. Like I said, even Sam's grenade launcher is useless."

"You're a long way from Tennessee," I said.

"Not really. Not if you use the Underground Highway, GI83" said Gormog.

"GI83?" I said.

"Of course, GI83: Goblin Interstate 83." Gormog said. Dutch just groaned. "My point," Gormog continued, "is that makes us U.S. citizens, though our fellow Americans haven't the slightest knowledge of our existence. We heard you five days ago when you first entered the tunnels. We found your front door, weeks ago, but had no idea what the password was, until Rufus opened it."

"We know all of your names. Senator, I mean Vice president-elect Ross has texted everyone's pic, too." said Farsog who waved her phone at us.

"That's just great," I said. "He's probably got his own spy satellite, too," I said.

"Launched it last year, as a matter of fact," said Gormog.

"No doubt, paid for with our dwarf gold, the bastard," said Arnie, who had death in his eyes when he saw Farsog smothering his chicken strips with *his* honey mustard sauce before taking a big bite out of one. "And how do we know you haven't betrayed us to your true lord and master?"

"Relax, Arnie," said Buck. "They'd be here already."

"Quite right. We'd like to have more children someday," said Farsog. "Children who will sit at our feet and watch *Jeopardy!* and *Wheel of Fortune* and *Charlie Rose*. Real American children. But after Sam was born we pledged never to have more children while the Demon Lord still enslaved our people. He's a monster. Every month he selects five unlucky goblins to have lunch with him. He televises this live on his personal network, Demon Lord TV. He broadcasts DLTV to all the goblin communities around the country."

"Did you say 'around the country?'" said Dutch, looking more and more depressed at each new piece of information.

"Yes," said Gormog. "But they live underground. They rarely bother anyone. Occasionally, a big goblin guard might pop up for a bit of fresh mountain air and lead a few hunters on a merry chase. How do you think the legend of Sasquatch or Bigfoot stays alive?"

"Please continue, Farsog," said Dutch, as if he didn't have enough to worry about.

"The five goblins invited for lunch *are* lunch." she said, with the saddest expression on her fluorescent yellow face. "He looks like good ol' boy Senator Bobby Ross," said Farsog, "until his jaw expands ten times its normal size and he breaks each goblin's body in half. He drinks their blood and eats their broken bodies live for his entertainment, and our horror. Then he says, 'Y'all keep doing a great job. Keep it up and don't forget to put your names in the drawing next month for "Lunchtime with your Demon Lord!" See you next month, same time, same place.' I don't want my future children to ever see this. We fled from our community. We've been wandering the tunnels for weeks, sneaking up to the surface for McDonald's and KFC. Fall and winter are our favorite seasons. You can hide your face underneath a scarf or a hoodie like everyone else this time of year. We do all of our shopping for the year. We were hiding inside one of the tunnels when we saw you." By the time she finished everyone was wiping away tears.

"As we said, the Demon Lord knows every member of your team," said Farsog, "and he's going a little crazy at how many times you've escaped his clutches."

"Every member?" Said Dutch.

"Yes, especially the Chosen One, the 'Fat White Fuck' — his words not mine." Gormog said.

"Gormog! What's wrong with you?! Apologize!" Farsog said, outraged on my behalf.

"I'm sorry, very sorry, but he really does wants the Fat White Fuck 'eaten dead or alive.'"

"That's Mr. Fat White Fuck to you." I said, strangely pleased that I was getting under the skin of the Demon Lord.

"Again, Sorry, Mr. Fat White Fuck," said Gormog.

"Apology accepted, but please, call me Rufus," I said, "or Chosen One or Big Man or just Chunk." Beca couldn't stop laughing, as was the case with more than a few of the dwarves. "Mr. Fat White Fuck" was pretty goddamn funny.

"I'm sorry, again, Big Man," Gormog said. I nodded to him, letting him know with my double chin and quivering gut that it better not happen again.

Farsog put her hand in Gormog's, the other around Sam's shoulder. Muppin was playing with Wendy.

"One last question," I said.

"Yes, anything," said Gormog.

"Are those cinnamon buns I smell?"

"Yes," said Gormog. "We thought you would enjoy them after your trip in the tunnels."

"Gormog has been trained at Le Cordon Bleu," Farsog said.

"It was an online certificate program," said Gormog, "I've been trained only online."

"He's too modest," Farsog said.

"Enough already, sweetheart."

"Smells heavenly. You should listen to your wife." I said. "I can't wait to taste one."

"You should know by now *a wife* is *always* right, Gormog," said Dutch. "Isn't that right, brothers?"

"Remember that, Mr. Fat White Fuck," whispered Beca for my ears only. My heart soared.

"Yes!" said every dwarf from the High Kingdom, all of whom already missed his wife more than King Thorax missed his beloved Grilda the Axe Mistress, his legendary dwarf wife who died wielding her axe at the very gate of the dwarf kingdom in the Battle of, *We're Gonna Fuck-U-Up!*

"Then I say, let's all relax and enjoy this delicious treat provided by our unexpected guests. I know they have much more to tell us," said Dutch.

"There's homemade hot chocolate for everyone and Farsog has turned down everyone's bed," said Gormog. "I promise by the

Son of the One, we mean no harm, but only seek sanctuary with you and an opportunity to help you kill the Demon Lord."

That was a new one, I thought: to hear goblins invoking the Son of the One, who gives hope where there was none. The Savior finds everyone who seeks him, and some who don't. Gormog was telling the truth. There was no ammunition in any of their weapons; and more importantly, no one was pounding on our door.

"It would be my great privilege to serve everyone cinnamon rolls and hot chocolate, hot tea, or coffee." Gormog said as he walked to the kitchen, with a slight limp.

With our bellies full of Gormog's delicious cinnamon buns, we went to bed. We found an extra bed for Gormog and Farsog. Sam slept on the floor in their room. Little Muppin slept curled up inside of Wendy by the front door. I've always said, "Trust your lupine: if she doesn't like someone, pay attention." I'd never seen Wendy in this maternal role before. She knew what it felt like to lose her mother and she was going to be there for little Muppin, always. They snored together in a deep sleep, a happy sleep for the first time in their young lives.

CHAPTER 50

The cinnamon buns, even the morning after, were delicious. For each of us, Gormog set out a small knife and porcelain cup filled with warm icing. In that way you could apply as much or as little icing as you desired, unlike so many bakeries and restaurants that drown their cinnamon buns in icing. He also made chocolate croissants and his own version of the Egg McMuffin: a drizzled, not drenched Hollandaise across the length and breadth of a perfectly poached egg, on top of which sat a thick slice of smoked Virginia ham with real maple syrup — and all sandwiched between a baked, homemade lemon poppy seed English muffin, the final thoughtful gesture from a Master Chef.

Gormog and Farsog insisted on cleaning up after seventeen hungry people. Sam dried the dishes. I sat at the dinner table eating a cinnamon bun, and feeding Wendy and Muppin scraps of chicken and cinnamon bun. Little Muppin played with Wendy under the table. I allowed Wendy to assume responsibility for little Muppin, and she shared her food with the baby Lupine. I'd never seen Wendy look happier. Burt got up. He couldn't stand it any longer and gently pushed Gormog aside and started washing dishes. He smiled at Farsog who dried.

"Do want to know what my favorite song is, Farsog?" said Burt.

"Sure, what's your favorite song, Burt?" said Farsog.

"It's called, 'You Don't Know Me,' by the late great Ray Charles."

"Why is it your favorite?" said Farsog.

"Because it reminds me of a beautiful dwarf maiden I once knew but briefly," said Burt, whose eyes welled up with tears. Farsog hugged him.

"We know that song," said Gormog, who sat at the table with me, feeding chicken scraps to Wendy and little Muppin.

"Would you sing it for us?" asked Farsog?

"I would love to," said Burt, who sang "You Don't Know Me" in a moving tenor voice, so beautiful that the dwarves turned the TV off to hear its timeless heartache, and the longing we've all felt for unrequited love.

Later, when Gormog, Farsog, and Sam were in the back making everyone's bed and washing their dirty laundry, we held a meeting in the kitchen. I volunteered to go back and help Gormog's family, but Arnie and Burt stepped up.

"We'll go back and help," said Arnie, "you can tell us what you've decided later."

"We're family, right?" said Burt. "And family members share the household chores." The cynic in me would say that the way to a dwarf's heart is through his stomach, but I believed there was true, heartfelt emotion in Arnie and Burt.

"Should we send Gormog and Farsog back to the hive?" Buck said. "They could spy on the movements of the Demon Lord and perhaps relay important information."

"Believe me, even now there are goblin teams searching for Gormog and his family," I said. "Even if they return and report killing us, they will be interrogated. They'll not survive it. How long do think these parents can keep our secrets when the Demon Lord or his demon assistants threaten to eat Sam? No, they're safer with us and so are we."

"Rufus is right," said Dutch. "The Demon Lord will begin his interrogation by eating Sam."

"Isn't possible they've already communicated our exact location?" Beca said. "Besides, we can't be sure they haven't been followed."

"You forgot what Buck said: they'd be here already." Dutch said. "Intentionally or not, they may have already led the Demon Lord to our door," said Beca, always the realist. "The enemy could be patiently waiting for the right time."

"If you're right, what do we do now?" Buck said.

"I still think you're overthinking this, Beca, my dear. To be cautious, let's make sure Wendy and Little Muppin sleep by the front door, which they do instinctively, right? Those pups will smell the enemy long before we see them and give us ample warning," said Dutch.

"And then we hightail it outta here in those pneumatic tubes in our bedrooms," said Buck. "That's a no-brainer."

"Buck's right," Beca said, "But where to? This is such a nice location. Would be a shame to leave the best damn safe house three miles beneath the earth."

"We have more than one safe house on the surface that we can retreat to." Dutch said. "And whether you believe Gormog or not, the bad guys probably think the three of them are dead, or AWOL. We can relax, ok? Those lupines look like they've got to crap. They've been farting their heads off. One lighted match and we're done for. "

"Did you know that methane gas from lupine shit powers the goblin communities in the High Kingdom, according to legend?" Petey said.

"Lupine farts may be the fuel of legend," said Dutch. "But if anyone lights his pipe, this quest will end in a mushroom cloud. Someone take those dogs out to crap."

"I thought it was your turn, Dutch," I said.

"I thought that it was your turn, Rufus," said Buck.

"I thought it was your turn, Buck," said Beca.

"I thought it was your turn, Arnie," said Burt.

"I thought it was your turn, Burt," said Arnie.

"I thought it was your turn, Petey," said Chad.

"I thought it was your turn, Chad," said Petey.

"Enough of this foolishness," said Dutch. "According to your schedule, Rufus, it's your responsibility to take those beasts out to crap!"

"You win," I said. "I'll take the little darlings out for their constitutional."

Six tunnels converged at our front door. I walked Wendy and little Muppin about 400 yards down a tunnel we had already explored, one we *wouldn't* be returning to. I hoped it would be far enough away not to smell the poop from our pad, but then lupine poop was quite potent. What's more, lupine crap did NOT glow in the dark, so their crap would also serve as an early warning mechanism, as I knew we'd hear goblins cursing even 400 yards out once they stepped in it.

I waited while Wendy released about five pounds of the worst smelling crap known to man, excluding dragon crap, or Buck's crap. Of course, I have no idea what the best smelling crap smells like — probably like the worst smelling crap. After all, a crap by any other name would smell as foul. Little Muppin deposited a respectable two pounds.

I let the lupines in while I took off my shoes, and returned to a family room that smelled like chocolate. I saw Sam on the floor with Wendy and little Muppin, petting them both while he was studying a large map, at least five feet in every direction. He was so focused on it that he didn't hear me sneak up on him.

"What'cha looking at little buddy?" I said.

"It's a Star Map of our galaxy," He said. "Did you know there are more than 200 billion stars in the Milky Way?"

"Yeah? I had heard it was closer to 400 billion," I said.

"You may be right. I only know that you sure can't see the stars from the tunnels," said Sam.

"An accurate observation. Then why do you care so much about something you've never seen?" I said.

"No, I saw them once when I was ten. That was six years ago when we traveled here from the Senator's coal mines in Tennessee. I popped up outside in the middle of the Smoky Mountains, just before we entered the Underground Highway, and I looked up at saw the Milky Way and I was never the same."

"Why are you so interested in the stars?"

"I want to be an astronomer," he said. "Our little planet travels around our little star, with billions of planets circling billions of stars across the night sky. I thought maybe there was a star with a planet, where a kid like me could look at them every night without having to hide underground his whole life."

"I hate to break it to you, Sam," I said, "but the light you see from the stars is really, really old light. Light that's been traveling for millions of years at 186,000 miles per second, just to reach us! It's possible all we see is the light and those stars are long dead, gone forever?"

"You're too pessimistic," Sam said.

"Maybe," I said. "I've been accused of worse."

"The stars are not gone!" Sam said defiantly. "They're not dead! I know how long their light's been traveling. They're still up there and I'm going to study them someday. I'm going to be an astronomer. I just know it."

A teenage goblin boy who had seen the stars once in his life, and who longs to become an astronomer. I thought I'd heard it all. Dammit, this kid was going to be an astronomer, if it was in my power. Besides, what the fuck do I really know about astronomy? Yeah, man, I'd love to meet some Vulcans some day. Could happen, right? I never expected to meet real biker trolls or elves from the The High Kingdom. Never say never, man.

As an afternoon snack, Gormog and Farsog prepared hot chocolate, espresso, crème brûlée, and raspberry blueberry fruit tarts. Also, homemade chocolate cookies, brownies, cinnamon rolls and ice-cold lemonade. Sweet. For dinner Farsog grilled Rib eye steaks and Gormog whipped up some garlic French Fries, with large chunks of delicious garlic stuck on every fry. Sam joined us while we talked about goblin fighting tactics in close quarters and how to best position ourselves to take advantage of the element of surprise in tunnel fighting. Yeah, we weren't strangers to that.

Beca was sleeping next to me, but it was platonic, just like a soldier in a combat situation. Even when women were finally allowed to fight on the front lines, my men and I always behaved with honor. She moved close to me and I said something I feared was stupid, that might turn her off, but I said it anyway.

"In the army I was in love with another soldier," I said.

"What was his name?" Beca said with a grin. I laughed.

"Sergeant Elizabeth Monroe," I said. "She was the supply sergeant in our unit. I was always requesting additional condoms and she thought that was funny, especially when she saw that the condoms were for water balloon fights I organized on the base."

"Oh," said Beca. " That is silly."

"Yeah, well anyway, I invited her to share her two weeks of shore leave with me in Oahu, Hawaii."

"I know where Oahu is, Rufus."

"Yes, of course. I thought Sergeant Monroe, Elizabeth, and I had a wonderful time. We held hands, walked along the beach, and made love three or four times a day."

"Wow, Rufus, I never knew you were such a stud," said Beca.

"I don't like to brag," I said. "But hardly a stud. Just your average red blooded American male."

"Three or four times a day?" Beca said. "Nothing average about that Stud Master. But please continue."

"On the day we were to return to Iraq she said to me, 'I love you Rufus, but I can't see you again.'"

" 'Why?' I said. 'I thought we loved each other. I thought we both pleased each other. You pleased me. You've made me the happiest man on planet earth, in our solar system, across the Milky Way.'

" 'I'm gay, Rufus.'

" 'So you're gay. I'm ecstatic!'

" 'Be serious, Rufus. I'm gay and I prefer sex with women. It's better for me.'

" 'Could have fooled me,' I said.

" 'I *did* fool you — because I love you. But you did not fool me, you see?'

" 'I see,' I said. 'It or I wasn't good enough for you?"

" 'Women are just better for me. They please me in a way no man can. I know that now because I've been with you.'

" 'Glad to be of service,' I told her. I was kind of bitter.

" 'Please Rufus. Don't make this more difficult for me. I wanted to please you. You're so funny, kind, and strong.'

" 'I'm not that strong,' I said, 'Because right about now I want to die.'

" 'I'm so sorry, Rufus. I'm so sorry,' she said.

"Then she left me at the gate and boarded her plane. That was the last time I saw Sergeant Elizabeth Monroe. When I returned to Iraq she had transferred. I didn't try to find out where. I just prayed that I'd die in battle and end the pain."

"Well, I'm *not* gay," said Beca as she pulled off her shirt, her bra and revealed her large beautiful brown breasts that looked me in the eyes. Then she wiped away my tears (of joy) and kissed me on the lips. I wrapped her in my arms and kissed her deep and removed the rest of her clothes. We made love three times before we fell asleep in each other's arms. I don't trust happiness, never will; but I was, in that moment, the happiest I ever expected to be in life.

The next day was quiet. We watched TV, read, napped, and played monopoly, scrabble, and chess until it was dinner. Then we set up the TV trays and turned on *Wheel of Fortune,* like millions of families in America. There were a couple of foldout chairs in the hall closet and Gormog and Farsog sat on these. Sam liked to lie on the floor with Wendy and little Muppin.

The dwarves wouldn't hear of Farsog or Gormog sitting on foldout chairs, not after the Coq au Vin she and Gormog prepared for everyone — and cleaning up after we all ate! Arnie gave his red velour La-Z-Boy recliner to Gormog, Petey his blue recliner to Farsog. I think I was never so proud of the dwarves as when they did this. Funny how you think you know someone until he surprises you — delightfully so. We ate a light dessert of lemon cake, with a thin, yet tart lemon frosting. Gormog and Farsog created less-is-more gastronomic miracles: frostings were thin not thick; hollandaise was drizzled not drenched; bacon was crisp not burnt; steaks were rare, never raw. They had the master chefs' touch and understood cooking in all its subtlety.

Farsog solved the Wheel's song lyrics puzzle, Neil Diamond's "Brother Love's Traveling Salvation Show in MAUI!" Well, Wheel wasn't sending Farsog to Maui anytime soon, but it got us all talking about one day taking a trip together to Maui when the quest had been fulfilled. There would be great places in Maui for Sam to stargaze. We drank another toast to those of our family we had lost: Ornery and Theo who were in our memories, and not forgotten.

Farsog even solved the final puzzle in the bonus round and would have won a brand new BMW Mini Cooper. We were all impressed with Farsog's talent at *Wheel* and pledged that if we survived this adventure we would do everything in our power to get her on "America's favorite show." Although, I wasn't sure whether America was ready for Farsog's fluorescent yellow skin. What the hell, she could wear long sleeves and cop to a bad tanning salon. It could happen.

Everyone was getting pretty damn fond of Gormog's family. Some might say it was the culinary skills of Gormog and his wife that opened the hearts of the dwarves. I'd seen almost the same exultation on their faces at Clucker's Chicken. But I fervently prayed that all of the dwarves truly loved Gormog's family. That their love went beyond their gastronomic infatuation with Farsog and Gormog's culinary skills. Was I expecting too much?

CHAPTER 51

tupid or not, when I considered how imminent my demise might be and had been on this quest, I decided to see the nation's capital before I was killed on the job, or on our next foray into the tunnels, or in some other unexpected encounter with monsters. My companions would be angry, but they'd get over it, assuming I returned alive. I had to get away and nothing was going to stop me. I wanted to see the Lincoln Memorial more than anything else, even more than the White House. Why? From everything I knew about Lincoln, more than any man in American history, I felt he had been chosen by God to be President of the United States at the most dangerous time in our history. He was also, along with Thomas Jefferson, the best presidential writer in history. The odds seemed astronomical to me that a one-term congressman, and self-educated country lawyer, could defeat a dozen Harvard trained politicians with every conceivable advantage (except brains), to win the Republican nomination and then defeat Stephen Douglas, his lifelong rival, for the Presidency. Lincoln was appointed by God and, like Christ, he paid for the sins of his people with his life. Perhaps an overstatement, but not by much.

Everyone was asleep. Beca was asleep next to me. What's the expression? Abstinence makes the heart grow fonder. It was true for us. My love for her was so intense, so immeasurable, and I adored her so that I could wait, although I didn't have to, until we pledged our eternal love before our friends and family: the dwarves, Dutch, and God. Did those last few sentences sound like horseshit to you? Reads like horseshit to me. We made love again and it was the best experience of my life. She had a rockin' body and didn't need to shape-shift into anyone else. She couldn't get any hotter. Just standing next to her gave me a pulsing hard-on like a jackhammer. And no one said a word about our lovemaking: not ten snoring dwarves or a 1,500 year-old wizard sleeping in the next room. It was the best thing about this crazy quest. I only hoped I lived long enough to marry her and that she would consent to be my wife, as she hinted before.

With that thought, I tiptoed over to a pneumatic tube, opened its door, and stepped inside. I decided to leave at night when everyone was asleep and hang out at an all-night coffee shop until morning. There was a Denny's not far from the entrance to the garage where we parked the limo. At daybreak I'd take a cab to the National Mall and see the National Archives where the Constitution and the Declaration of Independence were housed. I also wanted to see the animals of the world at the Smithsonian, stuffed though they were, poor little buggers. From there I'd walk down the Mall to the Lincoln Memorial, making periodic stops along the way before my White House tour. I had contributed fifty bucks for President McClintock's reelection. I wanted to see if he had spent my money wisely.

I entered a pneumatic tube in one of the empty bedrooms and pressed the "escape" button. It actually said, "PRESS NOW TO ESCAPE." Where was the *NOW* button? I didn't see it anywhere! Just kidding. I was impressed with the pod's operational simplicity. I pressed the button and with a schwooosh I flew through four miles of solid rock. I prayed that I wasn't too *portly* and that it didn't get stuck somewhere in the middle of the journey. I was confident that unsticking a pneumatic tube in solid rock was beyond the expertise of my companions. Thank God the tube stopped at ground level at precisely my height, in an obscure section of the underground parking lot. I saw the limo off in the distance, with its missing sunroof and mangled trunk — still parked in the same spot. Geez, that handicapped placard commanded respect.

As soon as I stepped out, the tube schwoooshed back down, and a piece of concrete slid over the opening leaving no trace of its existence. How the hell do I recall the tube when I need it? Hadn't figured that one out yet. Probably something simple I overlooked, I hoped. Just in case, I pulled a couple of uneaten Cheetos I had in my shirt pocket and stepped on them where the tube was. At least I had an approximate location.

I was right. Denny's was 200 yards from the garage. It was still dark when I emerged from the underground and I walked quickly in the cold. I looked up at the night sky and the bright stars and tried to feel the wonder Sam felt the first time he saw them. How much we take for granted. How wonderful it was to be above ground, out of a subterranean safe house buried miles underground. The freedom from the claustrophobic feeling even of our comfy little home was a miracle. I breathed deeply of the night air and thanked God for his deliverance.

Had to be 45 degrees outside and that's damn cold for a Californian. The street was deserted as I went into the restaurant. I ordered the Grand Slam Slugger: two buttermilk pancakes (well done), two bacon strips, two sausage links, two eggs, and hash browns. It also included orange juice and free coffee refills — all for only $10.95! The deal of the century. You can't beat it. True, nothing was as good as Gormog's pancakes, but I smothered my Denny's pancakes in butter and "healthy," but pretty damn tasty sugar-free syrup.

From my booth, I looked outside, up to the heavens while I ate, as if the pancakes were manna, a blessing from the Lord, as indeed they were. The sugar-free syrup was a nod to a healthier lifestyle that I was thinking more about since Beca and I were now a couple. Although, healthy or not, in my experience sugar-free anything was a dicey proposition: often enough, it could give you supernova-like anal explosions.

With a full belly, I relaxed, drank my third coffee refill, and read the *Washington Post* until 8:30. Then I took a cab and was initially planning to see the National Archives first, which opened at 9am and then on to the Natural History Museum at the Smithsonian, which opened at 10. As I was riding in the cab I was suddenly assailed by my thoughts. I was feeling like an idiot for leaving. Who was I doing this for? Myself? Or someone else? It was a huge risk I was taking and my better instincts said I was being a fool by putting the quest in jeopardy just to satisfy an itch to see the Lincoln Memorial and The White House. Why? Could the Demon Lord be fucking with my mind again? I was closer to him now than I had ever been since I first encountered him. I was in Washington, D.C.. He was in Washington, D.C. and now the vice president. Could he, the new VP be influencing me — even directing my thoughts somehow?

I decided to have the cab drop me off at the Vietnam Memorial, which was only a few hundred feet from Abe. It was too late to turn back now, even if the Demon Lord had reached inside my mind to affect my judgment, never my strongest quality. And judgment is everything, isn't it? I thought I'd spend less time at the Lincoln Memorial than at the National Archives or the Natural History Museum. Besides, I would get some good exercise on the Washington Mall trekking back to the Natural History Museum. Plus I had five hours before my White House tour began and that should be plenty of time to see everything. But the question lingered in my mind the entire time: was I being set up — or just setting myself up? Time would tell.

It was early November, just a week or so after the election, and many of the trees were barren, but a few retained their beautiful fall colors of red and gold, but it was damn cold, which is any temperature below 60 for a Californian.

At the Vietnam Memorial I spent most of my time wiping away my tears reading the names of the thousands of men and women, really boys and girls, killed in that pointless war. The black marble memorial rose from the ground like Death himself to accuse the living. More than 50,000 lives were lost in the Vietnam War. And what memorial would the government erect to hide its shame from the families of the men and women who lost their lives in two pointless Iraqi wars, with another ongoing, unwinnable war in Afghanistan? I tried to pay my respects without spending too much time at the Vietnam Memorial, worried I might slip into a PTSD fugue of my own. And that could be catastrophic because I had to stay alert to survive my little outing, or what felt more and more like poor judgment. So I paid my respects and walked quickly to the Lincoln Memorial.

The steps leading up to the Lincoln Memorial were only a few hundred feet from the entrance to the Vietnam Memorial. I was wearing a Boston Red Sox windbreaker, and my old BoSox cap pulled down low to cover my face. That's right, I'm from L.A. and love the Dodgers, but I wear a BoSox hat; for when they broke the Curse of the Bambino in 2004, and won the World Series, beating the mighty St. Louis Cardinals, I was forever a fan. Anyway, I noticed a strange looking man and woman sitting on the steps of the memorial eating store bought tuna sandwiches, drinking Coca-Colas, and watching everyone as if they were waiting for a sign from someone or something. They made me nervous because their faces were also hidden by hats. I was afraid. I knew from Farsog that the Demon Lord had texted my picture to his crew. I only hoped that they weren't waiting for me to appear on the steps of the Lincoln Memorial. That would be too coincidental, even for this paranoid Chosen One.

I was in the middle of the 58 marble steps leading to Abe. I was looking at Abe's thoughtful and sad face before I was aware that a woman had approached me; her red straw hat covered most of her face. Her face was protected from the cold by a crocheted grey shawl, and she wore what I guessed was an 18th century skirt down to her ankles. Not that I know a damn thing about

18th century women's fashion. Was she part of a historical reenactment troupe? She sure looked the part. Except for her straw hat she looked like Dolly Madison on a Hostess Bakery package. *God,* I thought, *I'd love a Hostess Dolly Madison Zinger right now, with a big glass of cold milk, whole milk, not that tasteless, nonfat 1% watered down swill.* A Zinger is a Twinkie with vanilla frosting on top. A Zinger could be a panacea for most of the world's ills, if only mankind understood that peaceful, joyful feeling after consuming five or ten with a couple of glasses of cold milk. At any rate, the old broad wasn't more than five feet tall. In a squeaky, halting, high pitched, irritating voice she croaked, "Excuse me, kind sir, do you have the time?"

"It's 10:15 ma'am," I said.

"Thank you very much!" she said.

"My pleasure and may God bless America," bullshit that I said for no earthly reason other than to be nice and acknowledge the old hag's 18th Century Colonial threads. It was my undoing. I should have kept my big mouth shut.

She left and I continued up the stairs, huffing and puffing, when I heard my voice again. I turned around and the same old hag held a tape recorder and was replaying our conversation to a tall man whose face was hidden by a blue straw hat. And then, of all things, they replayed part of my conversation with the demon I'd killed on the road and compared it to my, "And May God Bless America" horseshit. That dead demon's partner in the sky had recorded our conversation! Geez, technology could fuck you up royally these days.

And what's worse, you ever get that loosy-goosy acidic feeling in the pit of your stomach in stressful moments? Should have never used that sugar free maple syrup shit at Denny's. It's just pure chemicals and now, goddammit, I had a case of the squirts. You try to be good with your diet and, goddamn it, you windup with the shits. You know the feeling. It practically guarantees an anal explosion with the blast radius of Mount St. Helens. And I had it big time, but it had to wait when I heard: *"Aiiee!! Aiiee!!* The Chosen One!!" said the now hysterical hag.

Aiiee always made me laugh, whenever it appeared in *The High Kingdom*, functioning as a cry of dismay and maybe a battle cry for, "Kill! Kill!! Kill!!!" It's an absurd literary expression that only appears in fantasy novels. No soldier, no fighter, in fact *no one* in real life would scream *Aiiee!* He might say, what dah fuck! Or, for fuck's sake. Or, fuckity fuuuucccck! Or, oh fuuuucccck! Or, I'm going to fuck you up! Or, oh, fuck me! Or, fuck you! Or, fuckity fuck. Or, a simple drawn out, fuuuuuuccccccckkkkk! Or, I'm so fucked. Or, I just *shit* my pants. Or, I'll kill you muthafucker. Or, you mutherfucker! Or, you fucking motherfucker! Or, fuck you! Or, my personal favorite, MOM! Whatever. I found it funny and calming in a fucked-up situation to imagine someone shouting *Aiiee! Aiiee!* Though until now I never thought I'd hear it in public.

It wasn't so funny, though, when I turned and saw the woman in the blue hat running up the stairs, *fast*. Problem was, she was twice her original height, carrying a Glock 9MM in her left hand and a three-foot hatchet in her right, a she-troll with a Glock. Fuckity Fuck! Why are Glocks the weapon of choice for every crazy, murderous motherfucker? Why? Because there's no weapon of mass destruction easier to conceal. In the wrong hands you could kill thirty people in less than thirty seconds.

"Trolls," I said. "What rotten luck." They'd found me. I could only assume more were on the way.

My father once said to me, "There is no such thing as an ugly woman." He obviously never met a troll bitch. I'd heard female trolls were nastier than the males, if that was possible, and that they would do nasty sexual things to their male captives. I'll spare you the details. This one just wanted to cut off my head. Her hat blew off and I could see her face with its black boils and one large yellow cat's eye in the middle of her forehead, which explained the hat. I met her in the middle of the staircase. Not the best location for a fight. Her male companion, also a one-eyed troll was at the bottom of the stairs and got off three rounds from his Glock. Demon Slayer blocked two of the bullets and bounced one back into his eye, blinding him. I retreated quickly down the steps just in time to cut off his head before his eye grew back.

I must have killed the troll's mate because she screamed loud enough to hear her from the Oval Office, plus it attracted a group of Japanese tourists. She followed me down the stairs seeking revenge. At least I was fighting on level ground. I knew more of the Demon Lord's troops were on the way. I didn't have much time before I'd be overwhelmed. I had to kill the troll-bitch ASAP.

She was fast and got off six rounds from her Glock. Lucky for me Demon Slayer reacted faster than thought, parried, blocked, and obliterated the bullets on impact. Then she blitzed me, thinking her height and weight advantage were enough to overwhelm me. I backed up a few steps and flowed with my enemy. I took advantage of her hurried forward motion to deftly step to my side and cut off her wrist, sending her wrist and Glock flying into the middle of the tourists, some of who snapped pictures of the severed wrist. I think they were attaching the pic to an email for friends and family back home. Thank God, no one, yet, asked for a selfie or tried to get close enough to take one.

The Japanese tourists must have thought it was some kind of show put on by the Smithsonian, some bullshit historical reenactment. That is until the green pus-blood from the troll's wrist, flew on the women's shoes; a few of the women puked in the nearby planters. But the men thought it was all great fun. They must have just arrived from a theme park because they shouted, "Unraversal Studio! Ha!Ha! Unraversal Studio!! Hai! Hai! Domo Arigato!! Hai! Hai!!" Then more continuous camera shutters popping off like automatic weapons. Fucking tourists. Oh, wait, I was a fucking tourist, too. Fucking tourists are all the same. They all want a show.

The troll-bitch held a medieval ax in her left hand. At one end of the ax was the ax blade, but at the other end was a six-inch pike with a chain attached to a mace, with four-inch razor sharp spikes, looking oh so very painful. So I cut off that arm, too. But by this time the wrist and hand had grown back and she held a sword in that hand. Trolls were nothing if not resilient scum.

"Banzai! Banzai!" said three Japanese men from a safe distance. The muthafuckers knew this was the real deal, not some goddamn Revolutionary War reenactment. A few of the women were also taking continuous pictures, snapping away in delight. Fucking tourists and their cameras.

But back to the fight: The freaking troll bitch was pretty handy with a sword. I underestimated her. I blocked most of her blows, but one slipped in and sliced my left arm.

"Ouch," I said without emotion.

From the corner of my eye I could see Japanese men exchanging money. In general, I knew Asians loved to gamble (try getting a hotel room in Vegas in December, much less a poolside cabana). It seemed in poor taste to handicap my survival chances, especially while my life hung in the balance.

A crowd was building on the National Mall, all stopping to watch the action. I couldn't believe that everyone looked so nonplussed about a one-eyed troll bitch, and her ten-foot headless boyfriend — and all the green pus and blood. Maybe they thought it was all special effects. You know, fake blood and pus. Those Hollywood special effects bastards can do anything, right? Whoever had to clean up the mess wouldn't think so.

We fought back and forth and I could see the Demon Lord's troops in the distance getting closer. I had to finish her off fast. When she tried to slash my stomach, I pinned her sword to the ground and stepped on her blade with my Nike All Pros. She had nowhere to go. To her credit, her other arm had grown back and she pulled a hidden gun under her blouse, but I was faster and cut off her head. The green pus-blood sprouting from her neck like a geyser had the Japanese photographers in a shark-like frenzy.

"Domo Arigato, domo arigato," shouted the winners who had bet on me and were counting their winnings. The cavalry was now only about 500 yards in the distance. Some of the Japanese surrounded me for my autograph, and a selfie. I couldn't linger. I was about to sprint when a voice rang out:

"Drop the sword and put your hands in the air where I can see them. NOW!" Damn! A D.C. Mall cop had his weapon trained on my head. The autograph seekers dropped to the ground. Fucking cowards.

I lifted my sword and took one step towards him before he shot me. I blocked the bullets with Demon Slayer, and ricocheted a bullet into his shooting arm, which prevented him from shooting me again or chasing me. I could never seriously hurt him. Cops are heroes in my lexicon.

With the cop incapacitated and the Demon Lord's minions only 200 yards out, I ran due north, west of the Lincoln Memorial on Henry Bacon Drive as fast as my legs would carry me, again, surprisingly fast for a fat dude. I was dismayed to see at least twenty monsters gaining on me. Then my cell phone rang. "You're alive," said Dutch. "I was sure you'd be dead by now."

"Sorry to disappoint. Ok, I fucked-up."

"Where are you now, Mr. Fuck-up?"

"I'm on Henry Bacon Drive, running North pursued by five trolls in pink sweatpants, fourteen goblins dressed as old ladies, and one demon George Washington impersonator. I'm not kidding, Dutch, and they're closing in fast."

"Have you killed anyone?"

"Two trolls."

"Are you injured?"

"A nasty scratch on my arm that's mostly healed."

"Make a right on Constitution, a left on 17th street, and a right on Pennsylvania where you'll see a man in a canary yellow sports jacket and a green bow tie. He's a friend. He will help you from there. Good luck," said Dutch who hung up. Frankly, I expected a little more moral support.

On the corner of 17th street and Pennsylvania was a middle-aged man in a canary yellow sports jacket, a Yankees' cap, and an emerald green bow tie. His scarf was a rainbow of woven silk, and he wore bright purple earmuffs against the cold. He looked like quite the dandy, except for shoulders like a linebacker. He didn't say a word, just motioned to follow him. I was exhausted and slowed down when he spoke.

"If you want to survive, friend," he said, "pick up the pace."

"'Friend,' I just ran five blocks and killed two trolls. I'm a little winded, Ok?" I said, barely keeping up with him as he dashed halfway down Pennsylvania Avenue before making a quick right, down a flight of stairs leading inside the backside of an unknown white building.

"You're out of shape," he said.

"No shit, Sherlock. Who are you?" I asked. He just laughed.

By the time the enemy made a right on Pennsylvania, we were traveling underground.

"Are we where I think?" I asked.

"Yes, we're five stories below the West Wing, about to walk past the White House kitchen. Would you like something to eat?"

"A ham sandwich would be nice, with deli mustard."

"Funny, that's how the President likes it."

"Who are you?" I said, again.

"James Winters, Assistant to the Assistant to the Assistant Deputy Chief of Staff," he said. "At your service."

"All right, James Winters, Assistant to the Assistant to the Assistant Deputy Chief of Staff — where's the closest bathroom?"

"Right behind you," he said.

"Back in ten," I said, and went inside. Fortunately, there were grab bars for the handicapped. I held on to them with all of my strength and set off an anal explosion worthy of the Chosen One. Good thing for the grab bars. Without them I would have shot through the roof like an ICBM. "All better," I said with a smile on my face, happy with the result, and happy I had a chance to catch my breath while sitting on the throne.

"I'm so relieved," Mr. Winters said with a painful frown as he breathed in the fumes from the bathroom.

"Me, too."

We walked up four more flights of stairs and into an office just small enough to be the office of the Assistant to the Assistant to the Assistant Deputy Chief of Staff. James Winters' office was as neat as the man himself. Books in his bookcase, pictures on the wall, folders, and papers on the desk were all arranged with precision by this quiet, secretive, and uncommunicative man. I say secretive because the *Reader's Digest*, *People Magazine*, and Harlequin Romance novels in his office obviously belied his intelligence and his title, or so it appeared. My ham sandwich with deli mustard arrived soon after I was seated. The chef also added a bag of potato chips, half a dill pickle, and an iced tea with lemon. Very thoughtful. Mr. Winters took off his hat, scarf, and his earmuffs. His ears looked funny as if the natural curvature had been altered. His sky blue eyes, and an all but hidden, until now, purple aura confirmed my suspicion.

"You're a bloody elf!" I said.

"Indeed he is," said a voice from behind. I turned around and my eyes practically popped out of their sockets.

"Lord Reggie! Are you the..."

"The Assistant to the Assistant Deputy Chief of Staff, Rufus, and at your service, Oh Chosen One," said Reggie, with a grin as wide as the Potomac.

"And I'm his assistant," Mr. Winters said.

"But why?" I said.

"Why what?" said Lord Reggie.

"Why doesn't the President and Congress know what we know about the Demon Lord and his goblins and trolls chasing me in the middle of Washington, D.C.?! To say nothing about the infestation throughout this great country."

"Elf SEALs are even now destroying the monsters who chased you. As for the 'national' infestation, Congress can't agree on the precise location of 11 million illegal immigrants," said Mr. Winters.

"For thirty years," said Lord Reggie, "we've postponed immigration reform in the United States. Do you think the President or Congress would know what to do with *two million goblins* living under our national parks? Or with the man- eating biker trolls crisscrossing the nation's highways?"

"But they are here," I said. "You can't ignore them!"

"The President wouldn't believe us, Rufus," said Reggie. "That said, we do have soldiers hunting both. The goblins keep to themselves mostly. But the trolls are a bigger problem."

"Shouldn't we at least tell President McClintock he's in great danger when he is in the company of Vice President Ross?" said Dutch, who had just entered the room.

"You mean Vice President-*elect* Ross," I said. "I'm sorry I screwed up."

"Strange, but it may have been a blessing that you called out the hidden strength of the Demon Lord in the city," said Dutch. "At least we know with certainty that a great many of his agents roam freely in the nation's capital."

"Yes, the forces of evil are gathering," Reggie said. "We couldn't stop Ross' election as Vice President, but we still can protect the President and give the Chosen One a chance to kill the Vice President-elect before he is sworn into office."

"How so?" I said, regretting the question and afraid of the answer.

"Funny you should ask," said Mr. Winters.

"We have a job for you and your comrades," said Lord Reggie. "There is a new housing development for veterans; it's far enough away from Camp David to meet the law, but still close enough for easy access by a rogue strike force. Last year Senator Ross attached a rider to a Veterans' Benefits bill, which included a new affordable housing development for veterans and their families. But the homes are not for vets. Fell creatures occupy the homes. We suspect the Demon Lord is trying to get as close to Camp David as legally possible. He will try to kill the president before the inauguration. The president doesn't know we've surrounded him with an Elf SEAL detail, even though my men know it's a suicide mission. At least they'll give the President his best chance at survival.

"The Demon Lord, now Vice President-elect is trying to schedule a meeting with the President at Camp David. But the Demon Lord first wants a small, tough, specialized army nearby to protect him if, especially if he can't get past my men and murder McClintock. House trolls are that specialized force: they're flexible, smart, and strong. He's housing a small strike force near the Presidential compound, approximately twenty houses occupied by an unknown number of house trolls. Your team will destroy the trolls, burn the houses, and remove the threat. A few members of Captain Danny's Navy SEALs have volunteered to serve as backup. You'll coordinate with them as the time approaches."

"House trolls?" I said. "Are they different than Biker Trolls?"

"Not much different," said Dutch. "Just smaller."

"No, Dutch, that's not accurate," said Lord Reggie. "House trolls are smaller than Biker Trolls, but also smarter and faster: fast as a striking snake. Otherwise you kill them the same way: cut off their heads."

"Smarter and Faster: fast... as... a... striking...snake," I said. "Cheez Whiz! Yeah, to me that doesn't sound like 'not much different,' but a 'whole lot different.' Inasmuch as biker trolls are slow and stupid, 'smarter and faster' sounds like a quantum fucking-leap of difference."

"You *are* the Chosen One, correct?" said Mr. Winters, with an expression of disbelief and disdain.

"That's right, bub," I said, pissed. "Why? Do you want to fight the house trolls? You're welcome to join us, Mr. Assistant to the Assistant to the Assistant Deputy Chief of Staff...Yeah, that's what I thought."

"Rufus, you and your comrades will have the Elf SEAL backup," said Lord Reggie, who looked like he was struggling not to laugh, or maybe cry. Tough to say: I inspired both.

"Personally," I said. "I'd rather have Elf SEAL frontup, not backup, Lord Reggie. What the fuck is up with that? They're government employees, right, like *you*. You both work for the good of the American people and I'm one of those people."

"Rufus, you're out of line. You forget to whom you are speaking," Dutch said, angry at my tone with the Elf Lord.

"No I haven't. Not in the land of *E Pluribus Unum*," I said. "I'm an American citizen and it's my right, my duty to speak truth to power, all due respect to the Assistant to the Assistant Deputy Chief of Staff, Lord Reggie. I love Lord Reggie and respect him. And don't forget to whom you're talking, *Dutch*. I'm the *Chosen One*. You show me some respect. I'm the guy who's been drafted to kill this Demon Lord-fuck. I want Elf SEALs front and center baby, full participants, not hanging back until the battle's done."

"Well spoken, Rufus. It will be as you've requested," said Lord Reggie, calmly, unperturbed. Such was the measure of the elf.

"Regards to Lady Katherine," I said.

"She sends her regards as well," said Lord Reggie.

"Really?"

"No."

CHAPTER 52

Of course, everyone was pissed at me when I returned to our hidey-hole, including Dutch who had less respect for me, and more for Lord Reggie after our recent exchange, which was fine. I was right and they were wrong. Dutch would get over it. Lord Reggie was long past it.

"What the fuck were you thinking?" said Beca who punched me in the arm, *hard*. The bruise lasted weeks.

"I had to see the Lincoln Memorial," I said. "Lincoln is my hero. He saved this country from destruction."

"Yeah and you almost doomed our quest to destruction with your selfish desires," she said. "We've all been worried sick about you."

"Yes, very selfish of you, Mr. Chosen One," said Gormog.

"Gormog, you can call him Mr. Fat White *Fuck-up*," said Beca.

"Heard you chopped the heads off two trolls," said Buck.

"I did," I said.

"Good work, laddie," said Buck. "What's this I hear about house trolls near Camp David?"

"Lord Reggie is monitoring their activity," said Dutch who took a big bite out of a Gormog famous Cinnamon Danish. "It's a fake veteran's housing development that the Demon Lord is filling with house trolls. The Demon Lord is creating a house troll strike force close to Camp David to assassinate President McClintock."

"Guess whose job it is to kill them?" I said.

"The perfect mission for Lord Reggie's Navy SEALs, right?" said Burt.

"Wrong! Next guess," I said, as I cut into the super thick honey smoked ham steak and perfectly poached egg on one of Gormog's lemon poppy seed muffins.

"Not us I hope," said Arnie.

"Ding, ding, ding, ding, ding, ding! Give that dwarf an extra cinnamon bun," I said. "Yep, it's us. We get to destroy the trolls. Lucky us, lucky me, lucky you, lucky fucking quest!"

"House trolls are a bitch to kill," said Buck. "Slippery, fast, and tough for their size. Damn, what an evil fortune."

"Ah, they're not so tough," said Beca the Optimist. "I've killed plenty without too much effort."

CHAPTER 53

Seven days came and went and no one was eager to leave our comfortable little hideaway and no one asked us to. It was beginning to feel like the good old days long before this insane adventure, long before I'd even heard of Mosul, Fallujah, and Kabul — those rat holes where so many of my buddies died.

It felt like I was unemployed again, looking for a job, but only half-ass. Ah, the joys of unemployment, that much maligned state, that seasonal bliss, that happy time, that true blessing. After my tours of duty, I never had a moment's guilt making a few extra bucks at the government's expense. If the rent hadn't been due every month, I'd still be on the dole. I never woke up before eleven, Monday through Sunday. Then I'd walk down to Johnny's News & Magazine stand, right next to Benny's Falafel & Schwarma stand, where I'd buy an *L.A. Times*, a lamb schwarma, homemade hummus, and study the latest issue of *Juggs* magazine. Talk about paradise. The only thing better would be buying two schwarmas: one for me, one for the Juggs model, and making love to them both back at my place. Sadly, you can't always get what you want.

From Johnny's I might go to Starbucks, or better still, walk off the schwarma on a two-mile stroll down Ventura Blvd to Denny's.

If I felt like lunch, I'd order the Bacon Avocado Cheeseburger, medium rare, with a side of Thousand Island dressing as dippin' sauce. Everything is better with bacon and Thousand. Or if I felt like breakfast, I'd order Moons Over My Hammy, Denny's classic ham and scrambled eggs sandwich, featuring melted Swiss and American cheese, embedded hash browns on grilled sourdough. Over the years I think I've memorized most of the menu. But I digress.

Evenings were spent with Beca, Dutch, the dwarves, and Gormog's family talking over the finer points of close quarter combat, small arms fire, battle tactics, and the quickest way to cut off a house troll's head.

Later, Gormog taught Arnie and Burt how to make the Cinnamon Danish we had come to love. But it just didn't taste the same. It didn't have Gormog's love baked into it. You know what I mean. At night there was always *Jeopardy!*, or *Wheel*. Some nights we'd all watch a *Law & Order* marathon. Sam spent a lot of his time with his star charts. Most of the dwarves sat in front of the TV the entire day watching reruns of the *Twilight Zone, Cheers, I Love Lucy*, classic *Star Trek, Blue Bloods*, and *Gunsmoke*. They were glued like five year-olds to the lousy 15 inch black and white TV. According to Farsog, they got lousy TV reception in the Demon Lord's hive, except for *Lunch with Your Demon Lord* on DLTV.

Unfortunately, the time had arrived. We gathered our weapons in the early morning and headed out to destroy the house trolls. We took the escape pods to the surface where Lord Reggie had two limos waiting to take us to a large guardhouse on the perimeter of Camp David. The housing development was finished. Lord Reggie said most of the House Trolls had moved in. This was our best opportunity to destroy them all at once. We had all the trolls, all the rats in one nest, although that's an insult to rats everywhere.

We hoped to kill them all in one very long day of fighting. We had the Elf SEALs as backup (and frontup) to help us destroy the trolls.

We decided that Farsog, Gormog, and Sam would stay behind. The guardhouse was fully stocked with food and drink, but Farsog and Gormog made personal brown-bag lunches for each of us for the daytrip and you won't believe what they included, but I'm going to tell you anyway because it was such a blessing that we spared their lives and I don't mean just because they were good cooks: In every bag was their secret recipe for fried chicken that Gormog learned at the Cordon Bleu: fried chicken that put Clucker's to shame. In every brown bag there was a cinnamon Danish, Lays BBQ potato chips, twelve slices of sharp cheddar and sesame seed crackers, and fresh squeezed lemonade, hand-poured into fourteen individual thermoses. There were M&M peanuts for quick energy and the People's Choice Teriyaki beef jerky, everyone's favorite. Gormog's family would stay at the safe house, but we would take Wendy and little Muppin, who wasn't so little anymore.

Besides, dwarves had never sent women and children into battle, and Gormog was trained as a chef, not a soldier. Dwarves had 5000 years of experience killing trolls in the High Kingdom. It was in their DNA. Although none of the dwarves had ever seen a fighting shape shifter like Beca in battle or her take-no-prisoners attitude toward the enemy. However, everyone's attitude, including Beca's, was different toward Gormog and his wonderful family. The dwarves wouldn't risk losing such a blessing. It was the first time they had ever seen goblins as they saw themselves, right down to Sam's aspiration to be an astronomer.

As we were getting ready to leave, we watched TV coverage of President McClintock and the Vice President-elect. Both men lifted their hands together in unity at a barbecue on the President's ranch. All of the President's family, friends, and neighbors came out to celebrate their native son's reelection. Then we turned it off, depressed and frightened for the President's safety.

"Looks like we have our work cut out for us tomorrow," said Dutch.

"If nothing else," I said, "At least the Demon Lord won't be able to seize power by assaulting Camp David with a strike force of house trolls."

"I'm worried he may not need to," said Dutch. "If the Demon Lord gets past McClintock's Elf SEAL detail, he'll eat the President when no one's looking."

"*Now* you're telling me this? Yah gotta tell me this NOW! That's just fucking brilliant," I said, "We risk life and limb to eliminate a house troll military strike force that's all but superfluous if the Demon Lord decides to have the President for lunch instead."

"Don't tell me this is your first military campaign with a less than perfect objective," said Dutch.

"Nope. I've been on plenty of stupid missions, including this one." I said.

"Then deal with it my friend," said Buck. "Deal with it."

CHAPTER 54

One of the first signs that a neighborhood is infested with house trolls is the disappearance of pets. Even big dogs like the Great Dane and ferocious dogs like the Rottweiler have little chance against them. One house troll will allow the poor pooch to fasten its jaws on its rubbery troll's leg while the other troll sneaks up from behind and clubs the poor pooch to death. House trolls are five to six feet shorter than biker trolls, between 5 and 5 foot 3 inches for females and 5 foot 5 inches for males. However, it's a bitch to kill one because they're fucking fast. Like your biker troll, you've got to cut off their heads, but unlike your biker troll, they bob and weave like a prizefighter, making them tough little bastards to hit, much less decapitate. Plus they have social intelligence, too.

One curious fact about house trolls is that they're suckers for chocolate, especially See's dark chocolate with caramel and vanilla nougat, and See's dark chocolate raspberry truffles. More than See's candy, house trolls can't resist Girl Scouts or Girl Scout cookies, especially Thin Mints and Do-si-Dos. Nothing a house troll enjoys more than a dozen boxes of Thin Mints *and* a Girl Scout, both washed down with a couple gallons of cold (2%) milk.

Of course, if you don't have a Girl Scout or Thin Mints handy, House trolls are suckers for Jujubees, licorice, especially Red Vines, Big Hunk nougat bars, Milk Duds, Cherry Pez, Big League Baseball gum, Sweet Tarts, gummy bears, Raisinettes, peanut M&Ms, juicy fruit gum, Snickers, Milky Ways, Twinkies, Snow Balls, and People's Choice teriyaki beef jerky. BTW, me too.

There were only fifteen homes in the new housing development, not the twenty- five we had first thought. What a relief. Our plan was to go house-to-house selling Girl Scout cookies and candy. The homes in the new development ranged from 2,000 to 2,700 square feet, with three different floor plans that we studied while we waited for their completion and occupation. Each house had a large kitchen, which included a breakfast nook; there was a family room in front of the kitchen, facing the breakfast nook, a dining room adjoining a large living room facing the backyard, and one downstairs bathroom next to the staircase and front door. The upstairs had either three to four bedrooms, including the master bedroom. We had no idea how many trolls we'd encounter.

We used our guardhouse at Camp David as a staging area. Our intel failed to disclose, however, if was a major infestation, which meant more House trolls than we were expecting. House trolls were known to be independent and self-reliant, so we prayed there would not be any demons housed with them.

The Demon Lord created a real housing development, including streetlights, paved roads, plumbing, utilities, basketball hoops, lawn gnomes, and two car garages. The trolls were there to stay. Buck and I reconnoitered the neighborhood that night. We hid in the pine forest with our night vision goggles and scoped out the neighborhood.

"Cheez Wiz, Buck," I said, "Everything looks pretty quiet. Look at that! There's a Ford Minibus in every driveway. What the fuck does that mean?"

"It means there are more than two trolls per house," he said. "I'm sure glad we got two SEALs in each of our teams. Thanks for speaking up, Rufus." I guess he heard what I said to Reggie.

"Right," I said. "Two Elf SEALs *will* make a difference, but we'll be on our own, mostly, Buck."

"Agreed," he said, and shook his head. "When has a soldier not had to do more with less?"

"Ain't it the truth, brother. Ain't it the truth," I said, but still relieved like Buck that two SEALs on each of our teams would kill trolls right alongside us. Could save us worlds of hurt.

The house trolls were provided with everything to make the neighborhood look as American as apple pie. Adding to the logistical challenges was the fact that not only did mommy troll and daddy troll not drive to work everyday, but they also prowled the countryside and forest for stray dogs, cats, and hikers to eat. I'd never seen so many missing people and pet signs in the neighborhoods bordering this new troll community. This meant we had to also find and destroy house trolls prowling the area at night. Fortunately, Elf SEALs would handle it, quietly and efficiently.

The first house in the development was a beautiful two-story Tudor style home with large green shutters covering the windows on the first and second story. You couldn't a damn thing going on inside the home. There was an emerald green ivy bordering the sloping front lawn. Picture perfect like a house straight out of *Better Homes and Gardens*. They even had a three-foot metal lawn elf, which bore an uncanny resemblance to Lord Reggie! The house sat at the top of a short hill where the driveway sloped down to the sidewalk. The troll "family" had planted pink roses around their mailbox, which said "The Sacks." Every house had a "Vendors Welcome" sign glued just above the doorbell. "Dinner Welcome" would have been more accurate. I wondered how many free meals came right up to the door selling solar panels, magazines subscriptions, homeowner's insurance, or Girl Scout cookies? Whoever said no to free food? Not me.

Beca shapeshifted into a Girl Scout with Goblin-like features, with the scent of a Girl Scout goblin in "season." House trolls loved goblin meat in the High Kingdom. So why not a goblin-like Girl Scout, selling cookies? She was a genius.

Beca and I approached the first house.

Here's the thing: troll women, troll bitches, unlike goblin women, were more skilled and savage fighters than troll men. They were faster, more cunning, and ruthless. They did "stuff" to the body part of their living adversaries that are, frankly, unmentionable in polite, or any company. They possessed a rubbery strength that made them a bitch to kill (no pun intended). Thus Buck and the other dwarves warned me not to let my naturally tender heart lull me into a fatal attitude of compassion.

"When you've seen one, that's right, just one troll bitch cut off the testicles of your brother dwarf in battle and eat his balls like sushi, you'll know what to do. Or when you surprise two house troll bitches throwing soy sauce on dwarf tongue they're barbecuing on a hibachi grill, you'll know what to do." said Buck to me on the eve of battle.

Enough said. Ok, perhaps more than enough said. It's just like seeing an Iraqi woman running down the street toward your comrades. Do you yell at her to stop and hope she stops? If she doesn't stop, do you shoot her, hoping it's really a man disguised as a woman; or pray that she's wearing a suicide vest before you shoot her; or do take a chance that she just needs help and allow her to come within the kill zone before she pulls the pin on her grenade and murders all of your buddies? Let me tell you, the wrong decision can cost you a lifetime of regrets, of penitence, of guilt, of fucking PTSD dreams in the middle of the freakin' morning, afternoon, and night. Life is such a fucked-up thing. I gotta ask Christ about that when — or *if* I get to see him — which might be sooner than later. Didn't he say, "Those who live by the sword, die by the sword"? One more thing: House trolls usually have two eyes, but sometimes they only have one. You hoped that you'd encounter the one-eyed variety because the one-eyed house troll has lousy peripheral vision.

In each group, only two of us approached the door so as not to arouse suspicion. House trolls are wary fuckers. Beca rang the bell and a husband and wife troll team opened the door.

"Good morning, Mr. and Mrs. Sacks?" Beca asked.

"Hi there! Yes, I'm Harold Sacks and this is my wife Sandra," said Mr. Sacks with a burning cannibalistic lust in his eyes at the sight of Beca, who was balancing seven boxes of Thin Mints and Do-si-Dos, and wagging her ass at the same time.

"Hi Mr. and Mrs. Sacks! My name is Beca Gillespie and I'm with Girl Scout Troop 577. This is our troop leader and my dad, Robert Gillespie. Would you like to buy some Girl Scout cookies today?"

"Very nice to meet you, Beca and Mr. Gillespie," said Mr. Sacks, "We'd love to buy your cookies, but only if we can share some with you and your dad over a pot of delicious jasmine tea or cold milk. Do you have the time?"

"You bet!" said Beca, laying it on a little thick. Mrs. Sacks couldn't take her eyes off of me. She couldn't wait to sink her teeth into my fat gut after decapitating me. Yum, yum.

I couldn't blame Mr. Sacks. He wanted to eat Beca, and I wanted to make love to her in her cute little Troop 577 Girl Scout uniform. For now, though, I was her overweight, hapless father in a green Boy Scout's uniform two sizes too small, with "Troop Dad" in bold letters on my shirt covered in Merit Badges, five Bic pens in a pocket protector, pleated green shorts, black knee-high socks, black army boots, and for that added touch of authenticity, a genuine pot belly. As we entered the house, I made sure to leave the front door slightly ajar for the dwarves hiding just down the street.

"You both must be tired from all that walking," said Mrs. Sacks. "Why don't you dears have a seat on the couch while I prepare the tea and delicious cookies." Mr. Sacks followed her into the kitchen. We, Beca and her fat dad, must have looked like easy pickings for the Sacks and their relatives hiding upstairs — a veritable feast considering my girth alone.

House trolls are blitz attackers and these fuckers were no different. The second they entered the kitchen Beca reached for a Glock 9MM under her skirt, strapped against her pink panties (I watched her strap the gun to her panties that morning when she dressed. I still hadn't recovered).

"We ran out of Jasmine. I hope you enjoy Earl Grey my dears," said Mrs. Sacks, who sprang out of the kitchen with a three-foot machete and a Glock 7. Mr. Sacks had an MTech combat hatchet for up-close work. They both screamed "Aiieeee!!!" and lunged at us.

Beca shot out the eyes of Mrs. Sacks, blinding her long enough before her eyes could grow back to cut off her head with Mrs. Sack's own machete. I blocked Mr. Sacks's ax with Demon Slayer, stepped to my left, and cut off his head with a sideward motion.

To our dismay, four more House trolls leaped down the stairs to join the fight.

"HAVE ANOTHER COOKIE!" I yelled, which was the dwarves' and SEALs' cue to enter the fray. They came in front door behind the four trolls and cut off their heads posthaste.

When we arrived at the next house we were still dressed in our scouting uniforms, wiped clean of troll blood, as best we could. In this instance, we wore our official scouting backpacks that held our chainsaws. Our Glocks we kept more accessible: Mine was tucked into the back of my pants, held secure in my butt crack (TMI?). Beca's was, as I mentioned earlier, strapped to her baby-skin soft but muscular inner left thigh.

The name on the red mailbox said "The McCombs," which gave me an idea. Beca had shape shifted this time into a female adolescent mixed-race 15 year-old Girl Scout, with troll-like features. Hard to believe, but house trolls eat their own, especially a troll girl dressed as a Girl Scout.

A pretty woman (for a troll) with brown hair, dressed in khakis, penny loafers, and a cardinal red and gold USC sweatshirt answered the door. For free samples, I had an open box of Do-si-Dos. Who could resist?

"Good morning, I said. "I'm Jon McCallister, scoutmaster and leader of Troop 436, and this young lady is my very own daughter, Rebecca McCallister, Girl Scout extraordinaire, Special Grade

X46, with merit badges in self-defense, map reading, reconnaissance, astrophysics, housecleaning, and baking. Please, have a cookie."

"Good morning, Ma'am. We're selling Girl Scout cookies!" said Beca who saluted Mrs. McComb with an unofficial Girl Scout backward goosestepping greeting she invented as we stood at the door. She was a genius.

"Indeed," said Mrs. McComb.

"Indeed, greetings to the McCombs! I bring you good news and Do-si-Dos from Camp Girl Scout," said Beca, and bowed as she presented the McCombs with the small plate of Do-si-Do cookies.

"Hello darling, I'm Mrs. McComb, but please call me Betty," said the lady of the house. "And this is my husband Irving McComb. *You*, I mean *those* cookies look delicious."

"You did say, McComb, didn't you?" I said.

"Why yes, laddie, we're the McCombs from Dundee, Scotland," Irving McComb said, laying on his own bullshit Scottish accent a wee too thick.

"Why we're the McCallisters from Perth, Scotland. We must be related clans!" I said.

"CLANLY!" we all shouted together.

"Aye, 'tis a small world indeed," I said, with a terrible Scottish burr.

"Aye, indeed!" said Irving McComb, his red eyes burning at the sight of Beca, who was doing a wee little sexy Scottish jig in her excitement over our shared heritage — and also calculating that a hunger- and sex-crazed house troll is a careless house troll.

We the "McCallisters" and they the "McCombs" were tossing "indeeds" and "ayes" around like free cookies.

"Aye indeed, Ma'am, or should I say Clan McComb? said Beca. "How many boxes of Thin Mints and Do-si-Dos would like you to buy today? Did you know that 15% of the proceeds go to support Girl Scouts in the Scottish Highlands?"

Beca was pouring on the bullshit at epic levels. She held up her assorted boxes of Girl Scout cookies. She was less than five feet now in her tight fitting Girl Scout uniform, by far the sexiest scout I'd ever seen.

Mr. McComb's eyes were fixated on Beca; and by the mad look in his eyes, he was already eating her.

"We'd love to help you *and* the girl scouts in the Scottish Highlands," said Mrs. McComb. "Please, come in and we'll buy all of your boxes of Thin Mints, Do-si-Dos, Savannah Smiles, and whatever else is in your backpacks. I'm going to the kitchen to get my checkbook. Honey, please bring our guests into the family room. Back in a flash with the check and some nice, hot, Earl Grey tea. Do you take sugar, Mr. McCallister? Sweetheart, could you put out some placemats for our guests?"

"Of course, sweetheart," Mr. McComb said, his nostrils flaring uncontrollably as he stared at Beca.

"Please, a little milk for my tea, if it's not too much trouble," I said.

"Straight up for me," said Beca. "With a splash of Glenlivet, if it's handy. Just kidding, haha."

"How's the Earl Grey coming, sweetheart?" said Mr. McComb,

"Can't do two things at once, sweetie pie," said Mrs. McComb from the kitchen.

We sat down on the couch in the family room. The lady of the house wasted no time in the kitchen.

"Find your checkbook, sweetikins?" said Mr. McComb to his wife who was making noisy metallic sounds in the kitchen, not exactly the sound teacups make.

"Be right there, lovey-dovey," she said to her husband.

Several things happened at once. Something flashed and thumped: it was a large, fat house troll that landed at the bottom of the staircase. And then another. And another. At the same time our companions, Arnie and Chad, burst through the front door, chain saws a blazing and cut off the heads of the three male trolls faster than you can say, "Thin Mints."

As they were decapitating the upstairs, now downstairs trolls, Mrs. McComb sprang from the kitchen wielding a four-foot scimitar, and foot long serrated steak knife. I was surprised it wasn't an Uzi, or at least a Glock, until I remembered Beca's earlier explanation: "Trolls are like us in one respect. They don't like bullets in their meat." However, her husband trained his Uzi on my head, just for convenience's sake.

Mrs. McComb swung her sword once at my head and I ducked and automatically swept out Demon Slayer, parried her next blow, stepped to my left and cut off her head. Her troll's head hit the floor like a bowling ball.

Beca ran to the front door where the rest of our friends, Larry, Buck, and Petey streamed in with their chainsaws, all except for Petey raced upstairs to kill four more house trolls. Mr. McComb first shots went wild as I dispatched his wife; but then he lost his Uzi and his hand when Petey cut it off with a chain saw. I finished the job by cutting of his head, which spurted green and black pus-like blood all over the McCombs' pristine white carpeting.

Alas, so much for the "wee" McCombs of Dundee.

It was tough, exhausting work going house to house. After the fifth house we didn't bother with "Earl Grey, if you please" or "You must try a Do-si-Do" or "Have another cookie" or any other pleasantry. We immediately killed the trolls who answered the door and the dwarves with their chain saws were followed by Wendy and little Muppin, both of whom were surprisingly good at ripping off trolls' heads. After we killed all of the trolls in each house, we doused the house with gasoline to burn down later. We discovered every garage was filled with MAC-10s, Glocks, ammunition, bazookas, a tank, and stinger missiles to shoot down any pain-in-the-ass helicopters the government might send to protect Camp David from assault.

Much to my surprise, I discovered I was a celebrity. Taped to the refrigerator in every house was a poster with my name and picture:

WANTED DEAD OR ALIVE
Rufus Timmons
AKA: "The Chosen One"
REWARD OFFERED

There were so many trolls that we weren't sure our chain saws would holdup. Thankfully, house trolls had less sophisticated battle skills, nothing like the dwarves' fight skills or the Total Quality Improvement (TQI) philosophy dwarves passed down to their children like mother's milk for the last hundred generations. You could count on house trolls following the same blitz pattern. However, unless you countered quickly, before you'd knew it, three trolls would be on you like flies on shit: one troll would be eating your arm, another a leg, and a third pulling out your eyeballs and eating them like Jujubees — unless one of her pals beat her to it. Eyeballs were a well-known house troll delicacy. I don't care how famous or skilled a warrior you are, or think you are, you never faced house trolls alone. They were just too damn fast.

Those were my thoughts as we made our way from house to house. You may be wondering: "How did a sheltered academic acquire such a detailed a knowledge of house trolls?" Buck gave me ten-minute lectures every night at bedtime on fighting methods, various historical troll battles, and troll infestations in the High Kingdom. One night it would be battling house trolls on the open plain, another night a lecture on fighting house trolls in caves and in trees, or an enchanting bedtime story on five effective decapitation strategies for house trolls. My God, I had some unforgettable nightmares. Still do. But I was prepared.

We were divided into two teams of seven each with two SEALs, with a third backup team of Captain Danny's Elvish Navy SEALs ready to come to our aid, if needed. The SEALs waited in the forest outside the housing development and would destroy any trolls who escaped the house-to-house slaughter.

Dwarves, too, occasionally go berserk when battle lust was upon them. Burt was a perfect example. There was no better dwarf to have at your side in the heat of battle than Burt. But sometimes you couldn't call him off in a fight and he would kill everything in sight, even goblin children if they were present. Even after a battle, when Burt was tanning a goblin or troll skin for his collection, you interrupted him at your peril. I loved Burt like a brother, and he took personal responsibility for my safety, but like I said, he could get carried away. He could go ape-shit. You simply had to know when to stay the fuck away and give him his space.

For some reason he loved Gormog, Farsog, and Sam and honored them. Maybe it was his love of Gormog's cinnamon Danish or his eggs Benedict. He swooned over Farsog's Coq au vin, which Burt the Gourmand swore was better than Julia Child's legendary Coq au vin recipe. But still it was a damn good thing that neither Gormog nor Farsog participated in the battle with the house trolls. Burt would have killed both in the heat of battle and regretted it the rest of his life.

Life saving for us during the troll fight was the fact that our beloved Chainsaw Master, Petey, had attached his own self-made silencers to all the chainsaws in our company. Apart from the usual screaming that takes place between husband-and-wife trolls, just like their human counterparts, the next-door neighbor trolls heard nothing unusual.

We were prepared for more than four trolls per house: two parents and their relatives hiding upstairs. Like I said earlier, we learned our intelligence was flawed; certainly when we saw the minivans parked in every driveway. Our earlier ground reconnaissance saved our bacon there. We encountered no fewer than four trolls in every house and sometimes as many as twelve. But no house troll kids, thank God. I don't think I could have killed troll children, unless four or five of them ganged up on me and tried to eat me. I guess the Demon Lord wanted only adults in his House Troll Strike Force. But here's the deal, if you can believe it. Buck said that troll kids weren't safe in a house with so many adult trolls: they often ate their own when the food supply got low or all they had left in the cupboard was macaroni and cheese, or pretzels, or pork rinds. Sometimes they'd whip up a little Hamburger Helper with troll kids instead of ground beef!

You've seen all these cop shows on TV, right? Lots of blood, guts, and dead bodies: but they never tell you the truth about dead bodies. They never tell you that when a person, even a troll, is dead, his or her sphincter muscle relaxes and all the shit and piss in their bodies are emptied. Now multiply this by a factor of fifty and you'll start to approximate what ten dead house trolls smells like in a confined area, even with central air conditioning. TMI? Sorry.

Now, everyone showed great courage, and each of us acquitted himself (and herself) with honor and distinction. Arnie had a bad cut over his left eyebrow and was bleeding throughout the ordeal, but was hot with revenge on the remaining trolls. Even our mighty wizard Dutch had a serious gash on his arm and across his leg. Buck hand was heavily bandaged after almost leaving two fingers in one of the houses. Even Beca was limping. One of our Elf SEALs, Bosworth, nearly lost his arm. His arm was hanging by a tendon. I don't know what possessed me but I laid Demon Slayer across the wound and it healed him. Why Demon Slayer didn't burn him, I don't know. Maybe it was because Elves are without Original Sin and my heaven-crafted sword recognized this. Sounds like bullshit, I know. Who can say, really? Thank God, it worked.

"Beca, were you hit?" I said.

"Nothing serious," she said. "Just a couple of shotgun pellets in the ass. NBD. I'll take care of it back at camp."

"You're in pain. Are you sure?"

"Come on, we've got five more houses to torch." Beca said, giving me a withering look as if to say, *Don't bring up the subject again.*

We returned to the guesthouse at Camp David where the Elf SEALs repaired most of our hurt, and it was a good thing, because no one returned from the fight unscathed. Beca was still in pain. But she wouldn't say anything, so Captain Danny, and his team, didn't stick around for our thanks, but took off to his next assignment.

"They're going to get infected," I said.

"It'll be ok. My body usually absorbs this type of injury. It just takes time," Beca said.

"You can't even sit down without grimacing in pain."

"I don't grimace," she said.

"Those are tears of joy?"

"What's going on?" asked Dutch.

"STFU, Rufus." Beca said.

"STFU?" Dutch said.

"It's her sweet way of saying, '*Shut The Fuck Up*.'"

"Shut The Fuck Up about what?'" said Dutch.

"Beca caught a little buckshot in the ass during the fight. I'm worried it'll get infected if she does nothing about it."

"Thanks a bunch, Rufus." Beca said. "I told you to keep your mouth shut."

"I can't have a wounded warrior unprepared for what lies ahead." Dutch said, raising his voice so that everyone could hear him. "Beca, you have an easy decision. Removing buckshot is a minor procedure for anyone with battle experience and a first aid kit. Anyone in this room can do it. We all have emergency battle-field experience. Just choose someone, now!"

"Pick me! Pick me! Oh, please pick me!" shouted every dwarf who waved his hand. We all laughed, including Beca. She took my hand and we stepped into one of the empty bedrooms.

CHAPTER 55

Perhaps it was fitting, perhaps it was poetic justice that after exterminating the house trolls and burning down their homes, that we should return to our comfy little safe house to find it violated by the enemy. The enemy hadn't entered through the front door, but they had entered. The front and back doors were made of three feet of solid steel and only we knew the password. In a two-pronged attack somehow the enemy had dug his own tunnel somewhere into our safe house.

Our cozy little hide-a-way had been destroyed and defiled; our man-cave was in ruins: half-eaten food everywhere, tables over-turned, defecation on our bedroom floors, and in our beds, and what's worse, our little RCA 15 inch TV was gone, ripped off, stolen, probably manhandled, as well. What possible appeal could a TV from the Jurassic Age have for anyone?

At first, my worst instincts kicked in. I was certain Gormog and his family had betrayed us, until we found poor Gormog nailed to the kitchen wall with sixteen Bacasu steak knives: four in each hand and foot, spread out like Da Vinci's Vitruvian Man, with a goblin spear sticking out of his side; he'd lost a lot of blood, and didn't have much time. Some of the dwarves were crying. I think they were more upset over the empty refrigerator and the fact that without Gormog there would be no more piping hot chocolate croissants or Eggs Bene. I guess the thought occurred to me, too. We were all heartbroken about Gormog, but also about all the great home cooking we'd be missing. I'm ashamed to admit it. Plus Gormog was a decent, gentle goblin and just nice to have around. His family felt like our family.

"'Verily, I say unto you, A thief never enters through the front door,'" said Gormog, who tried to smile. "We think goblin scouts saw Sam taking out the trash. They returned with reinforcements and guessed, but guessed right and tunneled into one of the bedrooms. They surprised us during Final Jeopardy."

"You are very brave, Gormog, and a true friend," said Dutch. "Try not to talk. Let's get you down from there."

"No! I'll only bleed out faster. We told them nothing. They took Farsog and Sam prisoner; The Demon Lord will eat them at the next *Lunch with Bobby Ross*. It's only three days away. Please! You must save them."

"We will," I said, having no clue where they might be.

"I held back important information from you," said Gormog. "Please forgive me. I didn't tell you the entire truth. The Demon Lord set up another kingdom."

"Where?" We all said.

"Here!" said Gormog. "You're five miles south of the Demon Lord's Second Kingdom. It's right below the White House. Your President is in the gravest danger."

"Ah, crap!" we all said.

"Please save my family."

"Where do we begin our search?" said Beca.

"Follow the yellow goblin scat. Should lead you straight to the Demon Lord's kingdom," Gormog said, and died.

"Follow the yellow shit road." I said.

"Follow the yellow shit road!" said Buck.

"Follow the yellow shit road!" said Petey.

Dutch covered poor Gormog with a blanket. We'd been living in the heart of the Demon Lord's kingdom and never knew it?

Made perfect sense. Why reinvent the wheel? The tunnels had already been built at the taxpayers' expense. The Demon Lord could save the dwarf gold he'd stolen, and launch his own goddamn satellite and DLTV. Remember? The dwarf gold I hadn't seen so much as a fucking flake of. Perfecto. The Demon Lord had a ready-made bolthole once he started World War III. But the question remains: what would he do in an empty world, turned to ash? Fill it with his monsters, who probably weren't half as tasty as humans? Who knows what goes through the mind of a mad fucker. There are those who revel, take great joy is the happiness of others; and then there are evil fucks like Ross who delight only in the suffering of others, and my path lay directly across his. I was going to cut his head off and probably feel guilty about — for about a nanosecond.

All at once we heard laughter from outside our door: the kind of laughter a goblin makes when he thinks he's got you by the balls.

"It's a trap!" Petey said.

"Yah think?" said Beca. "Let's hope they left only a small contingent force, otherwise we're all in deep shit."

"Let's hope they haven't sabotaged the escape tubes," Buck said. "Some of us should leave now, especially you, *oh, Chosen One.*"

"Not yet," I said, fingering Demon Slayer's razor edge. "First we will make them fear, the House of the Cinnamon Buns."

"For Chef Gormog!" said Petey, who revved his chain saw.

"For beautiful Farsog!" said Burt, who slashed the air with his axe.

"For Sam the astronomer!" I said removing Demon Slayer from its sheath.

"Sounds like the laughter came from a bedroom," I said. Wendy, Beca, and I entered our room. Wendy smelled something and pulled a dresser off the wall. Sure enough there was dirt and goblin shit on the floor and the wall had been quickly repaired and painted over. They must be morons, too leave all this shit behind them and then attempt to cover it up with a little drywall.

Who was leading these idiots? Not to mention the dumbass goblins laughing in the tunnel outside our bedroom, waiting for us to fall asleep to attack us.

"Dutch! Look! The scum tunneled through our bedroom wall," I said. "Wendy found their entrance. Good job, Wendy. Good girl!" I grabbed her muzzle and kissed her on her head. Wendy loved kisses, though no one except me was brave enough to give them to her.

"Brings in six of those La-Z-Boys in and turn them over!" said Dutch. "Lock and load everyone. Be sure your Kalashnikovs and your M-16s are fully loaded. We'll nail these bastards when they come through."

We could feel and smell the goblin shit under our mattresses while we sat on the bed in the dark. Everything stank. We said a loud "goodnight" to each other around midnight and waited.

We weren't disappointed. Buck and five of the dwarves went to the family room, turned the remaining La-Z-Boy armchairs on their sides, and took up positions at the front door, just in case they had the password (and the key, which was missing). Dutch, Beca, Wendy, and I trained our weapons on the newly painted wall. The wall soon burst and the first goblins sprang out yelling, "Aiiiee!" and "Dwarf-fuckers!!" before we blasted them.

Beca fired a rocket-propelled grenade into the mass of goblins waiting to follow their comrades.

"Fire in the hole!" I said, just for fun before it exploded. And then there was silence, not so much as a single frickin' "Aiiiee!" from any goblins. So we pushed back the dirt and shoved the dresser against the wall, buttressing it with several beds from the other rooms.

Dutch and Buck were in the family room. Goblins and two trolls breached the front door, despite blocking it with seven La-z-Boy chairs. Dutch and Buck were getting the worst of it fighting two 12-foot trolls, but the trolls had their backs to Beca, who matter-of-factly jumped on them and cut off their heads, faster than you could say, "bye-bye." All the goblins were slain: those who entered through our bedroom and those who breached front door. I fired another rocket- propelled grenade at those gathering outside the front door: Bad luck for us as a demon was maybe fifty yards beyond our front entrance.

"A demon is come! You're mine muthafucka," screamed Petey who, before we could stop him, rushed to it with his Stihl MS 250 chainsaw.

"Petey, NO!" said Buck.

But Petey was in his bat-shit war frenzy groove and had his Stihl revved to the max and couldn't hear a damn thing. He was in berserk mode and attacked the demon's sword arm. The belt flew off the chainsaw as if Petey had tried to cut down a steel tree. The demon grabbed Petey by the head and pulled it off his shoulders, drank the blood and rolled the head at us as if it were a bowling ball. The he ripped off his arms and threw his body on the heap of dead goblins. Then he strolled toward us, as if he hadn't a care in the world.

Beca threw two fragmentation grenades at it, but to no effect.

"Why'd you do that?" I asked.

"Just for shits and giggles," she said.

"You know you can't damage it with a grenade."

"Maybe I can annoy it, ok?" said Beca, filled with battle rage and revenge. The demon fucker walked right through the blast like a cloud mist.

"All right, everyone, you know the drill," I said. "Dutch, load up everyone in the tubes and take off. Beca go with Dutch and take Wendy, too."

"I'm not going anywhere without you, Rufus, *my* Chosen One," said Beca, who bowed, and gave me the finger as she took ten tiny steps behind me. Wendy also wasn't moving from my side. Beca had to drag the lupine with her to a safe distance behind me. That's love for you: those were my girls and that bastard demon wasn't going to touch either one. The demon stopped around twenty-five feet from me. I went out to meet it.

"Dammit, Demon-dude," I said, shouting at him until he came closer. "You smell worse than your brother demon-fuck. You know, the one I decapitated. You guys got something against bathing?"

"I'll bathe in the Chosen One's blood," said the Demon, coming within ten feet, which was close enough.

"Geez, haven't heard that before," I said.

The demon-fuck withdrew his sword from its scabbard, which was at least two feet longer than Demon Slayer, which was fine. I didn't want to get any closer than I had to. "I think soap and water would pleasantly surprise you." I added. Once again, I was the only one standing in its path before it slaughtered my friends, my family. It had already ripped poor Petey to pieces. But this demon wasn't hungry. He wanted revenge. He didn't look as nondescript as the last demon I'd killed. He was my height, easily 6ft 4inches, broad shouldered. He wore yellow tennis shoes, tuxedo pants, a red Hawaiian shirt, and a black penguin jacket, and actually looked fashionable, spiffy, especially with the yellow running shoes, always a good contrast to black. I still had at least fifty pounds on him. I have at least fifty pounds on most people.

"Meet Black Mamba," the demon said, and held up his long sword; sure enough, a black mamba slithered back and forth inside his blade.

"Hey, why doesn't my blade have a groovy black mamba? You lucky pup! Demon Slayer, at your service," I said, showing him the translucent blade. He swung his sword before I could finish my sarcastic remark. The serpent in the sword lost about three feet of its tail when I cut off his sword by the same length. There was now snake blood moving to each side of his sword, plus my heavier weight leaning in with the force of Demon Slayer knocked the demon on his ass.

"Now it's a fair fight," I said. "Look! Our swords are the same length now." He was furious. In the background I heard the *swoosh* of pneumatic tubes, like missiles leaving their silos. I was glad that my companions made good their escape. Whatever happened, I knew Dutch and Buck would look after everyone. In life or in death I knew Beca and Wendy, my girls, would never leave me.

Beca shot another rocket-propelled grenade past the demon while he was still flat on his ass, just to dissuade any troll or pain-in-the-ass goblin from joining the fight. "Get up, you lazy piece of shit," I said to him, and had one pissed off demon when he got up. I hoped, in his anger, he might make a mistake in his swordplay.

"I'm going to enjoy eating you," he said, and pulled out a short, supplemental knife, a chef's knife, a Henckel, good German quality.

"Hey you, bastard, that's Gormog's Henckel!! You stole it from our kitchen, you jerk."

"Play fair, now. No extra blades," said Beca who shot the knife out of his hand.

He was a pretty good swordsman and parried most of my blows, and even cut my shoulder. But I'd seen most of his moves from Beca and Buck. I pushed him back on his ass with the brute force of Demon Slayer. Beca jumped on my back and took the few seconds she needed to suck the soporific poison from the demon's blade, meant to slow my reactions. We'd talked about this possibility and Beca wasted no time implementing our plan. She spit out the poison and it burned a hole in a dead goblin nearby. I was surprised it didn't hurt her. I guess shape shifters were immune to it.

I don't know who taught these demons swordplay, but their training was far from comprehensive. No doubt the Demon Lord was a better swordsman. His demon guard was still no match for a classically trained dwarf arms master, like Buck, or a professional assassin like my sweet Beca. I'd been attacked and scarred the length and breadth of I40 by the best.

The demon must have his lost temper and patience because he lunged at me, trying to stab me through the stomach. It was such an amateurish move, I almost laughed when I trapped his sword on the ground and cut off his head.

"I'm surprised these demons aren't that tough," said Beca. "Guess, you can achieve a lot through fear and intimidation. So-called tough guys are never as tough as they pretend to be."

"And some tough guys shake like a bowl of jelly before battle," said Beca. "Very true. Funny that the Demon Lord did a lousy job training his demon-guard," I said. "Let's hope the trainer isn't any better than his trainees."

"I wouldn't assume so, my darling. I know I wouldn't want my subordinates thinking they were my equal."

"That's a rather brilliant observation," I said.

"Brilliant to an academic, perhaps," said Beca. "Commonplace for an assassin. Come on, they're waiting for us up top." She took my hand while Wendy rubbed up between us and we left. I was one lucky guy.

Our friends shouted with joy when we stepped out of the escape tubes. The designer of the tubes never planned for a full-grown lupine. Thus poor little Wendy was stuffed into her own tube like a sardine, and none too pleased about it when she emerged.

By the time she reached the surface, Wendy was ready to destroy the world, but settled for a businessman, rather a businessman's brief case, which he dropped before screaming in horror, running for his life down Madison Avenue. Wendy vented her anger on his leather briefcase. When she finished with it, ripped papers, bits of leather, and shredded files blew down the street like confetti.

"It's ok, sweetheart," I cooed to Wendy and kissed her nose and petted her head. "You're so brave and good and all mine."

CHAPTER 56

We had serious issues to decide: Farsog and Sam were captives; Senator Ross was now *Vice President-elect Ross*. But what the hell, we were all going to enjoy a night out on the town, as much as we could; and hold a memorial dinner for Petey, Gormog, Theo, and Ornery. Reggie's assistant, Mr. Winters, had told us about a fabulous Middle Eastern restaurant called Abu's Mediterranean Feast near Dupont Circle, only a few miles from our escape tubes. Somewhere between the humus appetizer and the lamb shish-ka-bob, I decided no one else would die. There were 12 of us *still* alive, and still a lucky 14 if Farsog and Sam hadn't been eaten. There was real hope: our lucky number 14 was *still* in play while Farsog and Sam were alive.

"Greater love hath no man, than this: that a man lay down his life for his friends," I said. "I'm not sure if Christ said that before or after the apostles bolted, but it doesn't matter. He forgave them. He forgave them their overwhelming, overcoming, overmastering fear. But our brothers Ornery, Theo, Petey, and Gormog mastered their fear; they didn't bolt, but stood beside their friends and comrades in life and in death. So it is fitting that we honor them

tonight. So raise your flagons my brothers to the dearly departed."
We all drank to their memory.

"But what do we do about Farsog and Sam?" said Dutch,
strangely noncommittal.

"Yes," I said. "Now that our bellies are full, and we have sung
powerful songs in memory of and to the mighty ancestors of
Petey, Ornery, Theo, and yes, even Gormog, I say let us now plan
how to rescue Farsog and Sam."

"You can't be serious. Need I remind everyone that Gormog,
Farsog, and Sam are goblins? Goblin Hitters, assassins no less,"
said Buck. "And please, Rufus do not compare in the same breath
Gormog to our brother dwarves or our mighty ancestors."

"You didn't feel that way when you were eating Gormog's
Cinnamon Danish or his Eggs Benedict, or his Coq au vin." I said.
"You praised him mightily then."

"It was *Farsog's* Coq au vin," said Buck, not a little chagrined.
"And don't forget that was in payment for the sanctuary we gave
them. If we hadn't taken them in they would have wandered
in the tunnels until a goblin scouting party killed them. Am
I wrong? Get a grip, Big Man, they're just goblins."

"That was some Coq au vin," say Chad.

"Oh, that's a powerful argument, Buck, for abandoning Farsog
and Sam to torment and death," Dutch said, with no small amount
of irony in his voice. "I'm sure Gormog would be pleased."

"I know that Buck, my brother, is a better dwarf than the one
speaking now. I know it," I said. Buck was not pleased and turned
beet red.

"I really liked them both, Sam, too," said Burt, "and Gormog's
cinnamon rolls and his chocolate soufflé will always be the stuff
of gastronomic legend; and they were pretty damn nice for
goblins, but to risk my life and my share of the dwarf gold — for
goblins? That's asking too much."

"Agreed," said Buck. "There is too much at stake. Why the
whole quest is at risk if we *risk* everything for goblins, who basi-
cally intruded, no, *broke* into our safe house with the original
intent of killing us all, especially you Rufus. Ok, all right, I admit

I liked them, but I am not risking my life, or my gold for them." Buck took a piece of pita bread and dipped it into a plate of hummus and ate it but dripped a large portion of hummus on his chin.

"Risking everything for an honorable end is what this quest is about," I said. I'm going to risk it and I'm going to follow the yellow shit road and at least try to rescue Sam and Farsog. They're our friends, part of our little family and I won't abandon them to torture and death. Who's with me?"

"You're kidding, right?" Arnie said. "By the beard of my grandmother, they're *goblins*. You're nuts, oh Chosen One."

"I don't need a reason," said Beca. "If Rufus is going, I'm going."

"I ain't going. No fucking way," said Burt shaking his head with a mouth full of lamb shish kabob. "Dwarves saving goblins? Absurd. How could we face our friends back home?"

"Man, what are you thinking?" said Larry, who along with Buck chowed down on more of Gormog's Cinnamon Danish than anyone.

"Besides, they're already dead, most likely," said Buck. "If not, they're obviously being used as bait to get you to rescue them. That's what the Demon Lord expects *you* to do? Yah big ol' softy."

"No, he *expects us* to let them die," I said. "Dwarves risking their lives to rescue two goblins is a thought that would never occur to the Demon Lord. He understands too well the dwarves' hatred of goblins. It's the last thing he expects. That's why we have the element of surprise on our side; and a better shot of recovering your dwarf gold — though I think your gold's been converted it into cash and sits in an unassailable money market account, or blue chip dividend yielding stocks, or AAA state bonds earning state and federal tax free interest. Regardless, we'd need to know someone in government with a long enough reach to seize it? Uh, do we know anyone like that?"

"Reggie?" said Beca.

"Bingo!" I said. "Lord Reggie, the puppet master."

"Makes sense to me," said Dutch, mostly silent until now. "A good deed, Buck, may provide just the opportunity we need to recover your gold — in whatever form it currently sits."

"You'll never recover a penny of it." I said, "not until the Demon Lord, the new Vice President-Elect of the United States, is dead. Here's our chance to accomplish both of our goals. And if an opportunity to complete this quest and to return to your wives doesn't move you, I will say only this: '*What you do for the least of Mine, buddy, you do for Me.*' I'm going back to the hotel. I'm tired of this quest and tired of everyone around this table, with two exceptions. Goodnight and God bless you all, every one."

I decided they could sleep on their decision though I knew it wouldn't change. Wendy and I would return to the tunnels in the morning to rescue Sam and his mom. I'd have to leave without telling anyone. The dwarves' decision came as no surprise. Dwarves think twice before risking life and limb for anyone but their own. Certainly not for a family of goblin hitters whose lives we reluctantly spared in the first place, no matter how tasty their masterly prepared cinnamon rolls, eggs bene, and chicken dinners had been. I still loved the dwarves, despite their flaws, which were many; and they loved me despite mine; and I loved Beca despite the fact she was a ruthless assassin. I loved Dutch 'cuz old Dutch was cool and fair and wise and a standup wizard; I loved Wendy when no one wanted her because I knew she loved me when I first cradled her in my arms and she rubbed her wet muzzle all over my face, just to scent me and to make me her own. I loved Farsog and Sam and Gormog because they loved us and decided to make us their own (and I promised Gormog I'd rescue his wife and child and Chosen Ones don't break promises).

I knew immediately that when Dutch raised the subject of rescuing Farsog and Sam that the dwarves would be horrified at the prospect of entering the labyrinth of tunnels in the heart of the Demon Lord's realm for goblins that had forced themselves on us. And I knew they might be right. What's more, we could attempt a rescue only to find that Farsog and Sam were already dead. But the thought of Sam being eaten in front of his mom by the Vice President Elect was more than I could bear. I had to do something even if it meant dying. In fact, to be honest, dying was infinitely preferable to the shame of doing nothing.

CHAPTER 57

Reggie had made reservations for us at the Washington Four Seasons. Each of us had his (or her) own luxurious suite, even Beca, who I think welcomed a little alone time, and slept with little Muppin, bereft without Sam. Little Muppin needed comforting, and some special alone time with Beca. I could have used some special alone time with her, too. But I understood. Wendy slept with me and wouldn't let me out of her sight. We were all confident there were no hollow walls at this Four Seasons. A very elegant hotel, and call me cynical, but I knew not one dwarf was waiting for his rescue-the-goblins wake-up call.

I would take Wendy and we would go it alone. We would bring the fight to the Demon Lord. I was counting on the Demon Lord's vanity. I knew he was obsessed with killing me and probably couldn't decide whether to eat me first or to kill me and then eat me. At 3 AM my wake-up call came. Wendy and I hurried down 12 floors using the emergency staircase. I would ride her back to Dupont Circle where our escape pods waited. We came out in an alley just west of Pennsylvania Avenue. I mounted Wendy when I heard a voice say: "Where the fuck are *you* going?"

"No one sounded all that eager to join me," I said. "Although, I'd hoped you might show up."

"Hey, Mr. Fat White Dumbfuck, dwarves risking their lives for goblins? Really? You should have known better than to ask." Beca said.

"I had to make the argument for rescuing Farsog and Sam. So you don't think it made any difference?" I said.

"Do you see anyone here? Even I didn't like the idea," said Beca. "Though Farsog and Sam deserve a life free from the Demon Lord, it's not my problem. *You're* my problem. But like me — we made Farsog and Sam family and we promised Gormog. I don't break my promises, even to goblins."

"Neither do I," I said, happier than I could explain. "Well, then, let's go and embrace our fate." I jumped on the back of Wendy, Beca on Muppin. Beca shapeshifted into a sexy goblin bitch and we raced down a deserted Pennsylvania avenue.

⁘═══⁘

We arrived at the escape tubes and found them as we had left them, gone. I searched for the crushed Cheetohs I'd left there to mark their location and found some orange crumbs next to what I hoped was a nearly invisible retrieval button. Then I found three more tubes close to that one. They all said, "PRESS TO RETURN," so I pressed and prayed. Geez-Louise, I did a lot of goddamn praying on this quest. Five minutes later I was packing Wendy and Muppin into separate cylinders, trying to calm them down, as much as one could calm 550 pounds of frightened lupines. Then I activated their tubes. Beca and I stepped into the other two and we descended down into the belly of the beast. We were reassured by knowing that any goblin greeting party would be scattered in pieces from our lupine greeting party.

We reached our former safe house to find Wendy grooming Muppin who purred and grumbled like a well-tuned Harley Fat Boy. Our little home away from home was empty. The dead goblins had been removed and talk about a shit-fest, all that remained was goblin scat wherever you looked. Our wonderful, happy man-cave was a desolation of fluorescent yellow goblin shit. I almost cried.

"Suck it up, darling," Beca said. "When this is all over, we'll get the government to fix her up like new. I know where to find the money!"

"That's right, honey," I said. "We'll make our home away from home beautiful, again — but first we'll build our own little heaven above."

We left the house and followed the yellow shit road, which led even deeper into the earth and through countless tunnels. We found surprisingly little resistance leading to the Washington headquarters of the Demon Lord, now *Vice President-elect*, Bobby Ross. The goblins we met fled before us, leading us on or so I felt. Finally the yellow scat stopped before a large metal wall. "This must be the place," I said, "Pretty quiet. Maybe no one's home."

"I'm afraid," said Beca, who had shown no fear up to now.

"Be not afraid, my love," I said, echoing the admonition of Our Lord throughout the Bible. But I was afraid, too; just too proud to admit it to the woman I loved more than life itself.

Wendy roared a challenge to the wall that you could hear in heaven above, and hell below. It must have been heard on the other side of the wall because a door appeared where there was none before.

"Wendy darling and Muppin, wait here for us. If we're not back in 15 minutes run away and get help. You know the way," I said knowing Wendy would know what to do. She tried to come in with us, until I looked at her sternly. She whimpered. I could see tears in her eyes. She and little Muppin sat by the door, waiting.

Against our better judgment we entered. No one saw me as I dropped a metal pipe that prevented the door from closing all the way. Just in case the cavalry arrived, but what could Dutch and a handful of dwarves do against a legion of goblins, trolls, and demons, if that's what awaited us. I was glad that Dutch and the dwarves weren't here. It was a suicide mission. There wasn't much hope of escape, but I missed them right now. They never failed to give me hope. Thank God Beca was with me.

I could feel we had entered a vast the cavern-like structure. It was pitch black and I couldn't see a damn thing. Though it felt like the entire structure was breathing: the hot, collective breath of those inside inhaling and exhaling, waiting for the show to begin.

"I think we're surrounded," I said with a trembling voice.

"Be not afraid, my love," said Beca, right back at me.

It was so quiet I could hear my heart pounding. Then the floodlights came on, blinding me. When my eyes cleared, we found ourselves on a large round stage, surrounded by goblins, trolls, lupines, demons, and a couple of baby dragons circling above.

"Welcome, Rufus and Rebecca," said the Demon Lord in a soft voice, with true southern hospitality. "I've been expecting you both. I've been following your many accomplishments with great interest."

It was hard not to like this guy, despite what I knew about him. He didn't talk like a psychopathic, cannibalistic, murderous madman. His soft, southern, gentlemanly appeal was so incongruous with his demonic deeds, unlike his demon captains who were uncouth creatures.

"Welcome? Really?" I said. "Vice-President-Elect Ross, you've been trying to kill me since I began this quest."

"An unfortunate misunderstanding, oh Chosen One," he said in a soothing voice, not that I believed him for a second.

"Could have fooled me," I said.

"I guess you haven't heard the news," he said. "Pity about President McClintock. He's been missing now for 48 hours. In his absence, please address me as President-Elect Ross, if you would be so kind."

"I don't believe it," I said. Ross turned on an overhead monitor to CNN with Wolfy Blitzer.

"Wolf Blitzer here. With the mysterious death of President McClintock, Vice-President-Elect Bobby Ross will be the first *Vice President-Elect* in U.S. history to become President-Elect between now and his swearing in on January 20 as 48th President of the United States of America. Until such time, Vice President Fordham has been sworn in as President."

"I guess if Wolfy says it's so, it must be so. But you'll never get away with it," I said.

"Already have. He was a tough old bird, President McClintock; Very stringy meat and hard to digest," said the Demon Lord, who picked at his teeth, and belched. "I've saved some of his skin and I'm going to make some presidential man jerky from it."

"Man jerky? Never had man jerky. Plain man jerky or teriyaki?" I said.

"Sriracha!" he said. "You have much humor, Rufus."

"Presidential man jerky... you are one sick fuck," I said.

"Don't knock it until you've tried it," he said. "I appreciate your open mind, which is why I brought you here to say that you alone could help me rule this troubled world. If only you would kneel before me and pledge thy loyal service. You would be a true son to me. And a great help. You've already proven yourself by dispatching two of my best demons. I'd like you to be a part of my team, my family. Join me. It'll be fun."

"I guess it's expensive to hire and train new demons. You don't fool me. You'd kill me the moment I pledged my allegiance."

"Maybe, maybe not," said President-Elect Ross, with a smile. "What have you got to lose? You're a dead man anyway."

"How about my eternal soul," I said.

"Overrated, right fellas?" he said to the demons around him.

"Right, Mr. President!" They said in unison.

"Gosh, you know there was another fellow who was made the same offer for his allegiance," I said. "Not that I'm comparing myself for an instant. But then we all have our tests of faith."

"Yes, my uncle made him an honest offer and look what happened to him."

"It turned out ok in the end. You'll forgive me if I follow my Lord's example." I said and withdrew Demon Slayer from its sheath.

"Don't expect to rise from the dead," he said.

"I don't expect to die, muthafucker," I said, and kissed my blade.

"Suit yourself. Beca, *come!*" said the Demon Lord.

My heart stopped.

"I brought him my Lord, as commanded," said Beca who knelt before the Demon Lord, now President-Elect of the United States of America.

"What the fuck!" I said. "Say it ain't so. You?! I won't, I refuse to believe it! Our love wasn't real then? None of it was real? Oh God, Beca. I never would have guessed." I felt like a man struck by lightning, my insides turned to jelly.

"I'm sorry, Rufus. There has ever been one Lord for me," she said, then took five steps and on bended knees knelt at the right hand of her Demon Lord. Her Demon Lord placed his hand around her neck, as if his hand were a slave's collar. His hand was on fire and yet the fire didn't burn Beca, who suddenly had a mane of her own — and a tail, both on fire. Was she, too, a demon?! I couldn't believe it! At that moment I wanted to die. Not eaten alive, mind you. No fun there. But dying I longed for.

I couldn't look into the face of my beloved as she took her place at her true lord's side. I just put Demon Slayer back in its sheath. I couldn't accept her betrayal. I never felt more alone in my life, a good life up to now. I refused to believe that our love was one-sided. I would go to my grave believing Beca loved me. I had never known such despair. I couldn't go on. But I had to. There was still the Quest, my responsibility and I wasn't going down without a fight. I couldn't let this demon muthafucker destroy humanity.

"That's all right, my angel," I said. "If I have to die, I will die for love, mine for you and yours for me. So don't give it a second thought, sweetheart." I thought I saw something in her eye. Was it a tear forming? Was her heart breaking, too? Did she want to die right here, right now — with me?

"Step back, my servants," said the Demon-Lord making it sound like a big deal to those watching on DLTV and in the "studio audience." "This Fat Fuck is mine. I'm tired of this fool for God. I weary of his many escapes. I'm going to kill you and eat you now!"

"Talk, talk, talk," I said, mocking him to his own peeps. "Does this guy ever shut up? Bring it on, baby."

All of the goblins, trolls, dragons, and demons, all poised to strip the flesh from my bones, stepped back. This asshole was really going to fight me; I was in the middle of a circle the size of a boxing ring.

I took four long steps back to give myself room on the outer edge of the arena to maneuver. There were thousands of spectators in the audience, millions more watching on DLTV. Sam and Farsog were sitting in the first row. I smiled at them, but they were both too terrified to move. I even saw our RCA Black & White TV sitting on a ledge right next to his huge theater sized DLTV! As if this billionaire demon-fuck couldn't afford his own TV? He had to steal my tiny RCA. That really pissed me off.

"Hey, you big jerk, that's my RCA TV, you son-of-a-bitch," I said for all of the cameras around the room. "You've got billions of dollars and you steal my worthless, 1950s black and white TV?"

"What can I say? I collect antiques. Besides, Rufus," he said, "It's the little cruelties that give the most lasting pleasure. When I drop a hydrogen bomb on the Chinese and the Russians, will it be *as* pleasurable as eating you or stealing your little RCA TV? No, because I don't know a single Chinese or Russian by name. Turning three billion people to ash will never be as pleasant, or as much fun as seeing the expression on your face just now, when you saw your very own RCA on my wall."

"You are one sick prick," I said. "And don't you ever shut-the-fuck-up?"

"You know what day it is today, Rufus? Why it's *Lunch time with Bobby Ross!* We're streaming our fight to all of my centers around the country. Look up at the screen: You're on Demon Lord TV — DLTV, LIVE!! You're the Main Event on *Lunch time with President Bobby Ross!*"

"Nothing would please me more than to cut off your head you in front of all your poor suffering monsters," I said.

"Yes, I can well imagine. You know, I had planned to eat little Sam first," said the Dark Lord pointing his sword at Farsog and

Sam. "But right now I'm not that hungry. However, when I eat you I'm sure to be stuffed. But if I have a little room, I'll have Sam for dessert while his mom watches. Ain't life grand?"

The Demon Lord stepped down from his dais and slowly entered the ring. I'm six foot three, but still the Demon-Lord towered over me. The Demon-Lord smiled as he drew his sword, its black steel forged in the depths of Hell.

"My Uncle forged this sword a billion years ago, after he was thrown out of Heaven," said the Demon Lord, and held the sword in front of my face.

"Pretty impressive sword," I said. "To be honest, I don't know much about old Demon Slayer. I do know it decapitated two of your demons. You didn't train them very well. I hope you're more of a match."

Demon Slayer leapt out of its sheath into my hand. It startled and pleased me. Demon Slayer wanted a piece of this guy, too, and wasn't about to let me go down without a fight.

"I guess it must be a shock to learn the love of your life is really my girl," said the Demon Lord, who lunged at me on the word "my girl."

"Take her. But be kind to her. She quite wonderful, you know," I said, overwhelmed with misery. He was doing a great job getting under my skin. I parried his blow and with my sword and my superior body weight I pushed him and he fell on his face, hardly a position of invincibility.

There was a collective intake of breath from the monsters in the amphitheater. No one laughed, but many of them smiled, thrilled at his embarrassment. I kicked him in the ass for good measure as he tried to get on his feet and there was a deafening silence. I was going to die anyway so why not fight dirty.

In Afghanistan a fight may have started clean, with bullets or fists, but always ended dirty. It was either gouge the enemy's eye out or lose your own; it was shatter the bastard's kneecap or lose your own; crush his skull with a rock or suffer the same. War turns men into savages. You'd gladly shoot an insurgent in the back if you caught him about to plant an IED. In battle the man who strikes first usually wins. I killed his demons. Was it possible the master was not much better than his students? It was too much to hope for.

The Demon Lord tried to spring to his feet but I kicked him in the ass again, only harder. This time he rolled literally out of the ring and popped up like a Jack-in-the-box, smiling, but really pissed off at the embarrassing fall and ass kicking before his slaves.

"I see it's been a while since you've had your ass kicked," I said. "I always thought the master was superior to his students, but I guess you're no better than your demon flunkies I already killed. Get back in this ring and fight, you coward."

The crowd was eating it up. But I knew this was just preliminary stuff. He said nothing, just glared at me moments before he pulled out a second blade, a three-foot dagger. I was used to that trick. Buck demonstrated the response up and down I40. It was a good time to give him a better look at Demon Slayer's capabilities and in a quick adjustment, I faked him out with the beginnings of a slashing blow to his right and came left at the last second, cutting off his short blade in his left hand at the hilt, along with three of his fingers.

"Ouch," I said. "Sorry, only one blade at a time, President Fuckhead." Calling him a fuckhead in front of his people felt great. His expression changed from the amiable southern Senator to one pissed off opponent, embarrassed that all the monsters in his kingdom saw him suddenly as weak. Then he gave the *look*, the same one he used to paralyze me back at Cooperman Hall, but he couldn't paralyze me or take over my mind this time. I think Demon Slayer, my sword made in Heaven, simply wouldn't allow it. I can think of no other explanation.

"You look hungry," I said, "and that can slow you down. Did you check your blood sugar this morning? Maybe you should have had breakfast first. You don't want to your blood sugar to crash." True my heart was broken, but even in my misery, kicking this bastard's ass was fun, if somewhat hollow compensation — and yet everyone watching was enjoying the spectacle of seeing this prick get his comeuppance.

"I'm going to smother you with Peanut Butter and Jelly before I eat you in front of Beca, your once not-so-true-love, Beca."

"Ooo, I love peanut butter. May I have the first bite?" I said, ignoring the insult to my Beca.

He straightened his shirt and circled me, as I circled him, and so we circled each other.

"I couldn't find your mother and father."

"That's because they're dead, you idiot," I said. He lunged at me with such force that his blade penetrated and nearly cut off my right hand, which was spurting blood and hanging by a tendon, literally. I won't describe the pain, other than to say it hurt like a son-of-a-bitch.

"You're bleeding," he said, with a huge smile. That was an understatement. I bled like a stuck pig. It would take too long for Demon Slayer to heal it. The fight would be over by then. I took a yellow washcloth I keep in my pocket and wrapped it around my hand and the wrist it was barely attached to. I put Demon Slayer in my left hand, and prepared for his next attack, which wasn't long in coming.

He laughed and danced on the periphery, poking his sword from Hell at me from a safe distance. He was still afraid of me. But then he played to the crowd with some fancy but stupid move, parrying me, but I got underneath his sword and it flew out of his hand and into the corner of the ring. He wasn't laughing and smiling then. I was about to cut off his ugly head when he shot a lightning bolt at me right from his hand and delivered a searing wound into my left shoulder and Demon Slayer hung limp by my side, useless.

So much for fair play. I knew he possessed other powers. Hell, he was the Devil's own son or nephew or second cousin or some bullshit relation. His vain belief that he was some sort of master swordsman would play only so far, even for his ego. He wasn't about to lose the fight, even if he couldn't win with his sword alone. Demon Slayer had almost healed my severed wrist, but the hole in my shoulder made lifting Demon Slayer impossible. In that moment the Demon Lord sent a bolt of lightning through my right shoulder, too, and I couldn't move either arm. He picked up his sword. I was on my knees, helpless. Isn't that a son-of-a-bitch? You spend the whole fucking quest training with your sword, up and down I40, morning, noon, and night for this one goddamn moment and the motherfucking Demon Lord shoots you with bullshit lightning bolts. How fucked up is that? Quests, heroic or otherwise, have their own logic.

"Should I eat you where you sit? Or cut off your fat head first and drink your hot blood? Ooo, tastylicious," he said.

"So many choices," I said, and waited for the inevitable. I said my favorite prayer when I was in trouble: *Hail Mary, full of grace, forgive Us Sinners now and in the hour of our death.*

"I'm thirsty," said the Demon Lord. "I think I'll go with the latter," His came at me, his sword in both hands. Somehow with both hands I was able to lift Demon Slayer and block his blow, but Demon Slayer flew out of my hands at my last desperate effort and lay at Beca's feet. It was over. Despite all my training with Buck, Beca, Dutch, and the dwarves, I was never any match for him. Instead I closed my eyes, bent my head in supplication, and prayed for a swift death.

Then I heard a scream as if it stuck in someone's throat, then a thump and felt something rolling between my legs. I opened my eyes and saw the surprise and terror in the Demon Lord's face as his head rolled between my legs and off the stage. Beca stood above me holding Demon Slayer, grown taller than I'd ever seen her before.

"I knew you loved me; I just knew it, my darling girl."

"Rufus, you big goon. Ever doubt me? Never doubt me," said Beca, who planted a wet one on my lips.

"Never, my love," I said. Beca protected me from the Demons drawing a circle around us, though a respectful one given Beca's prowess with the blade. Demon Slayer had almost healed my wounds. Then the roof collapsed.

A dozen Navy Elf SEALs dropped down bearing Uzis and sacred swords of their own and killed all of the demons quickly and efficiently. Three helicopter drones, each the size of a vending machine, spread panic as they mowed down Goblins and Trolls with their integrated 50 caliber machine guns.

Without the Demon Lord, the monsters in the audience were mindless and fled in every direction rather than face the SEALs and the dwarves. Yes, the dwarves, too, had followed us. Dutch and the dwarves broke through the door I had left ajar and induced more panic in the goblins and trolls, killing about a third of them while the others looked for any hole they could crawl into.

Luckily, the diamond bracelet Reggie gave to Beca contained a microscopic tracking device. It led Captain Danny and his Navy SEALs directly to us. And when Dutch and the dwarves woke up to find us both gone, they contacted Lord Reggie and got here as fast as they could. In my heart I knew they wouldn't desert us. It was over. Hey, man, the quest was a success!

EPILOGUE

Here's how a few things turned out in the end. True to his word, Dutch, and his lovely wife Giselle, gave me and Beca his personal tour of the High Kingdom, where I actually got to meet the great grandson of King Fesbucket. Swell guy.

Six months later Beca and I got married, officiated by Dutch and Lord Reggie, King of the Elves. Dutch gave Beca away at the marriage like the father she never had. Beca was able to meet some of the most talented shape shifters in the High Kingdom. One of them even knew her mother, which gave Beca a better appreciation of her heritage. We always suspected that one of her relatives had slipped past the barrier. Although we never realized until then it was her mother, who Beca knew so little about.

When we returned to the U.S., I learned that Professor Blakeslee had died in his sleep, but not before approving my doctoral dissertation with distinction, as well as his recommendation that it be published by the Middlebrook University Press! His glowing review of my work made its defense effortless, a foregone conclusion, especially when I was autographing copies of "F.S.S. Bartlett's Disappearance on the Western Front and the Birth of *The High Kingdom*" in the university bookstore, two weeks before my defense committee even met. Home free as they say.

What was left of President McClintock was laid to rest at Arlington National Cemetery. The short-lived presidency-elect of Senator Bobby Ross and his "disappearance" was officially classified as Top Secret. With President McClintock dead, the Speaker of the House, a Republican, succeeded to the Presidency. With the House of Representatives and the Senate controlled by the Republicans, what was once divided government was now controlled by one party, a party only too happy to inherit power without investigating how they lucked into it. There was the usual congressional investigation that led nowhere.

Beca and I were back at Middlebrook University where I'd been offered an Assistant Professorship in the English Department. Farsog and Sam came to live with us. Farsog was our paid gourmet cook and like a second mother to Beca. We enrolled Sam in the university's evening extension program in Astronomy. If all went according to plan, in three years Sam would complete his BS in Astronomy through Middlebrook University's online Distance Education program. Then we would find (or buy) him a job at a local observatory, on the graveyard shift.

My days flew by teaching. I read the nation's newspapers online to see what was happening around the country since we defeated the Demon Lord. One thing I never expected. Out of the blue, Beca and I started receiving checks from a mysterious source. The first check was for $1,000,000.00 from an unnumbered account at Charles Schwab. I guessed right: Reggie had located the dwarves' stolen gold hidden in a series of shell corporations owned by the Demon Lord; and through some clever move by the IRS, orchestrated by Reggie, the IRS seized the money and moved it to Schwab, minus taxes, naming Reggie the sole trustee. Of course Reggie named the dwarves, Dutch, Beca, and me as beneficiaries of the trust. I would not have to raise a family on an Assistant Professor's salary. It also meant we could take more trips to the High Kingdom to see the dwarves and Dutch and follow the progress of their families.

The national parks around the country still reported the decimation of the local animal population. Most of the damage occurred at night without any witnesses. We debated how we should inform the new President that there was an infestation of goblins, trolls, and lupines, which presented an invasive species problem that required a sociological, as well as a military response. I thought and still do that with the exceptions of the trolls, goblins and lupines would make wonderful citizens.

One night Beca said to me, "Stouffers or sex, Rufus? Stouffers or sex? Your choice." I lost sixty pounds on the "Stouffers or Sex?" diet, a physician approved diet that you don't hear much about in the press. Stouffer's Lobster Newburg gave way to Stouffers' Lean Cuisines.

The following spring our son was born. Beca wanted to name him after me, but I insisted we call him Dutch, son of Beca and Rufus Timmons, in honor of our dear friend. We named Buck his godfather. Beca rented out the backroom of our favorite pub, "The Dancing Grizzlies" and we had a joyful celebration tossing Dutch's namesake around the table, with every dwarf pledging his and his family's service to baby Dutch, son of Beca and Rufus until the end of days.

We tucked little Dutch into bed. Beca glowed with contentment as she covered him with his tiny blanket and endless kisses. I pinched my beautiful wife's cute bottom and whispered, "So, my little shape shifter, who are you going to be for me tonight?" She took my hand and looked almost shy when she smiled at me.

One night I was grading papers into the early hours of the morning and watching baby Dutch with Wendy and little Muppin, who functioned as his official bodyguards. Both woke up and growled whenever they heard baby Dutch crying. I took little Dutch into my arms, cuddled, cooed, and sang to him, "Ninety-nine Demon Skins on the Wall." I held his sweet little head against my neck and I thanked the Son of the One for this great blessing of fatherhood, when I felt something decidedly hairy against my neck. I looked down and for a fleeting moment

I was looking down at a hairy lupine pup, but the image changed quickly back to my baby boy. I held him in front of me and looked at him, making sure all of his legs and arms were still there. He just smiled and started laughing. I mean it: little Dutch was laughing. Had he played a joke on dear old dad and enjoyed it? Fatherhood would be another great adventure.

THE END